Julian Hawthorne

The Laughing Mill and Other Stories

Julian Hawthorne

The Laughing Mill and Other Stories

ISBN/EAN: 9783744748155

Printed in Europe, USA, Canada, Australia, Japan

Cover: Foto ©Andreas Hilbeck / pixelio.de

More available books at **www.hansebooks.com**

THE

LAUGHING MILL

And Other Stories.

BY

JULIAN HAWTHORNE.

London:

MACMILLAN AND CO.

1879.

[*The right of Translation is reserved.*]

PREFACE.

WHAT is called the human interest in fiction is doubtless more absorbing than any other, but other legitimate sources of interest exist. The marvellous always possesses a fascination, and justly; for while it is neither human nature nor fact, it ministers to an æsthetic appetite of the mind which neither fact nor human nature can gratify. Superstition has been well abused; but that were a sad day which should behold the destruction in us of the quality which keeps superstition alive. Fortunately that day can never come—least of all under a Positivist administration.

Such works as "The Tempest," "Faust," and "Consuelo" show their authors at their best, because, being obliged by the subject to soar above the level of vulgar possibility, the writers catch a gleam of transcendent sunlight on their wings. And he who would mirror in his works the whole of man

must needs include the impossible along with the
rest. Whoever has lived thoughtfully feels that there
has been something in his experience beyond what
appears in "Tom Jones," "Adam Bede," and "Vanity
Fair." They are earth without sky. I do not refer
to that goody-goody Sunday-school sky which weeps
and smirks over the mimic worlds of so many worthy
novelists, male and female ; but to that unfathomed
mystery opening all around us—the sky of Shakespeare and Dante, of Goethe and Georges Sand. A
reader with a healthy sense of justice feels that an
occasional excursion mystery-ward is no more than
he has a right to demand. And such excursions are
wholesome for literature no less than for him. For
the story-teller, sensible of the risk he runs of making
his supernatural element appear crude and ridiculous,
exerts himself to the utmost, and his style and
method purify and wax artistic under the strain.

These remarks must smooth the way to the
confession that in the present volume no "human
interest" will be found, or has been attempted. The
gist of the work (or at least of three-fourths of it)
is to show how the impossible might occur. Now
in order to appreciate the delicate flavour of a ghost,

it is indispensable that the palate should not be cloyed by a contemporary diet of flesh and blood. In other words, the reality of the personages amidst whom the disembodied spirit appears should be insisted upon no further than is necessary to the telling them apart; only that side of the human figures which is most in accord with the superhuman should be made prominent. If the writer has managed this part of his business properly, he is open to criticism only in so far as he may have sinned in the way of conception and literary execution; and upon those points he is happily spared the necessity of pronouncing judgment. He may however be permitted to observe that the following stories are among the very lightest and least profound of their class; there are no tears or terrors in them; barely even a smile or a sigh; and, in short, their success—should they achieve any—will be mainly due to the fact that with such small pretensions failure would actually become difficult.

One of the tales, it should be added, is a mere *jeu d'esprit*, the presence of which in the collection is justifiable only on the plea that it makes believe to be what the others are—relieving a note too monotonously sounded by lowering it to the key of mockery. Possibly, nevertheless, it may turn out to be the float which will save the weightier portion of the cargo from going too speedily to the bottom. All the stories have appeared, during the last four years, in various periodicals, to the editors of which my acknowledgments are due for leave to reproduce them.

January, 1879.

CONTENTS.

THE LAUGHING MILL.

THE LAUGHING MILL.

I.

AMONG the pleasantest memories of my earlier days is one of an old gabled farmhouse overlooking the sea. It is a July afternoon, calm and hot. The sea is pale blue and its surface glassy smooth; but the passage of a storm somewhere to the eastward causes long slumberous undulations to lapse shorewards. They break upon the Devil's Ribs—that low black reef about half a mile out—and the sound is borne to our ears some seconds after the white-foam line has marked itself against the blue and vanished. There is a fine throb of sun-loving insects in the air, which we may hear if we listen for it; but more immediately audible is the guttural drawing of old Jack Poyntz's meerschaum pipe, and the delicate clicking of his sweet daughter Agatha's polished knitting-needles. From within doors comes the fillip of water and the clink of chinaware—good Mrs. Poyntz

washing up the dinner-things. For we have just
dined, and the blessing of a good digestion is upon
all of us.

Yes ; there we three sit, in my memory, side by
side upon the stone bench outside the farmhouse
door. The projecting eaves throw a quiet, transparent
shadow over us. Two or three venerable hens are
scratching and nestling in the hot sandy soil near
yonder corner, and conversing together in long-drawn
comfortable croakings. The fragrant smoke from
Poyntz's pipe-bowl circles upwards on the air, until it
takes the sunlight high over head. Truly a pleasant
time, whose peacefulness is still present with me after
so many years. I am old, who then was young ; but
that July sunshine is warm in my heart to-day.

Poyntz was an ancient mariner—not lean and
uncanny, however ; but burly, jovial, and brown ;
with a huge grizzled beard spreading over his mighty
chest, a voice as deep and mellow as a sea-lion's, and
eyes as blue and clear as the ocean upon which they
had looked for more than sixty years. He had been
a successful sailor, had visited many lands and
brought home many cargoes, and was, in a rough
simple way, a thorough cosmopolitan. After his last
voyage he had settled down in the ancestral farmhouse, and applied himself to agriculture. He was as
prosperous, contented, and respected a man as any in

the neighbourhood ; and during the fortnight or so
that I had lodged beneath his roof, I had grown into
a hearty liking for him. While as to Agatha—ah,
it was not liking that I felt for her ! Strange that
that fair, finely-moulded, queenly creature was only a
sailor's daughter ! Much as I honoured Poyntz, I
could not help sometimes feeling surprised at it. At
all events, she was as perfect a lady as ever stepped
on high-arched feet ; and I fancied that the old
mariner and his wife treated her in a manner more
befitting a distinguished visitor than a child of their
own. There was sturdy little Peter, now—he whose
brown legs were visible beneath the low spreading
bough of a scrub-oak beside the mill-stream yonder
—there could be no doubt as to *him*. But what a
brother for Agatha !

How well I recall her aspect, though it is more
than twenty years since that day. Her shapely head
was bound about with a turban of her bright yellow
hair, but her eyes and eyebrows were dark. Her
neck was round and slender, and supported its burden
in unconscious poses of maidenly dignity. The contours of her figure were full, yet refined ; her wrists
were small, and her hand was shaped like that
which lies on the bosom of Canova's Venus. Her
manners breathed simplicity and sweet composure,
yet were reserved and serious withal, and sometimes

they were tinged with a shadow of melancholy. At such moments her hands would fall into her lap, her head would droop a little forward, and her dark eyes gravely fix themselves upon some sunlit sail that flecked the pale horizon. So would she remain until, perhaps, the sail sank below the verge, or became invisible in shadow; then, with a sigh, the soft fetters of her preoccupation would seem to fall away from her. What were her thoughts during those reveries? and why should they be sad ones? I had never ventured to question her much as yet; her mystery was itself a fascination.

One thing about her had attracted my particular notice from the first—the curious pearl-shell necklace that she always wore clasped round her smooth throat. It was composed of very small shells of a peculiar species, not found in that part of the world. These were woven into a singular pattern of involved curves, and were fastened with a broad gold clasp, in the centre of which was set a large pearl. Handsome as the ornament was, however, and becoming to its wearer, it would not have so riveted my attention but for a circumstance to which I must here make a passing allusion.

Among my most precious possessions at that time was a fine oil portrait of my great-grandmother, who was a famous beauty in her day. My family, I should

have said, is of Danish extraction, though the name
—Feuerberg—was, after the emigration of the elder
branch to America, translated to the present Firemount. In my great-grandmother's days there had
been a bitter family quarrel; the younger brother
had attempted to cast doubts upon the legitimacy of
the firstborn, and when he failed to make good his
claim, he had fraudulently seized upon a large portion
of the inheritance and made his escape—whither was
not known, for no effort was made to pursue him. It
was believed that he went to Germany and married
there; and that afterwards he or his son had made
another remove, since which even conjecture had been
silent concerning them. But to return to the portrait.
It was a half-length, and had the quaint headdress
and costume of the period, one detail only being out of
the fashion; but this it was that had always possessed
most interest for me. It was the curious pearl-shell
necklace, woven in a strange pattern, and fastened
with a golden clasp, which was represented upon my
great-grandmother's statuesque bosom. This necklace
had for centuries been a family heirloom, and many
quaint traditions were connected with it. It was said
to have been given to the founder of our race by a
water-witch, or some such mythologic being; and
sundry mysterious virtues were supposed to belong to
it. Precisely what these virtues were I cannot tell,

nor does it happen to be of much consequence. One saying only I remember—that the wearing of it would ensure us happiness and prosperity so long as no member of the family brought dishonour on the name; but thereafter it would bring ruin. Now the necklace had been handed on from one prosperous generation to another, until the date of the quarrel above alluded to; and then, all at once, it had disappeared; and my great-grandmother was the last person known to have worn it. She mentioned it on her deathbed, and foretold that no good fortune was to be expected for the Feuerbergs until the sacred heirloom was recovered, and made a symbol of the healing of the family feud.

The negative part of the prophecy had certainly been verified. The elder branch of the Feuerbergs never got over the effects of the blow inflicted upon it by the younger brother. They gradually subsided from their original high estate; and were at last compelled to abandon the ancestral homestead, and try their luck in the New World. At the time of my birth we were in decently comfortable circumstances, which improved upon the whole as I grew towards manhood. I passed through college, and was afterwards admitted to the Bar, which by-and-by afforded me a tolerable income. But one spring I fancied myself ailing, and resolved to try the sea air; and so it happened that I became acquainted with Jack Poyntz, and with Agatha, and with her pearl-shell necklace.

Of course, all idea of recovering the original necklace had long ago been abandoned. It had been conjectured that the seceding brother of old times had appropriated it along with many other things that did not belong to him ; but there was no proof of this, other than that its disappearance had been simultaneous with his own. Moreover, if the fact must be told, I had outgrown the easy credulity of boyhood, and rather inclined to suspect that the whole picturesque old tradition was three parts imagination to one of truth. It might soothe my family pride to ascribe our decadence to the loss of a trinket, or I might excuse my indolence by declaring that fortune was attainable only on condition of its being found again; but if I descended to hard matter-of-fact, as a lawyer should do, I must admit there was nothing cross-questionable in such an old-wives' tale.

Cross-questionable or not, it will readily be conceived that the sight of Agatha's pearl-shells gave me a thrill of surprise, and deepened my interest in one who needed no such accidental attraction to render her irresistible. The necklace so closely resembled the one in the portrait, that the latter might have been painted from it. It was possible, no doubt, that my great-grandmother's necklace was not unique; that a duplicate—nay, many duplicates—existed. But it was not upon the face of it probable, nor was I disposed to accept any such commonplace solution of the problem. I loved Agatha, and I loved to think (for have I not hinted that I was romantic, though a lawyer?)—I say it suited me to believe that the necklace linked her, however unaccountably, with me. It was evident that she herself looked upon it as a most precious possession. She wore it continually, as she might have worn a talisman, and touched it often, twisting the golden clasp about, or following the woven pattern with meditative finger-tips. Once, when suddenly alarmed, I saw her grasp it quickly in her hand, as if either seeking protection from it, or instinctively yielding it protection ; and another time, during a storm, when a vessel was labouring in the offing, and seemed in danger of being carried upon the Devil's Ribs, I came upon her just as she kissed the great pearl in the clasp, as a Catholic would have kissed the crucifix to avert misfortune.

"Water-witch ! water-witch ! be thy spells wholesome ?" I said in Danish, for a knowledge of the ancestral tongue has always been kept alive in the family.

She turned round, started, and to my no small

surprise, answered in the same language: "Doubt not the spell, if the danger be daunted!"

And then, seeming to recollect herself, she blushed, and said in English: "It was a song my old nurse taught me. I should like to be a witch, if I might save people from being shipwrecked."

I made no reply, and we stood silently watching the struggle of the vessel with the storm for perhaps ten minutes. At length it succeeded in tacking at the very moment when all seemed lost, and bore safely away. Agatha's eyes met mine for an instant; there were both smiles and tears in them. She kissed her pearl again and moved away. But my digression has already gone farther than I intended. Let us return to the stone bench beneath the eaves, and the hot July sunshine.

II.

"Mr. Poyntz," said I, clasping my hands behind my head, and crossing one knee over the other, "how happens your house to be set up directly opposite the Devil's Ribs, and at least a mile and a half from the village? It's well enough in summer of course, but in winter, when the snow is on the ground, I should think you'd want to be nearer your butcher, not to speak of the meeting-house."

"Ay, surely!" answered Mr. Poyntz, taking the pipe from his mouth, and smoothing down the great sheaf of his beard. "But, d'ye see, sir, 'twas not I set the house here, nor my father before me, and maybe there was no butcher, nor yet no meeting-house along in those times. And another thing, since you've set me a-going, sir ; you see the lighthouse on the point yonder?" indicating an abrupt rocky promontory half a mile to the right of our position, which lay athwart the shore like a vast wall, separating us from the little fishing hamlet on the other side. "Ye see the lighthouse on tip-end of Gloam's Point, don't ye? Well, sir, old as that lighthouse looks to you now, I, that am a deal older than you are, can remember when 'twa'nt there. And that brings me round to what I was going to say. Along in those times, sir, when there wa'nt no regular lighthouse, but no bit less danger of craft running ashore, they used to rig up a sort of a jury-light, if I might so call it, in the front of our old gable. Ye may see the fixings now if ye steps forward a bit and look up there. Ay, ay, every dark night, more especially every dirty night, some of us would mount the garret shrouds, d'ye see, and show the lantern. And many a ship we saved, no doubt ; but they'd come ashore once in a while, for the best we could do."

"That's a suggestive name—Devil's Ribs. I suppose the bones of many a good man and vessel lie swallowed up in them."

"Ay, surely," returned the ancient mariner, swathing his head in a haze of tobacco-smoke. "The more since the currents and whirlpools thereabout mostly keep back the floating bits—spars, bodies, and such like—from getting to the beach. Whatever strikes there, sinks there, speaking in a general way. And forasmuch as there's five-and-thirty fathom clear water there, and always a tidy bit of surf on, 'tain't very popular work dredging."

"That's an ugly thought," I observed; "a great ship might go down there, and nothing ever be found to show what she was or who sailed in her."

I happened to glance at Agatha as I made this observation, and noticed that she paled a little and let her hands fall in her lap, and after a few moments she got up and entered the house, leaving Mr. Poyntz and me to ourselves. I fancied—but I may have been mistaken—that as she passed the threshold she laid her finger upon the pearl-shell necklace.

"Miss Agatha doesn't like to hear of wrecks," I remarked after a pause.

"Why no, sir," said Poyntz slowly, his blue eyes fixed upon the surf-whitened reef; "and perhaps 'tis natural she should not—specially those wrecks that the Devil's Ribs is to blame for."

"Has that necklace of hers anything to do with it?" I asked—though I cannot tell what possessed me to put so inconsequent a question. Partly to justify myself, I added: "It looks as if it might have been washed up out of the sea."

Poyntz threw a sharp look at me out of the corner of his weather-eye. "Ye've noticed the necklace, have ye?" said he; "and ye've a quick wit of your own, as they say is the way with lawyers. Howbeit, I think Jack Poyntz knows an honest man when he sights him, and hoping ye'll excuse the freedom, sir, methinks you are one. Now there's a bit of a yarn I'd like to spin ye—you being beknown amongst the great gentlefolks down to New York and elsewhere— about a wreck that once was on the Devil's Ribs. Maybe some of those you do business for can throw light upon it like; for what the ship was that was wrecked, or whence she sailed, was never known; for only that necklace that Agatha wears—only that and——something else, ever came to land. Ye guessed right, sir, d'ye see, and in hopes of your guessing yet more, I'll spin ye the yarn, leastways if ye've no objection. But afore starting, if ye'll kindly allow me, sir, I'll load my pipe, for with me the words come ever easier when there's smoke behind 'em."

I said nothing, but Poyntz saw well enough that I

was very much interested, and, like all incorrigible yarn-spinners, he found a humorous pleasure in prolonging his hearer's suspense. It was five minutes before his pipe was cleaned out, refilled, and lighted to his satisfaction, and then, having spread out his great arms along the back of the bench, stretched his mighty legs in front of him, and fixed his gaze upon the lighthouse—his favourite yarn-spinning attitude—he appeared to wait for an inspiration.

" How long ago was it ? " I asked at length, to set him going.

" Well, sir, it might be five-and-twenty years ago that that wreck took place. You was hardly more than out of your nursery then, I'm thinking. As for me, I was a chap of maybe forty—or maybe not so much ; my old father he had just parted his last cable, as I might say, and I had just come in from a voyage to the Pacific Coast for hides, and was living in this house alone by myself. I'd come home, sir, to find the girl as had given me her word spliced to another man ; and so it happened that I stayed a bachelor till after the age when many find themselves grandads. But I wedded at last, sir, as ye see, and never had cause to think the worse of myself for doing it ! "

" I should think not, indeed," I assented, laughing. But meanwhile I was telling myself that Agatha must

be nearly twenty years old, and that if Poyntz had
wedded only at the age of a grandfather, she could
hardly be his own offspring by marriage. Were the
doubts which her aspect had already suggested to me
well founded, then? I prudently waited, in the hope
that this question likewise might find its answer in
the course of my host's story.

"It was along about that time, sir," Poyntz continued, having acknowledged my compliment with a
friendly nod, "that I first came acquainted with
Scholar Gloam, as the folks called him ; him that
yonder point's named after, and that lived at the
Laughing Mill, over there, back of the wood. But
now I come for to think on it," broke off the old yarn-
spinner, pulling his meerschaum out of the corner of
his mouth and looking round at me, "did I ever
chance to speak to ye of Scholar Gloam afore ?"

"I don't think you ever did ; but I always like to
hear about anything that has a picturesque nickname,
as almost everything hereabouts seems to have."

The hale old man laughed, and raked his brown
fingers through his spreading beard. "In an out-of-
the-way place like this, sir," said he, "where's few
enough things anyway, nicknames come natural.
Well, now, as touching Scholar Gloam, he died nigh
a score of years ago ; leastways he knocked off living
in the body. For there be those," lowering his voice

and wrinkling his brows, "there be those—superstitious like—ready to take affidavit of having seen him, certain days in the year, a prowling round the Laughing Mill. His grave is near by, right under the Black Oak; and maybe the place is a bit skeery.

"Howsoever, that don't concern us now. When I knew Scholar Gloam, he was a middling-sized, slender-built young gentleman, having queer hair not all of the same colour, and a trick of talking to himself in a sort of a low mumbling way, as it might be the bubbling of water under a ship's stern, if ye know what I mean, sir. He was a comely favoured man of the pale sort, and grave and silent, though always the gentleman in his manners, as by blood and breeding. For the Gloams was the great family here fifty years ago, and was landlords of most of the farms roundabout; but they steered a bad course, as I might say, and died out, so as Scholar Gloam was the last of 'em. Old Harold, the Scholar's father, he was a reckless devil if any man ever was; and when he died 'twas found that Gloam Hall and all belonging thereto must go to the auction. The only bit left was the Laughing Mill itself, and an acre or two of land round about it."

"What did the mill laugh at, Mr. Poyntz? its own prosperity?"

"Nay, sir!" returned the burly mariner, shaking

c

his head. " I heard it laugh once, and I'd as soon
crack jokes with Davy Jones as listen to it again.
'Twas a mad, wild scream more than a laugh, and
like nothing human, praise goodness, that ever I
heard ! There was ugly yarns about that mill, d'ye
see ; folks said as how it had killed a man, and afterwards had got possessed with his evil spirit that
was always roaming about seeking whom it might
devour . . . . or maybe I've got things a bit mixed!"

"Who was it that was killed ?" I suggested.

" Ay, surely," said Mr. Poyntz thoughtfully, " I
should have told ye that. It was the man that was
married to old Squire Harold's housekeeper. And
that housekeeper, sir, when she was a young one, was
about as well-favoured a wench as a man would care
to speak with on a week day ; and 'twas said," hitch-
ing himself nearer to me on the bench and rumbling
in my ear, "that the Squire had a fancy to her, and
that after a time she was married off in a hurry and
sent to live at the mill, and that her baby was born
six months from the wedding. Well, all I know is,
little enough that child looked like him as passed for
its father ; and now comes the ugliest part of it. A
year after the child's birth the miller was found dead
one morning underneath his own mill-wheel. Seems
he'd fallen in the mill-race by some mishap, and so
had the life crushed out of him. But bad things was

said . . . . and the widow and child they went back
to the Hall, and lived there many years, till the
Squire died. The child got all his growth and train-
ing there, and folks used to say he'd have been more
like the Squire if he hadn't been most like his mother.
Well, the Squire being gone at last, and the estate all
sold saving just the mill, as I told ye, what does the
housekeeper and her son do but go back to the mill
again. The son—David he was called—was then a
likely young chap of maybe seventeen; and he took
right hold and began for to run the mill, and a very
fair profit he made out of it, taking one year with
another. And Scholar Gloam, he was living in the
mill-house along with them, having his room to himself, and his books and instruments quite cosy."

"Wasn't that rather an odd thing for him to do,
Mr. Poyntz, under the circumstances?"

"Ay, surely; but ye must keep it in mind, sir,
that Scholar Gloam was a wondrous odd man. He'd
been his whole life shut up with his books and
his studies, and no doubt had a vast deal of that
sort of learning; but of worldly knowledge, as I
might say, he'd none at all whatever, no more than
a child. Little he'd heard of his father's doings, be it
with the handsome housekeeper or anything else;
and little he dreamed—ye can make affidavit—that
her son had any claim to call himself his brother,

though 'twas told him once afterwards, as we'll come
to presently.　Nay, but my thought of him is, he was
a simple, honest gentleman at that time, kind of heart
and thinking ill of no one ; only a bit strange and
distant, d'ye see, as was no harm in the world for him
to be.　And being quite the same thing to him
whether he lived in a palace or a mud hut, so long
as he might study his fill, why, likely he'd an easy
enough time of it.

"And 'twould have been smooth enough sailing
for the whole of them only for one thing, which is to
say as how, ever and anon, in the mid of a big run of
luck, that there mill would take on a spell of its
laughing ; and with that folks would be giving it a
wide berth, and business would slack up again.　It
was no use the old woman and David a swearing
that a bit of rust on the axle was the cause of it all ;
for, mind ye, there was no steering round that black
fact of the old miller's having met his death on the
wheel ; and, too, though they was never done hunting
for that bit of a rust spot, they never found it, or if
ever they thought they had, lo ! there'd be the laugh
in their faces again, so to say, the next morning.
Ay, 'twas a bad, unholy sound that, sir ; but the
Scholar, strange to be told, seemed less to mind it
than anyone ; the cause being, mayhap, as how he
was a wondrous absent-minded man anyway, and the

only one as had never been told the true story of how the old miller came by his end.

"So now, sir, having dropped ye this bit of a hint of who Scholar Gloam was, I'll go on with the yarn of the wreck on the Devil's Ribs and the necklace.

•

III.

"But, first and foremost," continued Mr. Poyntz, after having revived his failing pipe with a dozen or so of quick whiffs, " first and foremost I must mention a queer habit he had—Scholar Gloam, I mean—and by which it was as I first came acquainted with him. As long as the sun was over the horizon line he'd stay indoors, behind the lock of his study door ; but at nightfall out he'd walk, foul weather or fair, and through the wood back yonder, down across the rocky pasture to the sea, a trip of maybe a mile and over. And often at midnight, as I've been pulling shorewards from the offing in my fishing dory, I've seen him standing a-top of the point, where the lighthouse stands now, the sky being light behind him, and he looking black, and bigger than any human creature ; and sometimes he'd be tossing his arms about, and shouting out some un-Christian lingo, though there was no one there to talk to—leastways that I could see. 'Twas a queer thing, I say, for a slender, delicate-looking gentleman like him to be out so by night, in all weathers, seeming not to know the difference whether it blew, or rained, or snowed, or all three together. Some folks used for to shake their heads over it, and say he was gone daft ; others there was (the superstitious kind, d'ye see) would have it as how Davy Jones, whose black bones had been the end of many a good ship and cargo, was in the custom of coming nightly to the point to hold parley with him, as it might be to strike a bargain whereby Davy should get the Scholar his estates and riches again in change for his soul.

"But Jack Poyntz never troubled his head with such fancies, sir ; and times, when I'd stowed my boat away, I'd hail him, and have him down to the house ; and sitting snug together by the kitchen fire, many a strange yarn has he spun me, the like of which never was heard before—leastways not outside of the books that were hid in his library—and of which many were writ in strange tongues as are not spoken in our Christian times. But it's not for me to be repeating of 'em now, only, as I was a-telling ye, it was such-like things brought us acquainted ; and very good chums we were, allowing for his being a young gentle-man scholar, and me a sailor as had no great book-learning, though knowing more of men and things than a hundred such as him. And by the end of a couple of years or so, meeting him that way off and on, I knew him as well as ever anybody knew him—as well, maybe, as he knew himself.

"Well, things being this way, one day, about the last week in September, it came on to blow. There was no rain, but no moon either, and the air was thick ; and night coming on, it was as black as my hat. It wasn't long afore there was a heavy sea running, and ye could have heard the surf on them Devil's Ribs five miles inland. I shipped the lantern up in the fore gable as usual, though knowing it couldn't show far in such a night ; and, thinks I, see it or not, any ship that gets caught in the tide this weather is bound to wreck ; so I'll hope, says I to myself, that they'll give us a wide berth. Howbe, I wasn't sleepy, so I loaded my pipe, and, thinks I, I'll have a snug smoke and a drop of grog alongside the kitchen fire afore turning in. No chance, thinks I, of my Scholar happening in this night ; he never could beat up against that wind, not if he had Davy Jones himself to pilot him. Well, there I sat for maybe an hour, the noise of the storm getting ever louder and louder, so at times I could hardly hear the rattle of my spoon as I stirred up the grog in the tumbler. Then all of a sudden there comes a knocking at the door, quick and heavy, and up I jumps and opens it, and lo ! there was the Scholar, with no hat and no coat, and that strange-coloured hair of his blown up wild about his head, and his eyes wide open and bright as a binnacle.

" ' Why don't you come in, sir?' shouts I, loud as if I was a-hailing him at the maintop, such a noise the wind made; 'ye'll get the heart and lungs blown clean out of ye if ye stop there!'

" Seemed like he answered me something, I couldn't make out what; but he laid hold on my sleeve with that thin white hand of his, that gripped like a vice, as if he'd pull me out into the storm with him, instead of coming in to me. And by his face I could see there was a storm within him as stirred him more than the one without; and then he pointed down seawards, and, thinks I, 'tis a ship he's seen or heard on the Devil's Ribs. And though I knew well we could no more help any poor wrecked souls. than if they was in the moon, yet it wasn't in me to back out of going with him to see what there was to see. So just laying hold of my tarpaulin and a flask of rum, off we starts on the run, dead in the wind's eye. How he managed for to scud over the ground at that rate is more than I could make out; the wind seemed to take no hold on him, but just let him through easy, though all the time it was near blowing my ears off.

" Well, down we came to the beach at last, at a

place about a cable's length this side of the point.
I'd kept my man in sight up to this time by reason
of the white shirt he had on, his coat, as I told ye,
being off him, but whither gone I'd not remembered
for to ask him. But now, all of a sudden, I found
he'd disappeared, and all I could see was the pale
froth of the surf that came leaping up the beach, with
a sound from the black wave behind it like the going
off of a big gun. Howsoever, I presently stumbled
round the corner of a big boulder—ye may see it
yonder, sir, in a line with the face of the lighthouse
and the top of the pine stump—and there he was on
his knees beside something wrapped up and still;
and when I looked, 'twas seemingly a young girl,
about twelve to thirteen years old, with no life in her.
She had come ashore on a bit of planking, and the
Scholar he had seen her coming, and had scrambled
down from the cliff in time to haul her in and under
the lea of the boulder. How he did it the Lord only
knows, for ten men working together might have
failed in it. But there she lay, with no mark of harm
or bruise upon her, and yet (as my heart misgave me)
lifeless from the washing of the waves through which
she had voyaged to land.

"I saw 'twould be no use trying to give her
rum yet awhile, so I stoops to lift her up along
with the bit of planking that she lay upon; and

Scholar Gloam he helped, though neither of us spoke, by reason of the thundering noise of the surf and the wind that half deafened us. It took us maybe a quarter of an hour, and then we were at home, and had her down before the fire, and wrapped in hot blankets, and everything done that could be done ; and after nigh a couple of hours' work, she moved the least mite in the world, and fetched a sigh. With that I sings out like I'd come upon a chest full of gold dollars, and says I, 'All's well, Scholar Gloam ; she's a-coming to, and she'll live to smile on us yet !' And then what does he do, sir, but just throws his head back with a little laugh, and topples over in a dead faint. 'Twas the exhaustion, ye must understand, as had come on all at once after the suspense of whether she was alive or dead was over. So there was I with the two of 'em to doctor. Well, I soon had the Scholar all right again ; but when he saw as how the child was a-doing well, he drops off suddenly to sleep, being tired right out and unable for to keep his eyes open ; and I didn't wake him, but just threw a blanket over him, and let him sleep it out.

"It was, maybe, half an hour after that that the little girl spoke ; she had been opening her eyes and then shutting them several times, and wondering where she was got to, I suppose, poor little dear. She was pretty and white, with yellow hair and big blue eyes, and soft little feet and hands, and pointed fingers; and round her neck was the pearl-shell necklace that ye've seen Agatha wearing, sir. Well, she looked at me for a bit, and seemed like to cry, not knowing who I was, or where she'd got to, d'ye see; and then she said something, repeating it over twice or thrice; but I couldn't understand her, by reason of her speaking some foreign lingo as was unknown to me. Howsoever, I took for granted that it must be some of her people she was asking after; so I pointed to the back room, and made believe as they were in there, but asleep, and not to be disturbed then. She believed me, poor little soul, and presently after dropped quietly asleep, with the tears yet under her eyelids, and the firelight flickering over her sweet face and yellow hair.

"Well, I sat there between the two, for I wasn't sleepy at all myself, and kept the fire alight, and my own pipe a-going, till morning, by which time the storm was mostly cleared off. So I got the old lantern down from the gable, and stirred about to get breakfast ready; and at sunrise, the two being still sleeping, I walked out to see if so be as anything of the wreck was visible. But the Devil's Ribs was only a bank of foam, and when I came to the beach there was naught there but a few shattered timbers and bits of spars and rigging; whatever else there

may have been had gone down within the whirlpool
of the Devil's Ribs, and would never see daylight
more ; nor was there anything to tell where the
wrecked ship hailed from, or what she was, or whither
she was bound. Nay, a man might well have doubted
whether there'd been any wreck at all ; and superstitious folks might have thought that the pretty
child we had found was a sea-nymph or a mermaid,
who had come on the shoulders of waves to bring us
good luck—or bad, maybe ! Not that I'd have ye to
think, sir, that I'm of the superstitious kind, being
a man as has seen much of the world, and lived
a number of years in it. But 'twas a strange thing
altogether, and stranger yet was to follow, as ye shall
hear.

"In my walk I happened by the boulder where
I'd been with the Scholar overnight, and there I
picked up a small iron box, with a big lock on it ; it
was lashed to four bits of wood, so as it might float,
and I think it must have come ashore along with the
raft that brought the little girl. Just as I laid hands
on it, and cut away the lashings, I sighted one of the
villagers a-coming over the cliff path towards me. So,
not caring to be hailed at that time, I slipped the
box in the pocket of my jacket, and steered for the
house.

"And lo ! there was the fair child sitting in the

chair, and the Scholar he was kneeling in front of
her, with her hands in his, and they were a-talking
together in that same foreign lingo as she had
spoken in to me; for, d'ye see, he had learnt it all
from his books, and understood it as well as she
who was born to it. The child was a bit scared
and tearful still, and he seemed to be a-comforting
of her; and as I came in, says he, ' Don't let on
that her folks are drowned, Jack; for I've told her
they're but borne away to another harbour, and will
return one day to claim her. So meanwhile,' says
he, ' she'll come to live with me at the mill, and be my
little girl; for is she not my little girl now, since 'twas
I brought her forth from the ocean that would have
robbed her sweet young life?' With that he kisses
her little hands, and says somewhat to her again in
her own tongue. It touched my heart to see the two
together, sir; for, d'ye see, the Scholar had never
seemed to be aware, as I may say, of women or
children until now; he had moved through life without seeing them or speaking to them, save at times in
an absent, dreamy sort of a way, as though they were
in different worlds. But now he was full of earnestness and a kind of joyful trembling surprise, as one
who had all of a sudden opened his eyes to a great
treasure, and was delighting in it all the more for that
he had been unknowing of it before. He was all in

all a changed man, and softened, and waked up
inside, so that his eyes seemed to be a-seeing the
things that was round him, and not things in a
dream; and methought there was a difference in his
voice, too; it was deeper and tenderer like, and made
you feel as how he had grown to be a man more than
a scholar. I thought he was as a ship that had long
been lingering in cold dark waters, baffled with winds
that set towards no pleasant harbour, but which had
at last found its sails filled with a fair fresh breeze, as
was blowing her to warm southern seas and tropic
islands full of heat and life. Ye'll maybe laugh, sir,
to hear an old sailor talk like this; but surely I had
loved the man, and pitied him, too, for his loneliness;
and it touched me, as I said, to see that he had
found a good thing in the world, and could feel the
happiness of it.

"Pretty soon, 'Jack,' says he again, 'ye must help
me carry her to the mill this morning, before the
village folks are astir; and don't tell them that she's
there, or whence she came. She's my own, and her
past is all gone for ever; God has sent her to me for
my own. I shall make her love me as I now love
her, and no other shall have any part in her. I
will be to her all that she has lost, and more; and
I will cherish her always and make her happy. And
when the village folks find out that I have her (as

soon of course they must), they shall be told that she is a good fairy come to bring me fortune and delight. I'd say that she rose up one morning out of the deep clear pool just above the mill-race; and that though appearing as a human being, she is in very truth not mortal, but has consented to live with me so long as I continue worthy of her companionship. But when the time comes—which God forbid it ever should!—that I prove unworthy, then shall she vanish back to her natural abode, and I be more desolate than before she came. And as for this necklace,' says he, 'it is a talisman; and should fate ever separate us, yet this be left me, 'twill be a pledge that' . . . .

" What's happened ? "

The yarn broke off abruptly enough. Poyntz and I had both started to our feet, our eyes and ears straining towards the mill-stream, where little Peter had during the last hour been quietly fishing. The sound of a quick scramble, a heavy plunge, and simultaneously a lusty scream, had sharply broken the repose of the summer afternoon.

"'Tis the brat has toppled in!" cried Poyntz, the sunburnt ruddiness of his complexion turning to a tawny sallow hue. "He can't swim; haste ye lower down, sir; I'll to the pool; but if as he's carried over the fall, ye'll stop him at the rapid."

· We had already set off on a run towards the bank, and we now separated in accordance with Poyntz's suggestion. I saw no more of the latter, being wholly absorbed in carrying out my part of the programme; and in a few moments I was standing panting beside the rushing water, trying to select the best point from which to take my plunge. Just then I heard a swift rustling step behind me, and there was Agatha, her lovely face and eyes aglow with terrified excitement. Then it passed through my mind that she had always evinced a particular tenderness and affection for poor little Peter; and at the thought I must confess that my resolve to save him at all risks became tenfold as strong as it had been before.

It was all a whirl and confusion; and only by comparing notes afterwards did we make out the order of events. Master Peter, it seems, after much unfruitful angling, had at last succeeded in hooking a huge trout, and straightway had lost first his mental and then his bodily balance. The fish being fairly on the hook, and pulling hard, the little man had rather chosen to go in after it, rod and all, than save himself at the cost of losing it. His scream, however, had startled not only his father and myself but Agatha and his mother likewise ; and the latter had followed her husband, as Agatha did me. When Poyntz reached the brink of the pool, the young fisherman had just risen for the second time, and was circling helplessly in the eddy. Poyntz sprang forward ; but his foot catching in a vine, he fell prone, his head in the water and the rest of his body on dry land.

Before he could disentangle himself (an operation which the well-meant but too convulsive efforts of Mrs. Poyntz only served to retard) the child had drifted into the current and was carried over the fall. It was now that Agatha and I first caught sight of him. She pressed impulsively forward, and had I not retained her would have leaped into the headlong rapids herself. As I caught her arm, I felt rather than saw her glance at me, as though measuring my ability to do what must be done. Apparently her decision was in my favour, for she stepped back ; and an instant after I was staggering breast deep in the boiling stream, watching the swift but topsy-turvy onset of Master Peter. Down he swept ; and to make a long story short, I succeeded in catching hold of him without losing my footing, and thereby in saving his life and my own. Agatha helping from the bank, we were soon landed high and dry, or

D

rather, very wet. Then ensued a great and indescribable hullaballo, wherein the first distinguishable words burst from Mr. Poyntz :

"Look ye here, wife!" cried he, laughing and weeping in the same breath, "look if the lad hasn't stuck to his fish through it all!"

And so it proved ; Peter had rivalled the childish exploit of his predecessor, stout little Kit North. There was the rod, still lightly gripped in his small fist; and a three-pound trout was flapping and gasping at the end of the line.

"He's but a chip of the old block, Mr. Poyntz," said I, when the shouts that greeted the discovery had somewhat subsided. "What is that sticking in the corner of your mouth?"

The old mariner put up his hand and took the thing out, and after staring at it for a moment in comical dismay, he burst into a laugh, in which everybody joined. It was the stem of his well-loved meerschaum, held unconsciously between his teeth throughout the entire turmoil; the bowl had probably been snapped off when he fell on the brink of the pool. So we all retraced our way to the house, the trout resting triumphantly in Peter's arms, who was himself carried by his father. Agatha and I walked side by side ; neither spoke to the other, and I knew not what thoughts were in her mind ;

but for my own part I had never been more light
of heart, and I regarded Peter and his trout as the
best friends that ever lover had. My achievement had
been trifling enough, Heaven knows ; but such as it
was, it had been done before her eyes, and partly
at least for her sake. When we had reached the
house-door, and the others had passed in before us,
she paused on the threshold and turned to me,
smiling, with her finger upon the necklace-
clasp.

"I kissed it to save you . . . . and Peter !" she
added hastily, and with a light in her dark eyes that
was half mischievous, half earnest.

"And now that we're saved, I suppose you are
going to kiss . . . . Peter ?" I dared to reply, for my
ducking had given me courage.

She blushed, but looked straight at me ; and the
next moment was gone into the house, leaving me
uncertain whether I had gone too far or not far
enough. But, ah ! happy Peter. A few bruises, and
the involuntary swallowing of a gallon or two of
water, were the extent of his injuries ; while his
blessings were beyond estimation. When I came
downstairs half an hour later, after changing my
clothes, I found him bundled up in an old pea-jacket
of his father's, and sitting in Agatha's arms. He was
watching his mother clean the big trout, the prize

of his valour ; and as I passed by, Agatha glanced up at me and kissed him !

I stole out by the kitchen-door and looked about for Mr. Poyntz ; for his yarn had, for several reasons, begun to interest me exceedingly, and I was most anxious to hear the end of it. But he was nowhere to be seen ; he had gone off to attend to something on the farm, and would as likely as not be absent till supper-time. It was a long time till then, and meanwhile I was without anything to amuse me. My mind was restless and excited, and I would have been thankful for any distraction. Nothing turned up, however, and at length—without being at the pains even to notice what direction I was taking— I set off on an objectless tramp, and was soon out of sight of the farmhouse.

I had plenty to think about—so much, indeed, that I could think coherently about nothing. Ideas crowded incongruously upon one another, now this one and now that catching my attention for a moment, and then receding to the background. From the picture of my late adventure in the mill-stream, I slid to a review of Agatha—my relations with her ; did she care for me ? had my lucky exploit really advantaged me ? and ought I to have stolen a kiss upon the doorstep ? Instead of considering these questions, I was pondering the tale which

Poyntz had begun to tell. Was it all true? would
he ever finish it? and what would be its up-
shot? But now the pearl-shell necklace ruled
my thoughts. Was it possibly the same as that
which my great-grandmother had lost? and if
so, would Agatha be likely to know anything
about it? The next moment a vision of Scholar
Gloam had risen before me. How had he come to
die, and be buried beneath the Black Oak? and why
was the old mill considered haunted? David—the
handsome housekeeper's son—what had become of
him? and, above all, what had been the fate of
the little sea-nymph? Then the necklace once more
—how came Agatha to attach such talismanic virtues
to it? and was not her doing so evidence that she
must know its ancient history? Again, was Agatha
Poyntz's own daughter? and if so, who and what
had been her mother? for she must be the child
of a union prior to that which had resulted in Peter.
The speculation gave place in turn to the idea of
the mill-wheel possessed by the devil, or by the
soul of the murdered miller—Poyntz had seemed
uncertain which. Had its "laugh" really been so
terrible? or had not an originally harmless, if disagreeable noise, acquired a supernatural horror only
because listened to across a gap of twenty years?
Ah well, what matter to me were all these idle,

unanswerable queries ? Behind all things—before all things, I seemed to meet the sweet fascination of Agatha's dark eyes, and to catch the gleam of her yellow hair. Yes, ever and ever, as the pendulum swings outwards and returns, does my thought come back to Agatha !

Immersed in such disjointed musings, I had journeyed on I know not how long, when all at once I became conscious, so to speak, of the outward world, and looked up and on all sides of me. Where was I ? In no place certainly that I had ever visited before. The sea was nowhere visible ; the surface of the ground was rocky and irregular, and in nearly every direction the view was shut in by thick growths of pine, birch, and oak. From beyond a clump of the latter, southward from where I stood, I thought I detected the noise of falling water ; and glancing eastwards, I could trace the course of a stream which was itself unseen, by the hedge of stunted timber that fringed its banks. The aspect of the neighbourhood was wild and remote ; it seemed to lie apart from men's ways ; and certainly he would have been an unsocial spirit who should have chosen such a spot to live in. On the other hand, anyone in search of a good place to do a murder in, or hold a witch meeting, need not have looked farther. A corpse might lie amongst these rocks and bushes

for twenty years without a chance of being discovered; and ghost and witches might scream their
eëriest unheard by mortal ear.

Meanwhile I walked on to the other side of the
clump of oak trees, when I suddenly found myself
gazing on a scene that involuntarily brought me to a
standstill.

v.

I was now standing on the bank of a stream
which, coming from the west, took its course past
my feet eastwards. For some distance its approach
was between gradually rising walls of rock, which
were highest just where I stood. Thence was a
precipitous descent into a small gorge about one
hundred paces in length, whose steep sides opened
out towards the east, their meeting-point being my
present station. Through the natural gateway which
it had cut for itself in the face of the precipice, the
stream fell cataract-wise into a deep pool below,
whence overflowing it rushed down a rugged incline,
and, having leapt another fall, raced along the middle
of the little glen, and so hurried with foam and noise
onward to the sea.

There were vestiges of a rude bridge, long
since broken down, across the natural gateway just

mentioned; and I even fancied that I could detect traces of an ancient footpath which had its beginning somewhere in the west, and, crossing the stream at this point, had then clambered down the slope to the bottom of the gorge. The bridge had not been entirely of stone; but a stout plank had probably spanned the flood, secured at either end by rough masonry. It must have been a ticklish passage without a handrail, for a false step, followed by a plunge over the cataract, would have been almost certain death. If Master Peter had tumbled in here instead of at the other pool miles lower down, not Poyntz, nor Agatha, nor I, nor all the luck in the world could have got him out alive.

The hollow of the gorge was much overgrown with bushes and brambles, and along the margin of the noisy stream the grass was high and rank. At the opening of the little valley farthest from where I stood rose an immense oak-tree—the only tree of anything like its size to be seen within a mile—whose wide-spreading branches cast a deep shadow on the earth beneath. So thickly clustered the leaves on the stalwart boughs, and so dark was their tint of green, the whole great tree seemed to have been steeped in night. The gorge, though full of sunlight and verdure, and vocal with the splash of the cataracts, wrought on me even at the first glance an impression of loneliness and desolation. The blue sky seemed farther away from this than from other parts of the earth's surface, and methought the sun shone upon it rather in mockery than in love.

Nearly midway down the hollow, and just under the second cataract, hung a huge water-wheel. It hung there motionless, and plainly many a year had passed since it had revolved upon its ponderous axle. It was built of wood, on a clumsy and old-fashioned model, and had become so blackened by age and weather that one might have fancied it charred by fire. Its parts were fastened together with great nails and clamps of iron, the strength of which, however, was now but a deceptive appearance, for the metal was eaten away by red rust, so that a hearty shake would probably have caused the whole structure to tumble into ruin. The rain and snow of unrecorded seasons had spread the rust in streaks and blotches over the swarthy rottenness of the woodwork until I could almost have believed it dabbled with unsightly stains of blood.

Side by side with these ominous discolorations, however, were growing patches of tender green moss ; and thick tufts of grass bent gracefully over the heavy rim of the wheel, where it impended above the rushing water. A delicate vine of convolvulus had become rooted somewhere above, and had wreathed itself in and out among the rigid spokes. It seemed as though Nature were striving, with but partial success, to win back to her own fresh bosom this gaunt relic of man's handiwork. With but partial success; for all the magic of her beautiful adornments could not annul the odd feeling of repulsion— or was it perverted fascination?—with which this sullen wheel began to affect me. I know not how to interpret, even to my own mind, the nature of this impression. Solitary as I stood there, I yet could not rid myself of the notion that I was not (in the ordinary sense of the word) alone. That wheel— there was something about it more than belongs to mere negative brute matter. It seemed not devoid of a low and evil form of consciousness—almost of personality. I recognised the morbid extravagance of the idea at the same time that I was powerless to do away with it. Everyone, probably, has had some similar experience; and the fact that reason cannot account for the sensation does not lessen its impressiveness.

The wheel had caught my eye from the first, and, as it were, commanded my main attention. But after a few minutes I looked away from it, not without a conscious effort of will, and gave a closer examination to other objects in the glen. The mill

to which the wheel appertained stood on the right
bank of the stream, but was now little more than
a heap of ruins. The wooden part was wholly
decayed, and the stone foundations were displaced
and shattered, and covered with weeds and rubbish.
A few paces farther back, huddled against the
southern acclivity of the gorge, was the carcase of
a dismantled and deserted house. The roof had
fallen in, the window frames and sashes were gone,
and the lifeless rooms stood open to the air. The
stone walls had formerly been overlaid with plaster,
but this had mostly fallen away, and what patches
remained here and there were stained with greenish
mould. A tall clump of barberry bushes was
growing just within the threshold of the doorway,
as if to dispute the entrance of any chance intruder;
and a vigorous plantation of some species of
yellow flowers was waving above the remains of the
chimney. The spectacle was in every respect forlorn
and depressing; no barren desert, that had never
been trodden by the foot of man, could have so
repelled and saddened the observer. Man feels no
sympathy for what has never known life; but that
which once has lived and now is dead, yet retains
in death some semblance of its extinct vitality,—that
it is which brings the true feeling of desolation home
to us.

After a time I climbed cautiously down from my coign of vantage, and making my way between loose stones and tangled shrubbery, I passed the black wheel and arrived at length beneath the shadow of the great oak. And here, for the first time, I began to feel very weary, with a weariness as much of the mind as of the body. In fact, what with my adventure with Peter, my long walk, and the excitement produced by old Jack Poyntz's strange yarn, I had been through a good deal for an invalid, and had earned the right to a little rest. Looking about me for a seat, my eye fell upon a small mound which lay between me and the base of the oak, with a bit of gray stone jutting out from one end of it. It might once have been a bench; at all events it would serve my turn, so I threw myself down at full length and pillowed my head and shoulders against it. As I lay, my face was turned towards the open end of the gorge, and away from the house and mill-wheel. These, however, dwelt in my memory; and on closing my eyes, I found that the scene of the ruin stood distinctly before my mental sight, more weird than the reality, because the phantom sunshine appeared pallid and ineffective.

The sound of a breeze stirring amid the thick leaves over my head mingled with the gurgle of the stream, until it seemed as if some voice were speaking in a low minor key—a tone without passion and without hope. As I listened, and fancifully attempted to fashion words and sentences out of the inarticulate murmur, that odd sensation of not being alone (which had all along been hovering about me) suddenly intensified itself to the pitch of conviction. Sitting up with something of a start, I glanced nervously towards the mill, and at once had the pleasure of seeing my conviction justified. The figure of a man was actually standing on the opposite side of the stream, one hand resting upon the wheel, while he fixed upon me the gaze of a pair of black eyes. He had probably been there from the first, or if not precisely there, then in the near vicinity ; there were hiding-places enough amongst the ruins. Nevertheless I felt an unreasonable anger against him. He had come upon me unawares ; and a surprise, if it be not agreeable, is apt to be very much the reverse.

He was a person of medium height, perhaps a little below it, and was clad in a shabby old-fashioned coat and small-clothes. He wore no hat, and the black hair which grew thickly upon his high head was curiously variegated with large patches of white. His countenance showed refinement and sensitiveness but the expression stamped upon it was singularly painful. I cannot better describe it than by saying that it seemed to indicate loss, loss beyond remedy either in this world or the next. Its effect upon me resembled that wrought by the desolate house, but was more potent, because humanised. The man seemed beyond middle-age, judging from the furrows on his brow and the stoop on his shoulders; and yet there was a kind of immaturity in his aspect. He was as one whose intellectual much outweighed his actual experience; who had dwelt amidst theories and eschewed reality. Such a combination of age and youth needs a strong seasoning of sincerity and simplicity to make it palatable; but in the present case these qualities were wanting, and instead there was an indefinable flavour of moral perversion.

When we had regarded each other for several moments, the man crossed the mill-race and advanced towards me, making a gesture of greeting with his hand. His manner was well-bred and quiet, and left no doubt that he was a gentleman; notwithstanding which I felt an antipathy against him, and was half-minded to admonish him that his presence was unwelcome. That I did not yield to this impulse was due, perhaps, less to courtesy than to the strong sentiment of curiosity with which the stranger had already inspired me. In other words, he was a magnet that attracted me with one pole while repelling me with the other; and the attraction was, for the moment, the stronger force of the two.

At this juncture it occurred to me—I know not how I had failed to think of it before—that these ruins must be what was left of the Laughing Mill, to which Poyntz had made allusion in his interrupted yarn. The recognition gave me a thrill of a kind not altogether agreeable; I was glad that the sun shone instead of the moon. Nor did I, under these changed conditions, so much regret the presence of a companion. I was in a nervous and abnormal state, and though far from superstitious—no lawyer could venture to be that—I preferred society to solitude in a place which had the reputation of being haunted. It was healthier to converse about such follies—even with an unsympathetic interlocutor—than to brood over them in private. This old-fashioned personage, moreover, had the air of being familiar with the neighbourhood; perhaps he was in the habit of coming here, and could give me some information about its former inhabitants—Scholar Gloam and the rest. I repented my former rude intentions, and resolved to be friends with him, and draw him out. Accordingly I returned his salute, and commanded my features to an expression of affability.

VI.

Within about three paces of me he stopped, and passed his hand two or three times through the black and white masses of his hair. He had the air of trying to rouse himself from a mood of painful preoccupation. At length he spoke in a faint, unaccented tone, like a voice heard far off.

" I want your sympathy," said he.

" Have we met before?" I asked, rather taken aback. " I really don't remember—but I believe I've been half asleep, and am hardly awake yet."

He shook his head slowly, his black eyes curiously perusing my face. "You have chosen an ill place to sleep in," he remarked after a pause. " Many a year have I sought repose there—in vain."

" Indeed? Well, I came here quite by accident, and judging by the aspect of the place, I shouldn't have supposed it would have been often visited."

" You are right, few come hither now ; but as many as do so are liable to meet with me."

I looked more narrowly at my queer companion, and all at once the thought struck me, the man is mad ! Yes, it must be so. How otherwise could the strangeness of his appearance, behaviour, and conversation be accounted for? He did not look dangerous, probably he was incapable of doing harm, and therefore permitted to wander about as he liked. In the moral atmosphere of these ruins he was sensible of somewhat congenial to his own forlornness, and [hence haunted them rather than any more cheerful spot. Certainly, this was an appropriate haunt for a madman—for one whose mind had fallen into that ugliest chaos which was once beauty and order. But I liked the spectacle of mental even less than that of material decay; and though the poor gentleman had asked me for my sympathy, I scarcely knew how to give it to him.

By I know not what faculty of divination, he appeared to suspect what was passing in my mind.

"I am not mad," he said quietly, but with a tremor of the finely-cut though irresolute lips. "I am not mad, I have passed beyond insanity. Let me sit down here and talk to you. Nay—do not rise! Recline as you were doing, and close your eyes if you will; I need only your ears."

While speaking thus he passed behind me, and apparently seated himself at the foot of the oak-tree, outside of my range of vision. But no sooner was he out of plain sight, than I was seized with an odd fantasy that he had actually vanished into thin air, and that were I to look round, I should not find him. His voice only was left, and even that now seemed unearthly. Was it a human voice? and not rather the rustling of leaves and the gurgling of .water, translated by my feverish imagination into weird speech?

"You were dreaming," resumed the voice; "what dreams had you of the wheel?"

"What dreams had I of the wheel?" I repeated, leaning back on the mound, and clasping my hands across my eyes. Here was another instance of my new friend's insight. How had he known that the wheel was in my thoughts at all! Yet it was true that I had given rein to all sorts of fanciful speculations concerning it, and was now, moreover, quite in the mood to give them utterance. And what better auditor could I desire than a madman, whom the wildest extravagance could not disconcert, nor the most palpable absurdities annoy? The opportunity was too fair to lose.

"What dreamt I of the wheel?" I exclaimed again: "I dreamt it was the mighty Wheel of Fortune, who, weary of trundling it about the world, had left it here amidst the sedge and spray of the waterfall. Henceforth, therefore, there shall be no more ups and downs in life, but mankind shall move for ever across one level plain, unchecked by darkness and uncheered by light!"

"Would you have it thus?"

"Oh no—not I! Come back, fair goddess! come back and wrest thy wheel from amidst those clinging vines and brambles—the arms wherewith reluctant nature strives to hold it back! Bring it forth once again upon the dusty road, and turn it as you go, lest our sluggish hearts forget to beat, and we cease to draw the very breath of life, and our souls, torpid and uninspired, grovel earthwards, nor dream of climbing higher than themselves! Bring forth thy wheel, and turn it for ever even as the world turns; for thy fickleness is the life of our lives!"

"Methinks the wheel of misfortune were its truer title; for it turns ever between a fool above and a corpse beneath; and the laugh of madness sounds before, and behind is a track of blood!"

"Nay, name it how you will; since all of human joy and grief, and life and death, have clustered round its course, as the moss and the vines cluster about it now. See how Nature seeks to make the awful symbol of destiny into a plaything for her own beautiful idleness! How fearlessly the light and shadow rest upon it! Yet it is bloodstained. Those rank ferns bend and peer in quest of some lurking horror? What is it? I feel its influence upon me."

"Aye, you feel it!" murmured my unseen companion, tremulously; "and how could you help but feel it? Do not the tragedies of human life instil their essence into the things we call inanimate? You have shuddered when handling the rack and the Iron Virgin of the Inquisition, and felt faint at the sight of the guillotine and the gallows. You were awed

E 2

by an evil influence breathed from the actual wood and iron—not by the mere knowledge of ghastly scenes in which they had borne a part."

"How came the influence there?" I asked, humouring his grotesque theory.

"That which has existed in an atmosphere of revenge, hatred, and despair, becomes at last impregnated with a malignant intelligence derived from them ; an intelligence both devilish in itself and able to endow you with its own deformity. And if you hold not aloof from it, you shall surely be destroyed —in soul, if not in body likewise!"

"But do we feel this influence unless aware beforehand that it is there?"

"Fix your thought constantly upon yonder wheel," was the reply, "and mark if it does not answer you."

Still with my hands clasped across my eyes, I concentrated my mind as directed, and presently felt my veins crawl with a slow chill of dismay—a chill which deprived me of control over my faculties, while awakening them to unnatural activity. That the wheel had a conscious personality, instinct with evil, seemed no longer open to doubt. Now the plash and gurgle of the water changed to the stealthy drip of blood ; and I shrank from the breeze that moved my hair as from a pestilential breath. Was I going mad too? My will seemed to falter; a tremor which I could not repress passed through me from head to foot.

"Aye, you feel it," murmured the voice again. "You are answered!"

By a determined effort I regained command of myself. Perhaps it was none too soon. Nothing is easier than to indulge this morbid vein, and few indulgences, I believe, are more perilous. With my change of mood came a change of tone; I cast aside the hysteric style, and adopted one more brusque and matter-of-fact, to which the reaction from sentimentality may have added a touch of asperity.

"Come, come!" I said. "We are overdoing this folly. I know well enough what place this is; Mr. Poyntz began to tell me about it this afternoon. An amusing story—all about the Laughing Mill, and the fellow who was drowned, and the nymph of the pearl-shell necklace. You see, I know what I am talking about! But the tale broke off in the middle; perhaps you can finish it?"

"It is you who must finish it?" returned the other. "But I want your sympathy; so let me tell my part."

"Do so," said I, "by all means. When I know you better, I shall be better able to sympathise with you. As to my finishing the story, I think I'm more likely to succeed as a listener than as a narrator; however, if it must be so, I'll give it the best ending I can. And I do sympathise with you already," I added, after a pause, in a less flippant tone. "I am a man, and I believe in human brotherhood."

My eccentric companion made no rejoinder, though I fancied he gave a sigh. Presently he began to speak in the same evenly-pitched, far-away voice that he had used throughout. The effect was rather as of a weary reader reading from a book than as of one who talks spontaneously, there was no hesitation, no rise and fall, no fire, no faltering. Yet the recital moved me more deeply than if it had been delivered with impassioned eloquence. Through the sad colourless medium I seemed to behold the direct movement of events, and almost to take part in them. Moreover, as the narrator proceeded, the notion more than once possessed me that his words reached my ears from some inward source—that I was merely thinking the things I seemed to hear. His tone was so attuned to the desolateness of the surroundings, as to appear like the mystic interpretation of their significance, such as might result from intense brooding over them. Indeed, taking into consideration all that I had seen, heard, and fancied that day, I almost believe I could have fallen asleep and dreamed just such a story as he told me.

Certainly no dream could have been stranger than the things he told.

VII.

They brought the yellow-haired little maiden to the mill (ran the story), and Gloam called her Swanhilda. Jael, the old housekeeper, looked at her sharply, and asked what good such a little creature could be among poor people? the girl was of no use herself, and would only hinder those who had to work.

Gloam answered, "Heaven has sent her to us. She shall be our inspiration, and the symbol of our good. Treat her with reverence, and tenderly, as you would treat the best and purest aspiration of your heart. If we wrong her, it will be our deadliest sin. If we cherish her, the sins we have committed may be forgiven us."

"She is a gentleman's daughter, at all events," said Jael. "Look at the shape of her hands and feet! No, she never worked, nor did her mother before her. Well, maybe her family will come after her some day, and pay us well for taking care of her. Or who knows but she may turn out heiress to some great estate, when she grows up? If that were so . . . . David, son, come hither. See—she's a pretty little thing."

Handsome David stooped down and took the child's small soft hand. "And so she is—a little beauty!" he exclaimed, looking into her blue eyes. "Can't speak English, eh? That's a pity; but live and learn. Right glad am I that you brought her here, sir," he added to Gloam. "Where did you pick her up?"

"She's the rainbow after the storm," Gloam answered, smiling. "But I shall not teach her English. Let her speak only the language which she has brought with her." And he led the child away.

"That may do for him," muttered David, "but it won't do for me. He can talk with her and I can't; so if he won't teach her English I will. Devil take me if she isn't a sweet little fairy; and she's quite enchanted the Scholar already. He's a changed man since yesterday. But he shan't have all the fun to himself."

. "She looks thirteen, don't you think?" said Jael. "She won't be a child much longer, David. Why, come three years or so, she'll be old enough to be married."

"Ay, old woman; but I shall be too old to marry her," he answered, with a keen look and a laugh.

"I tell you, son, she's a lady, and good enough to mate with any man."

"That's your notion, and likely enough it's true.

But good blood isn't all I want—I've got that already, thanks to your good looks ; what I want and haven't got is money. And Miss Swanhilda, pretty as she is, has less money even than I."

"But she has relations—rich relations ; her own father and mother may be alive for all we know. If she was saved off a ship where all the rest were lost, of course there'll be no telling for some time to come. But it's worth waiting for."

"Did no papers come ashore—nothing to help identify her ? "

"I asked Poyntz that," said Jael, "and so far as I can make out, I think there hasn't been anything."

"Well, I'll make sure of that next time I go over. We might advertise in the foreign papers after awhile. A right pretty little thing she is, and no mistake. But I'm not a-going to run any risks, old woman. Supposing I was to get tied down to her for life, and then find out that she'd got nothing, what would I do then ? "

"There's no need of supposing any such thing, David. As if you couldn't make the girl fond of you so as she wouldn't marry any but you ; then you'd have her safe, and if all turned out well, 'twould be time enough to put the ring on her finger."

"Ay, that's about the idea, I suppose. Well, the Scholar's got the start of us now ; and 'twon't do to let him see what we're up to; luckily he never did see what's going on under his nose. By-the-way, that's a quaint bit of a necklace the child wears; mayhaps that'll help us to find out something——"

He broke off suddenly, with an oath, and he and his mother stood listening, pale-faced. His eyes were angry, but terror lurked in those of the woman.

A strange jarring sound filled the air; it seemed to come from every side, and screamed harshly into the listeners' ears. If a fiend had burst into a long fit of malignant laughter close at hand the effect could not have been more hateful and discordant.

"The laugh again!" David muttered between his teeth. "It would be just our luck if it scared our best customer away. Devil take me if I don't begin to believe it is the soul of that cursed husband of yours, that you treated so affectionately. I'll swear there's not a spot of rust on the machinery as big as a pin's head."

"Oh, son, don't look that way at me," said the woman, in a shaken voice. "I would prevent it if I could; what can I do?"

"You might jump in and follow your husband; that's what he wants, I suppose," returned the son, angrily. "It's you that wronged him, not I; and as long as you're here we'll have no luck. That's the long and short of it!"

The laugh had died away, and Jael, pressing her hand above her heart, turned aside and passed out. She loved her son, and would have shed her blood for him; but this was not the first time he had spoken thus.

After she was gone, David stood at the window, biting his lips and muttering to himself. Suddenly he heard Gloam's step behind him, and looked round in surprise.

"What was that noise?" Gloam asked.

"Why, nothing new, sir. The same old story. Something wrong with the wheel again, I suppose."

"I remember no such sound before," said Gloam, excitedly. "It is hideous, like the shriek of an evil spirit. Let it never come again; it frightens Swanhilda, and comes between us like a prophecy of woe. Let it never come again!"

"You have taken to hearing through her ears and feeling through her senses—that's all the matter," answered David, smiling. "It sounds bad to you because it makes her head ache. As to stopping it, I'd do so, and gladly, if I but knew how. It loses us half our custom, for folks say the devil's at the bottom of it, sure enough."

"It is a wicked sound!" exclaimed Gloam again, "full of mockery and bitterness. Swanhilda was born to hear divine harmonies, and she will leave us if we greet her with such hideous discord."

"She was born to take her chance with the rest of the world, Mr. Gloam," replied the younger man, in a harder tone. Then he smiled again and added, in his muttering way, as he left the room, "She'll get used to it fast enough, never fear."

But a long time passed without the recurrence of the hateful sound, and meanwhile Swanhilda was recovering from her first melancholy and home-sickness. Gloam had told her that she would see her father and mother again some day, and by degrees her anxiety calmed down to a quiet and not uncheerful expectation. She seemed to know little of the history of her family, or else was averse from discussing it; for amidst all her winning sweetness and pure sincerity she retained a maidenly reserve and dignity not lightly to be overcome. But the guileless fascination which she unconsciously exercised upon all she met was impossible to resist. She gladdened all eyes and hearts, and the mill became a storehouse of beauty and gladness as well as of grain and meal. People came from all the surrounding neighbourhood to see Scholar Gloam's water-nymph; and at last, when the Laughing Mill was mentioned, they thought of Swanhilda's airy merriment—not of the ill-omened sound that had

first given it that name, but was already being fast
forgotten. So the prosperity of handsome David
increased, and was greater than it had ever been
before ; he had as many customers as the mill could
supply, and bade fair, in the course of years, to
become a wealthy man. He and Jael treated the
little water-nymph with every kindness, as well
they might ; and what Gloam had said seemed likely
to come true—that she would be the means of their
regeneration.

And Gloam himself was as a man transfigured.
He lived no longer amidst his books, but made
himself free to all ; and the neighbours wondered to
find him so genial and gladsome. He and Swanhilda
were constantly together ; they played and laughed
like children ; they went on long rambles hand-in-
hand ; in winter they pelted each other with snow-
balls ; in summer and autumn they gathered flowers
and berries and nuts. He treated her with the most
reverent and entire affection ; he was ready to
sacrifice anything for her sake, to give her anything
—unless it were, perhaps, the freedom to be to
another all that she was to him. But apparently
she was well content. Gloam was the only one who
spoke her language, and the only one, therefore, with
whom she could converse unrestrainedly. He would
not teach her English, and if others attempted to do

so it was without his knowledge or consent. He believed, it maybe, that no one but himself could appreciate her full worth, and thought it would be a kind of desecration to let another approach her too nearly. Certainly they were happy together. That part of his nature to which she appealed was not less youthful than she was herself; and in her society he felt himself immortally young. He forgot that there were lines upon his brow, and that his figure was bent, and that his hair had begun to be prematurely white. And he doubted not that as he felt so he seemed to her.

. Was his confidence justified? Had this child who was just beginning to be a young woman, penetration to see the fresh soul within the imperfect body? A more experienced man would have had misgivings, knowing that young women are apt to judge by appearances, and to be more swayed by downright power and passion than by abstract right and beauty. But Gloam's experience had not taught him this. He did not dream that she could ever learn to deceive him, or to give him less than the first place in her heart. But he dreamed that some day, distant perhaps, at least indefinite—they would be married. By all rights they belonged to each other, and when they had played their childish games to the end, and had wearied of them, then would they enter upon that new phase of life. Meanwhile he would not speak to her of the deeper love, lest she should be startled, and the frankness of their present intercourse be impaired. But women have been lost ere now through fear of startling them.

So more than two years slipped away, and the child Swanhilda had grown to be a tall and graceful maiden ; which seemed half a miracle, so quickly had the time passed. Her blue eyes had waxed larger and deeper, and in moments of excitement they became almost black. Her hair was yellow as an evening cloud ; her face and bearing full of life and warmth. Her nature was strengthening and expanding ; she was beginning to measure herself against her associates. Though so gentle, she was all untamed ; no one had ever mastered or controlled her. She knew neither her own strength nor weakness, but the time approached when she would seek to know them. Every woman is both weaker and stronger than she believes, and it is well for her, when the trial comes, if her strength be not the betrayer of her weakness.

VIII.

At this point in the story the voice of the narrator grew fainter and then made a pause. I still kept my reclining position, with my hands clasped above my closed eyes. In fact, it would have required a greater effort than I at the moment cared to make to have sat up and looked about me. The sun, I knew, had already sunk below the crest of the slope; the gorge lay in shadow, and beneath the oak it was almost dark. As I lay waiting for the tale to recommence, the sombre influence of the wheel asserted itself more strongly than ever. There it loomed, in my imagination, black, grim, and portentous. Its huge spokes stretched out like rigid arms, and the long grass which streamed along the gurgling water resembled the hair of a drowned woman's head. . . . . But now the voice began again.

One summer afternoon Gloam and Swanhilda were sitting on the wooden bench beside the mill, watching the heavy revolutions of the great wheel. They were alone. David was in the mill-room finishing the day's work, and Jael was preparing supper in the kitchen. For several minutes neither of them had spoken.

"Do you remember," said Swanhilda at last, using her native tongue, "the first day I came here, how there came a terrible sound that made me miserably frightened? I have never heard it since then. What was it?"

"Only a rusty axle; at least, so I suppose. That

careless David had forgotten to oil it properly. But I gave him such a scolding that there has been no more trouble."

"David is not careless—he works very hard, and I love him," retorted Swanhilda, tossing back her yellow hair. "Besides, such a noise could not be made by an axle."

"You may like David, but you mustn't love him ; you are a little princess, and he is only the house-keeper's son."

"What is the difference between loving and liking?" inquired Swanhilda, folding her hands in her lap, and turning round on her companion.

He took her hand and answered, "I shall teach you that when you are older."

"I am not so young as you think. I am old enough to be taught now."

"No, no, no!" said Gloam, shaking his head and laughing ; "you are nothing but a child yet. There is plenty of time, little water-nymph."

"If you will not teach me, I'll find someone else who will teach me. I will ask David ; he has taught me some things already."

"He? What have you learnt from him?" cried Gloam.

Swanhilda hesitated. "I should not have said that—but it's nothing, only that I am learning to

F

speak English. He didn't want you to know until I was quite perfect, so as to make it a surprise to you."

. "He had no right to do it. Why should you learn to speak with anyone but me?" exclaimed Gloam passionately.

"Do you think I belong to you?" demanded Swanhilda, lifting her head in half-earnest, half-laughing defiance. "No; I am my own, and there are other places besides this in the world, and other people. I will go back to my own country."

"Oh, Swanhilda," said Gloam, his voice husky with dismay, "you will never leave us? I cannot live without you."

"I will, if you are unkind to me. . . . Well, then, you must not be angry because David taught me English; and you must let him teach me the difference between liking and loving; I'm sure he knows what it is!"

"Do not ask him—do not ask him! That is my right; no one can take it from me! I saved you, Swanhilda; I brought you back to life, and that new life belongs to me!" The hand that held hers had turned cold, and he was pale and trembling. "I have kept you for myself; I have given up my own life—the life that I used to live—for you. But I cannot return to it, if you leave me."

"I did not ask you to give it up," she returned, waywardly. Then she relented, and said, "Well, you may teach me about loving, if you want to. Only, afterwards, you must let me love anyone I please!"

Gloam looked upon her for several moments, his black eyes lingering over every line of her face and figure. "You belong to me," he repeated at last. "If you left me for another, I should wish that your pearl-shells had drawn you down——"

Before he could finish uttering the thought that was in his heart, the words were drowned in a throbbing yell as of demoniac laughter. The evil spirit of the wheel, after biding its time so long in silence, had seemingly leapt exultingly into life at the first premonition of meditated wrong. Swanhilda shuddered, and hid her face in her hands. David thrust his head out of the mill-room window, and saw Gloam make a gesture of rage and defiance.

"Aha!" he muttered to himself, "so the children's games are over, are they? Can it be the devil's game that my beloved brother thinks of beginning now?"

Another year passed, and again a man and a woman were sitting together on the bench beside the mill. It was night, and a few stars twinkled between the rifts of cloud overhead. The gorge was so dark that the mill-stream gurgled past invisibly, save where occasionally a rising eddy caught the dim starlight. The tall wheel, motionless now, and only discernible as a blacker imprint on the darkness, lurked like a secret enemy in ambush. The man's arm was clasped round the woman's waist; her head rested on his shoulder, and her soft fingers were playing with the pearl-shell necklace that encircled her neck. They spoke together in whispers, as though fearful of being overheard.

"You silly little goose!" the man said; "a few months ago nothing would make you happy but learning what love was; and now you have found out you must ever be whimpering and paling. Why, what are you afraid of?"

"You know I am happy in loving you, David," was the tremulous answer; "but must lovers always hide their love, and pretend before others that they do not feel it? When I first dreamed of love, it seemed to me like the blue sky and the sunshine, and the songs of birds; but our love is secret and silent, like the night."

"Pooh! nonsense, and so much the better! Our love is nobody's business but our own, my lass. You wouldn't have Gloam find it out, would you, and part us? What! have you forgotten the fit he was in at my teaching you English a year ago? He wants you all to himself, the old miser! You weren't

happier with him than you have been with me, were
you?"

"Oh, David," whispered the girl, clinging to him,
"that was so different! I was happy, then, like a
wave on the beach in summer. I had no deep
thoughts, and my heart never beat as you make it
beat, and my breath never came in long sighs as it
does often now. Gloam used to say that he had
brought me back from death to life; but it was not
so. I lived first when I loved you. And the old
happiness was not real happiness, for there was no
sadness in it; it never made me cry, as this does."

He drew her to him with a little laugh. "When
you've lived a little more and got used to it, you'll stop
sighing and crying, and be as bright and saucy as
you were with Gloam. But you won't want to tell
him . . . . eh?"

She hid her face on his shoulder. "Oh no, no,
no; I could not; I should feel ashamed. But why
do I feel ashamed, David? Is not loving right?"

"Right? to be sure it is. Nothing more so!
And the pleasantest kind of right, too, to my thinking.
Eh, little one?"

"David, I have heard—are not people who love
each other married—at least sometimes? and after
that they are not afraid, or sad, or ashamed?"

A smile hovered on David's handsome lips.

"Married, yes, stupid people get married. Timid folks, who are afraid to manage their own affairs, and can't be easy till they've called in the parson to help them out. They're the folks that don't love each other right down hard, as you and I do. They're suspicious, and afraid of being left in the lurch ; so they stand up in a church and tie themselves together by a troublesome knot they call marriage. No, no ; we've nothing to do with that ; we're much better off as it is."

"But my father and mother were married, and they were not suspicious," ventured Swanhilda again, after a pause.

"Oh, ay, they were married," assented David ; adding, half to himself, "and if they were alive, too, and anxious to fill a son-in-law's pockets, I'd open mine, and gladly. But my father and mother were not married," he resumed to Swanhilda, with another smile, "so you see we've a good example either way."

She made no reply, but lifted her head from his shoulder and sat twisting the necklace between her restless fingers, her eyes fixed absently on the darkness. The clasps of the necklace came unawares apart, and it slipped from her bosom to the ground. She uttered a little cry, and stood up with her hands clasped, all of a tremble.

"I have lost it!" she said. "David, some harm is coming to me!"

"Nonsense! here it is, as good as ever." He picked it up as he spoke, and drawing her down beside him, fastened it again round her neck, and then kissed her face and lips. "There, there, you're all right. Did you think it was dropped in the mill-race?"

"Some harm is coming," she repeated. "It has never fallen from me since my mother put it on my shoulders, and said it would keep me from being hurt or drowned, but that I must never part from it. But I trust you, oh, my love! I trust you. Something seems wrong somehow; I have given you all myself . . . ."

"Lean close up to me, little one; rest that soft little cheek of yours against mine, and have done with crying now, or I'll think you mean to melt all away and leave me; and what would I do then?"

She turned and clasped her arms around him with a kind of fierceness. "I leave you, David? Oh—ha, ha, ha! Oh, but you must never leave me, my love— love—love! Oh, what should I do if you were to leave me?"

"Hush, girl; hush! you'll rouse the house, laughing and crying in the same minute! Don't you know

I won't leave you? There — hush! You'll wake
Gloam else."

" He loved me, too; he wouldn't leave me;
but he thought I wasn't old enough — not old
enough, ha, ha! . . . . David, does God know about
us ?"

"Not enough to trouble Him much, I expect,"
said the young man, with a short laugh. " If anything knows about us, it's the old wheel there, waiting
like a black devil to carry us off. Come, we must
creep back to the house."

They rose, Swanhilda stood before him, her sweet
sad face glimmering shadowy pale through the darkness. " Say, ' I love you, Swanhilda, and I will never
leave you ! ' " she whispered.

He hesitated, laughed, stroked her hair, and stooping, gazed deep into her eyes, as on the day when
they first met. Did his heart falter for a moment,
realising how utterly she was his own ? " You trusted
me just now," said he; "are you getting suspicious
again ?"

" No ; but I am afraid—always afraid now. When
you are not with me, I am afraid of everyone I meet;
I think they will see our secret in my eyes. When I
lie alone at night I am afraid to pray to God, as I
used to do. What is it? Why do I feel so? It
must be that we have done some wrong. My poor

love! have I made you do any wrong? I would rather be dead."

"Little darling—no! You couldn't do wrong if you tried. There is no wrong—I swear there isn't. Listen, now in your ear: I love you, Swanhilda, and I will never leave you! Satisfied now?"

Low as the words were whispered, they were heard beyond the stars, and stamped themselves upon the eternal records. But their only palpable witness was the mill wheel. A log of wood, carried over the fall, came forcibly in contact with the low-impending rim. It swung the heavy structure partly round upon its axle. And straightway, upon the hollow night, echoed a faint yet appalling sound as of jeering laughter. Slowly it died away, and silence closed in once more, like darkness after a midnight lightning flash. But it vibrated still in the startled hearts of the man and the woman, who crept so stealthily back to the house, and vanished in the blackness of the doorway, and it revisited their unquiet dreams.

IX.

Summer and winter came and went, and were followed by a gloomy and dismal spring. The late-lying snow was dissolved by heavy rains so that the mill stream was swollen beyond precedent, and rolled thundering through the gorge with the force of a full-grown cataract. But the mill was idle, and the wheel stood still. None came for flour now, nor to bring grist; for many a week all work had been foregone.

Yet the house was not deserted. An elderly woman, with a forbidding face that had once been handsome, moved to and fro behind the windows; and a man, bent and feeble, with strangely-grizzled hair, sat motionless for hours at a time in his study-chair. Sometimes, in his loneliness, he would set his teeth edge to edge, and clench his thin hands desperately, and utter an inarticulate sound of menace. But at a certain hour of the evening he would arise and walk with noiseless steps to the door of a darkened chamber. There he would pause and lean and listen. Presently from within would be heard the shrill, petulant crying of an infant, and anon the voice of its young mother, sad and tender, soothing and pathetic: "Baby, baby, don't cry; hush, hush, hush! father will come to us soon; he will come, he will come! he loves us and will never leave us; hush, hush, hush!"

At these sounds the pallid visage of the man would quiver and darken, and he would press his clenched hands upon his breast. Returning at length to his study, he got upon his knees and stretched his arms upwards.

"God—God of evil or of good, whichever you are —give my enemy into my power! Let my curse work upon him till it destroy him : let my eyes see him perish! He has robbed me of my love, and my hope, and my salvation; he has defiled and dishonoured that which was mine ; he has made my life a desert and an abomination! Yet I would live, and suffer all this and more, if he might perish by my curse, body and soul, for ever! Grant me this, God or Devil, and after do with me what you will!"

Such was his prayer. But he never entered the darkened chamber where the child and its young mother lay ; he never looked upon them or spoke to them, nor did his heart forgive them. He could not forgive till he had had revenge. Since that hour in which he had first learnt the truth, and with hysteric fury had sprung at the seducer's throat, his soul had been empoisoned against them and all the world. He was possessed by that devil to which he prayed, and good was evil to him.

One day he was standing in a kind of stupor at his window staring out at the black mill-wheel, which was now the only object in the world with which he felt himself in sympathy. There came a knock at the door, and Jael, the housekeeper, entered. Since the calamity which had befallen, her manner towards Gloam had undergone a change. She had before exercised a kind of authority over him, such as a compact and unsympathetic nature easily acquires over one of wider culture but more sensitive than itself. But Gloam had become more terrible in his desolation than a less naturally gentle man would have been; and Jael feared him. She felt that he might murder her; and minded her steps, lest in some sudden paroxysm he should leap out upon her.

She advanced a little way into the room, and stopped. He did not turn, or show that he was aware of her presence. After a few moments she said:

"Master, he is coming back; David's coming home again, sir. He's going to make it all right with Swanhilda—he means to marry her!"

Gloam did not stir; but as Jael watched him narrowly, she fancied that his limbs and body slowly stiffened, until they became quite rigid; only his head had a slight shivering motion. The woman shrank back a step, with a feeling of alarm.

It seemed a long while before Gloam spoke, and the same slight, involuntary shiver pervaded his voice. He still kept his face carefully averted.

"David coming back?"

"Yes, sir; I had a message from him this morning."

"To . . . . marry her!"

"Yes, indeed, sir; he'll make an honest woman of her. What he has done has laid heavy on his conscience ever since. And so he says he hopes you'll forgive and forget, and that we'll all prosper and be happy in the future."

Gloam's chest began to heave, and he folded his arms tightly across it. There was another long pause, as though he feared to trust his voice to speak. Finally the words came between his shut teeth :

"When—when—when ? "

" Did you mean, when will he be here, sir ? Well, he was expecting to reach the next town late this afternoon ; and from there he'd foot it over here ; and that wouldn't bring him here till nigh midnight. But likely he'll wait over, and get here to-morrow morning. Luckily though there's a moon to-night, to show him where to step, in case he comes right on."

Gloam unfolded his arms, and raising his hands to his head, passed them several times slowly through his hair ; staring downwards, meanwhile, at the wheel. The rigidity had passed away, and he seemed to be recovering from the agitation into which the first shock of the news had thrown him. Jael's mind was a good deal relieved at the absence of any signs of hostility on his part against David ; and she was just about withdrawing, when Gloam turned quickly about and stepped after her.

For the first time in the interview she now saw his face ; and the sight so far startled her firm nerves as to draw from her a short low cry. It was not that the face was pallid, furrowed, and wasted ; it had been all that from the first ; but what appalled her was the ghastly expression of the mouth and eyes. It was not a smile, unless an evil spirit smiles, foreseeing the destruction of its victim. Evil it was—delightedly evil, like the triumph of long-baffled hate. It was a cruel, hungry, debased expression, hideously at variance with the passionate and ill-regulated but refined character of the man. It suggested the idea that Gloam was possessed by a strange spirit, more potent and more wicked than his own, which commanded his body to what uses it pleased, in spite of all that he could do.

For it was evident that he himself understood the cause of Jael's dismay ; and he made a violent effort to drive the awful look out of his face. So far from succeeding, however, he was forced to break out into a frantic laugh, which echoed shrilly through the silent house, and seemed, to Jael's scared ears, a copy of the infernal cachinnation which was wont to issue from the bewitched mill !

"Don't mind it, Jael," he said, as soon as he could speak ; "it's nervousness—it's the reaction from suspense ! Wait,—have you told . . . . ?"

"Swanhilda, sir? not yet,—I thought I'd best break it gradually——"

"Don't tell her! don't hint it to her!" He spoke in a·harsh whisper, bending forwards towards her: "Because—because he might not come after all!", Then the mocking devil seized upon him again; and though he folded his arms and held down his head, the unholy laughter which he strove to suppress shook his whole body and turned his white face dark.

The housekeeper was glad to escape from the room; for she thought Gloam must have gone mad, and knew not what insane violence he might commit. Her first impulse was to run out and summon help, but after her immediate panic had cooled down, she thought better of such a proceeding. The explanation of his behaviour which Gloam himself had given seemed, upon reflection, reasonable enough. The abrupt manner in which she had told the news had thrown him for the moment off his balance. It was, upon the whole, rather a good sign than a bad one, for it showed him not so much deadened by suffering as he had appeared to be. When he had had time to rally, he would be his own gentle and manageable self once more.

Meanwhile she made preparations to receive David on his return. The young man's conduct towards Swanhilda had so angered his mother that she had more than acquiesced in the banishment which Gloam's rage had forced upon him. Not that she loved Swanhilda much; nor did the mere immorality of her son's deed greatly afflict her. But she had never ceased to have faith that, sooner or later, news would come of the yellow-haired maiden's relatives beyond the sea. It would come, perhaps, in the form of a wealthy and open-hearted gentleman; or of a lady, with diamonds sparkling on her hands and bosom. They would say, "We have learnt that the little niece or cousin whom we had thought lost, was saved, and is living here with you." "Yes," Jael would reply; "and she has been brought up as true a lady as if she were in a queen's palace; for we knew she had blue blood in her veins, and would come by her own at last." Then Swanhilda would appear, and captivate them with her beauty and simplicity. But when they offered to take her away, the girl would say, "Not without David, for I love him!" Whereupon, no doubt, there would be objections and remonstrances; but David's handsome face and engaging manners would half disarm them; and at the last Jael herself would arise, and sacrificing the woman to the mother, would declare openly, "He too is of gentle blood; his father was old Harold Gloam; he is the descendant of gentlemen, and not unworthy of the girl who loves him."

So would resistance finally be overcome, and all concerned be enriched.

Such had been Jael's dream; and her resentment at the revelation of David's crime had been mainly aroused by the fact that it involved the frustration of a chance of fortune her own espousal of which had rendered especially dear to her. When the scheme was first conceived, the young man had, indeed, acquiesced in it, but as time went on, and inquiries proved fruitless, he had abandoned the hope of obtaining wealth and station through Swanhilda's means. Yet the girl loved him, and was very beautiful; much of their time was of necessity passed in each other's society; and in the end the sin was sinned. Doubtless he had regretted her ruin; but to make her honourable amends had not been compatible with the projects of his ambition: and when Gloam's unexpectedly violent outbreak had driven him forth upon the world, he had perhaps deemed his banishment a not inconvenient pretext for freeing himself from the encumbrances, such as they were, which might otherwise have impeded him. He left Swanhilda behind, to pass her dark hour alone.

But, this being so, what was the occasion of his sudden change of purpose? Was he penitent? or had he found that honour and expediency could be

G

made compatible after all? The letter which he had
written to Jael did not explicitly answer this question ; but from hints which it contained, the housekeeper had drawn favourable inferences ; and she
looked forward to his coming with agreeable anxiety.
She had told Gloam the news, intending (should he
refuse a reconciliation) to acknowledge to him that
his father was David's likewise. But his strange
behaviour had frightened this purpose out of her
head ; and when she recollected it again, it seemed
most advisable that the revelation should for the
present be postponed.

X.

About sunset Jael was surprised by the beginning
of a jarring and rumbling noise, the like of which
had not been heard in the gorge for a number of
weeks past. Half incredulous of the evidence of
her own ears, she paused to listen. Certainly there
was no mistake—the mill was going! She stepped
to the window and looked out. Yes, there revolved
the great black wheel heavily upon its axle, churning
the headlong torrent into foam, and hurling the
white froth from its rigid rims. As she gazed,
astonished, she saw Gloam issue from the mill and
stand beside the boiling mill-race, watching, with

manifest excitement, the sullen churning of the huge machine. He wore no hat, his hair was tossed and tangled, his bearing reckless and wild. All at once (for the machinery, having been so long out of use, had doubtless become very rusty) an unearthly peal of laughter—or what seemed such—was launched upon the evening air. It partly died away; then it again burst forth, clinging to the listener's ears and stabbing them, and leaving a sting that rankled there long afterwards. In the midst of the infernal din, Jael saw Gloam toss up his arms and abandon himself to a sympathetic paroxysm of grisly merriment. The man and the machinery were possessed by one and the same demon.

"Master—Master Gloam!" cried the woman, throwing open the window and lifting her voice to her shrillest pitch, "what is the matter? Why have you set the mill going?"

He glanced up at her with wild eyes, and waved his hand. "It is a season of rejoicing," he answered. "The prayer that I prayed is coming to pass. Therefore let the wheel go round. Hear it, how it laughs and rejoices!"

"But there is no grist—the mill is empty."

"It will not be empty long; the grist is coming. It comes! it comes! Let the great wheel go round and grind it to powder!"

Jael drew back with a sickening apprehension at her heart. Gloam was too plainly in a state of delirious frenzy, if he were not actually mad. She longed for David's appearance, and yet dreaded it; she knew not whether the meeting between the two men would issue well or ill. And then her mind reverted to Swanhilda, and she asked herself what the effect of her lover's presence would be upon her. Ever since the first week following upon his departure the young mother had maintained a singularly passive demeanour, only occasionally disturbed by seasons of vague and tremulous anxiety. The housekeeper had looked in upon her several times that afternoon. She lay quietly in one position, her eyes open and fixed, save when the baby claimed her attention. She did not speak, and seemed scarcely aware of outward things. Even the uproar of the mill, when that began, commanded her notice but for a short time, and appeared rather to gratify than to distress her. She perhaps associated it with the thought of David, and fancied it in some way indicative of that home-return which she had all along never allowed herself to despair of. But she was as one partly entranced, whose ears and eyes, as some believe, are opened to things beyond the ordinary ken of human senses.

The evening was cloudy, and night came on

apace. Gloam had re-entered the house shortly after dark, and Jael presently went to his room to ask him where he would take his evening meal. But he met her in the upper passage-way. He seemed to carry something in his hand. She could not make out what it was, and he immediately hid it beneath his coat. To her inquiries he replied that he was going forth to resume his old practice of walking, and that he would sup with David after his return. Jael, in her uneasiness, would gladly have persuaded him to remain at home; but he was obstinate against all entreaties, and finally pushed roughly by her and was gone.

Meanwhile the mill was still in motion. The housekeeper had an impulse, soon after Gloam's departure, to go out and uncouple the machinery; but she feared lest he might resent her interference, and forebore. The noise, and the suspense she was in, combined to keep her in a state of feverish restlessness. Her thoughts busied themselves, against her will, with all manner of gloomy and painful memories and speculations. The vision of her youth rose up before her, and filled her with vain, remorseful terrors. She strove to cheer herself with picturing her son's arrival; but even that had now become a source of apprehension rather than of comfort. All the time she was oppressed by an indefinable sensation that someone was prowling about outside the house; and once, after the wheel had delivered itself of an outpouring of inhuman mirth, Jael fancied the strain was taken up in a no less wild, though not so penetrating key. Was it possible that Gloam was lurking in the gorge? And, if so, what could he be doing there? Cautiously she peered out of the window; but the moon was as yet obscured by clouds, and nothing was certainly distinguishable. She returned to the fireside; yet paused and listened again, because—or else her excited imagination deceived her—another and a different sound had reached her from without: a sharp, grating sound, like that made by a rusty saw eating its way through close-grained timber. Ere she could be certain about the matter, however, the noise stopped, and returned no more.

An hour or so later, it wanting then only a few minutes of midnight, Swanhilda suddenly awoke from her half-trance, and sat upright in her bed. The house resounded dully to the muffled throbbing of the machinery, but otherwise there was no stir. The little baby had fallen sound asleep, and lay at its mother's side, with its tiny hands folded beneath its chin, and grasping the pearl-shell necklace, which was its favourite plaything. After sitting tense and still for a moment, Swanhilda got out of bed, huddled on some clothes, kissed the unconscious baby twice or thrice, and then silently left the room. In another minute she had stolen down the stairs, and was standing between the house and the stream in the open air. She looked first one way and then another, and finally, without any hesitation in her manner, but with an assured and joyful bearing, bent her steps towards the top of the gorge. A narrow footpath led up thither, and at the highest point turned to the right, and was carried across the torrent by a narrow bridge formed of a single plank. When Swanhilda came to the turn, she did not go over the bridge, but sat down upon a stone amidst the shrubbery, and waited.

How had she known that there was anyone to wait for? Jael, certainly, had told her nothing; still less could she have learned anything from Gloam. Nevertheless, there she sat, waiting, and knowing beyond question that her lover was near, and was rapidly coming nearer. In a few minutes she would hear his steps; then he would be upon the bridge, and she would rise and meet him there. Had he not promised, months ago, that he would never leave her? and though he had been driven away for a time, she had never doubted that he would return. He loved her; soon, soon she would feel his arms about her, his kisses on her lips. Ah! what happiness after all this pain; what measureless content! How glad would be their meeting; and when she showed him their little baby, the cup of joy would be full. Nay, it was so already. In all Swanhilda's life she had never known a moment so free from all earthly trouble as was this!

It was near the end. She stood up; she had heard a footstep; yes, there again! He must be close at hand; if it were not so dark she would have already seen him. And now the clouds which had so long obscured the moon broke away, and the pale sphere hung poised in dark purple space, and shed a dim lustre over the little gorge. The light glanced on the curve of the cataract, and twinkled in the eddies of the pool, and danced along the tumultuous rapid, and glistened upon the froth of the mill-race. There the black wheel still plunged to its work, whirling its gaunt arms about as if grasping for a victim. In the bushes close beside it crouched a man with white face and staring eyes. He had laid his trap, and was waiting the issue. He had not seen Swanhilda leave the house and climb the little path; his eyes and thoughts had been turned elsewhither.

David came swiftly along the upland path, whistling to himself as he walked. We will not search his thoughts, seeing he was so near the end of his journey. When he arrived at the brow of the gorge, and was within a few paces of the bridge, he halted and peered forward earnestly. What figure was that that seemed to stand expectantly on the other side? It could not be Swanhilda—ay, but it was! He gave a little laugh, and then his hard heart softened and warmed towards her. "How she does love me, poor little thing!" he muttered. "And I've treated her devilish badly, no mistake. Well, well, I'll make it up to her, if all goes well, see if I don't!"

He came on to the bridge, and Swanhilda also hurried forward. Then the man below among the bushes started up, dry-mouthed and breathless. In an instant he sent forth a great, terrible cry of warning and agony; but before it could be uttered the lovers had met upon the narrow plank, and Swanhilda had received her kiss. While their lips yet touched, the plank, sawn in two all but a finger's breadth, broke downwards, and they fell, clasped in each other's arms—headlong down over the fall, down to the bottom of the eddying pool; up again, and over in the rapids, whirling round and round, dashed against the jagged stones, bleeding piteously; stunned, let us trust, already, but still clinging to each other. Now the last plunge: and so, at length, with a final shriek of heaven-defying laughter, the hungry demon of the wheel grappled its prey. Ay, snatch at them, tear, break, grind them down and hold them there; they are past feeling now. But not so the man upon the bank, with uncovered hair showing black and white in the moonlight, who has looked on at this scene, powerless to help, but awake to every swift phase of the tragedy, losing not a struggle or a pang, realising his own unspeakable horror and anguish, and foreseeing no comfort or pardon through all time to come.

The wheel stopped suddenly. Jael came breathless out of the mill-house, and shrinkingly approached the margin. A formless mass of something was wedged beneath the lower rim of the wheel and the bed of the stream, and a long mass of yellow hair floated out along the black water, and gleamed in the lustre of the untroubled moon. The man on the other side was kneeling down, and seemed to be gazing idly into the current.

"He was your brother," said Jael, sobbing with rage and misery. "Your father was his. You have murdered him. God curse you! I wish you lay where he is."

"Why, Jael," returned Gloam, smiling at her, "you invoke a curse and a blessing in the same breath! My brother?—well. Swanhilda loved him and not me. Thank God I was the brother of the man she loved; the same blood ran in our veins—

she loved a part of me in him. But why do you trouble yourself to curse me, Jael? I ask the charity of all men, and their sympathy!" . . . .

I unclasped my hands from above my eyes, and started to my feet. No, there was no one near me; I was quite alone. It was deep twilight, but objects were still discernible: yet nowhere, neither beneath the Black Oak, nor beside the Laughing Wheel, nor anywhere in the gorge, could I see a trace of my late companion—of him whose last words were even then ringing in my ears: "I ask the charity of all men, and their sympathy!"

XI.

The next morning I was down late to breakfast. It was glorious weather, and the blue sparkle of the sea came through the open window, bringing with it a limitless inspiration of hope and wholesomeness. It was difficult to believe that there had ever been any sorrow or wrong in the world.

"Ye're not looking right hearty," said Mr. Poyntz, with bluff geniality, while his good wife set before me a huge plate of daintily fried bacon and eggs, and a smoking cup of coffee. "Maybe ye walked a bit too far last night? 'Twas powerful late afore ye got home, anyhow."

"Yes," said I, glancing at Agatha, who was knitting a pair of stockings for Peter in the eastern window, the morning sun glistening on the broad plaits of her yellow hair. "Yes, Mr. Poyntz, I think I must have made a very long journey last evening. By-the-way, is not to-day Sunday?"

"Ay, surely!" exclaimed husband and wife in a breath; and then the former added, "Ye'll be wanting to go to church, I suppose?"

"No, not this Sunday; though I hope to go before long, if Miss Agatha is willing to show me the way." I glanced at her again as I said this, but she would not look up, and I could not even be sure whether she were listening. "What I want," I continued, "is for you, Mr. Poyntz, since you'll be at leisure, to take a stroll with me a little way up the stream. It will be a novelty, perhaps almost as much so to you as to me."

"Up the stream, is it?" returned he, pausing in the operation of cutting up a piece of tobacco, and turning his blue eyes on me; "why, truly, sir, that's a trip I've not made for a number of years. Howsoever, none knows the road better than I do, and if so be as naught else 'll do ye, why, I'm your man!"

Accordingly, so soon as I had done breakfast, the sturdy old mariner mounted a wonderful glazed hat and a new pea-jacket of blue pilot cloth, took a fresh clay pipe from the mantelpiece, with a sigh and a shake of the head over the destruction of his beloved meerschaum, and professed himself ready.

"Good-bye, Agatha," I said, passing the window. "Is there anything you would like me to bring you when we come back?"

"Oh, a great many!" answered she, looking up gravely; "but nothing, I'm afraid, that you can get for me. Though—you'll bring yourself back to dinner, I suppose, won't you?"

She bent over her knitting as she said it, and her mouth and downcast eyelids were very demure. Nevertheless, I was encouraged to fancy that my former remark about church-going had not fallen so entirely unheeded as it had appeared to do. Before I could hammer out a fitting answer (my brain always seemed to work with really abnormal sluggishness when I most wanted to do myself credit with Agatha), Poyntz rolled out in his deep, jovial voice, "Back to Sunday dinner? Well, I should hope so. Why, the old woman is baking a pie as I'd sail round the Horn to get a snack of! Come on, Mr. Firemount; it 'll go hard but we fetches back an appetite as 'll warm the women's hearts to look at."

We trudged off at a tolerably round pace, and soon struck into a narrow grass-grown lane which led towards the east; and had proceeded some distance along it before I said :

"Do you know, Mr. Poyntz, that your daughter is one of the loveliest women in the world ? "

"Ye mean Agatha ? Ay, surely, that she is, heaven bless her! She was always that. A tiny bit of a lass, I remember her, not so long as my arm ; as pretty a baby she was then as she's a woman now."

"Has she any thought of getting married soon ? Such a face and character must have suitors enough."

"Well, as touching that, sir," said Poyntz, taking his pipe out of his mouth and looking at it carefully, "ye mustn't think of Agatha just the same as of the fishermen's girls you meet round about. Good, honest girls they all are, I'm saying naught against that; but Agatha, d'ye see, is a bit different. Ye'll maybe think it queer I should say it, sir; but say it I will that Agatha is a lady. She may live in our house, and put up with our ways—nay, and love us too, which sure I am she does ; but all the same, if ye notice, she don't speak the same as me and the old woman do, nor she don't think the same neither. She's built on other lines, as I may say—a clipper yacht, while we're but fishing smacks, or trading schooners at best. And that being so as it is, the young fellows of our neighbourhood don't find they've got much show alongside of her somehow. They're afraid of her, that's the long and short of it. Not but she treats 'em kind enough, ye understand, as a lady should ; but 'tis the kindness of a lady, and not of an equal, and there's not one of 'em staunch enough to hold out against it. And how be they're fine lads, many of them, I can't truly say as I'm sorry for it, if so as Agatha is content."

"Nor can I," I echoed to myself, with devout earnestness. "She does seem of a different stock from most I see here," I said aloud. "I have seen women somewhat like her at Copenhagen ; though I don't know whether I should have thought of that if I hadn't happened to say something in Danish, yesterday, and she answered me in the same language."

"Did she now!" said Poyntz, tipping forward his hat and scratching the back of his head. "And if I might ask it, sir, how came ye to speak Danish your own self?"

"My family was Danish before I was born ; and I was taught the language almost before I knew English. Our name used to be Feuerberg ; but we've translated it since we've emigrated, you see."

"Ay, surely—Feuerberg," said Poyntz, puffing his pipe preoccupiedly.

We walked on for awhile in silence. So great

was my desire that the evidence I had been arranging in my mind should be borne out by the facts, that I was almost afraid to put the matter definitely to the proof; while Poyntz, on the other hand, was evidently taken by surprise, and had not got his ideas quite settled. At length, however, I thought I would hazard one hint more.

"I've been thinking of that yarn you were spinning yesterday afternoon—in fact, I believe I dreamt of it last night; and I should imagine that the little yellow-haired girl, if she grew up, would have looked enough like Agatha to be her sister—or her mother, at any rate."

"And I've been thinking, sir, of the accident that stopped me from finishing that there yarn ye speak of, and of the hearty thanks I owe ye for the stout heart and ready hand that saved my Peter. But thanks is easily said; and I mean more than words come to. I'd not have ye suppose as I'd give all trust and confidence to a man just because he's done a brave act for me and mine. But as I told you once afore, and speaking out man to man, I like the looks of ye, and ever did; and seeing as how ye've found out a good bit of our little secret already, and seem like you'd an interest to know more of it; for that, and likewise because of another thing, as I've just found out myself, and it may be as important as any

—well, I'll tell ye what about Agatha there is to tell."

At this moment, however, we passed round a clump of oak trees, and found ourselves right at the entrance of the little gorge where I had had my adventure the night before. Poyntz halted, and fixed his eyes gravely upon the scene for several moments. "Ay, the same old harbour," said he; "it's changed a bit now, but it brings it all back to me the last time I was here. This is the Laughing Mill, Mr. Feuerberg. And this here is the Black Oak, and here is poor Gloam's grave, d'ye see? with the bit of gray stone a-sticking out of the end of it."

"Why was he buried here?"

"Well, 'twas his wish; that's all. He was crazed the last years of his life, with grieving on the death of the young girl as he'd picked up on the beach, that I was telling you of. A sad thing it was altogether. She went wrong, d'ye see, with the fellow David, the Scholar's brother, and was drowned here along with him; but how that came to pass was never rightly known. 'Tis thought the Scholar had meant for to marry the girl himself. And so would David have married her, I doubt, if he'd known what I know."

"About the family?"

"Ay, sir, that. Ye maybe 'll remember the iron

H

box as I picked up? Well, I didn't tell anyone
about it then, not even the Scholar; and soon after
the night of the storm I shipped•for Rio, and was
away a matter of two years. When I came back
I heard as how David was thick with the girl—
Swanhilda they called her. Then I opened the box,
not having done it before, and found papers in it
telling who she was, and that folks of hers were
living in Germany, having emigrated there from
Denmark; and from what I could make out—for
'twas in a foreign lingo, and I was forced to borrow
a lexicon to it—it seemed likely as how they was
well off. Now, I had my opinion of David, that
he was a worthless sort of a chap, though clever
and handsome; so thinks I, I won't tell him of this,
for if so be as I do, he'll wed the girl in the hope
of money, and not for true love of her, who was
worthy the love of better than he. But what I'll do,
I'll write to those her folks in Germany, telling them
as how she's here; and when they come, then they
can do for her as they find best, and it'll be out of
my hands. And so I did, but had never an answer,
why I don't know. But it never came in my mind,
sir, that the fellow David would ever be so black
a scoundrel as to lead the poor innocent girl wrong.
How be, when he had done it, thinks I, I'll tell him
of her folks now, because now the best can happen

will be that they marry, though the best is bad
enough ; and if I tell him, maybe he'll make her an
honest woman, as the saying is. And tell him I did,
with a piece of my mind touching my thought of him,
into the bargain. And he promised me as he'd go
and make it right the next day—this being spoke
in the town above here, whither I'd gone for to see
him. And it can't be said but what he kept his
word ; only he and she was drowned in the night,
and crushed under that there wheel, as never has
turned since, to this day."

" What became of her baby—she had a baby ? "

" Ay, and so she did, sir. Well, 'twas cared for
by the housekeeper—she being grandmother to it
and so having first right, the more as the Scholar was
crazed, though not dangerous, but mild and melan-
choly-like. But in years the old woman she came to
the poor-house, and there died ; and I took the baby,
and gave her what best I had to give, and better
schooling than the lasses care for hereabouts. And
as luck would have it, an elderly woman of Danish
blood being come by a chance to the village, I got
her to be nurse to the little one, and so grew up
to a knowledge of her native tongue, d'ye see, and the
fairy tales and such like thereto belonging. And—ay,
I see you've guessed it long already, sir—that's
Agatha."

I had intended relating my vision to Mr. Poyntz on the spot where it occurred; but I know not what reluctance prevented me. It was too solemn and inexplicable an experience to bear discussion so soon. So, instead of that, I told him, as we trudged homewards together, the history of the Feuerberg family, and how all tended to ratify my conviction that Agatha and I were cousins, though far removed. And I may remark here that he and I between us had afterwards no difficulty (what with his documents and my knowledge) in establishing the relationship beyond a doubt. "But," I added, as we stood on the brow of the slope overlooking the old house, and saw Agatha appear round the corner and kiss her hand to us, "but she and I are the last of our race, and there is no great fortune awaiting us, that I know of. Only, Mr. Poyntz, I love her with my whole heart; if she can love me, will you trust her to me?"

"Nay, ye mustn't ask me," replied the ancient mariner, grasping my hand, with tears in his old blue eyes. "I doubt she loves you well, already. And so do we all, for ye're a man, all be a quiet one. 'Twill be hard parting with her, as has been sunshine to us this many a year; but ye'll bring her to see the old folks, as time serves; and I'm bold for to believe ye'll be as happy as the day is long."

It is twenty years since then, and old Jack Poyntz's prophecy has proved true. My wife is wont to say, with a smile in her dark eyes, that our prosperity is due to the restored virtue of the pearl-shell necklace, which still rests upon her bosom. To me, however, the necklace seems but as the symbol of the true love whose radiance has blessed our lives, and brought us better luck than any witch-craft can bestow.

CALBOT'S RIVAL.

CALBOT'S RIVAL.

I.

THE bitter cold weather out of doors made the cosy glow of my little library even more than usually grateful. I had carried the warm and bright anticipation of it close-buttoned under my top-coat throughout my cold drive in the hansom from the South-Western Railway Station to my rooms on the Thames Embankment. But now, as I stepped in and shut the door behind me, I found I had done it less than justice.

The four comfortable walls gave a broad smile of welcome, which was multitudinously repeated from the well-known back of every beloved book. Softly gleamed the Argand burner from the green-topped study table; hospitably flickered the blazing Wallsend from the wide-mouthed grate; seductive was the invitation extended me by padded easy-chair, fox-skin hearthrug, and toasted slippers; crisp was the greeting of the evening's *Pall Mall* lying on the table ; and solid the promise of the latest *Contemporary*, containing, as I knew, my article on "Unrecognisable Truths in their Relation to Non-existent Phenomena." Bethinking myself, moreover, of the decanter of matchless old port-wine in the right-hand cupboard of. the table, and of the box of prime Cabanas, made to my own order in Habana, in the drawer on the left, I was not so much disposed to envy Calbot his late betrothal to the beautiful Miss Burleigh, the news whereof he had triumphantly poured into my bachelor ears a week or two before.

"Never mind, Drayton, old fellow," I muttered to myself, as I pushed off my boots and slid my feet into the toasted slippers ; "what matter though love, courtship, and marriage be not for thee? Thou hast yet thy luxuries"—here I sank slowly into my easy-chair, "thy creature comforts"—here I got out the wine and the cigars, "and thy beloved offspring!" —here I glanced at "Unrecognisable Truths," &c., printed on the cover of the *Contemporary*.

While I am pouring out and tasting a mellow glass of port, let me briefly recall what and whence I am.

Snugness, comfort, and privacy are my *desiderata*. My visible possessions must be few, intrinsically valuable, and so disposed as to lie within the scope of two or three paces and an outstretched arm. My being a bachelor (and at the age of forty, I think I may add a confirmed one) enables me to indulge these and other whims conveniently and without embarrassment.

My forefathers kept large establishments and had big families—and plenty of bother and discomfort into the bargain. But when my turn came, I sold out everything (except a few old heirlooms, and a part of the library, and an ancestral portrait or two), put the cash proceeds in the Funds, and myself, with my literary tastes and æsthetic culture, into the rooms which I now occupy. I might live in a much more grandiose style if I pleased, but in my opinion I am very well off as I am. I can find my way to Freemasons' Tavern on occasions ; my essays are a power in the philosophic and theologic worlds ; and I can count on a friend or two worth their weight in gold, morally, mentally, and materially. Poor Calbot, to be sure—but more of him anon.

That is old Dean Drayton's portrait, over the mantelpiece—taken one hundred and fifty years ago : an ancestor and namesake of mine. He wrote a pamphlet on witchcraft, or something of that sort, which made a stir in its day. I had thoughts of entering the ministry myself a long while ago ; I

think it was about the time of my engagement to
Miss Seraphine Angell—the Bishop of Maresnest's
daughter. But when she jil—— when the affair
was discontinued I had second thoughts, ending in
the resolve to let both women and the ministry
severely alone for the future. So the name of
Drayton dies with me.

There is, I fancy, at once a curious similarity and
dissimilarity between the Dean and his descendant.
For one thing, we are both of us singularly liable
to be made confidants of delicate subjects ; with this
difference, however, that whereas the Dean is—or
was—an old busybody (I am quoting history, not
my private judgment), my natural tendency is not
only to mind my own business, but to tell other
people to mind theirs. It's no use, though—they
only babble the more ; and were I to lose all my
fortune, I could, by turning black-mailer, ensure a
permanent income twice as large as the one I have
now.

Another thing. The Dean was an alchemist—so
tradition says; and his descendant has a marked
taste for scientific subjects, though not of the occult
kind. One of the family heirlooms, by-the-way, was
a monument of the Dean's alchemic skill ; it was a
large sealed vase or phial, ornamented with cabalistic
figures and inscriptions, and affirmed to contain the

veritable Elixir Vitæ, manufactured after years of labour by the old gentleman, and corked up and put away for future use. It unfortunately happened, however, that he was killed by an upset of his coach, away from home ; and the vase remained sealed ever afterwards. I have often thought of taking a little out and analysing it ; for even should it turn out not to be the water of life, I thought it might possibly resolve itself into a bottle of excellent brandy. But I delayed too long ; and at last the mysterious phial very unexpectedly analysed itself, and dissipated itself at the same moment—but, again, let me not anticipate.

II.

I finished my first glass of wine, poured out another, and taking up the *Contemporary* turned to the masterly discussion of "Unrecognisable Truths," &c. Before I had reached the close of the opening period, however, I heard the postman's knock.

I ought to have mentioned that I had been down to Richmond that afternoon—an unusual thing for me to do at that time of year. But the fact was that a distant connection of mine had died a short time before, and his effects were announced to be sold at auction. I had reason to believe that among these effects were some old relics of my family—documents and so forth—which I was interested to recover; indeed, but that some foolish quarrel or other had parted my relative and me years ago, I might doubtless have had them at any time for the asking. Of the precise nature of the documents in question I was not precisely informed; Armstrong—such was my relative's name—had taken care not to enlighten me on the subject. When I read the announcement of his death in *The Times* I had half expected that he might have bequeathed me the old things; but it turned out that he had made no will at all, having, as it appeared, no very great property to dispose of. He was a queer fellow, and came of a queer family; half insane I always considered them; and I know they were suspected of witchcraft as long ago as the time of our old Dean. Nay, the Dean himself was whispered to have been the least bit overshadowed at that epoch, owing, I understand, to one fussy habit he had of encouraging confidences. One of these Armstrong witches had communicated some devilish secret or other to the reverend gentleman, I suppose, and thus brought ill-repute upon him. However, the Dean was no fool, and got out of the scrape by writing that pamphlet on witchcraft.

Well, I was about to say that when I heard of the sale I resolved to run over to Richmond and see what

I could pick up. I got there just in time to see the last lot knocked down. It was shockingly stupid of me to have mistaken the hour—such a cold day, too, and I so unaccustomed to running about the country at that time of year. But there was no help for it; I had to return as wise as I started, and the poorer by the loss of my temper and expectations. I was beginning to get in a good humour again, however, what with my fire, and my cigar, and my article on " Truths," &c., and partly, no doubt, by reason of the genial effect of that old port-wine; besides, I am by no means of a sour disposition, naturally; when all of a sudden came the postman's knock, making me start so that the ash of my cigar fell on the open page of the *Contemporary* and scorched a hole in it. Postmen have always been a horror to me; I have never enjoyed receiving letters since the date of a certain missive from—from someone who is now the wife of another man; and on this particular evening I was more than commonly averse to any such inter-ruption. I laid my book on my knees, leaned back in my chair, and blew an irritated cloud of smoke towards the painted countenance of my ecclesiastical ancestor over the fireplace. It curled and twisted about his respectable visage, until I could almost have believed that he winked one eye and moved his ancient lips as if to speak.

The servant brought in a square packet done up in brown wrapping-paper, and sealed in half-a-dozen places. It was about the size and shape of the magazine I had been reading—a little thicker, perhaps, and heavier. I put my name to the receipt accompanying the parcel, and the servant went out.

At first I was disposed to let the thing lie unopened till the next day, being well assured that it would not repay examination : and I actually did put it aside and attempt to resume my reading as though no interruption had occurred. But I found it impossible to get on, or to fix my thoughts upon anything except just that parcel. What could be in it? Who could have sent it? I looked at the direction, but could make nothing out of that; it was written in an ordinary business hand, quite characterless and non-committal. I felt it carefully all over; it was stiffer than ordinary paper, but not hard like wood. Meanwhile I glanced up at my pictured ancestor, and was struck with the expression of anxious interest which appeared to have come over his features. Perhaps he knew what the packet contained ; or more probably his ruling passion of curiosity, strong in death, was making his old painted fingers itch to break the seals and take a peep at the mystery. The idea provoked me, and with a sudden impulse I held the packet out over the blazing

Wallsend, two-thirds minded to drop it in. But the next moment I was more provoked at my own childish folly. I drew the thing back, took my pen-knife from my pocket, and cut the strings that tied it. Unwrapping the paper, there was disclosed to view a very antique-looking leather case or cover—a pocket-book or portfolio to all appearance. I undid the worn strap that fastened it, and it fell open, showing a number of leaves of musty parchment, written over with a quaint and crabbed chirography, such as could not have been in vogue for a good deal more than a century, to say the least.

III.

I am something of an antiquary, and not entirely without experience of MS. older even than this appeared to be. Having convinced myself by a cursory inspection that the matter was worth looking into, I lost no time in composing myself to its perusal.

It was written in Latin—a fortunate circumstance, since there was none of the difficulty attendant upon old-fashioned bad spelling to contend with. The substance of the writing consisted, so far as I was able to make out, of extracts from a number of private letters, supplemented by passages from the

I

pages of a journal and by occasional observations made apparently in the transcriber's own person. The combination formed a tolerably consecutive and logical history of three individuals—a woman and two men—who lived and loved and hated with the antiquated vehemence of a century and a half ago.

An odd circumstance which was immediately noticeable in the compilation was a systematic omission of the names of all the actors in the events narrated. A blank space of some length was left for each one, as though the writer had intended filling them in afterwards, but, for whatever cause, had failed to do so. Even the scribe himself—he was a friend or confidential adviser, as it seemed, of the principal figure in the narrative—had suffered himself to remain as nameless as the rest.

This omission affected me strangely. So far from alienating my interest, it greatly augmented it; and although the body of the writing was couched in terms sufficiently dry and matter-of-fact, the blank spaces gave rein to the imagination, and lent the story a present and almost a personal vitality and significance. It almost seemed to me that the matter was, in some way or other, my individual concern—that I was, or had been, involved in the incidents here set forth, and had still to look forward to the catastrophe. The potent port, I fancy, must have a little o'ercrowed my spirit; but I believe I ascribed it, at the same time, to the peculiar influence exerted over me by the portrait of my reverend ancestor. He seemed positively to be alive, and preparing to come down from his frame and take the MS. into his own possession.

I spent a long time in trying to find out whence the MS. came, and why it had ·been sent to me. But to this problem there was no apparent clue—no tangible evidence, external or internal. Of course I was sure that the secret lay in the blank spaces; and was half inclined to cut the knot by filling them up with my own name and with those of the first three friends of mine that happened to come into my head. However, after quite working myself into a fever, and ruining the flavour of my Cabana by letting it go out and then relighting it, I finally contented myself by ·stopping the pregnant gaps ·with the first four letters of the alphabet; and thus furnished forth, I buckled earnestly and steadily to my work, progressing so rapidly that in less than three hours' time I had mastered the whole narrative.

It was an unpleasant story, certainly, but there was nothing particularly weird or remarkable, after all, in the incidents related. From a literary point of view, it was greatly lacking in point and completeness; for though it ended with the death of the chief character and the marriage of the other two, yet the interest of the reader advanced beyond the written limits, and demanded a more definite conclusion. Things were left at such loose ends, in spite of death and marriage, that it was hard not to believe that more remained behind. In the heated and excited condition of my imagination, I felt strongly tempted to snatch up my pen and improvise an ending on my own responsibility.

The longer I mused over the matter the more convinced did I become that all had not been told. Moreover, I could almost fancy that I had some occult perception of what the true and ultimate conclusion really was ; nay, even that the authorship of this very MS., which had been penned considerably more than a hundred years before I was born, was nevertheless mystically my own. I repeat, there seemed to be something of myself in it ; and the events had an inexplicable sort of familiarity to my mind, as though they were long forgotten, rather than now known for the first time. And all the while that alchemic progenitor of mine kept up his mysterious winking and nodding.

It would be too long and tedious to transcribe the tale as I read it ; I will therefore give, as briefly as possible, an abstract of the leading points round which it was woven.

IV.

Shortly before the beginning of the last century, a wealthy gentleman—let us call him A.—made a proposal for the hand of a young lady living in the neighbourhood of London, the daughter of an excellent family, though at that time somewhat reduced in circumstances, probably in consequence of political jealousies. Judging from what is said of her, this young lady—Miss B.—must have been a famous beauty; and it would not therefore be surprising if A. had met with some rivalry in his suit. To all appearances, however, the course of true love flowed as smooth as oil. The B. family, in spite of their political disaffection, did not oppose the marriage of their daughter to so wealthy and respectable a suitor; and if she herself had any disinclination to him, she very probably and prudently said nothing about it, but treated Mr. A. very graciously.

A.'s property, and the general management of his business affairs, were entrusted by him to the care of a talented young barrister, C. by name; who, indeed, largely owed his prosperity and brilliant prospects to A.'s kindness, the latter having aided him in his preparation for the Bar, and afterwards put a great deal of business in his way, which otherwise he would have obtained but slowly. In fact, A.'s attitude towards this young man was almost parental; and no wonder if he felt himself secure in trusting his most private concerns to one who owed him so deep a debt of gratitude.

Nevertheless, it would doubtless have been wiser in him, a man somewhat advanced in life, not to have made C. the bearer and utterer of his loving messages to the lady of his heart, quite so often or so unreservedly as he appears to have done. C., who was probably a well-favoured and fascinating fellow enough, must have seen more of Miss B. than did her lover; and in his capacity of the latter's recognised confidant, he could easily have obtained access to her at any moment. Perhaps the young beauty was not averse to a little flirtation with the handsome and clever barrister. Perhaps she encouraged him; the evidence, such as it is, would seem to point that way. Be that as it may, we must admit that C. was exposed to pretty strong temptation. His virtue, be he who he might, must have had a struggle for it; and if we imagine him rather warm-blooded and tolerably weak-principled, we may be justly anxious as to virtue's victory.

Having made what allowances we will, there is no denying that C. turned out a great scoundrel. A. one morning took his carriage and went up to London, and the coachman stopped at the door of

the Court jeweller. Out steps Mr. A., with his velvet
cloak, his silk stockings, his plumed hat, and his
peaked beard ; and, with his long rapier dangling at
his side, and his lace ruffles half concealing his white
hands, he makes his stately entry into the bowing
tradesman's shop. There he spends a long time
examining, with all the whimsical particularity of an
elderly lover, the trays upon trays of rare, rich, and
costly nicknacks which are set before him. It seems
as though he would never be suited. The pompous
horses, standing outside, shake their rattling head-
gear and stamp their proud hoofs impatiently ; the
obsequious jeweller racks his brain and exhausts his
eloquence unavailingly. Never was there so difficult
a customer. At length the man of jewels picks up a
quaint-looking little locket, and is just on the point
of putting it down again, as not even worth the
trouble of offering, when Mr. A. exclaims :

"Hold, Mr. Jeweller, that is what we are looking
for. What is the price of that locket ?"

"Oh sir," replies the shrewd man of business,
quickly recovering from his first surprise, "I see you
need not be informed of what is truly valuable.
This little locket, which most persons would look
upon as commonplace, is in fact, in more senses
than one, the jewel of my stock. It is made, you
perceive, out of a simple brown tourmaline, ex-

quisitely cut in relief. The workmanship is really matchless, and the tourmaline itself—as perhaps you are aware—is believed to be endowed with certain mystic properties——"

"Yes, yes, Mr. Jeweller," interrupts the dark-visaged customer, in a somewhat testy tone; "I know the nature and properties of the trinket quite as well as you do. What I desired of you was to name your price."

The tradesman hesitated for a moment, and then, summoning all his audacity to his aid, mentioned a sum which made his own heart beat and his eyes water. But the composure of Mr. A. was not dashed a whit. He even appeared to smile a little satirically, as though to intimate that he considered himself as having altogether the best of the bargain. He paid the money without a moment's demur, and taking up the locket before the excited jeweller had time to put it in a box for him, Mr. A. saluted him gravely and stalked out of the shop.

"Well," thought the tradesman, as he watched the heavy coach roll away, "if he's satisfied, I'm sure I ought to be. And yet—I wonder what that locket was after all! I don't remember having ever noticed it amongst the stock before to-day. It really was finely enchased, and may have been more valuable than I supposed. But pshaw! fifty

guineas! Such a stroke of business was never heard
of before. If the locket had been a witch's amulet,
with power to drive men mad or raise the Devil, I
should still have made a good profit!"

Meanwhile Mr. A. was speeding on his way to his
betrothed. The fact is, they were to be married on
the morrow, and the honest gentleman had bought
the locket as a pre-nuptial gift. Probably the horses,
fleet and well-conditioned as they were, were somewhat put to it to keep pace with their owner's
eagerness to be at the end of his journey. In due
time, however, behold them reined snorting up at
the gateway of the B. mansion, and Mr. A., locket
in hand, preparing to alight.

But, alas! it is too evident that some disaster has
occurred. The servant who opens the door is pale
and scared; the household is in disorder. Twice
does the visitor demand news of the master and
mistress before he can elicit a reply.

"Present them my compliments, if they are at
leisure," continues Mr. A., "and ask whether I may
request the honour of an interview with their
daughter."

"Lord bless me, sir!" falters the trembling servant,
"haven't you heard——"

"Heard what?" says A., turning pale; "what is
the matter, fellow? Is the young lady ill?"

" Ill, sir ?   Lord bless me, sir, she—she's gone !"

Mr. A. recoiled, and seemed to gasp for breath
for a moment.   His face, from pale, became suddenly
overspread with a deep crimson flush, and the veins
on his forehead swelled.   At length he burst out in
a terrible voice :

"Gone ?   Where ?   With whom ?"

But at this point the appearance of the master
and mistress relieved the wretched footman from his
unenviable position.   The miserable story was soon
told.   The young lady to whom Mr. A. had entrusted
his heart and honour, to whom he was to have been
united the next day, whose wedding gift he even
then held in his hand, had eloped the night before
in the good old-fashioned manner, and was by this
time far beyond the reach of pursuit, could pursuit
have availed.   The flight had been six hours old
before it was discovered by the young lady's mother.

" But with whom ? with whom ?   Who was the
villain who dared to rob me ?" cried Mr. A., storming
up and down the hall in ungovernable fury.   "Who
was it, madam, I say ?   Stop your wretched whimpering and speak !"

"Dear me, Mr. A.," quavered the poor lady,
struggling with her sobs, "can't you think ?   Why,
it's that young Mr. C. of yours, of course.   Who else
could it be ?"

At this reply, which he seems not in the least to have expected, Mr. A. became suddenly and appallingly calm. During a short space he made neither sound nor movement. At length he slowly uplifted one clenched hand above his head, and shook it there with a kind of sluggish deliberation. To the frightened and hushed spectators it seemed as if the air grew dark around him as he did it. Still without uttering a word he now partly unclosed his hand, and there was seen to proceed from it a dusky glow or gleam, as of phosphorescence. Drawing in a deep breath, he exhaled it slowly over this phosphorescent appearance, as if desirous of inspiring it with the very essence of his being. If the account is to be believed, the glow became more lurid, and the tall figure of Mr. A. more sombre, with the action.

Whatever this odd ceremony might mean, it had the good effect of restoring the betrayed suitor to his wonted courteous and grave self-possession. In a manner at once earnest and dignified he besought Mr. and Mrs. B. to pardon and overlook his late violent and passionate demeanour.

"I have erred deeply," added he, "in permitting, even for a short time, that evil spirit which is ever at hand to ensnare the rash and unwary to gain dominion over me. For, alas! what right have I

to be angry? Your daughter, methinks, has better
reason to upbraid me than I her. What charm could
such a one as she is find in a graybeard like myself?
Truly, I blame her not, and sorrow only that she did
not frankly make known to me her disfavour, rather
than thus violently and suddenly cast me off. And
as for the partner of her flight, how can I do otherwise than pardon him? Have I not trusted him
and loved him as a son? Nay, nay, I have been
an old fool—an old fool; but I will not be an
unforgiving one. See," he went on, in the same quiet
and colourless tone in which he had spoken throughout, "here is a trifle which I had purposed presenting
to your daughter as a symbol of my affection. It
is a jewel, curiously carven as you see, and fabled
to exert a benign and wholesome influence over
the wearer. How that may be, I know not; but sure
am I that aught freighted, like this, with the deepest
prayers and most earnest hopes of him who had
thought (a foolish thought—I see it now!) to win the
highest place in her regard, will not be refused by
her when, acknowledging my error, I beg her to
accept it as the gift of elder friend to friend.
Permit me, madam "—he laid the locket in Mrs. B.'s
hand, she half shrinkingly receiving it; "you will soon
hear from your daughter and her husband "—this
word he pronounced with a certain grave emphasis—

"and your reply, let me venture to hope, will tend to a speedy reconciliation. Present her, in my name and with my blessing, with this gem; bid her transmit it as an heirloom to her descendants; and believe that, so long as it retains its form and virtue, my spirit will not forget this solemn hour."

Having delivered himself of this long-winded and not altogether unambiguous speech, good Mr. A. bowed himself out, and rumbled away in his stately coach. Shortly afterwards the abdication of James II. was known throughout England. The B.'s rose at once from their position of political obscurity to an honoured and powerful place under the new *régime*. C., who now turned out to have been for a long time a plotter for the successful cause, was not long afterwards installed as a Court favourite, and his beautiful wife became the idol of society. Poor Mr. A., on the other hand, had a sour time of it. He had been bitterly opposed to the Prince of Orange, and naturally found his present predicament an embarrassing one. He appears to have met with quite an Iliad of misfortunes and reverses; and a few years after William's accession he died.

The general opinion was that he had devoted his latter days to religious exercises. Certain it is, that he was on terms of intimacy with an eminent divine of the day; indeed, a careful analysis of references satisfied me that the compiler of the mysterious MS. and this divine could be no other than one and the same person. And the inference thence that he had died in the odour of sanctity would have been easy enough, save for one discordant and sinister circumstance.

This was reserved for the very last paragraph of the narrative, and shed a peculiar and ill-omened light over all that had gone before. It was related in the transcriber's own person; and after describing with some minuteness the last hours of Mr. A., it concluded as follows. I translate from the original Latin:

"Mr. A. having long lain without motion, breathing hoarsely, and with his eyes half open, and of a rigid and glazed appearance, as of a man already dead— all at once raised himself up in bed, with a strength and deliberation altogether unexpected; and having once or twice passed his hand over his brow, and coughed slightly in his throat, he said to me:

"'Take your pen, friend, and write. I will now dictate my last will and testament.'

"It appeared to me that he must be delirious both because he had, several hours previous, caused his will to be brought to him and read in his ear (this will bore date before the date of his intended marriage with Miss B.), and also because his aspect, notwithstanding the strength of his movements and voice, was more that of a corpse than of a living man ; and he might have been believed, by those who put faith in such superstitions, to be animated by some unhallowed spirit not his own.

"But when I showed him that former will, supposing him to have forgotten it, he bade me put it in the fire ; and when this had been done, and the will consumed, he bade me write thus :

"'I, —— A., being nowe about to die, yet knowynge well the nature of this my act, doe herebye bequeathe my ondyinge Hatred to C. and to his wife (formerly Miss B.), to them and to their Posteritie. And I doe herebye pray Almighty God that the Revenge which my Soule hath desired and conceived, be fulfilled to the uttermoste, whether soon or hereafter : yea, at the perill of my Salvation. Amen !'"

This Satanic composition was duly signed, sealed, and witnessed as A.'s last will and testament ; and the latest earthly act of the wretched man was the affixing his signature to an instrument which, whatever other end it might accomplish, could hardly fail of exercising its deadliest venom against himself.

V.

I lit a fresh cigar, poured out another glass of wine, and gave myself up to meditation. Those blank spaces completely mystified me. For what other object had this lengthy transcription been made than to record A.'s " last will," and the causes leading up to and (so far as that was possible) justifying it? Yet, on the other hand, the careful omission of every clue whereby the persons concerned might have been identified seemed to annul and stultify the laborious record of their actions. Or if the composition were a mere fiction, why not have invented names as well as incidents?

But fiction, I was satisfied, it could not be. It was not the fashion to compose such fictions a hundred and fifty or more years ago. ' And it was not within the scope of such an arid old specimen of the antique clergy as he whose stilted Latin and angular chirography I had just examined to follow such a fashion even had it existed. No, no. Account for it how I might, the things here set down were facts, not fancies.

The will was the only part of the compilation written in English, as though it were especially commended to the knowledge of all men; and it was certainly not the sort of thing a dying man would be apt to compose and have attested purely for his own amusement. Yet, as it stood, it was no more than a lifeless formula. But, indeed, so far as this feature of the narrative was concerned, the subtlest casuistry failed to enlighten me as to what Mr. A.'s proposed revenge had been, and how he expected it to be accomplished. An attempt to make the tourmaline locket serve as a key to the enigma promised well at first, but could not quite be induced to fit the lock after all. Either the problem was too abstruse, or my head was not in the best condition for solving it. The longer I puzzled over it, the more plainly did my inefficiency appear; and at last I came to the very sensible determination to go to bed, and hope for clearer faculties on the morrow.

I had just finished winding up my watch, which marked half-past ten, when there was a violent ring at my door-bell, followed by a rattling appeal to the knocker.

"A telegram!" I exclaimed, falling back in my chair. "The only thing I detest more than a post-man. Well, the postman brought an enigma; perhaps the telegram may contain the solution."

It was not a telegram, but Calbot, to whom I have already made incidental allusion. He opened the library door without knocking, came swiftly in, and walked up to the fire. This abruptness of manner,

K

which was by no means proper to him, added to
something very peculiar in his general aspect and
expression, gave me quite a start.

He was dressed in light in-door costume, and, in
spite of the cold, wore neither top-coat nor gloves.
His face had a pallor which would have been extraordinary in anyone, but in a man whose cheek was
ordinarily so ruddy and robust as Calbot's, it was
almost ghastly. He said nothing for some moments,
but seemed to be struggling with an irrepressible and
exaggerated physical tremor, resembling St. Vitus's
dance. I must say that my nerves have never been
more severely tried than by this unexpected apparition, in so strange a guise, of a friend whom I had
always looked upon as about the most imperturbable
and common-sensible one I had. He was a young
man, but older than his years, clear-headed, practical,
clever, an excellent lawyer, and a fine fellow. Eccen-
tricity of any kind was altogether foreign to his character. Something very unpleasant, I apprehended,
must be at the bottom of his present profound and
uncontrollable agitation.

Of course I jumped up after the first shock, and
shook his hand—which, notwithstanding the cold
weather and his own paleness, was dry and hot. I
fancied Calbot hardly knew where he was or what he
was doing; not that he seemed delirious, but rather

overwhelmingly preoccupied about something altogether hateful and ugly.

"What's the matter, John?" I said, instinctively
using a sharp tone, and laying my hand heavily on
his shoulder. "Are you ill?" Then a thought struck
me, and I added: "Nothing wrong about Miss
Burleigh, I hope?"

"Drayton," said my friend—his utterance was
interrupted somewhat by the nervous starts and
twitches which still mastered his efforts to control
them—"something terrible has happened. I wanted
to tell you. I can't fathom it. Drayton, I've seen——
May I take a glass of wine?"

He drank two glasses in quick succession. As
he hardly ever touched wine, there was no little
significance in the act. The rich old liquor evidently
did him good. To tell the truth, I would rather have
given him some brandy. He was not in a state to
appreciate a fine flavour, and my port was as rare
as it was good. However, I was really concerned
about him, and would gladly have given the whole
decanterful to set him right again.

He would not take a chair, but stood on the rug
with his back to the fire. As I sat looking up at his
tall figure, I caught the painted eye of my priestly
ancestor over his shoulder, and it seemed to me to
twinkle with saturnine humour.

" Well, what have you seen, Calbot ? "

" Some evil thing has come between Miss Burleigh and me, and has parted us. I have seen it—two or three times. She has felt it. It's killing her, Drayton. As for me. . . . . You know me pretty well, and you know what my life has been thus far. I've not been a good man, of course—quite the contrary ; I've done any quantity of bad things, but I don't know that I've committed any such hideous sin as ought to bring a punishment like this upon me—not to speak of *her!* I'm not a parricide, nor an adulterer ; I never sold my salvation to the devil—did I, Drayton ? "

" No, no, of course not, my dear Calbot. You have a fever, that's all. Don't get excited. Just lie down on the sofa for half an hour, and quiet yourself a little."

"I see you think I'm out of my head, and no wonder. I behave like a madman. But I'm not mad at all ; I wish I could think I were. This shuddering —it won't last—but I tell you, Drayton, when you see a man of my health and strength stricken this way in two days, you may believe it would have driven many a man to madness, or to suicide——"

" Let me pour it out for you ; your hand shakes so. I can give you some splendid French cognac, if you'd prefer it ? Well. Hadn't you better lie down ? "

"Come, I can control myself, now—I will!" said Calbot, through his teeth, and putting a strong constraint upon himself. For about a minute he kept silent, the blood gradually coming into his cheeks and the nervous twitchings growing less frequent.

"That's better," said I, encouragingly. "You don't look so much as though you'd seen a ghost, now. How is that Chancery case of yours getting on?"

"A ghost? You speak lightly enough, and I suppose your idea of a ghost is some conventional bogey such as children are scared with. We laugh at such things — heaven knows why! An evil, sin-breathing spirit, coming from hell to take vengeance, for some dead and buried wrong, upon living men and women—what is there laughable in that?"

"Really, Calbot," I said, with a smile—a rather uneasy smile, be it admitted—"I never laughed at a ghost, for the simple reason that I never saw one to laugh at."

"You never saw one, and you mean to hint, I suppose, that there are none to see?"

"Well," returned I, still maintaining a precarious grimace, "I'm not a spiritualist, you know——"

"Nor I," interrupted Calbot, in a lower and quieter tone than he had yet used. He took a chair, and, sitting down close in front of me, bent forward

and whispered in my ear: "But I saw the soul of a
dead man yesterday; and this afternoon I saw it
again, and chased it from the Burleighs' house in
Mayfair, along the Strand, and through the heart of
London, to its grave in St. G——'s churchyard. I
copied the inscription on the stone: it is a very old
one, as you will see by the date."

A far bolder man than I have ever claimed to be
might have felt his heart stand still at this speech;
and its effect on me was greatly heightened by
Calbot's tone and manner, and by the way he
fastened his eyes upon me. Nor were the circumstances in other respects reassuring—alone at night,
with a man three or four times my physical equal,
who was wholly emancipated from rational control.
I sat quite still for a few moments — very long
moments they seemed to me—staring helplessly at
Calbot, who took a small notebook out of his pocket,
tore out a leaf with something scrawled on it, and
handed it to me. I read it mechanically—"Archibald
Armstrong. Died February 6th, 1698." Meanwhile
Calbot helped himself to another glass of wine; but
I was too much unnerved to restrain him, and, indeed,
too much bewildered.

"Archibald Armstrong," muttered I, repeating
the name aloud; "died February 6th—yes; but it
was this present year 1875—not 1698. Why, I went

to the auction-sale of his effects this very after-noon!"

"Keep the paper," said Calbot, not noticing my observation, "it may possibly lead to something. And now I wish you to listen to my statement. I am neither crazy, Drayton, nor intoxicated. But I am not the same man you have known heretofore; my life has been seared—blasted. Perhaps you think my language extravagant; but after what I have experienced there can be no such thing as extrava-gance for me. It is an awful thing," he added, with a long involuntary sigh, "to have been face to face with an evil spirit!"

"In Heaven's name, Calbot," cried I, starting up from my chair, and trembling all over, I believe, from nervous excitement, "don't go on talking and looking like that. If you can tell me a straightforward, con-sistent story, I'll listen to it; but these hints and interjections of yours will drive me mad!"

"I'm going to tell you, Drayton, though it will be the next worst thing to meeting that——Thing—— itself, to tell about it. But the matter is too grim earnest to allow of trifling. You have a great deal of knowledge on queer and out-of-the-way subjects, Drayton, and I thought it not impossible that you might make some suggestions, for there must be some reason for this hideous visitation—some cause for it;

and though all is over for me now, there would be a kind of satisfaction in knowing what that reason was. Besides, I must speak to someone, and you are a dear friend, and an old one."

I was a good deal relieved to hear Calbot speak thus affectionately of our relations with each other; and indeed he appeared no way inclined to violence. Accordingly, having offered him a Cabana (which he refused), I put the box and the decanter back in the cupboard, and locked the door. Then, relighting my own cigar, and putting a lump or two of coal on the fire, I resumed my chair, and bade my friend begin his story.

VI.

"There was an intermarriage between the Burleighs and the Calbots four or five generations ago," said he; "I found the record of it in our family papers, shortly before Miss Burleigh and I were engaged; but it appears not to have turned out well. I don't know whether the husband and wife quarrelled, or whether their troubles came from some outside interference; but they had not been long married before a separation took place—not a regular divorce, but the wife went quietly back to her father's house, and my ancestor is supposed to have gone abroad. But this was not the end of it, Drayton; for, some years later, the husband returned, and he and his wife lived together again."

"Was there any further estrangement between them, afterwards?"

"It is an ugly story," said Calbot, gloomily, getting up from his chair, and taking his old place before the fire. "No; they lived together—as long as they did live! But it was about the era of the witchcraft mania—or delusion, if you choose to call it so—and it is strongly hinted in some of the documents in my possession that the Calbots were—not witches—but victims of witchcraft. They accused no one, but they seemed to have been shunned by everybody like persons under the shadow of a curse. Well—it wasn't a great while before Mrs. Calbot died, and her husband went mad soon afterwards. There were two children. One of them, the son, was born before the first separation. The other, a daughter, came into the world after the reunion, and she was an idiot!"

"An ugly story, sure enough," said I, shrugging my shoulders with a chilly sensation; "but what has it to do with your business?"

"Perhaps nothing; but there is one thing which would go for nothing in the way of legal evidence, but which has impressed me, nevertheless. The date of the second coming-together of my ancestor and his wife was 1698."

" Well ? "

" If you look at that paper I gave you you'll see the date of Armstrong's death is also 1698."

" Still I don't see the point."

" It's simply this : the—Thing I saw was the condemned soul of that Archibald Armstrong. Who he may have been I don't know ; but I can't help believing that my ancestor knew him when he was still in the flesh. They had a feud, perhaps—maybe about this very marriage—of course you understand I'm only supposing a case. Well, Calbot gets the better of his rival, and is married. Then Armstrong exerts his malignant ingenuity to set them at odds with each other. He may have played on the superstitious fancies which they probably shared with others of that age, and at last we may suppose he accomplished their separation."

" An ingenious idea," I admitted, "but what about your date ?"

" Why, on hearing of his death, they would naturally suppose all danger over, and that they might live together unmolested. And from this point you may differ with me or not, as you choose. I believe that it was only after Armstrong was dead that his power for evil became commensurate with his will. I believe, Drayton," said Calbot, drawing himself up to his full height, and emphasising his words with the slow gesture of his right arm, "that the soul of that dead man haunted that wretched couple from the day of his death until the whole tragedy was consummated—until the woman died and the man went mad. And I believe that his devilish malignity has lived on to this day, and wreaked itself, a second time, on Miss Burleigh and myself."

There was a short pause, during which my poor friend stood tapping one foot on the hearth-rug, his eyes bent downwards in sombre abstraction.

"Look here, my dear John," I said at length, speaking with an effort, for there was a sensation of heavy oppression on my chest; "listen to me, old fellow. You've had time to cool down and bethink yourself: so far as I can judge you appear, as you say, neither crazy nor intoxicated. Now I wish you, remembering that we are sensible, enlightened men, living in London in this year 1875, to tell me honestly whether I am to understand you as deliberately asserting a belief in visitations from the other world. Because, really, you know, that is what anyone would infer from the way you have been talking this evening."

"I see there would be little use, Drayton, in my answering your question directly; but I will give you a deliberate and honest account of my personal

experiences during these last two days : there will
be no danger of your mistaking my meaning then.
You won't mind my walking up and down the
room while I'm speaking, will you ? The subject is
a painful one, and motion seems to make it easier,
somehow."

I did mind it very much, it made me as nervous
as a water-beetle ; but, of course, I forbore to say
so, and Calbot went on :

"I said I found out all this ancestral trouble
some time before I was engaged ; and, as you may
imagine, I kept silence about it to Miss Burleigh.
I think now it was a mistake to do so ; but my
ideas on many subjects have undergone modification
of late. I believe I had forgotten all about the
discovery by the time I had made up my mind to
risk an avowal : at any rate, I had no misgivings
about it ; and when I came out from my interview
with her—the happiest man in England !—ah
Drayton, it seemed to me then that there could be
no more pains nor shadows in life for me thence-
forward for ever !"

I devoutly wished, not for the first time that
evening, that Calbot would not be so painfully in
earnest. In his normal state it was difficult to
get a serious word out of him ; he was brimming
over with quaint humour and fun ; but, as he

himself had remarked, he was another man to-day.
After walking backwards and forwards once or
twice in silence, he continued :

"You know how happy I was those first few
days. I daresay you wished me and my happiness
in Jericho, when I insisted on deluging you with
an account of it. Think ! Drayton, that was hardly
a week ago. Well, as soon as I had got a little
bit used to the feeling of being engaged, I began
to think what I should give her—Edna, you know—
for a betrothal gift. A ring, of course, is the usual
thing ; but I couldn't be satisfied with a ring : I
wanted my gift to be something rare—unique ; in
short, something different from what any other
fellow could give his mistress ; for I loved her
more than any woman was ever loved before.
After a good deal of fruitless bother, I suddenly
bethought myself of a jewel-box which had belonged
to my mother—God bless her !—and which she had
bequeathed to me, intending, very likely, that I
should use it for the very purpose I was now thinking
of. I got out the box, and overhauled it. There
was a lot of curious old trinkets in it ; but the
thing which at once took my eye was a delicately
wrought gold necklace, that looked as though it
had been made expressly for Edna's throat. There
was a locket attached to it, which I at first meant

to take off; but on examining it closely, I found it was quite worthy of the chain—was an exquisite work of art, indeed. It was made of a dark yellow or brownish sort of stone, semi-transparent, and was engraven with a very finely-wrought bas-relief."

"Calbot!" exclaimed I, starting upright in my chair, "what sort of a stone did you say that locket was made of?"

"What is the matter?" returned he, stopping short in his walk and facing me with a glance partly apprehensive, partly expectant. "I never saw exactly such a stone before—but why?"

"Oh, nothing," said I, after a moment's excited thought; "it certainly is very strange! But, never mind, go on," I added, throwing a glance at the old manuscript which lay open on the table; "go on. I'll tell you afterwards; I must turn it over in my mind a bit."

"The reason I described it so minutely," remarked Calbot, "was that I got a notion into my head that it had something to do with what happened afterwards, and the reason of that notion is, that almost from the very moment that Edna took the necklace—I clasped it round her neck myself—the strange awful influence—visitation—call it what you like—began to be apparent.

"Oh Drayton, you can never know how lovely, how divine she looked that evening. She had on what they call, I believe, a demi-toilette; open at the throat, you know, and half the arm showing. No woman could have looked more beautiful than she, before I put on the chain and locket; yet when they were on, she looked as handsome again. It was really wonderful—the effect they had. Her eyes deepened, and an indescribable change or modulation—imperceptible, very likely, to anyone beside myself, her lover—came over her face. I think it was a shade of sadness—of mystery—no, I can only repeat, that it was indescribable; but it gave her beauty just the touch that made it, humanly speaking, perfect. I daresay this is all very tiresome to you, Drayton, but I can't help it!"

"Oh, go on, my dear fellow," said I warmly; for, indeed, I was moved as well as excited. "Won't you sit down? Here, take my chair!"

But he would not.

"As I fastened the clasp, I said: 'You are fettered for ever now, Edna!' and she said, with her eyes sparkling: 'Yes, I am the thrall of the locket; the giver may lead me in triumph where he will!' Just as the words passed her lips, Drayton, I felt a sensation of coldness and depression; I gave an involuntary shudder, and looking quickly in Edna's eyes, I saw there the very reflection of my own feeling! We were alone, and yet there seemed to be a third person present—cold, hateful, malevolent. He seemed to be between us—to be pressing us irresistibly apart ; and I felt powerless to contend against the insidious influence ; and so was she. For an instant or two we gazed fearfully and strangely at each other ; then she said faintly : ' Come to me—take me! ' and half held out her arms, her face and lips all pale. Drayton, I cannot tell you what a desperate struggle I had with myself then! My whole soul leapt out towards her with a passion such as I had never known before ; and yet my body seemed paralysed. I had felt something similar to it in dreams before then ; but the dream pain was nothing to the real pain. A cold dead hand was on my heart, dragging it backward, deadening it ; and another at my throat, stifling me. But I fought against it—it seemed to me I sweated drops of blood—but I overcame. I put my arm round her waist—I kissed her ; and yet, though I seemed to hold her—though our lips seemed to meet —still that Thing was between us—we did not really touch each other! With all our love, we were like lifeless clay to one another's caress. It was a mockery —our souls could meet no more." Here Calbot covered his eyes with his hand for a short time. "It was the last time I ever kissed her," said he.

I said nothing ; my sympathy with my hapless friend was keen. Yet I must confess to a secret sensation of relief that there was to be no more kissing. It was natural, under the circumstances, that Calbot—poor fellow!—should speak recklessly ; but I am a bachelor, a confirmed bachelor, and such descriptions distress me ; they make me restless, wakeful, and unhappy. Yes, I was glad we had had the last of them.

"It all passed very quickly, and a third person would perhaps have seen no change in us ; probably the change was more inward than outward, after all. It was peculiar that we, both of us, by a tacit understanding, forbore to speak to each other of this dismal mystery that had so suddenly grown up between us. It was too real, and at the same time too hopeless ; but to have acknowledged it would have been to pronounce it hopeless indeed. We would not do that yet. We sat apart, quietly and conventionally making observations on ordinary topics, as though we had been newly introduced. And yet my betrothal gift was round her neck, moving as she breathed ; and we loved each other, and our hearts were breaking. Oh, it is cruel!"

In exclaiming thus, my friend (being at the farther end of the room at the time) struck his foot sharp against the leg of a small antique table which stood

L

against the wall. Like many other valuable things, the table was fragile, and the leg broke. The table tipped over, and a vase (the ancestral vase, containing the elixir of life), fell off to the floor.

Calbot—I think it was much to his credit—found room amidst his proper anguish to be sincerely distressed at this accident. On picking up the vase, however, he immediately exclaimed that it was unbroken. This was fortunate : the table could be mended, but the vase, not to speak of its contents, would have been irreplaceable. Calbot put it carefully on the study table, beside the MS. ; set the invalid table in a corner ; and then, to my great satisfaction, drew up a chair to the fire, and continued his sad story in a civilised posture.

VII.

"I did not stay long after this ; and ours was a strange parting that evening, if our hearts could have been seen. We felt it a relief to separate, and yet the very relief was a finer kind of pain. We knew not what had befallen us ; but, perhaps, we both had a hope, then, that another day would somehow set things right.

"I only took her hand in saying good-bye ; but again it seemed as if her soft fingers were not actually in contact with mine—as if some rival hand were interposed. And I noticed (as I had done once or twice before during our latter conversation) that, even while the farewell words were being spoken, she turned her head abruptly with a startled, listening expression, as though another voice had spoken close at her ear. I could hear nothing, nor understand the dimly terrified look in her eyes—a look appealing and yet shrinking. But afterwards I understood it all. When I reached the street, I turned back and caught a glimpse of Edna at the window. Beside her I fancied I distinguished the half-defined outlines of a strange figure—that of a man who appeared to be gesticulating in an extravagant manner. But before I could decide whether it were a shadow or a reality, Edna had turned away, and the apparition vanished with her."

. " Her father, of course," I threw in, with a glance over my shoulder; " or perhaps it was the footman." Calbot made no reply.

" I got up yesterday morning," said he, " convinced that the whole thing was a delusion. I took a brisk walk round Hyde Park, ate a good breakfast, and by eleven o'clock was on my way to her house, sure that I should find her as cheerfully disposed to laugh at our dolorous behaviour the night before as I myself was. I went down Piccadilly in the best of spirits; but on turning the corner of Park Lane, I very plainly saw three persons coming down towards me."

Here Calbot paused so long that I could hardly refrain from springing out of my chair. I had never heard him argue a case before a jury; but had I been the presiding judge himself, I was convinced that Calbot could have moulded my opinions to whatsoever issue he had pleased. But, on the other hand, I doubt whether he was aware of his own best powers. The effect he was now producing on me was certainly not the result of any premeditated artifice.

"I saw Edna," he finally went on, speaking in a husky labouring tone, and gazing intently over my shoulder, as if he saw her *there*. "She was walking in the centre, with a weary lifeless step, her head bent downwards: on her right was her father, as jolly and portly as ever; and on her left, Drayton, was the same strange figure of which I fancied I had caught a glimpse the night before. It was no shadow now, however, but looked as real and palpable as General Burleigh himself. It appeared to be diligently addressing itself to Edna, occasionally even stooping to speak in her ear; and once I saw it put its arm round her waist, and apparently press its bearded cheek to her own."

"Why, in Heaven's name, Calbot, didn't you——"

But there was something in my friend's eyes, as he turned them on me, which made me break off just there.

"When I first turned the corner the three were sixty or seventy yards distant. It struck me at once that Edna seemed to have no direct consciousness of the stranger's presence. That is, she did not act as if he were visible to her ; though, at the same time, I could hardly doubt that the *idea* of him was present to her mind ; and from her manner of involuntary shrinking and starting when the Thing became particularly demonstrative in its manner, I fancied that the words which it appeared to address to her insinuated themselves into her brain under the form of dismal and hateful thoughts. Perhaps, Drayton, the base or wicked notions that sometimes creep into our minds unawares, asserting themselves our own, are whispered to us by some evil spirit, invisible to our sight, but capable of impressing the immaterial part of us all the more effectively.

"As they drew near, I could no longer doubt that the Thing was viewless, not only to Edna, but to everyone else besides myself alone. Had it been otherwise, the figure's remarkable costume, no less than its many eccentricities, would have drawn a great crowd in a few moments. It was a tall fantastic apparition, clad in a black velvet cloak and doublet, silk hose, and high-heeled shoes. On its head was a broad-brimmed hat, with heavy plumes; there were lace ruffles at its wrists and round its throat. A long rapier dangled by its side; its beard was gray and peaked, but a copious powdered wig flowed out beneath the hat and rested on the shoulders.

"Its gait, as it stalked along the pavement, was mincing and affected, and under other circumstances I might have laughed at it. Its manner and gestures were absurdly exaggerated and fantastic. It was continually bowing and scraping to Edna, and seemingly making hot love to her; but as often as she winced or shrank from it, it appeared hugely delighted, throwing up its arms, wagging its head, and contorting its body, as if carried away by an immoderate fit of laughter.

"The sun was shining broadly, but none of its rays seemed to fall on the sable garments of this singular personage. In fact, though I saw him as plainly as I now see you, Drayton, I was, nevertheless, well aware that here was something more or less than flesh and blood. It was a being of another state than this mortal one of ours. I say I saw him; and yet I do not believe that it was with my natural eyesight. A deeper sense of vision had been temporarily opened within me, and this spectre came within its scope.

" For a spectre it was. General Burleigh, striding
bluffly along by the other side of his daughter, swing-
ing his cane, twisting his moustaches, and ever and
anon smiling and bowing to a passing friend, was
ludicrously unconscious of there being anything
supernatural in his vicinity. Moreover, I saw at
least twenty persons pass the apparition shoulder
to shoulder, evidently without seeing it ; though they
would often shiver, and wrap their top-coats or shawls
more closely round them, as if a sudden blast of icy
air had penetrated them. All this time the three were
approaching slowly, and were now but little more
than twenty paces distant. I had not moved a step
since first coming in view of them, and had kept my
eyes fixed point-blank upon the apparition.

"At this moment I was puzzled to observe that
the black-garmented figure was a good deal less distinctly discernible than when it had been farther off.
The sun was still as bright as ever, the air as clear,
but the outline of the shape was blurred and unde-
fined, as though seen out of focus through a telescope.
General Burleigh now caught sight of me for the first
time, and his cordial gesture of salute caused Edna
quickly to raise her eyes. We saw despair in each
other's looks, and then she dropped her eyes again, and
moved wearily onward. Simultaneously with her glance
the spectre (which appeared to be as unconscious

of everything save Edna and myself, as everyone
except us was of it)—the spectre also directed its
gaze at me. I can never forget that face, Drayton.
I seemed to grow older and more miserable as I confronted it. And all the while it was getting less and
less perceptible ; now it was magnified, clouded, and
distorted ; but the devilish expression of it was still
recognisable. Now it faded or expanded into vague-
ness ; only a foggy shadow seemed gliding by Edna's
side ; and when she was within ten paces, and her
father's voice was speaking out its hearty welcome to
me, every trace even of the shadow had disappeared ;
nothing was left but that chilliness and horror of the
heart which I had felt the night previous, but now
vastly intensified, because I was no longer ignorant of
the cause of it. Edna and I would never again be
alone together. This devil was to haunt us henceforth, mocking our love by its hideous mimicry and
derision, marring and polluting our most sacred
secrets, sickening our hearts and paralysing our hope
and reliance in each other. We could neither escape
it nor resist it ; and its invisibility when we were
together was not the least fearful thing about it.
To see it, awful as it was, must be less unendurable
than to imagine it, unseen ; and the certainty that, so
often as I left Edna, I should leave this devil in her
company, visible once more the moment he was out

of my reach, but never to be met and grappled with hand to hand—this was hard to bear! Had ever mortal man before such a rival?

"All this, of course, was but dimly apprehended by my mind at the time; but I had sufficient opportunity to muse upon it afterwards. General Burleigh seized my hand, and shook the head of his cane at me.

"'Shall be obliged to court-martial you, young man! What have you been doing to my daughter, sir? Why, no one can get a word or a smile out of her, since you came with your tomfooleries! She keeps all her good humour for you, confound you! It's witchcraft—you've bewitched my little girl with your lockets and your necklaces and your tomfooleries! You've bewitched her—and I'll have you court-martialed, and executed for witchcraft, by Jove! Ha, ha, ha! Ha, ha, ha!' And with that he gripped my hand again, and vowing that the club was the only place for him since I had appeared with my tomfooleries and witchcraft, he swung round on his heel and strode away, his broad military shoulders shaking with jollity; and left Edna alone with me— and my rival!

"We strolled off along Piccadilly, and I daresay every man we met was envying me from the bottom of his heart. But though her arm was in mine, I knew I might as well have been miles away from her. And we both were reticent of our words on all matters lying near our hearts, as if that third presence had been as palpable and visible as it was otherwise real. We spoke constrainedly and coldly; nay, we even tried not to *think* of our love or of our misery, lest it might possess power to see our thoughts as well as hear our voices. We walked on, seldom looking at one another, for fear of catching a glimpse of it in each other's eyes. I saw, however, that Edna still wore her locket—indeed, she had told me, the night before, that she would never take it off, until I bade her do so.

"'So your father thinks you bewitched, Edna,' I said at length, trying to throw off the incubus a little.

"'I am not very well, I think.'

"'He seemed to fancy the spell was connected with that old locket,' I continued; my very disinclination to the subject driving me to tamper with it.

"'Perhaps it is,' returned Edna listlessly, lifting her hand for a moment to her throat. 'I am not quite used to it yet.'

"'To witchcraft, do you mean? You have seen no phantoms, have you?'

"I felt her little hand clutch my arm with an involuntary start. I looked down, and she met my eye with a blush, and at the same time with a terrified shrinking expression that was bitter to behold.

"'I see nothing with my open eyes,' she said, scarcely above a whisper; 'but at night—I cannot help my dreams; and they follow me into the day.'

"It was as I had thought, therefore; the spectre was not objectively visible to her. She could not get away from her own self, and hence could gain no point of vantage whence her persecutor could be seen. There was little doubt, nevertheless, that her mental picture of him agreed with my ocular experience. It seemed to me, on the whole, that her burden must be far harder to bear than mine. There is a kind of relief in being able to face a horror; and my own feelings, since seeing this evil spirit which was haunting us, had been in a certain sense more tolerable, if more hopeless, than the night before. But how did I know what agony she might suffer? Even her innocent sleep was not sacred from this evil thing; all her maiden reserve and delicacy were outraged; she could be safe nowhere—no one could protect her; and with me, who would have given my life to please a whim of hers, her suffering and exposure must be less endurable than anywhere else. I could well understand her blush, poor girl— poor girl!"

Not for many years—not since, in fact, certain sad experiences of my own early days—had I been so deeply stirred as by this recital of Calbot's. His voice had great compass and expression, and the needs of his profession had given its natural powers every cultivation. He had a way of dwelling on certain words, and of occasionally pausing, or appearing to hesitate, which greatly added to the effect of his narrative. All this might be acquired by art, but not so the ever and anon recurring falterings and breaks, into which, as now, he was unexpectedly betrayed. I felt that it was unwise in me to listen to him, to sympathise with him, as I was doing; yet could I not find it in my heart to stop him. All fears of violence on his part had been for some time past allayed. I was well aware that my encouragement of his confidences could only result in my passing a feverish uncomfortable night, and a listless dismal morrow; and yet I forbore to interrupt him. Ah! it is we old bachelors who have hearts after all.

I blew my nose, Calbot cleared his throat, and continued.

VIII.

"Well, Drayton, I shan't keep you much longer. From Piccadilly we turned into Bond Street, and were walking up the side-walk on the left-hand side, when suddenly Edna stopped, and clasped both her hands round my arm. She uttered a low exclamation, and trembled perceptibly. Her face, as I looked at it, was quite rigid and colourless. I did not know what was the matter, but fearing she was about to swoon, I looked round for a cab. In so doing my eye caught my own reflection in a mirror, fixed at a shop entrance on the other side of the street. It was in this direction that Edna also was gazing, and the next moment I no longer wondered at her ghastly aspect. Close by her shoulder appeared the fantastic black-garmented figure which I had seen awhile before in Park Lane. He was making the wildest and most absurd gestures—grinning, throwing about his arms, making profound mock obeisances, and evidently in an ecstasy of enjoyment. I looked suddenly round, but the place which should have been occupied by the original of the reflection appeared entirely empty. Looking back to the mirror, however, there was the spectre again, actually capering with ugly glee.

"Meantime people were beginning to notice the strange behaviour of Edna and myself, and I was thankful when a passing cab enabled me to shield her from their scrutiny. No sooner were we seated than she fainted away, and only recovered a few

moments before we stopped at her door. As I
helped her out she looked me sadly in the face, and
said :

"'Come to me to-morrow afternoon—for the last
time.'

"I could say nothing against her decision,
Drayton ; I felt we should be really more united,
living apart, than were we to force ourselves to outward association. Our calamity was too strong for
us ; separation might appease the mysterious malice
of the phantom, and cause him to return whither he
belonged. The persecution of our long-dead ancestors now recurred to me, as I had read it a few
months before in those dusty old documents, and I
could not help seeing a strange similarity between
their fate and ours. Yet we had an advantage in
not being married, and in having the warning of
their history before us. You see," observed Calbot,
somewhat bitterly, "even I can talk of advantages !

"I went to her house to-day and had a short
interview. I cannot tell you in detail what we said,
but it seems to me as though the memory of it
would gradually oust all other memories from my
mind. I told her that passage of history. We
agreed to part—for ever in this world. I took back
the chain and locket which I had given her but so
short a time before. We said good-bye, in cold and

distant words. We could not gratify the evil spirit, which we knew was watching us, by any embrace or show of grief and passion. We could be proud in our despair."

"One moment, Calbot," said I, interrupting him at this point; "you say she gave you back the locket?"

"Yes."

"Is it in your possession now?"

"It is at the bottom of the Thames."

"Good! And have you or Miss Burleigh seen anything of your phantom since then?"

"You forget that we parted only this afternoon. But I understand your question. No, Drayton, it is there that the fate of our ancestors gives us timely warning. We must never meet again."

"I don't consider the cases parallel; and besides," I added, with a glance at my MS., "there is perhaps another point to be considered. However, finish your story, if there be any more to tell."

"A little more, and then my story will be finished indeed! I am going with the new expedition to the North Pole, and it will be my own fault if I return. Well, after leaving her, I came straight downstairs and hurried out. I felt as though I must go mad, or kill someone—myself perhaps. As I stood on the doorstep, mechanically buttoning up my ulster, I felt that creeping sickening chill once more, and knew that the unholy Thing had passed me. I looked sharply about, and in a moment or two I saw it, as plainly as ever. It stood on the sunlit pavement, about fifty yards away, and appeared to be beckoning me to approach.

"I watched it for perhaps a minute, and then a sudden fury took possession of me. My hatred against this devil which had blighted my life and Edna's must have leapt up in my eyes, for I fancied, from the way the phantom leered at me, that he meant to claim a sort of relationship with me—as though I were become a devil too. Well, if I were a devil, perhaps I might be able to inflict some torture on this my fellow. I sprang down the steps, and set off towards it. It waited until I had passed over more than half the intervening distance, and then it suddenly turned and walked onward before me. So a chase began."

"Good gracious, Calbot," remonstrated I; "you don't mean to tell me you ran after it—in the face of all London too?"

"I would have followed it to its own hell if it had led me there," he returned. "At first it stalked along swiftly but easily, only occasionally cutting a grotesque caper in the air, with a flourish of its arms and egs. It kept always the same distance in front of me—with no effort could I lessen the interval. Nevertheless, I gradually increased my speed almost to a run, much to the apparent delight of the hobgoblin, who skipped with frantic glee over the cold pavements, occasionally half facing about to waive me on. It turned the corner of Piccadilly, and I lost sight of it for a moment; but, hurrying up, there it was again, a short distance up the street. It made me a profound mock obeisance, and immediately set off anew.

"As I need not tell you, the figure which I was pursuing was visible only to myself. The street was full of people, there were all the usual noise, bustle, and gaiety of the city at that hour; but though it passed through the midst of the crowd, in all the fantastic singularity of its costume and manner, no one stepped out of its way or turned to gaze at it. That it should be so terrible a reality to me, and at the same time so completely non-existent to the rest of the world, affected me strangely. Here was a new bond of relationship between me and it. My misery and I were one; but the link which united us was a cap of invisibility for the demon.

"*I* was not invisible, however, nor unnoticed. I was conscious that everyone was staring at me—and no wonder! I must have presented an odd spectacle, hurrying onward with no apparent object, and with an expression of face which may well have been

M

startling to behold. But so long as no attempt was
made to stop me, I was indifferent to remark. I had
determined to follow my black friend in the plumed
hat, no matter where the chase might lead me.

" The pace grew quicker and quicker. We went
down the Haymarket, and were now in the throng of
the Strand. All the places which I know so well
passed by like remembered dreams. They seemed
illusions, and the only real substance in the world was
this Thing that I pursued. The dark shape continued
to glide forward with easy speed, ever and anon giving
me a glimpse of the pallid malignance of its evil
visage; but my own breath was beginning to come
hard, and the difficulty of forcing a path through the
press became greater as we neared the heart of the
city. Passing beneath Temple Bar, the spectre
stopped a moment and stamped its foot imperiously,
at the same time beckoning to me with an impatient
gesture. I sprang forward, yearning to grapple with
it; but it was gone again, and seemed to flit like a
shadow along the sidewalk. Its merriment, however, now forsook all bounds—it appeared to be in a
ceaseless convulsion of chuckling laughter. We fled
onward, but so absorbed in my pursuit had I now
become, that I recollect nothing distinctly until the
tower of St. G——'s came into view. I think
a premonition of what was to occur entered my

mind then. The hobgoblin disappeared—seemingly through the iron railing of the contracted graveyard which bounds the northern side of the church. I came up to the railing and looked within. It was sitting on an ancient headstone, blackened by London smoke and worn by time; it sat with its elbows on its knees, and its head in its hands. A sombre shadow fell about it, which the cheerful sunshine could not penetrate; but its awful eyes emitted a dusky phosphorescent glare, dimly illuminating the leering features. As I looked, a change came over them—they were now those of a corpse already mouldering in decay, crumbling into nothingness before my eyes. The whole figure gradually faded or darkened away: I cannot tell how or when it vanished. Presently I was staring fixedly at an old tombstone, with a name and a date upon it; but the churchyard was empty."

IX.

Of my own accord I now reproduced my decanter of port-wine, and Calbot and I finished it before either of us spoke another word.

What he was thinking of meanwhile I know not; for my part, I was endeavouring to put in order a number of disjointed ideas, imbibed at various epochs during this evening, whose logical arrangement, I was convinced, would go far towards elucidating much of the mystery. As to the positively supernatural part of Calbot's experience, of course I had no way of accounting for that; but I fancied there were materials at hand tolerably competent to raise a ghost, allowing such a thing as a ghost to be possible.

"I am glad, Calbot," I began, "that you came to me. Your good sense—or instinct, perhaps—directed you aright. Do not despair: I should not be surprised were we to manage between us to discover that your happiness, so far from being at an end, was just on the point of establishing itself upon a trustworthy foundation." Calbot shook his head gloomily. "Well, well," resumed I, "let us see. In the first place—as regards that locket. It will perhaps surprise you to learn that I had heard of it before you came this evening—had read quite a minute description of it, in fact."

"Where?" demanded my friend, raising his eyes.

"That will appear later. I must first ask you whether, in the old family documents you spoke of, the personal appearance of this Archibald Armstrong was particularly delineated?"

"I hardly know; I have no recollection of any especial passage—and yet I fancy it must have been given with some fulness; because when I saw the hobgoblin, its costume and aspect seemed curiously familiar."

"And had I seen it, there is little doubt in my mind that I should have recognised it also."

"Indeed!" exclaimed Calbot, sitting upright in his chair, "how happens that?"

Wait a moment, I am merely collecting evidence. Now, have you any reason to suppose that a connection of any sort—friendly, business, or other—subsisted between your unhappy ancestor and this Armstrong previous to the former's marriage?"

"Do you mean whether he was under any obligations to Armstrong?"

"Yes."

"He may have been—but the idea is new to me. How——"

"I am not done yet. Now, did it never occur to you—or, I should say, does it not seem probable—that the locket which you had found hidden away in your mother's jewel-box was in some way connected with the family tragedy you told me of?"

"I have thought of it, Drayton; there is no difficulty in imagining such a thing; the trouble is, we haven't the slightest evidence of it."

"I was about to say," I rejoined, "that there is direct evidence of precisely such a locket having been bought, in the latter part of the seventeenth century, by precisely such a looking man as the hobgoblin you saw to-day. It was to be a wedding-gift to the woman he was to marry the next day."

" Drayton ! "

" That woman deceived him, and eloped on the eve of her marriage with a protégé of his. He professed forgiveness, and sent the locket as a pledge of it."

" Odd ! "

" He died in 1698, and his last recorded words were a curse invoked upon those whom he had before professed to pardon—upon them and their posterity."

" But, Drayton—what——"

" It is my opinion that his forgiveness was merely a cloak to his deadly and unrelenting hatred. It is my opinion, Calbot, that the pledge he gave was poisonous with evil and malicious influences. The locket was made of tourmaline, which has mysterious properties. No doubt he believed it a veritable witch's talisman; and from the sufferings which afterwards befell his enemies (not to speak of your own experience), one might almost fancy witchcraft to be not entirely a delusion after all."

" One might, indeed ! But if, as you seem to imply, this locket enabled Armstrong to persecute Calbot and his wife, why did not they send it back or destroy it ? "

" Simply because they were not aware of its evil nature, and fancied that Armstrong's (if it were his) profession of forgiveness had been genuine. Very likely Mrs. Calbot habitually wore it on her bosom, as Miss Burleigh did again yesterday, more than a century later. The persecutor must have been a devil incarnate, from the time he learnt his lady's faithlessness until his death ; and after that——"

"A plain devil. But to come to the point, you think that the locket was the sole medium of his power over them ? "

"Undoubtedly. Then, after their death, it re-mained in the family, but never happened to be used again : it is not a jewel to catch the eye by any means. It remained perdu until you fished it out for Miss Burleigh, and thereby stirred up the old hob-goblin to play his devilish tricks once more. But by a lucky combination of accidents you parted with her in time ; she returned you the locket, thus freeing *herself* from the spectre ; and you, by throwing it in the Thames, have secured him against ever being able to make his appearance again."

"It may be so, Drayton," cried Calbot in great excitement. "I remember, too, that when I gave her the locket she promised fealty *to the giver !* Now, in fact, not I but this cursed Armstrong was the real giver ; and so Edna was actually surrendering herself to his power. But, supposing your explanation correct, why may not Edna and I come together again ?"

"Well, my dear fellow," replied I, as I lit another Cabana, "unless you have acquired a very decided aversion to each other during the last few hours, I really don't see why you shouldn't."

"Drayton, I'm afraid to believe this true! Tell me how you came upon your evidence, and what degree of reliance may be placed upon it."

I told him briefly about the MS., and added the conviction (at which I had arrived during his narrative) that it must have been sent to me by my former friend, Armstrong's executor ; and probably comprised the very papers which I had made an ineffectual attempt to secure at the auction sale. "The only lame point about the matter," I added, "is, that the MS. is wholly anonymous. All the names are blanks, and though I have no doubt, now, that they are Armstrong, Burleigh, and Calbot, there is no direct proof of it."

My friend's face fell. "There, it may be only a coincidence after all!"

"Nonsense! a coincidence indeed! If you have credulity enough to believe in such a 'coincidence' as that, you have certainly mistaken your profession."

"If your were a lawyer," returned he, "you would know that there is no limit to the strangeness of coincidences. But let me see the MS."

"It is there on the table, at your elbow."

Calbot turned and took it up.

"How's this—it's wet, soaking wet!" he exclaimed. "Drayton, I'm afraid I must have cracked that old vase of yours. It has been leaking, and the table is flooded."

It was too true. The precious water of life had been preserved through so many generations merely for the sake of spoiling the morocco of my study table at last. Vanished were my hopes of earthly immortality. Cautiously lifting the vase, in the hope that somewhat of the precious ichor might yet be saved, the whole bottom fell out. Calbot was sorry, of course, but he had no conception of the extent of the misfortune. He observed that the vase could easily be mended, as if the vase were the chief treasure.

"Never mind," said I, rather soberly, after we had sopped up the inestimable elixir, as well as we could, with our handkerchiefs. "I shall die an eternity or two the sooner, and shall have to get my table new covered, that's all. I hope, Calbot, that the good which your visit here has done you, will be a small fraction as great as the loss it has inflicted on me.

Well, and how has the MS. come out of the scrape? All washed out, I suppose."

With a penitent eye Calbot took it up once more, and ran his eye over the last page. I saw his expression change. He knit his brows—looked up at me with a quick questioning glance—looked back to the page, and finally said : " Oh ! "

" What ? "

" It seems you had filled in the blanks before I came ? "

" With the first four letters of the alphabet. Yes ! "

" With the names in full ! "

" What names ? "

" Why, Drayton, the first thing I looked at was this record of ' ondyinge Hatred,' &c. It contains all the four names—yours as one of the witnesses of Armstrong's signature. They are written out in pale red ink, as plain as can be——"

I had jumped from my chair and taken the MS. from Calbot's hand. It was impossible—it was inconceivable, but it was true. The page was thoroughly wetted through, but there were the three names—the *four* names, for my own was added, in the character of compiler of the work—plainly traced out in light red ink. Could I have done it in a fit of abstraction? No, for the chirography was not mine—it was identical with all the rest of the writing. In my utter bewilderment, I raised my eyes to the wall, where hung the picture of my ecclesiastical ancestor—he, the alchemist, the busybody, the death-bed confidant, the suspected wizard—and my own namesake—we were the only two Toxophiluses in all the line of Draytons. Once more, for the third or fourth time that evening, it struck me that he looked excessively knowing and sly.

Who can analyse the lightning evolutions of human thought? I knew the truth before I could explain it. It crystallised in my brain all in a moment. A glance at the front of the MS., which had not been wetted, confirmed me.

I threw down the MS., clapped Calbot on the shoulder, and burst into an immoderate fit of laughter, which his astonished and concerned aspect served only to aggravate. It was some minutes before I could speak.

"It is a simple matter after all," I said. "My old progenitor, there on the wall, was a friend—confidential friend—of Armstrong's. It was he who wrote that MS., and left the blanks, which are not blanks, but names written in invisible ink. He prepared, then, the chemical reagent for the purpose of making the invisible writing visible whenever the time should come. Perhaps he meant to apply it himself some day; but, unluckily, death snatched him all unawares from the scene of his pious intrigues. The

MS. got into the hands of Armstrong's heirs (from whom I this day received it). The reagent stayed with the Draytons. This evening you came and brought the two together in your own inimitable style. You see, wherever the paper is wet, the blanks are filled in : the untouched parts are blanks still. Oh John, John! I wish this had happened before I printed my article on 'Unrecognisable Truths :' it is a peculiarly apt illustration."

"Didn't I tell you," said Calbot, after a pause, "that there was nothing in the world so strange as coincidences?"

"There is the hobgoblin still unaccounted for," answered I ; "but I have done my part ; I leave the rest to you."

*   *   *   *   *

The next day but one came a note from my friend. It ran :

"What did I do at your rooms last night ? Was I queer at all ? I had intended calling on you that day, to tell you that Edna and I were going to be married April 1st, and to get you for my best man. *Did* I tell you ? Because, if not, I do now. The fact is, you see, I had been reading over some curious old family documents (I think I spoke to you about them), and then I went up to Edna's and frightened her half

to death with telling her ghost stories about the locket
I'd given her as a betrothal gift (a queer little thing it
is. Did I ever mention it to you?) Well, going
home I met young De Quincey, and he proposed—
he's always up to some devilry or other—he proposed
doing something which I shall never do again ; I was
a fool to try it at all, but I had no notion how it
would act. I'm afraid I may have annoyed you. I
have an idea I upset your ink-bottle, and that I got it
into my head that the ghost story I had been telling
Edna was true. How was it? I know I felt deathly
sick the next morning; I'm not certain whether it
was the port-wine I drank, or that confounded
hasheesh that I took with young De Quincey. I
promised Edna I'd never take any more. Well, you
won't object to being my best man, will you?

"J. C."

So far from explaining the essential mystery—the
Ghostly Rival—this letter of John's only makes it, to
my mind, more inscrutable than ever. Talk about
coincidences! For my part, I prefer to believe in
ghosts.

MRS. GAINSBOROUGH'S
DIAMONDS.

MRS. GAINSBOROUGH'S DIAMONDS.

"SUPERB! I don't know when I have seen finer, Tom, really!"

"Ah!" said Tom, complacently handling his left whisker. "And," he added, after a moment or two, "and thereby hangs a tale!"

It was after dinner—after one of Tom Gainsborough's snug, inimitable little dinners ; only we three —Tom, his wife, and myself : and a couple of negro attendants, as well trained and less overpowering than the best of the native English stock ; and that charming dining-room, just big enough, just cool enough, soft-carpeted, clear-walled, and the steady white radiance of the argand burners descending upon the damask tablecloth, crowned with fruits and flowers; and an agreeable shadow over the rest of the room, so that those sable servitors could perform their noise-

N

less evolutions unseen ; and a pervading sense of unconscious good-breeding and unobtrusive wealth ; and——but I will not speak of the china ; I will not descant upon Tom's wines ; I don't wish to make other people envious. Only it was all inexpressibly good, from fascinating Mrs. Gainsborough and her diamonds, down.

I felt a peculiar interest in Mrs. Gainsborough, because, in addition to her other attractions, she was a countrywoman of mine—that is to say, an American. She was brunette, slender, graceful ; with a weird expression of the eyes under straight black eyebrows, an expression which somehow suggested mesmerism —or perhaps a liability on her part to be mesmerised ; faultless throat and shoulders ; and hands and wrists that she could talk with, almost. Where had Tom found her ? I never had thought of asking him : she was a Virginian very likely—an " F. F. V." ; and they had doubtless met upon the Continent. This was the first occasion on which I had seen her in her diamonds. Indeed, Tom and she had only been married a year or two, and had been settled in that *bijou* residence of theirs scarcely six months ; and this was but my third or fourth dinner there. Well, her diamonds became her, and she them ; they somehow matched that weird light in her eyes ; and I told Tom as much when, after dinner, she withdrew and left us over our wine.

" And thereby hangs a tale," repeated he, thoughtfully reaching his hand towards the decanter, and filling my glass and his own.

Now, it seemed to me entirely in accordance with young Mrs. Gainsborough's " style " that there should have been something odd and romantic in the circumstances of her first acquaintance with Tom, and that diamonds should be mixed up with it. Therefore I was more than willing to give ear to the strange story which he proceeded to relate to me. Imagine the servants dismissed, a fresh lump of coal in the grate, the decanter between us, and our legs and elbows disposed in the most comfortable manner possible. Then, this is the story.

II.

" The diamonds, you must know, have been ever so long in our family. It is said they were brought from India, in the time of Marco Polo, by an ancestor of mine. But that is neither here nor there ; and sure enough they were only put into their present shape quite recently. I can remember when half of them were uncut, or cut in some barbarous oriental manner, picturesque enough, but not fashionable. And some were mounted as nose-rings, some as clasps, some in the hilts of daggers, and in all sorts of other ways.

When I was a child, I was sometimes allowed to play with some of the loose ones, as a treat ; until, at last, I contrived to lose one of the biggest. You may not believe it, but the governor actually horsed me and gave me a birching ; and the diamonds were locked up from that day. It was only a few years ago that my dear mother, now no more, got them out, and insisted upon their being made up into a regular set by some skilful jeweller. We were thinking of going to Rome at the time, to spend six or eight months, and the first idea was to give the job to Castellani. But then it appeared that my mother had got her eye fixed upon a certain man in Paris, whom she had been told was the first lapidary in Europe. He, and none but he, should set our diamonds. You know my mother generally had her way ; and she had it in this case. The fellow certainly did understand his business ; his work was well done, as you may have noticed this evening. A queer, pale, nervous little chap he was ; not a Frenchman at all, but a Saxon, born in Dresden, I believe, or some village in that neighbourhood. His name was Rudolph—Heinrich Rudolph. He lived and worked in a little dark shop in the Latin Quarter.

"He and I became quite intimate. You see, I had been commissioned to attend to this diamond business, and to remain in Paris until it was done. I was to watch it through all its stages, and be sure that my mother's directions regarding the style of the setting were accurately followed. When all was finished, I was to pay the bill and bring the diamonds on to Rome, where the family would by that time be established. Well, I was a young fellow, and probably I was not so much cast down at the prospect of spending a month or two alone in Paris as you might suppose. But I doubt whether I should have attended to my ostensible business so faithfully as I actually did, had I not been so greatly taken with my little friend Rudolph. He and I twigged one another, as boys say, from the first. I used to sit and watch him work for hours at a time; and as he worked, he would talk; and very queer captivating talk a good deal of it was. He was a thorough artist and enthusiast, and seemed to care for nothing outside of his profession. He did not appear to me to be in the way of making much money, and it occurred to me that it might be acceptable were I, in an unobtrusive way, to introduce him to some wealthy customers. I knew few people in Paris; but there was a Mr. Birchmore, an American gentleman, staying at my hotel, with whom I had forgathered over a cup of coffee and a cigar once or twice: he was a handsome middle-aged man, with an atmosphere of refined affluence about him such as would have befitted a duke. Not a bit like your traditional Yankee; in fact, I'm not sure that I should have suspected him, if I hadn't seen his address—'Fifth Avenue, New York City, U.S.A.'—in the hotel register, about a week after my arrival. He was an agreeable man enough, though not at all the sort to take liberties with ; however, I made up my mind that I would get him to Rudolph's on the first pretext that offered.

"Well, I had an excellent pretext before long. Mr. Birchmore came into the café one afternoon, with rather an annoyed look, and made some inquiries of the waiter. François raised his eyebrows and shrugged his shoulders ; there was some further conference, and then he and Mr. Birchmore began searching about the floor of the room. It presently transpired that he had lost a diamond out of his ring, which had contained three matched brilliants. It was nowhere to be found.

" 'I don't mind the loss of the stone itself,' said Mr. Birchmore at last, sitting down near my table ; 'but it's one of a set, matched with great difficulty, and I'm afraid I may never replace it.'

" Here was my opportunity. I set forth the wisdom, skill, and resources of my little Saxon friend in glowing colours ; mentioned the work he was doing for me, and declared that if any man in Europe could help Mr. Birchmore to repair his loss, Rudolph was he. Mr. Birchmore at first paid little heed to my representations ; but finally I induced him to accompany me to the Latin Quarter, and at least make the attempt. The next morning, accordingly, we set forth ; and as we sauntered along the wide pleasant boulevards, our conversation became more free and affable than it had been hitherto. I found my companion could be exceedingly entertaining when he chose it, and had a vast fund of experience and adventure to draw upon. He had been almost everywhere ; he had made himself familiar with all varieties of civilised and uncivilised men ; as a matter of course, too, he was a versatile linguist. The only direction in which he gave any evidence of comparative deficiency was in that of literature and the fine arts. His life had been essentially an active one ; he cared little for Tennyson and Swinburne, for Matthew Arnold and Carlyle. He had, however, read and appreciated 'Macbeth,' and some others of Shakespeare's plays ; and he was well acquainted with several of the romances of 'Unabashed Defoe.' I did not discover all this in the course of that one stroll over to the Latin Quarter, but it leaked out during our subsequent acquaintance, which was destined to become more intimate and prolonged than I had any idea of then. As I have intimated,

Mr. Birchmore was quite frank and open in his talk, except upon one topic—himself. Of his inner life and circumstances I could learn nothing. Though he never was obtrusively reticent, yet he contrived never to refer to his own private affairs. I could not satisfy myself whether he were married or single, whether he were a Catholic or Atheist—hardly whether he were rich or poor. Some shadow of grief, some incubus of fear or calamity, seemed to overwhelm him, and impose silence. The most I could do was to draw inferences; and my inference was that he was a bachelor, a millionaire, a sceptic, and a man who, at some period of his life, had committed, either deliberately or by force of circumstances, a terrible crime! You will see presently how far my estimate was from the truth, or how near to it.

"However, I am anticipating, as it is. We arrived in due time at Rudolph's little shop, and I introduced him to Birchmore. I had previously told the latter about my diamonds, and now I made Rudolph produce them. The man of the world examined the gems with evident interest, and with a knowledge of their value and qualities which surprised me, and caused the little jeweller to eye my friend with a jealous keenness.

"'These are all Indian stones,' was Birchmore's first remark. 'There is not an American among them—or stay! What is this? neither an American nor an Indian! An African, I declare, and one of the finest I have seen!'

"'Der Herr hat recht!' muttered Rudolph, with a glance at me. 'Er versteht ja alles.'

"'You know German?—he says, "What you don't know about diamonds isn't worth knowing," I put in. Birchmore nodded with a half smile.

"'I ought to know something about precious stones,' he said. 'I spent three years in a diamond mine, for one thing.' He seemed on the point of saying more, but checked himself, and went on scrutinising the stones, most of which were already in their ·new setting. 'A costly parure that,' he remarked at length. 'It wouldn't sell for a penny under thirty thousand pounds.'

"'Five hundred eighty-five thousand francs, with the setting,' replied Rudolph, to whom the words had been addressed. 'Monsieur's estimate would have been correct, but that this stone here is a little off colour, and this one has a slight flaw, which is now in part concealed by the setting.'

"'You travel under proper precautions, I trust?' said Birchmore, after a pause, turning gravely to me. 'I know the confidence you young fellows have in your courage and cleverness ; but a dozen or a score of thieves might conspire together for such a prize as this, and against their skill and address no single man would stand a chance. Ah! I know something of it.' I was robbed once.'

"'Do tell me about it!' I exclaimed, with an impulsive betrayal of interest that made me smile the next moment.

"'Another time,' said he, shaking his head; and presently he added: 'You will pardon me for presuming to counsel you?'

"'My dear sir, I am much obliged to you. My idea is that the simplest precautions are the best. I shall carry the stones in an inner pocket, and I shall go armed. No one will suspect me; and if I am attacked, I shall make a good defence at all events.'

"Mr. Birchmore said nothing more, and indeed seemed scarcely to listen to my remarks. I now suggested to him that he might show Rudolph his ring. He put his hand to his waistcoat pocket, and gave a half-suppressed ejaculation of disappointment and annoyance. He had left the ring at home!

"'No matter; I will call to-morrow, Herr Rudolph,' he observed. 'I've no doubt I shall find what I want here, if anywhere. Good-morning—that is, if you are ready, Mr. Gainsborough. By the way, Rudolph, I suppose you put your treasures in a safe at night?'

"'Oh, by all means, Herr,' replied the little Saxon.

'And I have a watchman also, who guards all night long.'

"'A prudent fellow: yes, that will do,' murmured Mr. Birchmore, in an undertone to himself. Then, with a parting nod and smile, to which the jeweller did not respond, he sauntered out, I following him. We walked back to the hotel. I did not see him again until after dinner, when he offered me a cigar; and when we had smoked together awhile in silence, he said abruptly:

"'I've found that stone.'

"I looked at him inquiringly.

"'The diamond out of my ring. In my trouser pocket, of all places in the world! Fell out while I was groping for my keys, I suppose. Sorry to have raised false hopes in your friend Rudolph. By the way, he'll have finished that job of yours before very long?'

"'In about a week, I fancy. I shall be sorry to leave Paris.'

"'Yes? Well, it is a nice place; but one gets tired of the nicest places in time. I do. I like to be moving.'

"'I shall have a month to spend on my way to Rome. This is almost my first experience of the Continent. I wish I had some travelling companion who knew the ropes.' This hint I let fall in the hope

that he might propose to join me ; but as he made no
rejoinder, I at length ventured to put it more plainly.
I gave a rough sketch of the route I proposed to
follow, asked his opinion upon it, and finally said
that, should his inclination lead him also in that
direction, I should be very glad of his company.

"'Well, sir, I'm obliged to you,' replied Mr.
Birchmore, after a pause of some moments. 'You
couldn't pay a man a better compliment than to
ask him to travel with you ; and I would accept
your offer as frankly and fearlessly as you make
it, only—well, the fact is, I'm not so entirely at
my own disposal as I may appear to you to be.
I have been through a good many experiences in
life, and some of the consequences are upon me
still. When you have reached my age—if you ever
do reach it—you will understand me better. I
suppose I may be fifteen years your senior ; well,
fifteen years means a good deal—a good deal.' He
puffed a meditative cloud or two, and then added,
'You're not hurt? You see how it is? I would
really like to accompany you—but I can't.'

"Of course, I warmly disavowed all resentment
and felt inwardly ashamed of having forced him,
by the freedom of my advances, into making this
explanation. Meanwhile, I could not help liking
him better than ever, and feeling more than ever

interested, not to say curious, about him. It was now certain that some mystery or other attached to him. I cast covert glances at him, in the vain attempt to read something of his secret through his outward aspect. But he was inscrutable, or rather, there was nothing especially noticeable in him. His face, as I have said, was handsome in its contours ; he wore a heavy moustache and a short pointed beard on his chin. His forehead was wide across the temples, but low ; and dark brown hair, rather stiff, and streaked here and there with gray, grew thickly over his head. His hands were large, and hairy up to the second joints of the fingers, but they were finely and powerfully formed, and the fingers tapered beautifully, with nails smoothly cut and polished. In figure he was above the medium size, and appeared strongly built, though he had complained to me more than once of rheumatism or some other bodily failing. In walking, he took rather short steps for a tall man, and without any swaying of the shoulders ; his hands being generally thrust in the side pockets of his coat, and his face inclined towards the ground. But his eyes, large, bright, and restless, were his most remarkable feature. They appeared to take note of everything : they were seldom fixed and never introspective. Compared with the general immobility of the rest of his countenance, these eyes of Mr. Birchmore seemed to have a life of their own—and a very intense and watchful one. Whenever they met mine fully (which was but seldom, and then only for a moment at a time) I was conscious of a kind of start or thrill, as if a fine spray of icy water had swept my face. What had those eyes looked upon? or what was it that lurked behind them?

"'We may run across each other again—hope we may,' said Mr. Birchmore, when he shook hands with me at parting, a few days later. 'Glad to have met you, Mr. Gainsborough—very glad, sir.'

"'Thanks; I am glad to have met you. Your acquaintance has profited me not a little.'

"'Oh, as to that,' said Mr. Birchmore, with a smile, and one of those startling straightforward glances into my eyes, 'as to that, the profit will have been mutual, to say the least of it. Good-bye!'

III.

"My route to Italy was rather a roundabout one. Instead of running down to Marseilles and so on *viâ* Civita Vecchia to Rome, I set off eastwards, and crossed Germany, passing through Cologne, Frankfort-on-the-Main, and Nuremberg; thence I proceeded to Leipzig, and at length brought up in

Dresden. It was my intention to go from there southwards through Switzerland to Venice, and thus to make my approach to the Eternal City.

"Dresden, however, detained me longer than I had expected. It was in August that I reached it: there were not many people in town, but I was delighted with the Gallery, with the picturesque sweep of the river, and with the green shade and good music of the Grosser Garten. There were several charming drives, too, in the neighbourhood; and as for the beer, it was really a revelation to a man who had never known anything less heavy and solid than Allsopp's pale ale.

"I had put up at the Hotel de Saxe, a broadsided old building on one side of a large irregular 'platz,' called, I believe, the Neumarkt. My landlord, who was a young gentleman of great personal attractions, interested himself a good deal about my amusements; and one day he happened to ask me whether I had visited a region known as Saxon Switzerland. This, it appeared, was a mountainous district some twenty miles up the Elbe, in which was solved the problem of putting the greatest amount of romantic picturesqueness into the smallest possible compass. It was a land of savage rocks, wild precipices, and profound gorges, conveniently grouped within the limits of a good day's tramp. It comprised all the sublime and startling features of your Yellowstone Valley in California with an area about equal to the summit of one of the table bluffs in that region.

"I packed my valise for a sojourn of two or three days among these pocket Alps, put my diamonds in that secure inner pocket, and took a droschkey for the railway station. The trip to Schandau (the principal village of Saxon Switzerland) can also be made by steamer; but after discussing the pros and cons of rival routes with my host of the hotel the evening previous, I had decided to go by rail, which provides nearly half as much pretty scenery as the river road, and takes up less than a fourth as much time. I alighted at the station door somewhat late, and having given my trunk in charge to a porter, was hurrying to get my ticket, when my attention was caught by a young lady, who was standing on the platform in an attitude that bespoke suspense and anxiety. Her veil was down, but from the slender elegance of her figure and the harmonious perfection of her costume, I could not doubt that her face was beautiful. Evidently she was not a German; had she been a thought less tastefully dressed, I should have said she was an English girl; as it was, she might be either an Austrian or an American. Even then, I rather inclined to the latter hypothesis.

"She appeared to be entirely alone; but she was scanning with ill-concealed eagerness the crowd that was entering the station, as if in search of a familiar face. When her glance fell upon me, I fancied that she took an impulsive step in my direction; but she checked herself immediately, and looked away. While I was hastily debating within myself whether or not it would be 'the thing' for me to go up and ask her if she needed any assistance, I saw a *dienstman*, or carrier, come up the steps, and taking off his cap, deliver her a note. She tore it nervously open, threw back her veil impatiently, and ran her eyes over the contents. Beautiful she was, indeed! My anticipations had been behind the truth on that score. Such strange, mystical, dark eyes underneath level black eyebrows I had never seen. But just then there was an expression of dismay and distress in them that made me half forget to remember their fascination.

"She now addressed the carrier, seemingly in broken German, for he evidently did not well understand her, and the answer he made appeared to increase her embarrassment. Her slender foot tapped the stone pavement; she read the note once more, crushed it up in her hand, and then her arms fell listlessly at her sides with an air almost of despair. She looked this way and that helplessly.

"By this time several persons besides myself had

o

observed her bewilderment, and I thought I perceived that a certain fat old Jew, wearing a number of glittering rings and a very massive watch-chain, was inclined to take advantage of it. This decided me on my course of action: I came quickly forward, as if I had just caught sight of her, and lifting my hat with an air of respectful acquaintanceship, I said in French:

" ' If mademoiselle will permit me, I may perhaps be of some use.'

" Her veil, either accidentally or of design, dropped again over her face as she turned it towards me. I knew that she was scrutinising me with a woman's intuitive insight, and I tried to look as guileless and respectful as I am sure I felt. In a moment she asked:

" ' Monsieur est-il Français ? '

" ' I'm an Englishman,' I answered, blushing a little, I dare say, at her implied criticism of my imperfect accent.

" ' Oh, I am glad ! I, too, am almost English—I am American. But I don't know how I can be helped, really ! '

" ' Some friend has missed an appointment——? '

" ' Yes, indeed ! Oh dear ! it's worse than that. It's my father.'

" ' You were going by the train—— '

"'There has been some stupid mistake. I'm sure I don't know what I shall do. We had arranged to start at ten o'clock this morning, and I started first, because I wanted to do some shopping on the way down. I understood that we were to rendezvous here. But he did not come at ten, and I sent a dientsman to the hotel; and now he has brought word from the hotel-keeper that papa started by the ten o'clock steamboat. I had not understood that it was to be the steamboat; you see; and I'm left here all alone.'

"'But if you took the next train, you would still arrive two or three hours before him; that is—may I ask where you were going?'

"'Oh, I think Schandau is the name of the place.'

"'Schandau? Oh, then it's all right. There is a train starts immediately.'

"'Yes—but—no; I'm afraid I can't do that.'

"I was puzzled. 'Perhaps you would like to telegraph him to come back here for you?'

"I don't know where to telegraph, so that he would get it; besides—— But, excuse me, sir. You are very kind; but I won't trouble you with my affairs. I dare say I shall get on very well.'

"She turned away with a slight bow; but she was so evidently nonplussed, that I determined to make another effort to gain her confidence. There was not much time to lose ; the first bell was already ringing.

"'I am going on to Schandau,' I said. 'If you like, I will send you back to your hotel in a droschkey; and when. I get to Schandau, I will hunt up your father and tell him the mistake he has made. Here is my card.'

"She looked at it, and her manner at once changed. A half-repressed smile glimmered on her face. I felt that we were on a right footing at last, though I could not at the time understand how it had happened.

"'I will confess to you, Mr. Gainsborough,' she said, glancing up at me with a charming trustfulness in her manner. 'My papa is so forgetful. We were not coming back to Dresden. After Schandau we were going on to Prague ; and he has gone off with all our luggage, and—and he has left me without even any money to buy my ticket ! At least, I did have enough, but I spent it all in my shopping.'

"This cleared up matters at once. 'How stupid of me not to have seen it all before !' I exclaimed. 'Now, we have just time to get the train.' I hurried her on with me as I spoke, bought our tickets in the twinkling of an eye, and without waiting for the change, convoyed her rapidly across the platform, and, with the assistance of a guard, we found ourselves

safely ensconced in a first-class carriage just as the
train moved off.   My beautiful companion, breathless,
smiling, and yet seemingly a little frightened, sank
back on the cushions, and felt for the fan at her girdle.
I wished to give her plenty of time to recover her
composure, and to feel assured that I had no intention
of taking undue advantage of our position ; so, having
arranged the windows to suit her convenience, I
betook myself to the other end of the carriage, and
diligently stared at the prospect for fully five minutes.
Nature could endure no more, and at the end of that
time I was fain to change my posture.   I stole a
glance at my fair American.   She, too, was absorbed
in the prospect on her side, which consisted at the
moment of a perpendicular cutting about ten feet
distant from her window.   Her attitude as she sat
there was the perfection of feminine grace.   Her left
hand, loosely holding the fan, drooped on her lap ;
her sleeve, slightly pushed up, revealed the lovely
curve of her arm and wrist.   I am a particular
admirer of beautiful wrists and hands, and here I saw
my ideal.   How exquisitely the glove fitted ! and
how artistically the colour harmonised with the rest
of her costume !   The other little hand supported her
chin : I could just see the rounded outline of her
small cheek, and the movement of the dark eyelash
projecting beyond it.   Beneath her hat the black hair

turned in a careless coil, and charming little downy
curls nestled in the nape of her neck. She was a
thorough brunette, pale, and yet pervaded with warm
colour. Beneath the skirt of her crisp dress peeped
the pointed toe of an ineffable little boot, which occasionally lifted itself and tapped the floor softly. Suddenly, in the midst of my admiring inspection, she
turned round upon me, and our eyes met. There was
an instant's constraint, and then we both laughed, and
the constraint passed away, not to return.

"'I was going to ask you,' said I, 'whether you
wouldn't prefer sitting on this side. You will find the
river better worth looking at than that stone wall.'

"'I am under your orders, sir, for the present;
you put me here; and now, if you tell me I am to go
elsewhere, I shall obey.'

. "She rose as she spoke; the jolting of the carriage
caused her to lose her balance; I held out my hand
to assist her, and so she tottered across and seated
herself opposite me.

"'Now are you satisfied?' she asked demurely,
folding her hands in her lap, and sending a flash into
me from those mystical eyes.

"'Yes, indeed, if you are. Did you ever travel
this way before?'

"'If you mean, alone with a gentleman I never
met before—no!'

"'Oh, what I meant was——'

"'I know—I was only making fun. Yes, I believe I was in this part of the country once, when I was a very little girl; that was before I went to the Convent, you know.'

"'To the Convent?'

"She gave a charming impromptu laugh. 'I wasn't quite a nun—I don't want to make you believe that! Only I was brought up in a convent near Paris; educated there, as many young ladies are. I was there seven years—wasn't that long? and I only got out a little while ago.'

"'It must have been awfully dull.'

"'Oh, I liked it in a sort of way; they were very kind to me there; but then I didn't know how pleasant it was outside! You would never believe how delightful the world is, if you were only told about it. My papa used to tell me about it sometimes; and he is a great traveller—he has been everywhere. But I didn't realise it until I saw for myself.'

"'Have you been to America since leaving the Convent?'

"'Oh yes. I went to New York, and saw my cousins there. Papa went with me, but he came back to Paris first, and I followed later. I met him again in Paris only a week ago. He will be surprised to see you here, Mr. Gainsborough. What a funny way you

have chosen to go from Paris to Rome—through
Dresden!'

"'Yes, I—but, by-the-bye, how did you know I
was going to Rome? and why will your papa be
surprised——?'

"Again she laughed, and regarded me with so
delightfully mischievous a glance that I felt convinced
I must in some way be making a fool of myself.
What did it all mean? I bit my lip, and the colour
came into my face from provocation at my own
evident thick-headedness.

"'If you had only waited a little longer in Paris,'
she continued, still smiling enigmatically, 'perhaps
we might have met in a more regular way, and
perhaps, then, you would have let me have had a look
at your—diamonds!'

"My diamonds! That explained the mystery in
a flash.

"'Is your father Mr. Birchmore?'

"'I am Miss Birchmore, if you please, sir. You
never asked me for my card, and I didn't like to force
it on you. It was so kind of you to take me on trust,
without making sure that I was all right first. I
thought Englishmen were more cautious and reserved.'

"I could now join in the laugh against myself with
full appreciation of the excellence of the jest. Mr.
Birchmore, then, had been a married man after all.

Of course he was ; why had I not before remarked the strong family likeness between him and his daughter? Take her on trust, forsooth! How I longed to retort that I was ready to take her for better for worse, then and there, if she would have me. If she were a fair specimen of American girls, what a nation of houris they must be, indeed! But, then, they were not all brought up in French convents. It was that that added to Miss Birchmore the last irresistible charm. That it was that gave her that naïveté, that innocent frankness, that unconscious freedom. And this lovely creature had actually known me, by report, before we met. Her father had told her of me, and evidently he had not given me a bad character. And this accounted for the favourable change in her manner when she saw my card. Well, it was altogether delightful; I had been guided by a happy destiny; thank fortune I had so conducted myself as at least not to prejudice Miss Birchmore against me. Verily, good manners are never thrown away; and, moreover, I prided myself (as I fancy most gentlemen do) on my ability to detect a true lady at a glance.

"We now resumed our conversation on a still more confidential footing than heretofore. Miss Birchmore related many amusing anecdotes of her late experience in New York, as well as of her earlier days

in the Convent, and even some passages of her child-
life previous to the latter epoch.   I observed, however,
that ever and anon she would check herself, seeming
to pass over certain passages in her history in silence ;
and this reminded me of the similar behaviour which
I had noted in her father. That secret—that mystery,
whatever it was, that weighed upon him—had cast its
shadow over her young heart likewise.   Honestly did
I sympathise with her unknown trouble, and ardently
did I long—all vulgar curiosity aside—to have the
knowledge of it imparted to me.   Few calamities are
so heavy as that, by earnest and friendly help, they
may not be lightened.   What could it be ?   In vain I
asked myself that question.   Here was this lovely
girl, in the first fresh bloom of existence, just
beginning to taste, with eager uncloyed palate, all the
sweet joys and novelties of life—health, youth, a
happy temperament, and ample wealth ranked on her
side ; and yet this bitterness of a misfortune, not
by rights her own, must needs communicate its
blighting influence to her !   It was tragical to
think of.   Yes, ever and anon I could mark its traces
in her vivid face and winning bearing.   A passing
gloom of sadness in those wonderful eyes ; a quiver
of apprehension about the lips ; an involuntary
gesture of nervousness or lassitude ; many trifling
signs, scarcely perceptible, perhaps, to a regard less

keen and watchful than mine had already become. Already?—but time in an acquaintance like this is not to be measured by hours or minutes. It is a trite saying, and yet how true, that those who are under the influence of a strong emotion may live years in a few heart-beats.

"'Please—oh, please don't look so solemn, Mr. Gainsborough! What has happened? I should think, to look at you, that you had been robbed of your diamonds at the very least?'

"'No; they are safe enough,' said I, calling up as cheerful a tone and aspect as I could muster, and putting my hand over the inner pocket as I spoke. 'Are you fond of diamonds?'

"'Oh, did you ever hear of a girl who wasn't? I think there is nothing so beautiful. Papa has a great many, but he says I mustn't wear them until after I am married. Isn't that hard?'

"'But perhaps you think of being married before long?' I inquired, with positively a jealous throb at my heart.

"'No; that's the trouble; I know I shall never be married.' These words were uttered in a lower and graver tone, and once more I thought I could discern the flitting traces of that mysterious melancholy. But she brightened up when I said:

"'Well, he won't object to your seeing my

diamonds, at any rate; not even to your putting
them on, perhaps!'

"'Just for a minute—may I? that will be splendid! Papa says that some of them are the finest he
ever saw.'

"'For longer than a minute, Miss Birchmore, if
you are willing—I mean if he——' What did I
mean, pray? Was I going to make an offer of my
hand, heart, and diamonds, on less than an hour's
acquaintance, in a railway carriage? and was I going
to forget that the diamonds did not belong to me
at all, but to my respected mother, who would
probably see me cut off with a shilling before grant-
ing me the disposal of them? Luckily for my self-
possession and self-respect, the train drew up just
then at the station known as Krippen, on the bank
of the river immediately opposite Schandau. The
guard opened the door; we alighted, and the first
person we saw was Mr. Birchmore, and close behind
him a short, ungainly, beetle-browed fellow, a valet
or footman apparently, with a campstool, an umbrella,
and a small basket of fruit on his arm.

IV.

"Mr. Birchmore shook my hand cordially, yet I
fancied that he betrayed signs of embarrassment or

uneasiness. He seemed glad to meet me on my own account, and yet to feel constrained by my presence. Had he any reason for wishing to conceal from me the fact that he had a daughter? It now occurred to me for the first time that in her conversation with me Miss Birchmore had never alluded to her mother. Perhaps her mother was dead—had died in her child's infancy. Perhaps the silence concerning her arose from some other and less avowable cause; there might be some matrimonial disgrace or tragedy at the bottom of the father and daughter's reserve. The idea had a certain plausibility, and yet I found it unsatisfactory. The true explanation of the mystery might not be worse than this, but I fancied it must be different—it must be something more unusual and strange.

"'This is an unexpected pleasure,' said I, for the sake of saying something, as we descended the steps down the river embankment to the ferry-boat.

"'The world is not so large a place as people pretend,' replied Mr. Birchmore. 'Have you been long in Dresden?'·

"'A week or so. I've been doing the neighbourhood, and was told that Saxon Switzerland must not be left out of the list. I came near going by the boat——' Here I suddenly recollected that if Mr. Birchmore had gone by boat, as his daughter said he had, his presence in Schandau before us was wholly inexplicable. 'How did you manage to get here so quickly?' I exclaimed; 'the steamer can't be due for three hours yet!'

"He looked at me in apparent perplexity; Miss Birchmore seemed to share my own surprise. There was a pause of a few moments; then she said in a low tone:

"'You know, papa, I got word that, from some misunderstanding, you had taken the steamer instead of the train.'

"'Ah, to be sure,' he rejoined, with a short laugh; 'I see the difficulty. You must look upon me, I suppose, as a sort of magician, able to transport myself about the country on some new telegraphic principle. Well, I'm afraid I can't lay claim to any such supernatural power. I shall lose credit by the explanation, but you shall have it nevertheless.'

"'No, no! give us room for the exercise of our imagination,' cried I, laughing. The fact was, I felt as if my query had been in some way unfortunate. There was a certain effort in Mr. Birchmore's manner, and a want of spontaneity in his laugh. In my ignorance of the true lay of the land, I was continually making some irritating blunder; and the more I tried to make myself agreeable, the worse was my success

"Mr. Birchmore, notwithstanding that I deprecated it, chose to make his explanation. 'Kate was right,' said he; 'my first intention was to go by train. Afterwards I decided on the boat, and left the hotel with the purpose of getting our passage that way, and sending Kate word to meet me at the landing. But the boat turned out to be so crowded that I changed my mind again: it was then so late that I hadn't time to reach the central railway station; my only chance of catching the train was to jump into a droschkey at the steamboat landing and drive as the *kutcher* never drove before, for the lower station, which was half-a-mile nearer. I got there barely in time; and Kate, it seems, was waiting at the central all the while!'

"'And of course,' added Miss Birchmore, 'the people at the hotel fancied he *had* gone by the boat, and sent me word so. Oh yes, I understand it all now; don't you, Mr. Gainsborough?'

"'I don't take it kindly of your father to strip away the illusions from life so pitilessly,' returned I, in a humorous tone; 'I should have been much happier in believing that he had flown through the air on the Arabian king's wishing-carpet.' This sally sufficed to raise the smile of which we all seemed so greatly in want, and so we got into the ferry-boat in a comparatively easy frame of mind.

"The valet to whom I have already alluded sat
on a thwart near the bows, in such a position that
I had a full view of him.   A more unconciliating
object I have seldom beheld.   His body and arms
were long, but his legs were short, and bowed outwards.   His features were harsh, forbidding, and
strongly marked ; but there was an expression of
power stamped upon them which fascinated my gaze
in spite of the ugliness which would otherwise have
made me glad to look away.   It was not the power
of intellect, for although there was plenty of a
saturnine kind of intelligence in the countenance,
it was not to be supposed that a fellow in his position
of life would be remarkable for brains.   No, this
power was of another kind ; I do not know how
to describe it ; but I believe some people would get
out of the difficulty by calling it magnetic.   Whatever
it was, it produced a very disagreeable impression on
me, and I could not but wonder that Mr. Birchmore
should have chosen to take such a creature into his
employ.   I had the sense, however, on this occasion
to keep my speculations to myself ; I was resolved
not to make a fool of myself again if I could help it
—at least, not with this particular family.   I noticed
that whenever Mr. Birchmore had occasion to address
this man, he did ·so in a peculiarly severe and
peremptory tone, very different from his usual low-

voiced style. There was seemingly no great affection for him on his master's part, therefore ; and certainly the valet looked incapable of a tender feeling towards any human creature. Possibly, however, he was invaluable as a servant, and his unpropitiating exterior might cover an honest and faithful heart. Only should such turn out to be the case, I would never again put faith either in physiognomy or my own instinct of aversion. I disliked to think of this ill-favoured mortal being in daily association with my lovely Kate Birchmore—for already, in my secret soul, I called her mine! and I made up my mind that if ever fortune granted me the privilege of making her what I called her, I would see to it that monsieur the valet formed a part of anyone's household rather than ours.

"Meanwhile the ferryman had poled and paddled us across the river, on the shore of which a swarm of hotel-porters stood ready to rend us limb from limb. But Mr. Birchmore put them all aside save one, to whom he pointed out my trunk, and gave him some directions which I did not hear.

"'I take the liberty,' he then said, turning to me, 'to so far do the honours of this place as to recommend you to the most agreeable hotel in it—the Badehaus, at the farther end of the village, and about half a mile up the valley. These hotels that front the river would give you better fare, perhaps, and less unpretending accommodation; but if quiet and coolness are what you are after—not to mention the medicinal spring water and a private brass band—the Badehaus is the thing.'

"'The Badehaus be it, by all means.' This attention surprised me, not because I misdoubted my friend's courtesy, but because I had imagined that his courtesy would not stand in the way of an unobtrusive attempt to withdraw himself and his daughter from my immediate companionship. Yet so far was this from being the case, that he had taken some pains to secure our being together—for of course the Badehaus must be his own quarters. I glanced at Kate, who had taken her father's arm, and was pacing beside him thoughtfully, with downcast eyes. Was she glad as well as I?

"We passed through a narrow alley between two friendly buildings, which seemed strongly inclined to lean on one another's shoulders; crossed the rough cobble-stones of the little market-place, and, gaining the farther side of the bridge, found ourselves on a broad level walk which skirted the southern side of the small valley wherein the village lies. On our right hand was a series of stuccoed villas, built against the steep side of the hill; on our left a strip of meadow, with a brook brawling through it; and beyond this again the straggling array of the village, and the hill on the other side. Overhead, the spreading branches of low trees kept off the glare of the sun. Had Kate and I been there alone, methought, the charm of the place would have been complete.

"'What delightful little villas these are!' I exclaimed. 'Aren't they better than any hotel—even the Badehaus?'

"'If you think of spending any great time here—I believe they don't let for less than a week. But probably these are all full at this season. Higher up the valley, two or three miles beyond the hotel, you would find detached farmhouses, whose owners no doubt would be glad of a lodger. If you are not broken in to a traveller's hardships, though, you'll prefer the Badehaus.'

"'I think I shall prefer it as long as you are there.'

"'Well, I'm sorry to say that won't be long—we shall move to-morrow morning. If I had expected you, I—I should have been happy to have arranged matters otherwise. But the fact is, I have engaged rooms at one of the farmhouses I spoke of, and to-morrow they will expect us.'

"My spirits fell at this news like a feather in a vacuum, and I daresay my face showed it. There could be no doubt now that Mr. Birchmore was resolved to get rid of me. That he would go to-morrow to some distant farmhouse I did not question; but as to his having intended any such thing before he saw me alight from the train, I confess I didn't believe it. It was an unpremeditated expedient; and his inviting me up to the Badehaus was only a polite mitigation of the shock.

"'I am very sorry!' was all I could say.

"Kate turned her face a little towards me at the words, and her eyes met mine sidelong. Only that look—she did not speak; but I saw, or thought I saw, enough in it to make our parting at such brief notice a sentimental impossibility. At whatever sacrifice of the laws of ceremony and civilised reserve, I determined that my acquaintance with her, so well begun, should not thus be nipped in the bud. I would sooner win her as a barbarian than lose her as a man of the world. How to execute my determination was a problem to be solved at my leisure.

"We sauntered on to the hotel, chatting discursively; my mind was too much preoccupied to be thoroughly aware what we were talking about. Arrived at our destination, I followed my trunk to my room, having arranged to take an early dinner with my friends. It was nearly two hours before we met again. The dinner passed with the same sort of desultory conversation that we had affected during our walk. Mr. Birchmore's manner was serious and rather cold. Kate, too, was subdued and grave; not the brilliant laughing Kate of the railway carriage. We were waited upon at table by the saturnine valet whom his master called Slurk—a name that seemed to me to suit him excellently well. He waited on us in perfect silence from the beginning. of the meal to the end, though several times peremptorily addressed by his master. There was to me something disagreeably impressive in the fellow's very taciturnity—it seemed to indicate reserved power. Kate, I noticed, was careful never to speak to him, but I saw his glance several times directed fixedly upon her.

"After dinner Mr. Birchmore produced a cigar and said :

"'I must take a droschkey over to our farmhouse. Do you young people care to come, or would you rather stay here ?'

"'I think I'll stay, papa, please,' answered Kate.

"'And I, to see that nobody runs away with her,' I added with an easy smile.

"'Slurk, get me a carriage,' said Mr. Birchmore ; and nodding a good-bye to us he went out.

"'How far is it from here—this farmhouse, Miss Birchmore ?' I asked, when we were alone.

"'I believe about two miles.'

"'I should like to know its exact situation.'

"'Why didn't you go with papa, then?'

"'Can't you imagine?'

"She had been absently puckering her handkerchief into folds in her lap. Now she looked up.

"'Why do you wish to know where we are going?'

"'Because I've taken a great fancy to—to Mr. Slurk, and I can't bear to think of losing sight of him!'

"I had expected her to laugh and perhaps blush; instead of that an expression of something like terror swept over her face, and she laid her finger on her lip.

"'Don't talk of him!' she whispered.

"Her emotion had so surprised me that I could only stare in silence. Here was another mystery—or stay! could it be that Slurk was at the bottom of all those strange signs and enigmas that I had been puzzling myself over from the first? I was prepared to believe whatever amount of evil concerning the fellow might be required. But what could he have done, or have it in his power to do, that could so affect Miss Birchmore? Had he held her life or fortune at the mercy of a word she could hardly have betrayed more dismay at my jesting satire.

" ' It's nothing,' she said, recovering herself after a moment. 'Only I don't like him much, and you—and I wasn't expecting to hear his name just then.'

" ' Heaven knows, it is a very different name I should have spoken !'

" ' No, no, no. You have amused yourself with me to-day; and to-morrow, you must find someone else to amuse you, that's all !'

" ' Amused myself, Miss Birchmore !'

" ' Well, Mr. Gainsborough, I'm sorry if I failed to entertain you. I'm sure I tried hard. But it's so difficult to entertain an Englishman !'

" ' Upon my word, I believe you've been laughing at me from the beginning ! But however ridiculous I may be, Miss Birchmore, I can have thoughts and feelings that are not ridiculous——'

" ' Oh, please—please don't be angry. And I'm sure I never thought you ridiculous, I—oh, anything but that !'

" The tone, the look which accompanied these last words made me forget caution and self-possession for the moment. 'Miss Birchmore—oh Kate ! I cannot lose sight of you—I cannot lose you ! Do you care —is it nothing to you if we never meet after to-day ? Kate, I love you !'

" Had the confession come too soon ? Was she

offended ?   She shrank away from me with a
searching glance.

"'Do not forget yourself, sir! You are an
honourable English gentleman. What have you
said ?'

"'I love you—yes, love you !'

"'Love me!' she repeated slowly, and caught her
breath ; her eyes fixed themselves on me with an
inward look, as of intense reverie.   'It must not be—
it must not be! but he does love me !'   Her hands
fell in her lap; there were tears now in her eyes, but
a smile quivered over her lips.

"'Why do you say it must not be, Kate ?   It is!
It shall be !'   I took her hand, which she scarcely
attempted to withdraw; I felt that I had won her,
and would hold her against all comers.   Just then
a knock came at the door; she snatched her hand
away and rose to her feet.   Mr. Slurk entered.

"'The band is going to play in the court,' he said
in German.   'I have kept chairs and a table for the
lady and gentleman beneath the trees.'   He made a
low obeisance as he spoke, but his malignant glance
never swerved from Kate ; and she, half turning
towards him, seemed impelled by a power stronger than
her own will to meet it, though slightly shivering the
while with pure aversion.   For my own part, I longed
with all my heart to kick the varlet into the hall, or

throw him out of the window. But prudence warned me to bide my time. If I obtained the footing to which I aspired in Mr. Birchmore's family, I would settle summarily with Mr. Slurk ; meanwhile, I should best consult my interests by conducting myself with all due quietness and decorum. I offered Kate my arm to lead her from the room ; but with a barely perceptible gesture she declined it, and walked swiftly before me through the doorway, Slurk making another deep obeisance as we passed. The fellow had a smooth unimpeachable way of getting the better of one that made my blood boil ; I commanded myself not without an effort, and nursed my wrath to keep it warm.

"When we reached the court, the brass band had established itself in the little pagoda erected there for its accommodation, and was just striking up ; and there, sure enough, were a table and chairs awaiting us beneath the trees. But neither of us was in a humour to face a crowd of people ; and by a tacit agreement we turned to the right, and crossing the little plank bridge which spanned the narrow stream that skirted the hotel grounds, we found ourselves in the high-road leading up the valley. Along this we walked for some distance, both of us silent ; at length the opening of a path presented itself, which climbed by a zigzag route to the summit of the pine-clad hill.

Into this we turned, and in a few moments were out
of sight of alien eyes amidst the thick-growing
hemlocks. The ascent was steep, and at the first
turning in the path my beautiful companion paused
for breath.

"'Will you take my arm now, Kate?' I said.

"With a faint smile she complied. 'Just for this
once,' I heard her murmur, seemingly speaking to
herself. 'Never again—but this once I will!'

"'Now, Kate,' I said resolutely, bending forward
so as to catch her eye, 'let us have done with
mysteries. No more "never-agains" and "just-this-
onces," if you please! First, I want you tell me
whether you love me?'

"She drew her breath hard. 'I can tell you
nothing, Mr. Gainsborough——'

"'You shall not call me "Mr. Gainsborough." If
you can't call me "Tom," call me nothing; but I will
never be "Mr. Gainsborough" to you again!'

"'I thought we were to have no more "never-
agains?"' she rejoined, with a passing sparkle of the
former playfulness in her air.

"'None of yours, I meant.'

"'I will call you "Tom," if you please, on one
condition.'

"'What condition?'

"'That you let it be "just this once!"'"

" 'Kate, do you love me?'

" 'Oh, you are cruel!' she cried, with passionate emphasis, slipping her hand from my arm and facing me with glowing looks. 'I wish I could say I hate you! You are a man of the world, and I a poor girl from a convent, who know nothing. I am trying to do right, and you oppose me—you make it hard and bitter to me. If you loved me as I—as I would love if I were a man, you would not press me so. I tell you, it must not be!'

" 'What is, shall be, Kate! Dear Kate, we love each other; and who in the world shall prevent it, or forbid our being married?'

" 'Hush! hush!' She came a step nearer to me, and caught my sleeve with her little hand, as a timorous child might do; glancing nervously over her shoulder as if something fearful were hidden amongst the trees. 'Did you hear nothing?' she whispered. 'Did not someone call me?'

" 'Only I have called you, dear. I called you "Kate;" and I want to call you "wife!"'

"She continued to stand motionless, with that frightened listening expression still on her face; and yet my words had apparently passed unheard. What was it, then, that her ears were strained to catch? To my sense, the forest was full of shadowy stillness, tempered only by a faint whispering of leaves, and now and then a bird-note high over-head.

"Gradually the strange preoccupation left her. Her breathing, which had been irregular and laboured, now came evenly and gently once more. She glanced sidelong at me for a moment; then, with a swift tender movement she came yet a trifle closer, and laid her other hand upon my arm.

"'Tom—Tom dear! I will say it, for we shall be parted soon, and then, if I am alive, I shall be comforted a little to think that I did say it! Listen—Tom dear, I love you! Never forget that I said it—Tom, I love you!'

"I was taken deliciously by surprise. You must not expect me to tell how I felt or what I said. I can only remember that I took her in my arms and kissed her. The bird that warbled over our heads seemed to utter the ecstasy that I felt.

"Presently we began to move on again. I don't know why I didn't speak; perhaps I thought that our kiss had been the seal of her surrender, and that there-fore words were for the moment impertinent; by-and-by the converse would be renewed from a fresh basis. Besides, my thoughts were flying too fast, just then, for speech to overtake them. I was thinking how singular had been the manner and progress of our acquaintance. It was scarcely in accordance with what I believed to be my normal temperament and disposition to plunge so abruptly and almost reck-lessly into a new order and responsibility of life. I had fancied myself too cautious, too cool-headed, for such an impulsive act. But it was done, and the fact that Kate's feelings had responded to my own seemed to justify the apparent risk. We were meant for each other, and had come together in sheer despite of all combinations of circumstances to keep us apart. Knowing, as we did, scarcely anything of each other as worldly knowledge goes, we had yet felt that inward instinct and obligation to union which made the most thorough worldly knowledge look like folly. What would my mother say to it? How would the news be relished by her father? I cared not; I fore-saw difficulties enough in store, but none that ap-palled me. After all, an honourable man and woman, honestly in love with each other, are a match against the world, or superior to it. Union is strength, and the union of loving hearts is the strongest strength of all.

"'And do you want to marry me really, Tom?'

"We had gained the summit of the steep hill, and were now pacing along the ridge. The narrow winding valley lay sheer beneath us on the right, with the white road and the dark stream lying side by side at the bottom of it. The crest of the opposing hillside seemed but a short stone's-throw distant; the aroma of our privacy was the sweeter for the pigmy droschkey, with its mannikin inmate, which was crawling along through the dust so far below. We commanded the world, while we were ourselves hidden from it.

"'I should rather think I did, Kate!'

"'I thought Englishmen only married as a matter of business; that they married settlements and dowries and rank and influence, and added women merely as a matter of custom and politeness.'

"'I am satisfied to marry for love; if that's un-English, so much the better for me!'

"'You would take me without anything but just myself?'

"'What is worth having, compared with you?'

"'Oh Tom! But then, you cannot have just myself alone. Nobody in the world is independent of everything—not even an American—not even an American girl who has lived seven years in a convent! I may not be able to bring you anything good—anything that would make me more acceptable; but what if I were to bring you something bad—something terrible —something that would make you shudder at me if I were ten times as lovable as you say I am?'

"'Why then, I should have to love you twenty

times more than ever I suppose, that's all!' I answered, with a laugh.

"'You don't mean what you say—at least you don't know what you say. You are not so brave as you think you are, sir! What do you know of me?' She spoke these sentences in a lower, graver tone than the previous ones, which had been uttered in a vein of half-wayward, fanciful playfulness. Almost immediately, however, she roused herself again, as though unwilling to let the lightsome humour escape so soon.

"'Well, let us pretend that you have married me, for better or worse, and that it is all settled. Now, where will you take me to first?'

"'Where do you wish to go?'

"'Oh, it must be somewhere where nobody could come after us,' she exclaimed, with a curious subdued laugh. 'Nobody that either of us has ever known; neither your mother, nor my father, nor—nor anybody! And there we must stay always; because as soon as we came out, we should lose each other, and never find each other again. And that would be sadder than never to have met, wouldn't it?'

"'But, my darling Kate,' interposed I, laughing again, 'where on earth, in this age of railways and steamboats and telegraphs and balloons, are we to find such a very retired spot? Unless we took a

voyage to the moon, or could find our way down
to the centre of the earth, we should hardly feel safe,
I fear!'

"'Oh, well, you must arrange about that; only it
is as I tell you; and you see marrying me is not such
a simple matter after all. Well, now, suppose we
have reached the place, wherever it is—what would
you give me for a wedding present?'

"'What would you like?'

"'No—you are to decide that. It wouldn't be
proper for your wife to choose her own wedding
present, you know.'

"'I believe such a thing does sometimes happen
though, when the people are very fashionable and
aristocratic.'

"'But I am not aristocratic; I am an American.
Now, what will you give me?'

"'What do you say to the diamonds?'

"'Well, I think I will take the diamonds,' she
said meditatively, as though weighing the question
in her mind. 'Yes, papa said I might wear diamonds after I was married. But might not your
mother object?'

"'Not when she knows whom they are for; and, at
any rate, she is going to leave them to me in her will.'

"'Oh! and you expect that the news of our marriage will kill her?'

"'It ought rather to give her a new lease of life. But you shall have the diamonds all the same. Will you try them on now?'

"'Why, have you got them with you?'

"'Certainly: I always carry them in this pocket.'

"'How careless! You might lose them.'

"'No: the pocket buttons up; see!' and turning back the flap of my coat, I showed her how all was made secure.

"'But what if robbers were to attack you?'

"'Then I should talk to them with this,' I rejoined, taking my revolver from another pocket, and holding it up.

"'Oh, that's a derringer! they have those in America. What a pretty one! Let me look at it.'

"'No,' said I, replacing it in my pocket; 'it has a hair-trigger, and every barrel is loaded. You shall look at something much prettier, and not dangerous at all. Here—sit down on this stump, and take off your hat, and I'll put them on for you.'

"The stump of which I spoke stood at the end of the path we had been following, and within a few rods of the brink of a precipitous gorge, which entered the side of the steep mountain-spur nearly at right angles. Across this gorge (which, though seventy to one hundred feet in depth, was scarcely more than half as wide at the top) a wooden bridge

Q

had formerly been thrown; but age or accident had broken it down, until only a single horizontal beam remained, spanning the chasm from side to side, and supported by three or four upright and transverse braces. The beam itself was scarcely nine inches in width; and the whole structure was a dizzy thing to look at. My nerves were trained to steadiness by a good deal of gymnastic experience; but it would have needed a strong inducement to get me across that beam on foot.

"Kate sat down on the stump as I directed; but her manner had become languid and indifferent; the brightness and sparkle of her late mood were gone. As she looked up at me, her level eyebrows were slightly contracted, and the corners of her mouth drooped. Her hands were folded listlessly in her lap. She was dressed in some soft white material, through which was visible the warm gleam of her arms and shoulders; the skirt was caught up in such a way as to allow freedom in walking; she wore a broad-brimmed white hat over her black hair; a yellow sash confined her waist, and her hands were bare. I untied the ribbons of her hat, she permitting me to do so without resistance; and then, kneeling before her, I unbuttoned the diamonds from my pocket, and laid them, in their case, upon her lap.

"'Now, dear, shall I put them on you, or will you do it yourself?'

"She opened the case, and the gems flashed in the checkered sunshine that filtered down between the leaves of the trees. The sight seemed to rouse her somewhat; a faint spot of colour showed in either cheek, and she drew in a long breath.

"'They are splendid!' she said. 'I never saw anything like them. No, your mother would need to die before giving up these.'

"'They won't look their best until you have put them on. Come!'

"'Oh, I'm afraid! what if——'

"'Afraid of what?'

"'What if someone were to come and see——'

"'Nonsense, my darling! There's no one within half a mile of us; and if there were, they would only see a lovely girl looking her loveliest.'

"'How nicely you talk to me! Well then—you put them on me. I won't touch them myself.'

"The parure consisted of a necklace and a pair of earrings. I lifted them, flashing, from the case; clasped the necklace round her throat, she sitting motionless, and hung the earrings in her ears. A light, that matched their marvellous gleam, seemed to enter into her eyes as I did so.

"'You and these diamonds were made for each

other!' I said; and bending forwards, I kissed her
on the lips.

"For more than a minute she sat there quite still,
I kneeling in front of her; we were looking straight
into one another's eyes.   Then, all at once, a troubled
anxious look came into her face.   She rose with a
startled gesture to her feet.

"'Hush! hush! did you hear?'

"'What's the matter?' cried I, jumping up in
surprise.

"'Hush! someone calling—calling me!'

"Again that strange fancy!   What did it mean?
I could not repress a certain thrill at the heart as I
gazed at her.   It was very weird and strange.

"As I gazed, a singular change crept over her.
Her face was now quite colourless, and its pallor
was intensified by the blackness of her mystical eyes.
Those eyes slowly grew fixed—immovable, as if
frozen.   The lids trembled for a moment, then
drooped, then lifted again to their widest extent,
and so remained.   Her lips, slightly parted, showed
the white teeth set edge to edge behind them.   The
rigidity descended through her whole body; she
was like a marble statue.   She breathed low and
deeply, as one who is in profound slumber.

"'Kate, what has happened to you?' I cried in
alarm, putting my hand on her shoulder.   Her arm

was fixed like iron; she seemed to hear nothing, feel nothing. She was as much beyond any power of mine to influence her as if she had been dead. The diamonds that glittered on her bosom were not more insensible than she.

"I must confess that I was somewhat unnerved by the situation. Kate was evidently in some sort of trance; but what had put her into that state, and how was she to be got out of it? For aught I knew, it might be the prelude to a fit or other seizure of that nature, involving consequences dangerous if not fatal. In the bewilderment of the moment the only remedy that I could think of was cold water; to dash her with water might be of use, and could scarcely make matters worse. About thirty paces from where we were standing a small rill meandered amongst the roots of the trees, and trickled at last in a tiny cascade down the rocky side of the gorge. Towards this I ran, and stooping down, attempted to scoop up some of the refreshing element in the crown of my straw hat.

"Rising with the dripping hat in my hands, I turned to go back; but the sight that then met my eyes caused me to drop everything and spring forward with a gasp of horror.

"Moving as if in obedience to some power external or at least foreign to herself, as a mechanical figure might move, steadily, deliberately, and yet blindly, Kate had advanced directly towards the narrow chasm, and when I first beheld her she already seemed balancing on the brink. Before I could cover half the distance that separated us, she had set foot on the long beam which spanned the abyss, and had begun to walk along it. By the time I reached the hither end, she was halfway over, stepping as unconsciously as if she were on an ordinary sidewalk, though the slightest deflection from a straight course would have sent her down a hundred feet to the jagged boulders below.

" Standing on the hither verge, every nerve so tensely strung that I seemed to hear the blood humming through my brain, I watched the passage of those small feet, which I had admired that morning as they peeped coquettishly from beneath her dress in the railway carriage—I watched them pass, step after step, along that awful beam. I suppose the transit must have been accomplished in less than a minute, but it seemed to me that I was watching it for hours. I uttered no sound, lest it might rouse her from her trance and insure the catastrophe that else she might escape ; I did not attempt to overtake her, fearful lest the beam should fail to support our united weight. I saw her pass on, rigid, unbending, but sure of foot as a rope-dancer ; and at last I saw her reach the opposite side, and stand once more on solid earth, preserved from death as it seemed by a miracle. I have no distinct recollection of how I followed; I only know that a few seconds afterwards I was standing beside her, with my arm round her waist.

"I led her forwards a few paces out of sight of the ravine, the mere thought of which now turned me sick, and brought her to a plot of soft turf, beneath a tree with low spreading branches. The trance was evidently passing away; her limbs no longer had that unnatural rigidity; her eyelids drooped heavily, and her jaw relaxed. A violent trembling seized upon her; she sank down on the turf as if all power of self-support had gone out of her. At that moment I fancied I heard a slight crackle among the shrubbery not far off; I looked quickly up, and saw—or thought I saw—a short ungainly figure obscurely stealing away through the underbush. Almost immediately he vanished amidst the trees, leaving me in doubt whether my eyesight had not after all played me false.

"As I turned again to Kate, she was sitting up against the trunk of the tree, the diamonds flashing at her throat and ears, and a puzzled questioning expression on her face.

"'What makes you look so strange?' she murmured. 'Where is your hat! How did we come here, Tom? I thought——'

"She stopped abruptly, and rose slowly to her feet. Her eyes were cast down shamefacedly, and she bit her lip. She lifted her hand to her throat, and felt the diamonds there. Then, with an apprehensive, almost a cowering glance, she peered stealthily round through the trees, as though expecting to see something that she dreaded. Finally she turned again, appealingly, to me, but said nothing.

" I thought I partly understood the significance of this dumb-show. She was subject to these somnambulistic trances, and was ashamed of them. She knew not, on this occasion, what extravagance she might have committed in the presence of me, her lover. She feared the construction I might put upon it, yet was too timid—or, it might be, too proud—to speak. But her misgiving did me injustice. Shocked and grieved though I was, I loved her more than ever.

" 'You were faint, my dear, that's all,' I said, cheerfully and affectionately. 'I brought you under this tree, and now you're all right.'

"She shook her head, with a piteous smile. 'I know what has been the matter with me, Mr. Gainsborough,' she said, with an attempt at reserve and coldness in her tone. 'I had hoped I might have parted from you before you knew, but—it was not to be so! It is very good of you to pretend to ignore it, and I thank you—I thank you. Here,' she added, nervously unclasping the necklace and removing the earrings, 'I have worn these too long. Take them, please.'

"'Kate, you shall wear them forever!' cried I, passionately.

"'I must not begin yet, at all events,' she returned more firmly. 'Take them, please, or you will make me feel more humiliated than I do now.' She put them in my unwilling hands. 'And now we'll get our hats and go back to the hotel,' she continued, with a smile which was pathetic in its effort to seem indifferent and unconstrained. 'Where are they? Ah!'

"She had just caught sight of her white hat lying beside the stump on the farther side of the gorge. The suppressed scream and the start indicated that she now for the first time realised by what a perilous path she had come hither. She remained for a moment gazing at the beam with a sort of fascination; then, moving forward to the brink, looked down the sheer precipice to the rocks below.

"'I wish I had fallen!' she said, almost below her breath; 'or,' she added, after a short pause, in a tone still lower, but of intense emphasis, 'I wish he had!'

"'You wish I had?'

"'I did not know you were so near,' she answered, drawing back from the verge. 'No, no—not you!

Come, we must walk round this place. Tell me,'
she said, facing me suddenly, 'did you see anyone?'

"'I think not. I fancied I heard——'

"'We must get back to the hotel,' she interrupted
excitedly; 'at least, I must get back. I don't like
to be here. I wish you would leave me. I would
rather say good-bye to you here than there.'

"'I never mean to say good-bye to you at all,
Kate. If this is the trouble you hinted at, you over-
rate it entirely. Why, two people out of every seven
are somnambulists. It is as common as to have
black hair. Besides, you will outgrow it in a few
years; it is only a nervous affection, which any doctor
can cure.'

"'It is not that; you don't understand,' she said,
with a sigh.

"'Whatever it is, I'm determined not to lose you.
I shall tell your father, when I see him, that I love
you, and that wherever he takes you I shall follow.
No one can or shall keep us apart.'

"The resolution with which I spoke seemed to
impress her somewhat. 'You can speak to him if
you will. But, oh! it is no use. It cannot be; you
don't understand. Let me go; good-bye. No, do
not come with me; please do not! I have a reason
for asking it. I will see you once more—to-morrow,

before we leave. But let me go alone now, if you love me.'

"She went, walking quickly away through the wood. I watched her for a few moments, and then returned to the grass plot beneath the tree, and threw myself down there in a very dissatisfied frame of mind. The sun had set before I returned to the hotel.

V.

"I saw nothing more of Kate that day; but I came across Slurk several times, and there was a peculiar look on the fellow's countenance which made me renew my longing to chastise him. I was anxious to know whether Mr. Birchmore had returned; but, as I could not bring myself to make any inquiries of his valet, and did not care to let him see me asking any-one else, I was obliged to remain in ignorance. However, as I sat out under the trees at dusk, a tall figure, with a lighted cigar in his mouth, appeared in the doorway of the hotel, and, on my saluting him, he sauntered up to my table, and complied with my invitation to sit down.

"The waiter brought us coffee; and under its stimulus I ventured to introduce the subject which lay nearest my heart to Mr. Birchmore's notice. No doubt I put my best foot foremost, and spoke as eloquently as was consistent with my downright earnestness and sincerity. Mr. Birchmore heard me almost in silence, only giving evidence by an occasional word or interjection that he was giving me his attention. Once or twice, too, I was aware of his having given me one of those sharp icy glances for which he was remarkable. When I had spoken, he fingered the pointed beard on his chin meditatively, and puffed his cigar.

"'This is a very fair and honourable offer that you make, Gainsborough,' he said at length. 'I liked you before; I like you better now. You take it for granted, I suppose, that I'm pretty well off. There, you needn't say anything; I've no doubt of your disinterestedness; but these matters would have to be mentioned, sooner or later, if the affair went on. I say "if," because—I may as well tell you at once; it will save us all pain—because it can't go on: it must stop right here; and I can only regret, for both your sakes, that it has gone so far.'

"'Mr. Birchmore, I cannot take this for an answer. You have given me no reasons. If you want confirmation of my account of myself, I can——'

"'I want nothing of the sort; on the contrary, I feel complimented that you should accept *us*, not only without confirmation, but without question. But you can't marry my daughter, Gainsborough, much as I

like you, and much as I daresay she does. When
you are older, you will understand that men cannot
always follow that course in the world which appears
to them most desirable.'

"' However young or old I may be, Mr. Birchmore,
I am old enough to know my own mind, and to require good reasons for changing it. If you have any
such reasons, I wish you'd show your liking for me
by telling me what they are.'

"' Do you remember a talk we once had in Paris,
when you hinted that I should accompany you on
your jaunt? I told you then that the past life of a
man sometimes had a hold over his present, con-
straining his freedom, whether he would or no. And
can't you imagine that those circumstances, however
cogent they may be, or, very likely, just because they
are so cogent, might be very inconvenient to talk
about? To speak plainly, Gainsborough, I don't
see how your loving my daughter obliges me to tell
you all the secrets of my life.'

"' I don't want to know your secrets, sir; I wish
to marry Miss Birchmore.'

"Mr. Birchmore laughed.

"' Well, you're a pretty determined wooer,' said
he. 'I can't give my consent to the match, because—
well, because I cannot; but if you won't take No for
an answer, nor profit by the warning I hereby give

you, I'll tell you what I will do. I will allow you
yourself to discover and acknowledge the causes
which make your marriage with Kate impossible.
You must not blame me if the discovery gives you
pain, and the acknowledgment causes you mortification. I have given you fair warning. And I will
only add, sir, that the pain and mortification won't
be all on your side. I could not give you a stronger
pledge of my friendship and liking for you than in
thus letting you find out what has hitherto been
hidden from all the world. And I only demand one
condition—that you promise, when you have made
your discovery, and left us, never to mention to any
human being what our secret was.'

"'I give that promise with pleasure. As to my
leaving you of my own free will, that is—begging
your pardon—impossible and absurd.'

"He laughed again, and shot another of his startling looks at me. 'Very well, young sir, I've nothing
more to say. Come with us to the farmhouse to-
morrow; there's plenty of room there, and they are
used to being accommodating. Stay with us until
you're satisfied, and then—don't forget your promise!'

"He rose as he finished speaking, and flung away
the remains of his cigar.

"'Good-night!' he said, holding out his large
well-shaped hand.

"'Good-night! and thanks for your confidence, which you will never regret, Mr. Birchmore.'

"'Qui vivra, verra!' was all his answer, as he walked away, with his hands in his coat-pockets and his singular short steps. He was an enigma sure enough, and yet my belief in him was as intuitive and inalienable as in Kate herself. His mysterious hints and warnings were powerless to disturb me : I trusted in the ability of us three combined to overthrow any antagonist. I sat late beneath the trees, smoking, and brooding over my passion, as young men will, and ever and anon glancing up at a certain window, behind the lamp-illumined curtain of which I had reason to suppose my darling was. Was she thinking of me now? Even as I asked myself this, and gazed upwards, a shadow fell upon the curtain ; it was pushed aside, and the window was swung back on its hinges.

"With a throb of the heart I sprang to my feet and wafted a kiss from my finger-tips towards the face that peeped out upon me. Stay! was it Kate's face after all? The arms and shoulders now appeared, and the form leant upon the window-sill. A lucifer-match flashed, and I had the pleasure of beholding the sinister visage of Mr. Slurk lit up by a sulphurous gleam, as he leisurely lit his pipe and stared down at me.

"'Schöne gute Nacht, Herr Gainsborough!'

VI.

"We made a late start the next morning, and did not reach the farmhouse before four o'clock. I had little opportunity of speaking to Kate on the way; in fact, the presence of Slurk, who sat on the box of the vehicle, and once in a while threw a glance at us over his shoulder, irritated me to such a degree that more tender sentiments were temporarily pushed into the background. Kate herself, though she attempted to appear cheerful, betrayed signs of inward anxiety and nervousness; while Mr. Birchmore conversed with a volubility and discursiveness greater than I had ever remarked in him before.

"The farmhouse stood quite alone, on an unfrequented by-road, in a little angle of the hills. It was not exactly a picturesque building, with its four walls covered with rough plaster and pierced with dozens of small windows, and its enormous red-tiled roof, with those quaint narrow apertures, like half-opened eyes, disclosing a single pane of glass, which do duty as dormers. It stood flush with the road, as German houses are fond of doing; but behind was a large enclosed farmyard, roughly paved with round stones and well walled in. The front door, though rather pretentiously painted and ornamented, with some religious versicle or other written up on the lintel, was not used as a means of entrance or exit. It was, as I afterwards discovered, not only locked and bolted, but actually screwed up on the inside ; and the only way of getting into the house was by a side door opening into the courtyard. As the courtyard itself was . provided with a heavy gate, you will see that the farmhouse, close to the road though it was, was by no means so easy of ingress or egress as it appeared, supposing, of course, that it was the humour of the inmates to declare a state of siege. I mention these particulars merely by the way : they are common to three houses out of five in this region.

"The Birchmores' luggage had, it appeared, already been carried over from the hotel ; but a man, in rough peasant's costume, who announced himself as the master of the house, now came out to take charge of my trunk. I was, or fancied myself (as you may have noticed), a quick judge of faces, and this peasant's face failed to commend itself to me. It was at once heavy and gloomy, while a scar at one corner of his mouth caused that feature to twist itself into a per-functory grimace, grotesquely at variance with his normal expression. In person he was much above the common size, and to judge by the ease with which he slung my heavy trunk over his shoulder, he must have been as strong as Augustus the Stark himself, whose brazen statue domineers over the market-place in Dresden.

"'Guten Morgen, Herr Rudolph!' said Slurk, hailing this giant affably. The two seemed to be on some sort of terms of comradeship, having, perhaps, struck up an acquaintance during the previous negotiations for lodgings. I must say they looked to me to be a not ill-matched pair.

"We alighted, and were welcomed in with surly courtesy by Herr Rudolph. Kate, confessing to a headache, went at once to her room, whence she did not again emerge; Slurk disappeared into the kitchen regions with the landlord; Mr. Birchmore presently went out for a stroll before dinner: and I, finding myself thrown temporarily on my own resources, decided to make a virtue of my loneliness by writing some letters which had been long owing. I accordingly groped my way up the darksome stone staircase, and so along an eccentric passage to my room.

"I did not know then, nor could I, even now, accurately describe the arrangement of rooms in that farmhouse. There were at least three separate passages, not running at right angles to one another, but seeming to wander about irregularly, now and then turning awkward corners, descending or ascending short flights of steps, or eddying into a little *cul-de-sac*, with, perhaps, only a closet door at the end of it. The consequence was, it was nearly impossible to say whose room adjoined whose. It might be a long distance from one to another, measured along the passage, and yet they might actually be separated only by the thickness of a wall. Where the farmer and his family slept I know not, but I have reason to believe that all our party, including Slurk, were accommodated upon the same floor.

"On opening the door of my room, I found some-one already there. This person was a comely young woman, the farmer's daughter evidently, busy in the benevolent occupation of putting things in order. She had moved my trunk beneath the window, she had put fresh water in the ewer, she had straightened out the slips of drugget on the rough-board floor, she had placed some flowers in the window, and she was now engaged in tucking a clean sheet on the bed. I said she was comely; on second looks she was better than that. She was positively pretty, with the inno-cent blonde prettiness of some German peasant-girls. Her fair hair, smoothed compactly over her small head, and wound up in a funny little pug behind, possessed a faint golden lustre; her eyes were of as pure and serene a blue as any I ever looked upon; her smooth cheeks, slightly browned by much sun-shine which had rested on them, were tinged with healthful bloom; her mouth might have been smaller, but the full lips were well-shaped, and there were white even teeth behind them. Her figure, like that of most Saxon peasant-girls of her age, was robust and vigorous; she wore a simple bodice and skirt, and her feet and legs were bare. Altogether I thought her a very agreeable apparition.

"'Good-morning, honoured Herr Gainsborough,' she said gravely, in German, as I entered.

"'Good-morning, pretty maiden,' returned I gallantly. 'You seem to know my name, though I don't know yours : what is it ?'

"'I am called Christina—Christina Rudolph. It is some time that I have known Herr Gainsborough's name,' she added.

"'Really! how comes that ?' I asked, by no means displeased.

"'The honoured Herr has been kind to a relation of mine—a very near relation,' replied Christina, with the same gravity.

"'Have I? I'm glad to hear it! Was she as pretty as thou ?' inquired I, venturing upon the familiar form of address.

"She blushed, and answered : 'It was not a woman —it was my brother.'

"'Oh, thy brother! And where did I meet thy brother ?'

"'In Paris, Herr Gainsborough.'

"'In Paris! Rudolph! What, art thou the sister of Heinrich Rudolph, who lives in the Latin Quarter, and is considered the cleverest jeweller in the city?'

"'Yes, honoured Herr,' returned Christina, smiling for the first time, and showing her pretty teeth and a dimple on either cheek. 'My brother Heinrich cut and arranged the diamonds in the parure of the honoured Herr's mother.'

"'So he did, Christina, and he did it better than anyone except him could have done it. And so thou art really his sister! How did he tell thee of me?'

"'He wrote to me while you were still in Paris, and described the pretty stones, and told how Herr Gainsborough used to come and sit with him, and see him work, and talk a great deal with him.'

"'Yes, he was well worth talking with! And I remember now that he said he was born in this neighbourhood, and that he had a sister and a father living here. It was stupid of me not to have thought of that when I heard your name. Well, Christina, I'm afraid I wasn't of much use to him after all. I tried to get him customers, but I knew very few people in Paris; and the only person I did succeed in introducing to him—by the way! it was this gentleman who is with me now.'

"'Herr Birchmore; yes, my brother spoke also of him,' said Christina, her gravity returning. 'But he did not speak of the young lady, or of the servant.'

"'No, I believe they weren't with him at the time. I only met them myself since I came to Schandau.'

"'The young lady is Herr Birchmore's—wife?'

"'His wife? Dear heavens, no! His daughter, of course, Christina.'

"Christina said nothing, being occupied in neatly smoothing out the pillow, and laying the wadded counterpane over the sheet.

"'Will Herr Gainsborough stay with us long?' she asked, after a pause.

"'As long as Herr Birchmore does, I suppose,' said I carelessly.

"'And Herr Birchmore's daughter?' subjoined Christina, with a twinkle of mischief so demure that I could hardly be sure whether she meant it or not.

"'Thou art as clever as thy brother, Christina, I laughed, colouring a little too however, I daresay 'It is true I have not known them long, but—but people see a good deal of one another in travelling together.'

"'I have heard it said that travelling makes people acquainted with——' she paused, and looked down thoughtfully at her bare feet. Presently she lifted her blue eyes straight to mine and asked :

"'Herr Gainsborough has his diamonds with him?'

"'Undoubtedly! They are never away from me.'

"'In going about this place, the Herr should be cautious. Some of these hills and valleys are very lonely. There are spots, not far from here, where no one goes for sometimes many months.'

"'Well, I'll be very careful, Christinchen,' I rejoined laughing, and in truth not a little amused at the care my friends took of me. 'But thou must remember that no one in Germany, except Herr Birchmore, and his daughter, and thyself, knows that any such diamonds as these are in existence—much less that they are in my pocket!'

"Christina raised her finger to her lips, as if to caution me to speak lower. 'There is at least one other who knows—the man Slurk!' she said.

"'Well, perhaps he may,' I replied, somewhat struck by her observation; 'and as I see thou hast taken a dislike to the fellow, I will confide to thee that I consider him an atrocious brute. But brute though he is, there's no harm in him of *that* kind. He is an old servant of Herr Birchmore, I believe, and would of course be dismissed at once if there were anything serious against him.'

"'Naturally!' was all Christina's answer; she made no pretence of arguing the point with me.

'Adieu, honoured sir!' she said at the door. But with her hand upon the latch she paused, turned round, and added rather confusedly :

"'Will Herr Gainsborough go on any expedition with his friends to-day?'

"'Why, I hardly think so, Christina.'

"'But to-morrow, perhaps?' she persisted, lifting her blue eyes to mine again.

"'Perhaps,' I admitted, with a smile.

"'Then—if he can trust me—would the Herr mind leaving the diamonds with me, until he comes back again?'

"'Nay, Christinchen, I cannot give them up, even to thee—and although I trust thee as much as thy brother, or myself. But thou mightst lose them—and if they are to be lost at all, I would rather the responsibility should be mine. Besides,' I continued, showing my revolver, 'I go always with this. But I thank thee all the same, Christinchen, and I would like to do something—to——'

"I stepped towards her : the fact is, I suppose I meant to kiss her. But her expression changed in a manner not encouraging to such an advance; she looked both grave and hurt, and I paused.

"'I was going to say—if thou wouldst like to see the diamonds, it would give me great pleasure to show them to 'thee.'

"'Many thanks, honoured sir! I would rather not.' And with a formal curtsy the fair-haired little maid opened the door and disappeared, leaving me feeling rather foolish.

"'The pretty peasant has a pride of her own!' I said to myself, as I opened my trunk and got out my writing materials. 'She's actually offended because I wouldn't constitute her guardian of thirty thousand pounds' worth of diamonds. Good gracious! why, that father of hers, if I know anything of faces, would cut all our throats for as many groschen. But what an unmistakable scamp my friend Slurk must be to have aroused the suspicions of such an innocent unsophisticated little creature as Christinchen! By Jove, though, anybody might be suspicious of a leer and a slouch like his! What if there should be anything in it? Just suppose such a thing for a moment, eh? It's impossible, to be sure; but the impossible does sometimes happen. How on earth did Birchmore ever happen to have such a fellow about him? I tell you I've always had a notion that he may be at the bottom of all this mystery that Birchmore and Kate are so much exercised by. Now, what if he—but pshaw!

"'There is one thing I'm resolved to do, however,' I continued to myself, as I settled down with paper, pens, and ink at the table in the window. 'I'll buttonhole Birchmore this very afternoon, and get out of him everything he knows about his precious valet. It can do no harm to have the matter cleared up. The thing is absurd, of course ; still, the situation out here is rather lonely ; and with two such lovely neighbours as Papa Rudolph and Slurk—*par nobile fratrum*—it may be as well to be on the safe side. Yes, that shall be cleared up to-day ! '

"Having arrived at this sapient determination, I set to work writing my letters, and scribbled away diligently for an hour or two. At length, as I was looking vacantly up from my paper, at a loss for something interesting to set down upon it, my eyes happened to rest upon the pane of my open window.

"Like nearly all German windows, it opened inwards on hinges, instead of running up and down in grooves. The pane on my left, therefore, having the dark room as a background, acted as a mirror of the sunlit landscape outside on the right, showing me a portion thereof which was directly invisible to me from where I sat, and to any person standing in which I must myself be invisible.

"Now my window was on the southern side of the house, which fronted westward on the road. On the opposite side of the road was a narrow strip of land planted with vegetables, and above this rose the abrupt side of a hill, ascended by a winding path partly hidden by the trees. I could not see this hill and path without leaning out of the window and looking towards the right ; but a considerable part of it was reflected in my window-pane mirror, and could thus be readily observed without rising from my chair. Happening, then, as I said, to cast my eyes upon this mirror, I saw two persons standing together on the path upon the hillside, and conversing in a very animated manner.

"I had no difficulty in recognising them : they were Mr. Birchmore and his valet. So far there was nothing surprising in the spectacle. That which did surprise and even astonish me, however, was the mutual bearing of the two men towards each other.

"I have already mentioned the peremptory tone in which Mr. Birchmore uniformly addressed the man Slurk, and the generally overbearing attitude he assumed towards him ; but in the conversation now going forward all this was changed. To judge by appearances, I should have said that Slurk was the master, and Mr. Birchmore the valet. The former was gesticulating forcibly, and evidently laying down the law in a very decided and autocratic way. His square ungainly figure seemed to dilate, and take on a masterful and almost hectoring air ; while Mr. Birchmore stood with his hands in his coat-pockets, undemonstrative and submissive, apparently accepting with meekness all that the other advanced, and only occasionally interpolating a remark or a suggestion, to which Slurk would pay but slight or impatient attention. Both were evidently talking in a low tone ; for though they were not more than fifty or sixty yards from where I sat, I could not catch a single word, nor even so much as an inarticulate murmur, unless by deliberately straining my ears. But I did not need nor care to hear anything : what I saw was quite enough to startle and mystify me.

"After a few minutes the two interlocutors moved slowly on up the path, and were soon beyond the field of my mirror. But the unexpected scene which I had witnessed did not so soon pass out of my mind.

"I got up from my table and began walking about the room, with the restlessness of one who cannot make his new facts tally with his preconceived ideas. Who and what was Slurk, and how had he obtained ascendancy over a man like Birchmore? Certainly it could not be a natural ascendancy. Birchmore must have put himself in the other's power. In other words, Slurk must be blackmailing him. And this was the trouble, was it?—this was the mystery? It was an ugly and awkward business, certainly; but the main question remained after all unanswered. What was it that Birchmore had done to give Slurk a hold upon him? and had that act, whatever it was, compromised his daughter along with him? For now that I gathered up in my memory all the hints and signs which had come under my notice in relation to this affair, I could not help thinking that Kate's attitude had in it something suggestive of more than mere filial sympathy with her father's misfortune. In that misfortune or disgrace she had a personal and separate in addition to a sympathetic share. And yet, in what conceivable way could a low villain like Slurk fasten his gripe upon a pure and spotless young girl? and what a hideous thought—that such a girl should be in any way at his mercy! The more I turned the matter over in my mind, the more ugly did it appear. No wonder that father and daughter had warned me away. Some men in my position, having seen thus far, might have shrunk back and given up the enterprise. But I was not in that category. I was more than ever determined to see the adventure to its end ; nay, to gain my own end in it too. The conditions of the contest were at all events narrowing themselves down to recognisable form. It was to be a trial of strength mainly between myself and Slurk—between an educated plucky Englishman, and a base German ruffian—between one, moreover, who had right, moral and legal, on his side, and love as his goal—and one armed only with underhand cunning and terrorism, and aiming at nothing higher than the extortion of money. This was the way I read the situation, and I flattered myself that I was equal to the emergency.

"Upon consideration, however, I decided to alter my intention of asking Mr. Birchmore about his valet. It was tolerably clear that he was not in a position to give me any information ; and besides, I had already learnt everything except the particulars. Those particulars, if I did not succeed in discovering them unaided, must be extracted from Kate. She would not withhold them from me, if I questioned her resolutely and directly, enforcing my inquiries with disclosure of the knowledge I had already obtained. This then should be my next step. I sealed up my letters, locked them in my desk, and, it being now nearly seven o'clock, I went down to supper.

VII.

"But at supper there was no Kate; Mr. Birchmore and I were served by Christina, while the voices of Slurk and our landlord could be heard in the kitchen. My conversation was naturally somewhat constrained; Mr. Birchmore had a good deal to say about some excursion which he had in view for the morrow, but I failed to pay very close

attention to his remarks. Once, however, I caught
Christina's eyes fixed upon me, and smiled as I
remembered her warnings respecting the supposed
danger of solitary rambles.

"After supper I felt more restless than ever. Mr.
Birchmore brought out his invariable cigars, expecting
me to join him in a smoke; but I was not in the
mood for it, neither did I feel at ease in his company
until things should have begun to look a little more
comprehensible. I left him, therefore, and wandered
aimlessly about outside the house, exploring the
farmyard and buildings, and then coming round to
the road, and pacing up and down on a beat about a
quarter of a mile in length. It was a clear moonlight
night, and so warm as to be almost oppressive. At
length I returned to the house, it being then after
nine o'clock. Mr. Birchmore had apparently retired ;
Christina was nowhere to be seen ; so I got a lamp
from my surly landlord, and found my way without
much difficulty to my own chamber.

"The warmth within doors was still more oppressive
than outside. I opened both the windows, drew up
my bed between them, and placed the table with the
lamp on it near the bed's head. I had previously
thrown off my coat and waistcoat, and laid them
across one end of the table. The diamonds were still
in the pocket of the coat; I intended taking them

out before going to sleep, and putting them under my
pillow, or in some equally secure place. My revolver I
also placed beside the lamp. Then, having provided
myself with a book out of my trunk, and drawn the
bolt of the door, I reclined on the outside of the bed
and began to read.

"I could not, however, fix my mind upon the page.
First my attention and then my eyes would wander:
I took a futile and absurd interest in scrutinising all
the details of the room. I recollect them distinctly
now. The walls were not papered, but the plaster
was washed over with a dark gray tint, which rubbed
off on the fingers, and the uniformity of which was
relieved by vertical bands of dull red painted at
intervals of about five feet from floor to ceiling. The
ceiling was low—about eight feet from the floor—and
whitewashed. In one corner stood the china stove, a
glistening, pallid structure of plain tiles, built up four-
square nearly to the top of the room. On the side of
the room opposite the two windows and the bed was
fastened a tall looking-glass, formed of three plates
set one above the other, edge to edge, in such a
manner as painfully to cut up and distort whatever
was reflected in them. In front of the looking-glass
was a lilliputian washstand, and beside it a straight-
legged chair without rungs. In a word, a room more
utterly devoid of every kind of picturesque or orna-

mental attraction could not be imagined ; yet I could not keep my eyes from vacantly traversing and re-traversing its vacancy. The door was behind me, as I lay turned towards the little table on which the lamp stood, but I could see the free edge of it brokenly reflected in the mirror, with the cracked black porcelain latch-handle and the iron bolt which I had shot into its place.

"I was anything but sleepy: the heat, and the pest of midges and beetles which the light attracted in through the windows, would have sufficed to keep me awake even had my mind been at ease. In order to disperse the insects I finally extinguished the lamp ; the moonlight in the room was so bright that I could almost have seen to read by it. I closed the book, however, and clasping my hands under my head, I gave myself up to meditation. Not a sound of any kind was audible except the muffled ticking of the watch in my waistcoat pocket, and the faint rustle of the pillow as I breathed. The white moonlight seemed to augment the stillness ; the whole great night, and the house with it, seemed silently and intently listening ; and at length I found myself listening intently too ! For what ? I could not tell ; but I listened nevertheless.

"By-and-by I fancied a sound came—a sound from somewhere within the house. It was a very faint sound, and did not come again; but it was such as might have been caused by the light pressure of a foot in one of the passages outside. Instinctively I reached forth my hand and laid hold of my revolver; but I did not rise from the bed nor otherwise alter my position. I still lay as if asleep, with the revolver in one hand, the other beneath my head, and my eyes fixed upon the edge of the door, which was obscurely visible in the mirror.

"Several minutes passed thus, and there was no return of the noise. Then I saw the handle of the door move and turn. The latch clicked slightly; the door, bolted though it was, opened as if on oiled hinges, admitting an indistinct figure in a long robe of soft gray. So much I saw in the mirror. Then the door was closed again, and the figure, advancing towards the bed, ceased to be reflected in the glass. It advanced close to the bed, and paused there a moment; I could hear its deep regular breathing. All this time I had not moved, but lay with my back turned, feigning slumber.

"Presently the figure passed round the foot of the bed and came up the other side. The full white light of the moon fell upon it. It was Kate, as I had known it was from the first moment she entered the room. She was clad in a dressing-gown of soft flowing material, which was fastened at the throat and trailed on the ground. It had wide sleeves, one of which fell back from the bare smooth arm and hand that carried a lamp. The lamp was not lighted: Her black hair hung down on her shoulders, and on each side of her pale face. Her eyes were wide open, but fixed and vacant. Her breathing was long and measured, as of one sound asleep.

" She put the lamp down on the table beside mine, and then stood quite still in the moonlight, her face wholly expressionless and without motion. It was an appalling thing to see her thus. I, too, remained motionless, but it was because I knew not what to do. To awaken her might bring on the worst consequences. If she were not disturbed, she might possibly retire as quietly and unconsciously as she had come. But the mystery of her being there at all appeared utterly inexplicable. What had led her, in her trance, to visit my room? how had she ever known where it was? What had she dreamt of doing here? and above all, how had she contrived to enter through a bolted door with as much ease as though she had been a spirit? Perhaps this was but a spirit—or a phantom of my own brain! Was I awake?

" She stretched out her hand, not following its motion with her eyes, but mechanically and as it were involuntarily. She laid it on my coat—on the pocket which contained the diamonds. Then, slowly and deliberately, and still with averted face and eyes, and that long-drawn, slumberous breathing, she unbuttoned the fastenings one after one, and her soft tapering fingers closed upon the case.

"Meanwhile my mind had been rapidly canvassing all the pros and cons of action; and I had come to the conclusion that it would be better for her that I should interfere. Of my personal interest in the matter I believe I did not think; indeed, knowing that the diamonds would not be lost, there was no reason why I should. But it would not do to risk compromising Kate. It was dangerous enough that she should be here at all; but that she should carry away the diamonds with her was inadmissible. I rose from my bed and laid my hand gently on her wrist.

"She was no spirit, but warm flesh and blood. For a few moments the restraint in which I held her seemed to baffle and distress her; I fancied I could feel her pulse beat under my fingers: a kind of spasm crossed her face, her eyelids quivered and the eyes moved in their sockets. Then her breathing became irregular, and caught in her throat in a kind of sob. The moment of her awakening was evidently at-hand, and I dreaded its coming, lest she should scream out and rouse the house. But fortunately she uttered no sound. Slowly speculation grew within her eyes; she fixed them on me, first with an expression of strange pleasure, soon changing to bewilderment and fear. Then, with a cry that was none the less thrilling because it was a whisper, she drooped forwards into my arms. It was a delicious moment, for all its peril.

"'You are perfectly safe,' I whispered in her ear; 'only make no noise.'

"'Tom,' she said, suddenly freeing herself from my arms, and putting a hand on either shoulder, while her wild black eyes searched my face, 'you understand—you don't think——?'

"'Of course I understand, my poor darling!'

"'What shall I do—what shall I do? Let me kill myself!'

"With a motion swift as the glide of a serpent, she reached towards the revolver, which I had left on the bed. I was barely in time to catch her arm. The look in the girl's face at that moment was terrible.

"'Let me!—I will!'

"'Hush, Kate! You never shall.'

"'Oh, what shall I do!' she murmured again slipping down on her knees and running both hands through her thick black hair. 'Tom, if you loved me you would kill me!'

"'Kate, everyone in the house is asleep. You can go back to your room, and no one know. Only be calm.'

"'And no one know? You think that?'

"'I am sure of it!'

"'I know better! Someone knows it now: he made it happen!'

"'Don't kneel there, dear. You're not yourself yet. You don't know what you're saying.' I said this reassuringly, but her words had inspired me with a vague alarm that I ventured not to define. I brought a chair and made her sit upon it, and sat down beside her.

"'Not here!' she whispered, drawing back out of the moonlight into the shadow. 'Come here, Tom. He may be looking!'

"'Why, Kate, who can see us here? The door is shut.'

"'Oh—why was not the door bolted?'

"'It was. I can't conceive how you opened it.'

"'Oh the villain! how I hate him!'

"'Kate, I love you, and whoever you hate must have to do with me.'

"'You can do nothing—no one can do anything! —unless you'll help me to kill him!'

"'Whom? Do you mean Slurk?—tell me that!'

"'Yes!' she answered with a shiver; not looking me in the face, but with her hands clasped tight between her knees. 'I do mean—him!'

"'Now tell me all that he has done, dear,' said

I, quietly. 'I must know everything; and then I promise you that you shall be freed from him.'

"'He is my master!' she said, in a frightened whisper. 'He has been so ever so long! He makes me do what he will—he sent me here to-night. He shames me and destroys me—he loves to do it! He makes me sleep, and then I cannot help myself. I wake, and find it done; and he has no mercy.'

"'Why does he do this?'

"'It was when I was only a little girl that he first got that power over me. He knew my father was rich, and he wanted me to be promised to him for his—wife, Tom. Then my father put me in the convent, and I stayed there seven years, till we thought he had lost the power, or was dead perhaps. But he found me in America, and made me come back; and now it's worse than ever.'

"'Why doesn't your father have him arrested and imprisoned? It can be done.'

"'Oh my poor father! He cannot, Tom; do not ask me that!'

"'I must ask it, Kate. Remember, I love you! Why is it?'

"'My father is afraid of him too,' she said, chafing one hand with the other with a piteous expression of pain. 'If he did anything against him, he would be ruined. My father cannot help me, Tom.'

"'But I do not understand. What has your father done that he should be afraid of such a scoundrel as Slurk?' I demanded sternly.

"She hesitated long before answering, moving her hands and head restlessly and fetching many troubled sighs. At last she laid her hand shrinkingly on mine, and I grasped it firmly. 'I will tell you, Tom,' she said in a faltering voice; 'but you know I would tell no one in the world but you. My dear papa did not do wrong himself; but there were people connected with him who did, and made the blame seem to be his. And there were some papers of papa's which—which—oh——'

"'Yes, yes, I understand, darling; and Slurk stole the papers?'

"'Yes—that is—no; it was worse than that, for he didn't know where the papers were kept; no one knew that but I. Tom, he made me sleep, and in my sleep he made me go to the place where they were, and take them out, and give them to him. He made me rob my own father—put my own dear papa in his hateful power. I would rather have died! And papa forgave me—think of that!'

"'Then Slurk has the papers in his possession? and he uses them for blackmail? But have you never thought of trying to—it sounds badly, but it would be perfectly justifiable—to steal them back again?'

"'I can do nothing. He can make me helpless by a look ; and he always carries them with him. But, Tom, if it could be done without being found out, I would tell papa to kill him. But I cannot let my dear papa be hanged for that wretch ; and, you see, we have no evidence.'

"'Good God! What a fearful thing it is!' I muttered. What help, what consolation could I offer? A refined and sensitive girl under the mesmeric control of a ruffian ; her father subject to his extortions and insults ; and the only escape a worse misery even than this—Kate to yield herself to him in marriage! Faugh! the thought sickened me ; but it enraged me, too! Kate was right ; death, sudden and merciless, was the proper measure to be meted out to Slurk. If he had appeared at that moment, I believe I would have shot him unhesitatingly, and rejoiced in the deed. Murder would be a righteous work when wrought on such as he ; and if the murder were brought home to me, could I suffer in a better cause?

"Kate had risen slowly from her chair, and was now fronting me, scanning my face and bearing with curious eagerness. She held her hands across her bosom, alternately interlacing the tips of the fingers and pulling them free again. Her lips moved as if in speech, but no sound came from them.

"I got up presently, looking I daresay very solemn, as indeed I felt.   Her eyes followed mine as I rose ; and now we gazed straight at each other for some moments.

"'I promised you that you should be freed,' I said, 'and you shall be.   I shall be sorry to have any man's blood on my hands ; but if you can be saved in no other way, it must be so.'

"'You do love me, indeed!' she murmured, with a sort of sad exultation in her tone.   But she added : 'I cannot let you do it.   I cannot lose you, even to be freed from him.   It is my father's fault, after all.   Besides——'

"'I take it upon myself,' interrupted I, with a dignity which may have been absurd, but which did not seem so to me at the time.

"'But it would be murder—at any rate, the law would call it so.   No, you must not be called a murderer, Tom.   But I—they would not hang a woman : let me do it !   I should love to do it !'

"And she spoke with a look that confirmed the words.

"Before I could reply, however, her expression changed again.   She appeared to think intensely for a few moments, and then her face lighted up. Suddenly she caught my hand and kissed it !

"'And kiss me, Tom !' she cried, excitedly.   'Kiss

me, for I deserve it ! I have thought of a way that will save us all !'

"Much startled, and half fearing that the girl's mind had given way under the pressure of trouble, I was attempting to quiet her ; but she silenced me by an impetuous gesture, and went on speaking eagerly and rapidly.

"'To-morrow we had planned to go to Kohlstein for a picnic. It's a great, immense rock, where robbers lived hundreds of years ago. Hardly any-one ever goes there now. I have been there, and I remember that on the top it is full of deep clefts and holes ; and I thought how, if anyone were to fall into one, they might lie there for months without being found ; and they could never get out of them-selves. So now—listen ! We will go up there—you and I and—he ; and I will lead him near the brink of one of those clefts, and then you must rush forward and take him, and drop him down—down to the bottom ! So we shall get what we want, and yet there need be no murder.'

"'Not be murder, Kate ?'

"'It need not be ; for when he was safe down there, rather than be left to starve, he would give up those papers. Don't you think he would ?'

"She was trembling with excitement, and her state communicated itself in some degree to me, so that I was scarcely able to think coherently. But there certainly seemed to be plausibility in her scheme ; at the worst, it would be better than shooting the man outright. But would the recovery of the papers put an end to Slurk's persecution of Kate as well as of her father? Would not his power over her remain ?

"'But we can have him imprisoned then, you see,' was her answer to my objection ; 'and for fear of that, he would never dare to trouble me again. He would have been in prison long ago but for the papers.'

"'It certainly seems a good plan,' I said, after a confused attempt to turn the matter over in my mind. 'We'll ask your father's opinion to-morrow.'

"'Oh, he must know nothing of it!' she exclaimed, with a gesture of vehement dissent. 'He would betray it. You don't know how—what a power that villain has over him. Slurk treats him like a child when they are alone. No, Tom ; we must do it all ourselves, or it will fail. Only when it is done will dear papa get back his courage.'

"I knew more about how Mr. Birchmore was treated by his valet in private than Kate was aware ; but I made no allusion to this. The more I reflected upon the enterprise, the more inclined I was to assent to it. It was wild, fantastic, unconventional ; but it had important practical merits nevertheless. Moreover, it possessed the powerful recommendation (as I deemed it) of allowing for a fair man-to-man struggle between Slurk and myself. I was to overpower him by main strength; and from what I had observed of the fellow, I fancied he would be able to make resistance enough to save my self-respect. On the other hand, he might be able to do more than this; and if the worst came to the worst, of course I might be compelled to maim him with my revolver. But altogether, the prospect kindled my imagination; I was stimulated by the thought of distinguishing myself by my personal prowess before my mistress's eyes, in conflict with her dastardly oppressor. And as I looked at her standing there before me, so lovely and so full of courageous fire, I said to myself that no knight of yore ever did battle in the lists for a worthier lady-love!

"However, I realised that this was neither the place nor the hour to enter upon a detailed discussion of our plans. Every moment that Kate remained with me increased her peril, especially if, as she seemed to think was the case, Slurk had despatched her thither. As to his motive in so doing, I had no difficulty in forming an opinion. There was little doubt that he meant to use her as an unconscious cat's-paw to steal the diamonds, as, before, to purloin the papers compromising her father. Had I been asleep, the device could hardly have failed of success. But as Kate seemed herself not to suspect the real nature of her involuntary errand, I would not additionally distress her by alluding to it; it was enough that it furnished me with a sufficient pretext, had others been wanting, for inflicting chastisement on the valet.

"Kate said, in answer to my inquiry as to the proposed time of our starting on the picnic expedition the next day, that it would probably be about eleven in the forenoon; we would, therefore, have ample time to settle the particulars of our scheme before the hour of action arrived. At parting, she clung to me with peculiar tenderness; nor had I ever loved her so well as that moment, when I looked forward to liberating her for ever from the evil spell that had been blighting her young life.

"After she had gone, I had the curiosity to examine the bolt on the door. The explanation of its mysterious opening proved simple enough. The screws whereby the socket of the bolt had been fastened to the door-frame had been removed, and the holes so enlarged that they could be slipped in and out without difficulty. Socket and screws had then been replaced, so that the bolt could be shot as readily as before. But the security was only an illusion; for, the latch being turned, a slight push would bring away the socket and screws attached to the bolt ; and thus the supposed means of safety be ingeniously used to disguise the real absence thereof.

VIII.

"It occurred to me next morning that, considering the nature of the work that was cut out for me, it might be prudent to depart from my usual custom by leaving the diamonds at home in Christina's charge, as she had herself suggested ; and I took the earliest opportunity of mentioning this proposal to Kate. To my surprise she at once expressed a decided dissent from the arrangement, and indeed seemed so much perturbed by it, that I at once relinquished the idea. But I begged her to tell me the reasons of her objection.

"'Not now,' she said hastily; 'I hear papa coming ; wait till after breakfast, and then you shall know.'

"We were standing at the gate of the courtyard, breathing the fresh morning air. She left me, and returned to the house, whence Mr. Birchmore almost immediately issued, and saluted me with more than his usual cordiality. I wondered what his behaviour would have been had he known of the transactions of the past night, or of what was in store for us during the day! He began to talk about Kohlstein, and related several anecdotes of the bandits, by whom it was said formerly to have been inhabited. 'I have been up there more than once,' he remarked, 'and the traces of their occupation are still visible. I remember one feature that particularly impressed me—a narrow cleft or chasm of considerable depth, into which the old fellows are said to have thrown their prisoners when they became refractory.'

" 'Would the fall kill them?'

" 'I should say not; the bottom seemed full of chopped brushwood and other such rubbish. But no human being could have got out unaided; and probably a day or two's lonely sojourn there would bring the most resolute malcontent to terms. It would be a ghastly fate to fall in there, nowadays, and have one's skeleton fished out again the following year, perhaps, and a sensational paragraph in the newspapers. You young folks must pick your steps carefully to-day.'

" 'Forewarned is forearmed!' rejoined I, with a short laugh. Further conversation was cut short by a summons to breakfast. On this occasion Slurk waited at table, and I observed him with more than usual attention and toleration, as one with whom I was so soon to try desperate conclusions. He was certainly a villanous-looking character; but he appeared to be, for reasons best known to himself, in excellent spirits this morning; a circumstance which stirred up an unwilling kind of compassion within me, reflecting what a speedy and final end was going to be put to all his possibilities of enjoyment. Vile though his life had been, it was the only one he had.

"Kate likewise had the semblance of unusual gaiety, but I could see that it was either feigned, or the result of nervous excitement. And my judgment was justified when, after breakfast, she overtook me as I was on the way upstairs to my room to make my final preparations, and said, in a voice unsteady with emotion:

"'Tom dear, you asked me why you might not leave your diamonds with Christina. You do not know what danger you were in last night! On my way back to my room I heard—two people talking together, and they mentioned your name; so I stopped and listened. One said: "The bolt is all right: I had better go in and risk it; he'll be certain to be asleep by this time!" And then the other said: "He has his revolver; leave it to me; he believes he can trust me. To-morrow, when he goes out, I'll get him to leave them with me for safety!" and then they both laughed. My darling, this house is a den of thieves!'

"'Were the persons you heard—who were they?'

"'Christina, and that creature she calls her father. Hush! there she comes. She must not see us together;' and in a moment Kate had glided away. I went on up the stairs with a heavy heart. I would almost rather not have heard this last revelation; my confidence in my penetration had received a humiliating shock. To think that Christina's innocent face and modest maidenly air concealed the heart of a thief, or, worse still, of a decoy-duck, was a blow to my vanity as well as to my faith in human nature. How artful she had been, when I fancied her most ingenuous and kind! And then it all at once flashed upon me—what if Heinrich Rudolph himself were in the plot! what if he had written them to be on the look-out for me! and what if Slurk, being secretly in league with him, had contrived to get the Birchmores, and me along with them, into the house, intending to divide the spoil with Herr Rudolph and Christina! Many signs seemed to point to this as a true deduction from the circumstances; and even as I was rather grimly considering the matter, a new confirmation of Kate's discovery awaited me. Christina was standing at my room door, and, as I came up, she curtsied and said:

"'I was wishing to speak a moment to Herr Gainsborough, if he would permit me.'

"'What do you want?' I asked somewhat roughly.

"'Does the honoured Herr remember what I said yesterday——?'

"'That you wished me to give you my diamonds for safe keeping? Yes; and I have to answer, that I am not quite so trustful as you seem to think!'

"The scornful and severe tone in which I spoke evidently startled her; but she still affected not to understand. 'It was for Herr Gainsborough's own sake——' she began; but I interrupted her.

"'Do you remember what *I* said yesterday? that I went armed; well, I am armed to-day, and whoever tries to teach me how to take care of my diamonds may happen to get a bullet instead; so let him beware. If Herr Rudolph is anxious about me, you can tell him that!'

"'Herr Gainsborough will be sorry to have spoken so,' said Christina, colouring deeply, and with tremulous lip.

"'I am sorry to have to say it, Christina. But, can you tell me how the bolt of this door came to be in this condition?' and I pulled out the loose socket as I spoke, and the screws fell to the floor.

"'Indeed I did not know this!' exclaimed she; but the dismay and confusion which were but too plainly visible on her face belied her words.

"'You will understand, however, that a house whose fastenings are so much out of order would not be a proper place to keep treasures in. Well, good-bye, Christina. I am going to Kohlstein, and probably I shan't spend another night here. When you write to your brother in Paris, you may tell him that the diamonds are quite safe, though they may have been in danger.'

"'Will Herr Gainsborough let me say one word?'

"'It's too late—I have no time,' returned I, with an emphasis all the more coldly contemptuous because of the secret inclination I felt—in view of her youth and prettiness—to be compassionate and forgiving; and perhaps I was half sorry that she attempted no further self-vindication; but, obeying my gesture of dismissal, passed out of the door and down the passage, with her bare feet, and her blue eyes downcast, and no backward glance. When she was gone, I shut the door in no enviable mood, and walked to and fro about my room like a surly bull in a pound. For the first (though not for the last) time I heartily cursed the diamonds; they seemed to raise the devil wherever I carried them. In the midst of my anathemas Mr. Birchmore knocked at the door, and told me that everything was ready downstairs for the start.

"'And, by-the-bye, Gainsborough,' he added, with one of his point-blank, icy glances, 'I have arranged that our luggage shall be removed to-day; and if you leave yours here, I advise you to seal it up in my presence. I found the lock of my door in rather a strange condition this morning. I have my own opinion of what our landlord may be.'

"'Who recommended you to this place, Mr. Birchmore?' I demanded curtly; for I was getting to feel something like contempt for my intended father-in-law. It was not easy to respect a man who, under whatever stress of circumstances, allows another man to make a slave of him.

"'It was that fellow Slurk; and he deserves a good horsewhipping for it!' replied Birchmore, thrusting his hands resolutely into his pockets.

"'I think he deserves at least that,' I rejoined with a significant laugh; 'and whenever you're inclined to operate on him, I'll stand by you.'

"Mr. Birchmore said no more, and we went downstairs in silence. Kate was already seated in the carriage; Slurk was on the box, with a large basket containing our provisions for the day beside him. Mr. Birchmore and I took our places—one of us at least with a heavy heart. The landlord stood at the door and nodded us a surly farewell.

"'Where is Christina?' I asked him.

"'She has gone to the town to sell eggs: did the Herr want anything?'

" 'I should like to have sent for a screwdriver; but probably I can get one on our way back,' was my answer ; and with that we drove away.

"In about half an hour, proceeding by unfrequented roads, we came in sight of Kohlstein. It was a vast four-sided mass of gray rock, seamed with deep clefts and fissures running horizontally and vertically, so that it appeared to have been built of gigantic blocks of stone. It was considerably over one hundred feet in sheer height, and it stood upon a rising ground of shifting sand. Slender trees grew here and there out of the crevices of its headlong sides, and straggled nakedly along its level summit, outlined against the sky. It was an ideal place for a robber stronghold ; impregnable, certainly, to any attack save that of the heaviest modern artillery.

" 'We must get out and walk from here,' remarked Mr. Birchmore. 'There's only one way of getting to the top, and that's on the other side. I have got a touch of my rheumatics to-day, and hardly think I shall be able to do the climbing. However, that needn't interfere with you young people, of course.'

" I exchanged a covert look with Kate as I helped her to descend from the carriage ; and she pressed my hand and smiled. I admired her courage as much as I lamented the apparent lack of it in her father. The horse having been unharnessed and tethered where some cool grass grew beside a stream, we struck off across the sandy upland; Slurk carrying the big basket, Mr. Birchmore walking with a rather feeble step near him, and Kate and I in front. It was an even hotter day than yesterday, and the tramp was a wearisome one. By the time we arrived at the foot of the Stein, we were quite ready to rest a few minutes in the shadow of the rock, for coolness and breath.

"'No, I can't do it!' said Mr. Birchmore, wiping his forehead and glancing hopelessly up at the narrow white footpath that seemed to mount almost straight upward to the distant summit. 'Just leave me here, with a few sandwiches and a bottle of hock, and I shall do very comfortably till you come back.'

"It was certainly very arduous work clambering up that ladder-like path, and I doubt whether Kate's determination and mine would have held out, had the motive which urged us been merely one of curiosity. But the top was gained at last, and we threw ourselves down on the dry grass to rest and to be fanned by the welcome breeze that blew there. Slurk placed the basket in a little hollow where some bushes kept off the direct rays of the sun, and stretched himself at full length beside it.

"'Now, let us walk about,' suggested Kate at

length in an undertone ; 'we must see what there is
to be seen.'

"We had already arranged all the steps by which
we were to proceed to the achievement of our purpose,
and we felt that the sooner it was ended now the
better.   The surface on which we stood, though preserving a general level, was full of irregularities and
unevennesses ; it was overgrown with low bushes and
parched grass, with perhaps half-a-dozen starved and
meagre trees.   Here and there the naked rock jutted
forth from the thin soil, crumbling and weatherworn,
its surface stained in places with dry lichens.   The
entire table was scarcely two-thirds of an acre in area ;
and a more forlorn and uncongenial spot, even in the
midst of summer, it would be hard to find.   The cave
in which the robbers lived was somewhere lower
down ; we had passed its entrance on our way up ;
but it was here, probably, that an outlook was kept
over the country, to spy out the approach of victims
or of enemies.   It struck me that it was hardly worth
while to be a bandit, if one must put up with such
bleak and unattractive quarters in which to carry on
the business.

"Kate and I wandered over this barren summit
hand in hand.   The moment was now very near that
was to make a great change in the world for both of
us.   We felt, somehow, as if we were taking leave of

a certain part of our lives then. At least, I remember gazing out across the wide expanse of sunlit country that stretched far away on every side, and wondering whether it would look the same an hour hence. Slurk all the while lay beside his basket, and appeared to be asleep.

"We came to the brow of a sort of shelf or shallow declivity, descending which we found ourselves on a lower level by some six or seven feet; and so much of the area as lay behind us ceased to be visible. Advancing a few paces farther, we paused abruptly on the edge of a dark, profound cleft, which gaped right at our feet. It was so narrow that one might easily leap across it at its widest part; but it was so deep that, for all that I could see, it might descend to the very base of the Stein. Peering downwards earnestly, however, my eyes, becoming accustomed to the gloom, could dimly discern what seemed to be a bottom at a depth of not more than twenty feet.

"'It's an awful thing to do, after all!' I murmured after a long inspection, looking up at Kate.

"'Are you ready?' was all her answer.

"'Yes,' said I, shamed by her resolution. 'Let him come.'

"She mounted the little ridge, and stood with her graceful figure silhouetted against the blue heavens.

I, below, turned up the cuffs of my sleeves and buttoned my coat across my chest.

"'Slurk!' called she, in a clear penetrating tone, 'bring the basket here, if you please. We mean to take our luncheon on this side.'

"She remained standing there, with her back towards me. From my lower position I could not see whether Slurk were answering her summons with alacrity or not; but since it would be his last opportunity of obeying her orders, I was content to let him take his time. By-and-by he appeared, with the basket on his arm; he descended the ledge, and Kate followed him, with her eyes on me.

"'Set it down there, near the edge of this pit; not quite so near, please. Now take hold of him!'

"The last words were spoken in a sharp, ringing tone; and at the same moment the girl drew a long knife from beneath the overskirt of her dress, and stood with it in her hand. Surprised at her action, I hesitated half an instant; in that half-instant Slurk had thrown himself towards me and grasped me round the body with his long powerful arms. Almost simultaneously with his attack, I felt myself borne down by a heavy weight from behind, and my arms pinioned. The struggle for a minute or two was tremendous, but I felt that I was overpowered. A hand was pressing hard against my windpipe. Kate stood there with her knife, a new and strange expression on her face ; but she did not stir.

"At length a panting voice close to my ear—a voice which I knew well, and which, heard now, so amazed me that I almost ceased to resist—said :

"'I've got him safe here, Captain ; have you got his legs ? '

"A grunt from Slurk intimated that he had.

"'Now then, Kittie,' continued Mr. Birchmore ; 'be quick there, will you ?'

"Kate came towards me with her knife. At that sight I uttered a yell of animal rage, and made one more desperate effort to be free.

"'Hold him tight, can't you ?' said Kate, in a voice that I scarcely recognised as hers ; 'I don't want to hurt him.'

"They mastered me ; and then, with a rapidity and deftness that showed the practised professional, Kate made a circular cut through the breast of my coat and drew out the diamonds.

"'That's all right,' remarked Birchmore. 'Now the rope !'

"She went to the basket, and took from it a coil of fine rope. The two men threw me upon my face, and bound my arms and my feet securely. I made little resistance, but submitted in sullen silence.

"'Don't forget his revolver,' said Birchmore,

when this was done ; and turning me over, they took
the weapon from my pocket.

"'How do you feel now, young gentleman?'
inquired the fellow, addressing me with a smile.
'This is the result of plotting to throw unfortunate
valets into deep pits, and of flirting with strange
young women. I warned you, you remember, to
keep out of our way ; but idle curiosity has been
your ruin. Kittie, put on the diamonds; he says
they become you!'

"Slurk grinned at this sally, but the girl said
moodily : 'Don't bother the boy, Jack; he behaved
like a gentleman all through; he'd make a great
deal better husband than you do ! Heigho!'

"'Well, Captain,' continued Birchmore, addressing
Slurk in English, 'what are your orders? Shall we
lower away now, and be off? It's nearly half-past
one, and we've a good distance to go before three.'

"'Listen to me, Mr. Gainsborough,' said Slurk,
also speaking in English, though with a foreign
accent ; 'we've got what we wanted out of you, and
we don't want to do you any more harm than is
necessary. But we must have time to get safe away,
and to do that we must allow twenty-four hours.
We shall leave you at the bottom of this pit, with
some provisions ; and I shall loosen your arms enough
so that you can feed yourself. After we are safe,

I shall write to your friends at the farmhouse, who are very honest persons I believe, and they will come here and get you out. That is the best we can do for you. Now then, Jack!'

"They loosed the cord a little round my arms; then, taking it by the slack end, they lowered me into that dark chasm until I rested at the bottom. Then I saw Kate's face above the edge, between me and the sky, with something wrapped up in paper in her hand.

"'Here's some sandwiches for you, my poor boy,' said she. 'I'm sorry to say good-bye to you in this way, really! But I don't suppose you'd have me now, even if Jack weren't my husband already. Well, good-bye. Don't flirt too much with that silly little Christina when you get out. There are the sandwiches.'

"She let them fall beside me, nodded, and was gone. I lay on my back, with nothing to look at but the narrow strip of blue sky overhead. It was quite cool where I lay, on a bed of sand and rubbish; and it was still as death. I was buried alive to all intents and purposes, and the chance of my ever being disinterred rested upon a basis of probability so narrow, that I judged it wisest not to hope. I lay there, gazing up at the sky, and thinking over my adventure; beginning at the beginning, with my meeting with Birchmore at the hotel, and tracing the progress of the conspiracy step by step to its conclusion here. It was very ingenious, and very well carried through. It had taught me a lesson that I was likely to profit by, if I ever got out.

"I don't know how long I lay there; probably but a short time. All at once another face intervened between me and the sky. It was not Kate's this time; it was a very different one—Christina's.

"After peering anxiously downward for several moments, she asked:

"'Is Herr Gainsborough there?'

"'Yes.'

"'The Herr is not badly hurt?'

"'Not a bit, Christina!'

"'Gott sei Dank!' she exclaimed, heartily; and adding: 'it is all well; you will be helped out immediately,' she vanished.

"Soon other faces appeared, with beards and helmets—the faces of the 'Polizei.' In a few minutes, by the aid of ropes and stout arms, I was drawn up once more to the light of day, blinking like an awkward bat.

"Before me stood nearly a dozen persons: a squad of police-officers, with their swords and carbines; Herr Rudolph and Christina; and three prisoners—a woman and two men, whose faces were unpleasantly familiar to me.

"Some little official ceremony of identification, and so forth, having been gone through with, we all started for our various places of destination. The trial took place not long afterwards in Dresden; the prisoners were all convicted, and sentenced to ——I don't care to remember what. They were a dangerous gang of thieves, whom the police of several countries had long been vainly endeavouring to capture. But meanwhile, I went back to spend the night at the farmhouse of Herr Rudolph. I need not say that I scarcely had the courage to look him and his daughter in the face. Herr Rudolph was a most excellent and blameless person; and as for Christina——! I knew not in what terms to begin my apologies to her.

"It appeared that my little friend Heinrich, in Paris, had had his suspicions of the man calling himself Birchmore from the first, and, in writing to his father and sister, had mentioned as much. When, therefore, the Birchmore party unexpectedly turned up at the farmhouse, along with the owner of the diamonds, a good deal of perturbation was created. Afraid openly to warn me, in the absence of direct evidence, Christina had done what she could indirectly to excite suspicions in my mind. Failing in this, the girl had actually gone down to Schandau, on the evening of my interview with Kate in my

chamber, and laid her information at the police
bureau. The next morning she met the officers by
appointment at some distance from the house, and
they followed us to Kohlstein. After seeing the
whole party of us to the top of the Stein (Birchmore
followed a few minutes after myself and the others),
they formed a cordon at the foot of the path, and one
of their number went up to reconnoitre. Peeping
over the edge of the plateau, he saw Birchmore just
making his attack, and immediately signalled to
those below to approach. Thus it happened that the
thieves, as they were making off with their plunder,
found themselves confronted by an impassable cordon
of six loaded carbines. Resistance was out of the
question, and they surrendered at discretion.

"'And what can I do, Christina,' I said, 'to show
you how much I thank you? Of course I don't speak
of cancelling the obligation—that nothing could do ;
but I should like to leave you something to—to
remind you that you saved my life and my diamonds.
Would you wear a diamond ring for me, or a pair
of earrings ?'

"'No, many thanks, Herr Gainsborough,' replied
the little maiden, gravely. 'You owe me nothing ;
and as for diamonds, I shall never like them, since I
have seen them the cause of so much trouble and
danger.'

"'But unless you let me do something, Christina, I must think you refuse to forgive me for my inexcusable impertinence and stupidity.'

"She looked down at her bare feet, and smoothed her apron. 'Well, lieber Herr, I would not like to have you think that, truly; I do forgive you with all my heart; and just before you go away to-morrow —just when you are ready to start—perhaps, if you please, I will ask you for something.'

"'You shall have it, whatever it is!' I answered.

"So, the next day, when the droschkey was at the door, and my trunk packed and put on the box, I left Herr Rudolph conversing with the driver, and went back into the house to find Christina. She was standing in a shadowy corner of the kitchen, so absorbed in scouring plates that she did not appear to notice me until I spoke.

"'I am come to say good-bye, and to claim your promise, Christina.'

"She put down her plate, and blushed, with downcast eyes.

"'Herr Gainsborough will not be offended? it is something I have no right to ask—only—it will show I am not unforgiving—and—it would be better for me than the diamonds.'

"'What is it, dear Christina?'

U

"She looked up in my face, shyly and yet frankly, and said:

"'Kiss me!'"

IX.

This (as nearly as I can recollect it) is the story told me by my friend Tom Gainsborough, as we sat over a decanter of claret after one of his inimitable little dinners. When it was over I gave a grunt, and flung the but-end of my cigar into the grate.

"There's one thing I don't understand about this story," I then remarked; "and it has misled me all along. Your description of that creature, Kate —her eyes and eyebrows, complexion, hands, and nationality—all persuaded me it was the present Mrs. Gainsborough. Yet it appears she was nothing of the sort!"

"I should think not, indeed!" exclaimed Tom, laughing. "They are as different, even in appearance, as two straight-browed brunettes could possibly be. It is not my fault if you were misled by a description —you who know so well how incurably vague the best descriptions are. Were you to see them side by side, you would acknowledge that they are as little alike as you and I are. As to the American part of it—the truth is they were not really Americans at all: Birchmore and the girl were French; and I in my ignorance mistook their French accent for the Yankee twang. When, several years later, I met some real Americans—and married one of them—I realised my error."

"Humph! Well, I daresay you were not more stupid than the majority of your countrymen would have been in your place. But another thing—was all that mesmeric business genuine, or a part of the conspiracy?"

"Conspiracy, of course! It was the stock expedient of the gang—and a very ingenious one, I think; for of course the mesmerised one might turn up anywhere, and if she were not discovered, well and good; while if she were, all she had to say was that she was in a mesmeric trance. As it happened, the latter alternative occurred in both their attempts on me; but I give the girl credit for turning it off excellently well. In fact, she took a real artistic interest in her business. You see, she had been trained as a rope-dancer in her childhood, and afterwards she was on the stage for a time. She certainly had marvellous dramatic talent, and thoroughly enjoyed "taking a part." The realistic element that entered into her performances no doubt rendered them much more exciting than ordinary stage work, and perhaps, sometimes, she almost deceived herself."

"Ah! I should not wonder. Well, and what was

the meaning of that confusion about the steamboat and the train, and Birchmore's explanations?"

"A mistake on their part—that's all. Accidents will happen, you know. I daresay my unexpected questions disconcerted them greatly; but I was unsuspicious enough, Heaven knows. What I admire as much as anything in their management of the affair was the skill with which they made me believe, from the outset, that I was forcing my company upon *them*, when in reality it was they who were leading me round by the nose."

"Missus Gainsborough say de tea ready, sah!" said the sable servitor, opening the door.

"Let's go up at once!" I exclaimed, rising from chair. "I shall hereafter feel a new interest in looking at Mrs. Gainsborough's diamonds!"

THE CHRISTMAS GUEST.

THE CHRISTMAS GUEST:

A MYTH.

THEY were ideal young people, and lived in a fairy farmhouse, in the Eldorado of lovers. Everything went happily with them; no troublesome grown-up people thwarted or annoyed them; they could be together as much as they liked, and had never in their whole lives heard of such a thing as impropriety. They had no enemies, nor so much as a single friend with conscientious ideas of duty. In spite of all this they were remarkably content with each other and with the world at large, and never did any wrong, to speak of, from week's end to week's end. For the rest, they had lived and played together ever since they could remember, had never quarrelled except to provide a pretext for a reconciliation; and she had always called him Eros, and he had always called her Psyche. They loved each other with all their hearts, and were a living refutation of the folly of those who would persuade us that pain and struggle are the necessary discipline of human beings. To see these two was enough to make one believe in the feasibility of setting up a new Garden of Eden on a durable basis.

‘ Notwithstanding their fanciful nicknames, and exceptional surroundings and circumstances, Psyche and Eros were as thoroughly human in their thoughts and emotions as if they had lived in the most commonplace of country villages, and, although they had always been together, their temperaments were as wide asunder as the poles. Psyche was imaginative, dreamy, and sensitive to both mental and physical impressions; her gentle brown eyes would fill with tears at the lightest touch of pity or pathos, and the delicate bloom in her cheeks would fade and her girlish figure droop after but an hour's illness. Yet she was entirely wholesome and healthy both in mind and body, and though her voice was low and soft, and her manner tender and appealing, she had a strength and courage in the cause of right and truth such as a son of Anak might have envied. Eros, on the other hand, took practical views of life, and prided himself upon his solid common sense. Being now on the verge of his twenty-first birthday, he affected a manly and dogmatic tone, as of one who knew the world, and had arrived at the maturity of his judgment. He was a red-cheeked, fair-haired, blue-eyed youth; sturdy, vigorous, and jocund. Psyche loved him devotedly, and took every occasion to persuade herself that he was the wisest as well as the dearest of mankind. But she could not help suspecting sometimes that he was not always quite amenable to reason, and would feel very guilty when the conviction was occasionally forced upon her that she had taken a higher view of this or that question than he had. On the whole, however, she continued to maintain the sense of her own inferiority unimpaired, and the more inferior she felt the better was she pleased.

Now it so happened that Eros would come of age on Christmas Day; and as if the falling together of these two celebrations were not enough, it had been decided to enhance their joyfulness by the addition of a third—which was to be neither more nor less than the young people's wedding! Here, surely, was bliss enough to be crowded into one short twenty-four hours; and moreover, as Psyche observed, looking into her lover's blue eyes with the frank shyness of her own brown ones, "What Christmas present could we make to each other so appropriate as the surrender of ourselves into each other's keeping?"

Yes, this was bliss enough even for ideal young people who lived in a fairy farmhouse in the Eldorado of lovers. .Nevertheless—if it will be believed—even this was not all! A fourth cause of rejoicing, and one to which Eros and Psyche looked forward with scarcely less delight than to their own near union, was the promised advent of an old and intimate friend of theirs, from whom they had been separated many years, but whom they had never forgotten, or ceased to reverence and love. He had been a young man when they were children, and they had looked upon him then, and did now, as a dear elder brother. He had been their confidant and adviser, the un-weariable promoter and companion of their childish merrymakings; a teller of splendid stories, a man ardent, gay, sweet-tempered, wise. They had adored him as only children can adore such a friend; all his sayings were to them oracular, and all his doings superhuman. They fancied—with cause or without, it matters not—that but for him they would not even have loved each other as they did. He had brought out the best that was in them, and inspired that best to become better. He had shown Psyche the man-liness that was in Eros, and had opened the eyes of Eros to the rare loveliness of Psyche. What did they not owe to him? And since he went away he had become transfigured in their memories.

Nine years had he been absent, a missionary among the heathen. But he had also travelled much in civilised lands, and had seen all manner of men and customs. Meantime he had written scores of delightful letters to the young friends who loved him —letters which they read and re-read scores of times, and thought more wonderful than his best stories in the old days. Throughout this long period he had never given up the purpose of seeing them again, and, if possible, to part no more. But still the intended meeting had been put off; for Mortimer—such was his name—had so much work to do in illuminating darkened souls, as to leave but a distant hope of ever being able to indulge his own personal desires. At length, however, the much-wished-for opportunity had presented itself, and Mortimer was really coming. A few days before Christmas the young people received a letter from him, telling the great news. This letter was addressed to Psyche, who, as was her right, insisted upon having it all to herself, and would not allow Eros to lay a finger on it. She indeed vouchsafed to read it aloud to him, but tantalised him by pretending to reserve certain passages to herself; because, as she archly averred, they contained secrets for her private ear. Eros, as her future lord and master, was half disposed to take umbrage at this exclusion, and, had the letter been from any other being in the wide world except Mortimer, there is no saying whether he might not

actually have been jealous! But since he was de-
barred from jealousy, he solaced his discomfiture by
putting on an air of complacent indifference, stroking
his eyebrows with his forefinger, and twisting the
ends of an almost imperceptible moustache. Psyche
saw through his pretences, and knew that he was
annoyed, and she hated to annoy him. Why, then,
did she not hand him over the letter?

"I am on the point of setting sail," the letter ran,
"and probably shall arrive soon after you receive
this. At all events, I am resolved to be with you on
Christmas Eve—your marriage eve! Death alone
can forestall me in that pleasure. I have said good-
bye to my barbarians, who were very sorry to lose
me, and fear that I shall never return to them. But
I will; and I mean to bring you two—or you one, as
you will be by that time—with me. Yes, my good
old people; for though your home is Eldorado, mine
is Paradise! Never was so beautiful a country—so
tender and serene a climate; such gentle-hearted
and Christian barbarians! It is a real Paradise,
large enough and lovely enough to tempt all good
souls to migrate thither; and I come forth into the
world to find colonists, and bring them back with
me. You will come, Psyche? and then I shall make
sure that Eros will follow you, sooner or later!

"And so you are waiting for me to marry you?

Well, I believe you are meant for each other, and I will do what I may to render your union sacred and perpetual. Not that I think mere earthly union is always the highest good for those who love. You know the old proverb; and there are lovers whose hearts never quite realise one another's worth until separation has taught it them. Do you love your old friend, who used to go nutting, boating, snow-balling, and story-telling with you, any the less because you haven't seen him for nine years? And would not you, Eros, love Psyche a thousand times better were some chance to part you from her awhile? You have never had her out of your sight, except when your eyes were shut, and you don't half know how dear she is to you. It would do you good were I to take her with me to my Paradise, and leave you behind. Until you know what it is to be alone, and to see what you most want beyond your immediate reach, you do not know everything. But perhaps you will be content not to know?"

All this, and much more, did Psyche read to Eros. But at the end of the letter there was a post-script, having glanced at which she looked up towards her lover with a sudden apprehension in her eyes. His own happened to be averted; and after an instant's hesitation, she folded up the letter and said, "The rest is a secret!"

"All right !" returned Eros, yawning, and getting up ; "no woman can be entirely happy without a secret. Every man knows that ; so I'll make you a Christmas present of this one." And with that he sauntered off, his hands in his pockets.

When he was gone. Psyche unfolded the letter and read the postscript again.

"I sail to-morrow," it said, "and am glad of it on more accounts than one. It is a long overland journey from my home to this port, and I did not know until I got here that a strange and fatal epidemic is wont to make its appearance in the town about this time of year. During the last few days it has broken out with great virulence, and people are dying all around me. It kills in a few hours, and gives no warning, save a passing chill. Well, I have no fears ; I have passed unharmed through a hundred pestilences. Still, if I should fail to sit by your fireside next Christmas Eve, do not blame my will."

" Dear old Mort !" Psyche murmured, tears standing in her eyes. "What if he had died, just as he was on his way to meet us after all these years ! I won't tell Eros ; no, not even if it makes him angry. It's better he should be angry than anxious. If anyone is to be anxious, let me be so. Only if Mort doesn't come on Christmas Eve, then

Eros must know. But he will come, I know; and we shall all be happy."

It lacked scarcely three days to Christmas, and the house had to be arranged and decorated for the festivities. It was a house of a thousand to hold merrymakings in, and seemed really to take a genial interest in the preparations that were going forward, and to give it all the assistance that was in its power. Gray and weatherbeaten without, within it was warm and home-like. Square oaken beams divided the low ceilings of the rambling rooms; the deep fireplaces were dusky with the smoke of ten thousand fires; the mellow old kitchen was a world in itself; and the shadowy bed-chambers, with their great four-post bedsteads, were just the place to play hide-and-seek in with ghosts and goblins. Moreover, the best of feelings prevailed between the venerable mansion and the natural and elemental surroundings amidst which it had so long existed. The forest grouped itself artistically in the background; the hillside sloped lovingly towards it on the right; at a little distance, a clear-eyed pond smiled placid goodwill. And the rough spirits of Wind and Rain, Snow and Frost, seemed to grow soft and tractable in their sports with this time-honoured structure. "Merry Christmas!" they whispered, wept, and glistened; and the house glowed back a hearty response out of its diamond-paned lattices, and its clustered chimney breathed forth smoky satisfaction.

Meanwhile Eros and Psyche laboured with all their hearts and hands, and made the rooms green with ivy, holly, and laurel. In the parlour, beneath the cluster of mistletoe that hung from the ceiling, was arranged a little platform, with a daïs, and an altar-table covered with white samite. It was here that the marriage ceremony was to take place. By mid-day of Christmas Eve all the preparations were complete, and the two lovers were sitting together in the deep bay-window, half hidden by the ample curtains, and head-over-ears in lovers' talk. They were big with the charming self-importance that belongs to young people in their condition. Love burned for them ˙in the centre of all things—it illumined, warmed, and perfumed the whole world. For them the great earth turned more smoothly on her axis, and moved in a fairer orbit ; the setting sun sank splendidly amidst his clouds for their sake ; for their delight yonder rosy-cheeked boy ploughed his whistling way through the snow, and the sleigh-bells jingled so merrily from the distant road. If only Mortimer were there, their happiness would be complete. And now he must arrive every moment, so Eros kept saying, looking out of the window with confident expectation ; but Psyche scarcely replied.

Her soft little hands were cold and tremulous, and the corners of her sweet lips drooped as she thought of the secret that harboured in her breast. It was the first secret she had ever kept from Eros. Oh that it might resolve itself happily, and not—not as she now began to dread! For evening was coming on apace, and their friend had not yet come. He did not come, though he had promised that Death only should forestall him. As minute after minute slipped by, Psyche felt an almost irresistible impulse to snatch forth the letter from her bosom, where she had hidden it, and give it to her lover, that he might share and perhaps cheer her suspense. But she forebore; she was strong enough to suffer alone, and she felt, though hardly admitting it even to herself, that Eros was not so strong in that kind of strength as she. He would laugh at a blow from a fist such as would knock her senseless, but the blows of mental pain and disappointment he was but ill-fitted to endure. Thus thinking, the gentle Psyche crushed her trouble down, and even strove to forget it, or believe it unfounded and imaginary, if so she might answer her lover cheerfully, and in no way cast a shadow upon his Christmas Eve. But still that strange coldness crept at intervals through her veins, making her hands and her voice vibrate.

x

"Why, it's quite dark already!" exclaimed Eros at length. "Surely the man means to be here by supper-time? I wonder how near he is now."

"There may have been a delay. The snow is very deep, you know, in some places. Perhaps he won't find it possible to get here before to-morrow."

"Pooh! my dear little Psyche. You have forgotten the kind of man that our Mort is. When he says he'll do a thing, he does it—if he's alive. And in that very letter of yours, which you make such a mystery about, but which I know perfectly well has nothing in it more than you read to me—he says in that very letter that only Death would stand in the way of his getting here to-night. And since he's a man in perfect health and in the prime of life, I don't see what doubt there can be that he'll keep his word. Only I do wish he'd told us the very hour, so that we mightn't have had this suspense to bother us."

"Do you suppose we shall recognise his face when he comes?" asked Psyche, after a little pause.

"Recognise him? Of course we shall!" returned Eros, positively, as became his masculine superiority. "He'll be considerably changed, to be sure; very likely he'll have a big black beard, and there'll be a few lines across his forehead and round his eyes; but you mustn't mind that. That sort of thing is bound to come on a man as he grows old. I'm beginning to find that out myself; and Mort—why he's nearly forty by this time!"

"How very wise he will be!" murmured Psyche, thoughtfully. "He was the wisest person in the world before he went away; we shall be almost afraid of him now."

"Well, as to that," said Eros, rubbing his downy upper lip and smiling, "as to that, my dear Psyche, you must speak for yourself. Undoubtedly Mort, the dear old fellow, has an immense deal of information, and plenty of good sense to back it— which is more than always happens, I can assure you. But when a man reaches his majority, and is on the point of becoming a family man into the bargain —give me another, dear——what was I going to say? Oh, well, I don't think *I* shall be much afraid of him, or of anybody else, that's all."

"Eros," whispered Psyche, feeling his strong young arm round her, and his hand on hers, "should you be willing to have him take us back with him to his Paradise, as he speaks of doing in the letter?"

"Well, my dear, that must depend a great deal

upon circumstances. I shall talk with Mort, and see what he has to say about his place. We mustn't forget that we're very well situated as we are, and ought not to move unless we're certain of bettering ourselves. The sort of society he speaks of might not suit us, you know; we're not missionaries, and don't care about barbarians as such. Mort, wise as he is, hasn't much practical sense in some ways; not so much as—some men I know. He's all for the loftiest and most ideal thing possible, without reflecting whether or not it's inconvenient or uncomfortable too. In short, unless his Paradise turns out to be a finer place than I think it will, I shall feel inclined to keep hold on what we have. Besides, Psyche, any place that you are in will be Paradise to me."

This compliment fairly merited the reward which Eros immediately claimed and took for it, and which, by its potent effect upon both giver and receiver, made speech seem impertinent for a time. Psyche sat gazing out across the darkened snow with her tender brown eyes, and Eros looked fondly on her, thinking that he loved her more than anything in the world, and that life would be a blank without her. Surely, were she to be taken from him, all his light and warmth would depart along with her. That passage in Mortimer's letter which suggested that it might be well sometimes for lovers to be parted had received his unqualified, though unuttered, disapproval. Why should such a thing have been written? Often, since Psyche had read it to him, Eros had resolved to dismiss the idea from his mind; but such is the perversity of human minds that the idea remained in spite of him. It made him feel now and then really almost uneasy. The feeling, of course, was a morbid one; common sense and wholesome reason forbade him to entertain it. Had he no more confidence in Providence than to believe that it would take his Psyche from him—his Psyche, who had grown up with him from infancy? Would the good God be so cruel as to deprive him—and at this moment of all others—of the companionship of her whom he so loved? But the misgiving was unworthy of him. If he could not forget it, why then he would face it, and face it down.

He bent towards Psyche, and discovered, by some method known to lovers, that her eyes were wet with tears. When Love is in supreme command, the soul is more tenderly alive to various influences, and hence more prone to sadness of a certain kind, than at any other epoch of life. But Eros had never understood Psyche's constitutional tendency to melancholy, and just now he found it especially inopportune.

"What makes you unhappy?" he exclaimed. "Aren't we together, and haven't we everything we want? And ought not this evening to be the most joyful we ever yet spent?"

She leaned her head on his shoulder, hiding a sigh. "I was wondering, dear," she said, "whether, when we go to the real Paradise, we shall meet and know each other there as we do now. Do you believe we shall?"

There were few problems too profound for the plummet of Eros's common sense to sound them. "Certainly we shall, my dear!" he answered emphatically. "What put such a question into your head?"

"But shall you love me then? And shall I be your own wife there, Eros, as I am to be here?"

"I really don't see the use, my dear little Psyche, of bothering our heads with such gratuitous puzzles as that. There's quite enough to attend to in this life, without trying to guess what may happen to us in the next. For my part, it's enough to know that we love each other in the body, and are to be husband and wife here in this farmhouse. There'll be time enough to speculate about other states when we are in them."

"Ah! but, Eros," said she, lifting her gentle face

from his shoulder and looking in his eyes, "suppose that I were to die to-night—this very night, before our wedding! Could you be content to wait—could you rest satisfied with the love that we have already loved in this world, and with the knowledge that I was still loving you in Paradise, and would be yours when you came there?"

Eros felt an impulse of impatience, which he repressed so far as not to give it words; but he turned his face away. Those theories of delicate tissue and transcendental application, which Psyche was given to entertaining, irritated and silenced him. He loved Psyche, as an honest man should love a woman— better than any other man ever loved a woman, he thought; and what more could be expected of him? Besides, was it not being ungrateful for the blessings in their possession to be borrowing trouble from an improbable or unimaginable condition of things to come? It was really too bad, thought Eros, and he turned his face away and looked down the avenue, leaving Psyche unanswered.

It would have been quite dark now but for the whiteness of the snow. The wind was rising, and the window-seat was getting chilly, and Psyche's hand, which still lay in his own, was cold as ice, and she herself seemed to shiver. The blinds must be closed, and they would go back to the fire, for Mortimer might not come till midnight, for all they knew. Stay!—what was that shadow moving this way up the avenue? Was it——

"Psyche! Psyche! look!" cried Eros, starting to his feet in joyous excitement. "That must be—isn't it? Yes, it must be Mortimer—it is our dear old Mort!"

"Oh Eros, I believe it is!" she answered, peering tremulously through the darkness. "I can't see clearly; I had a vision of Death—that Death was coming instead of him!"

"Death, indeed!" exclaimed Eros, with a laugh. "Let this be a lesson to you, my dear, not to indulge in silly fancies again. But come on! We must receive the dear fellow at the door."

He ran into the hall, Psyche following, and flung wide the heavy portal. A gust of icy wind burst in, as though it had been lying in wait for them on the threshold; and Psyche seemed to shrink away before it, and Eros himself could scarce repress a shiver. But they pressed forward again, and gazed out earnestly on the night. Yes, there could be no doubt about it now. There came their friend—he who was most honoured and trusted by them both, yet who, for nearly half their lives, had been a stranger to them—there he came, striding swiftly towards them across the snow. Only a dark, lofty shape he seemed ; but the step, the bearing, were unmistakable; they were Mortimer's own. By a simultaneous impulse the two young lovers threw one arm round each other, and extended the other to the advancing form. They could not cry out in welcome. Was it their great joy that silenced them? for joy will sometimes bind the faculties like awe. It was very dark, and neither had remembered to bring a light. Almost before they were aware of it their strange friend was standing close in front of them. How icy cold was the wind!

In moments of high feeling and excitement we do and say things as in a dream, and afterwards hardly remember how we acted. So was it now with Eros and Psyche. Did Mortimer take Eros's hand in a grasp as soft and cold as snow? Did he kiss Psyche's forehead with lips that sent a happy shudder to her heart? Did he speak to them in mellow, loving tones that sounded at once strange and familiar? And did they answer him? Or was it all a dream? Be that as it may, the spell soon passed off, and they found themselves in clear possession of their several senses once more. The long-expected guest had crossed their threshold, thrown aside his heavy cloak, and removed the soft fur cap from his black hair, and, Eros leading the

way, the three friends had entered the warm, firelit
parlour.

"Sit down, all of us!" cried the host, rubbing
his hands together. "Draw up to the fire, and get
warm, if you can. My stars, what a night! Psyche,
you look as if you'd been kissed by an icicle; and
you, Mort, you are as cold as death!"

They sat down round the broad hearth, the guest
between the lovers; and as the firelight flickered over
them, so flickered and fell and rose again their conversation. It often happens that, when we anticipate
saying most, we find the least to say; and somewhat thus did it fall out in the present instance: or,
perhaps, because in a meeting like this, however
thoroughly foreshadowed and anticipated, there is
apt to be a good deal of strangeness and unexpected
diffidence to be overcome,—perhaps it was for this
reason that speech flowed but intermittently for
a while. Nevertheless, the lovers could feel that they
were every moment growing more and more into
sympathy and understanding with their new old
friend, and doing so even more speedily and completely than might have been possible through the
uncertain medium of words. He diffused around
him, without effort, and apparently without being
conscious of it, a gentle and winning influence which
was fairly irresistible; so that by-and-by Psyche and

Eros fancied that never before had they known him so well as now. At the same time, however, Psyche was inwardly aware of a great, yet indescribable, change from that Mortimer who had bidden her farewell nine years before. The principle, the genius of the man remained; but it existed now within the sphere of such a mighty and grand personality as transcended all she had previously known or conceived. It was as if some beneficent angel had stooped from heaven to visit them, and, lest his celestial splendour should overwhelm them, had assumed the guise and tone of that human being in whom they felt the most affectionate trust. Through his manner and aspect, and the low resounding melody of his utterance, she seemed to catch glimpses of a power and wisdom almost superhuman; but blended with a deep kindliness and charity, and a sublimity of nature that were more human than humanity itself. She looked up to him, not in fear, but with a loving, familiar kind of reverence; and would have confided to him the choicest secrets of her heart.

The influence that he exercised was not of that kind which belongs to superior age. There was in him all the fire and vigour of unquenchable youth. His lofty figure was as alert and lightsome as it was majestic. His manner was instinct with gentle sprightliness and playfulness, and it was impossible not to feel cheery and hopeful in his company. The curve of his lips, and ever and anon the sudden kindling in his eyes, betrayed the fiery soul within; yet in everything that he said or did were visible the traces of a serene and absolute self-control.

"We are glad you came in time," observed Eros at last. "We should never have got married, I believe, if you had not been here to tie the knot."

"At least," added Psyche, in her clear, subdued voice, "you will make it seem more beautiful and indissoluble, and give it a deeper significance, than anyone else could have done. Yes, I am glad you came in time. Do you know, Eros, I did not think Mortimer would come at all? That passage in the letter that I did not read you spoke of a strange pestilence, and immediately it came into my mind that Mortimer was dead. And even now," she continued, turning to the guest, and half-timidly meeting his strong, unfathomable eyes with her own, "even now, though I see you here between us, I cannot feel as if our Mortimer were in this world. Are you really he? or a messenger come to tell us that he is gone?"

"I am alive—am I not?" answered the guest, with a particularly radiant smile; "and if I am, then your Mortimer is also. As to my getting here at the right time, I am always sure to do that; it would be a sad business, indeed, if I were not. But are you both certain that you are glad to have me here?"

"It would not be merry Christmas if you were not!" exclaimed Eros, heartily.

"I am not always so well received," the other resumed. "I have been in all sorts of places, and have met all sorts of people, and almost all have called me abrupt and unceremonious. But then, not many know me for what I really am."

"I think I know you," said Psyche, after a pause; "and I cannot imagine myself so happy that your coming would not make me happier."

"You need not fear to know me, Psyche," returned the guest, with grave gentleness; "and really I am not so unsympathetic as I must often seem. But I have a task in the world which brings me less credit in the performance than in the after result. Mankind, you know, Eros, are not always wise and far-sighted enough to recognise at the moment what is most for their good in the long run."

"Yes, I know that; but for my part I think I can tell what I need more quickly and surely than most people. For instance—that Psyche must be my wife, and that you must make her so."

"You rate my powers too high," rejoined their friend, smiling again. "God only can make a man and woman one."

"Oh, I don't trouble myself with such fine-drawn distinctions. If you pronounce the service over us, I will take the rest for granted. As I was telling Psyche the other day, it's not worth while looking beyond this world. If she is mine here, I'll risk our getting separated hereafter."

"Hereafter may not be far off," said the guest, more gravely than he had yet spoken. "You were best not to leave it out of the account."

"Death is my enemy—I can see no good in him!" declared Eros; "and I will do the best I can to have my happiness in spite of him."

"He doesn't mean it!" exclaimed Psyche to their friend, in a low, appealing tone. "He knows that only Death can make Love immortal."

"I must tell you," observed the guest, after a pause, "that I cannot stay here long; I shall be gone to-night. What I came to do, therefore, must be done soon."

"To-night!" cried Eros, in astonishment that was half incredulous. Psyche said nothing, but hid her face in her hands and shivered a little.

"I wished to make you happy—happier than you have ever been — if you would let me," resumed the previous speaker. " Whoever has lofty beliefs will have a lofty fate. If your idea of marriage is high enough, you will not hesitate to come with me to my Paradise. How is it with you, Eros ? "

"Not yet," replied Eros, laughing and shaking his head. " It's too far off, and the journey is too cold. If you are really determined to leave us, you must go without me. Surely you can't expect me to be ready to start at such short notice ? No, no! I mean to stay by this comfortable fireside for a long time yet, and so shall Psyche."

"Death has summoned men on shorter notice than this," said the other. " Think again before you decide."

"I have decided ; and I never change my mind," said Eros, obstinately.

And truly his preference was not an unnatural one. The old parlour presented a most attractive aspect. The great log which had been burning on the broad hearth had now fallen into glowing fragments, over which small yellow and bluish flames danced intermittently. Everything was warm, home-like, and familiar. Out of doors the stars shone crisp and white, and the snow glistened pure as a maiden's soul. But ah! it was so terribly cold ; the beauty of the prospect could be enjoyed much better from the genial vantage - ground of the hearthstone.

"If that is your decision, you must abide by it," said the guest, and something in the words, and in the manner they were uttered, awed Eros for the moment. Then, turning to Psyche, he continued: "But even your Eros cannot choose for you. What is your preference? Are you, too, willing to postpone Paradise for the fireside?"

Psyche was naturally more imaginative than most young girls, and possibly there was something in the shadowy mystery of the hour, and in her own physical and mental condition, that wrought upon her mood. A creeping languor and a chill which the heat of the embers could not counteract were gaining possession of her, and filling her brain with weird fancies. Insensibly, he who sat beside her, and whose icy lips she had felt upon her brow, had become clothed to her apprehension with an unearthly, superhuman personality. No man was he, but an angel of tender and mighty sway, stooping from heaven on the eve of Christmas, to hold high argument with two mortal lovers on those questions which most nearly concern their welfare. As she spoke her voice sounded faint and ethereal, while her eyes sought to penetrate the shadow which had fallen over the face of Eros.

"It is pleasant here," she said; "yet if, in Paradise, our union may be eternal and secure, it is surely better to be there."

"You will meet Eros where we are going," returned the strange friend, gently, taking her hand in his own. "If not this Eros whom you have known here, then another and a worthier one than he."

"Oh, not another," whispered Psyche, entreatingly; "it must be this Eros—my own dear Eros whom I have always loved. I have lived with him, and our hearts are grown together. He is better and nobler than he seems."

"It is not for me to decide," was the answer. "But do you speak to him, Psyche. If he loves you, he will lay your words to heart."

Psyche rose from her chair, and, stepping somewhat feebly, crossed to where Eros sat, and stood before him, her hands clasped. The room had become more dusky, so that the three figures appeared rather like shadows than beings of flesh and blood. For a moment or two there was silence, and only Psyche's beseeching attitude seemed to speak.

"Eros," she said at length, "I feel that I must go —I must go with this friend of ours. Do you know him, Eros? He is your friend as well as mine. You might have gone with us; but that was not to be. We shall not know marriage here, and we shall seem

Y

to be separated for a time. But if your love for me has been as great as mine for you, the memory of it, and the faith in what is to come, will heal the worst of the parting. Oh, my love, say it shall be so!"

"You are crazy—both of you!" cried Eros, wrestling with the fear that beset him, and striving to speak in an assured and masterful tone. "What has Mortimer to do with you, Psyche? You are mine, and whoever pretends to take you from me is my enemy!"

"Eros—Eros!" exclaimed the girl, with passionate earnestness, "it is you who are crazy, my poor darling. Mortimer is dead; and the letter which he wrote—the letter that I alone read and touched—had in it the contagion of the pestilence. It was the message of my death; and now my death has come."

"Death shall not have you!" cried Eros, starting to his feet; and such was the vehemence of his rebellious anger that he felt ready to defy even Omnipotence. "What have I done that I should lose you? I have loved you truly and faithfully— why should not my love have its rightful fulfilment? It shall not go for naught and end in dust and ashes! As for this future you talk about, what is it? a misty possibility—an indefinite surmise—nothing! I say

it is unjust and tyrannical, and I will not submit!
Come to me, Psyche!"

He reached towards her through the dusk, but she
seemed to falter backwards from him, and when he
would have followed, the tall form of the mysterious
guest rose between, and beneath that mighty and
majestic gaze the eyes of Eros wavered, though the
rebellion in him was unconquered still.

"You must yield her to me," said those deep,
reverberating tones; "yet it is not I that parts you.
True lovers can be parted only through want of
faith. Upon yourself alone, therefore, does it depend
whether she leaves you for a time or for ever."

Eros pressed his hands to his head. Every good
and evil impulse of his soul was in deadly struggle
for the mastery. Was his love greater than Death?
or had the past been a delusion? Was the future
to be a blank? He was but a man, with a man's
weaknesses. He must rise to higher levels through
bitter trial, if at all; and except there were in him
some elements of generous nobleness, to turn his
stubborn self-will at the crisis of the conflict, the
demon of mistrust would gain the victory. Had he
such allies?

"Speak to him again, Psyche," murmured the
lofty presence, "you may yet prevail."

"Eros," she said, throwing all the tenderness of

her loving soul into the word, "this is more than our friend—he is our brother. Love and Death should glorify each other. If they are enemies, Death becomes cruel and Love degraded. Yield me up now that you may possess me for ever. Oh, quick, my love—quick!"

The struggling man uttered a cry, heartrending, full of anguish. He was faint and giddy, and the world seemed to reel beneath his feet. He stretched out his arms. "I love you, Psyche," he uttered. "Do not leave me behind; let me go with you!"

He felt her hand again within his own. "You are my own Eros," she whispered in his ear. "I shall not altogether leave you; you will see me in dreams, and you will know that the Paradise I go to is near this earthly home of ours. At last—perhaps not for a long time—but at last we shall meet there. And now . . . . take me to our marriage-altar, and let us say farewell there."

They came to the little samite-covered table, Psyche supported between the other two. The lovers knelt down together, and the form of the mysterious guest bended beneficently above them. Then Psyche slowly drooped sideways, and Eros caught her in his arms. Yet no—she was not there!

Still kneeling, he looked upwards through the window into the clear winter night, and saw where two cloud-shapes seemed to flit hand in hand across the starlit purple of the heavens. A strange peace entered his lately tortured soul. The doubt in his love's immortality was gone, and the struggle was ended.

"Take her, friend!" he cried, in a voice trembling with a deeper than earthly happiness. "So great is my love, that not in this world, nor with this mortal body, can I give it fit and full expression."

He was left alone in the old parlour, with the dead embers of the fire upon the hearthstone. Christmas bells were ushering in what was to have been his wedding-day; but, like their sweet notes, his mortal hopes had been caught up to heaven, but were not lost there. It is many years since then, yet every returning Christmas has found the same light of peace in his face that first dawned there so long ago. No brooding sullenness or failing faith has changed it into gloom.

But who was the mysterious guest, and why did he bear the likeness of him whom, above all others, Eros and Psyche had loved? That is a question which answers itself in all our lives. For when the time comes—as come it must—that this majestic Presence is met face to face, shall we not trust that the countenance which will, perhaps, seem awful, may at least not be as that of a stranger whom we know not, and whose heart is indifferent towards us? Would it not be pleasant, at that hour, to recognise in him who must herald our entrance into a new society, the well-known features of one whom our previous life had made our most secure and faithful friend?

THE END.

CHARLES DICKENS AND EVANS, CRYSTAL PALACE PRESS.

MACMILLAN'S POPULAR NOVELS.

In crown 8vo, cloth, price 6s. each Volume.

By WILLIAM BLACK.

Green Pastures and Piccadilly.

A Princess of Thule.

Madcap Violet.

The Maid of Killeena; and other Tales.

The Strange Adventures of a Phaeton. Illustrated.

By CHARLES KINGSLEY.

Two Years Ago.

"Westward Ho!"

Alton Locke. With Portrait.

Hypatia.

Yeast.

Hereward the Wake.

By the Author of "JOHN HALIFAX, GENTLEMAN."

The Head of the Family. Illustrated.

The Ogilvies. Illustrated.

Agatha's Husband. Illustrated.

Olive. Illustrated.

By MRS. OLIPHANT.

Young Musgrave.

The Curate in Charge.

A Son of the Soil.

MACMILLAN AND CO., LONDON.

MACMILLAN'S POPULAR NOVELS.

In crown 8vo, cloth, price 6s. each Volume.

By CHARLOTTE M. YONGE.

The Heir of Redclyffe. Illustrated.

Heartsease. Illustrated.

The Daisy Chain. Illustrated.

The Trial. Illustrated.

Hopes and Fears.

Dynevor Terrace.

The Pillars of the House. 2 vols.

My Young Alcides.

Clever Woman of the Family.

The Young Stepmother.

The Dove in the Eagle's Nest.

The Caged Lion. Illustrated.

The Chaplet of Pearls.

Lady Hester; or, Ursula's Narrative.

By ANNIE KEARY.

Castle Daly.

Oldbury.

A York and a Lancaster Rose.

Tom Brown's Schooldays.

Tom Brown at Oxford.

My Time and What I've Done with it. By C. BURNAND.

Hugh Crichton's Romance By C. R. COLERIDGE.

Owen Gwynne's Great Work. By Lady AUGUSTA NOEL.

Patty. By Mrs. MACQUOID.

Rose Turquand. By ELLICE HOPKINS.

A Nile Novel. By GEORGE FLEMING.

Mirage. By GEORGE FLEMING

Old Sir Douglas. By the Hon. Mrs. NORTON.

Sebastian. By KATHERINE COOPER.

MACMILLAN AND CO., LONDON.

MACMILLAN & CO.'S CATALOGUE of Works in BELLES LETTRES, including Poetry, Fiction, etc.

Allingham.—LAURENCE BLOOMFIELD IN IRELAND; OR, THE NEW LANDLORD. By WILLIAM ALLINGHAM. New and Cheaper Issue, with a Preface. Fcap. 8vo. cloth. 4s. 6d.

An Ancient City, and other Poems.—By A NATIVE OF SURREY. Extra fcap. 8vo. 6s.

Archer.—CHRISTINA NORTH. By E. M. ARCHER. New and Cheaper Edition. Crown 8vo. 6s.

Arnold. — THE POETICAL WORKS OF MATTHEW ARNOLD. Vol. I. EARLY POEMS, NARRATIVE POEMS, AND SONNETS. Vol. II. LYRIC, DRAMATIC, AND ELEGIAC POEMS. New and Complete Edition. Two Vols. Crown 8vo. Price 7s. 6d. each.

SELECTED POEMS OF MATTHEW ARNOLD. With Vignette engraved by C. H. JEENS (GOLDEN TREASURY SERIES). 18mo. 4s. 6d.

Large Paper Edition. Crown 8vo. 12s. 6d.

Art at Home Series.—Edited by W. J. LOFTIE, F.S.A.

"*If the whole series but continue as it has been begun—if the volumes yet to be rival these two initial—it will be beyond price as a library of household art.*"—EXAMINER.

A PLEA FOR ART IN THE HOUSE. With especial reference to the Economy of Collecting Works of Art, and the importance of Taste in Education and Morals. By W. J. LOFTIE, B.A., F.S.A. With Illustrations. Fifth Thousand. Crown 8vo. 2s. 6d.

SUGGESTIONS FOR HOUSE DECORATION IN PAINTING, WOODWORK, AND FURNITURE. By RHODA and AGNES GARRETT. With Illustrations. Sixth Thousand. Crown 8vo. 2s. 6d.

MUSIC IN THE HOUSE. By JOHN HULLAH. With Illustrations. Fourth Thousand. Crown 8vo. 2s. 6d.

20,000, 11, 1878.

A

Art at Home Series—*continued.*

THE DRAWING ROOM; ITS DECORATIONS AND FUR-
NITURE. By Mrs. ORRINSMITH. Illustrated. Fifth Thousand.
Crown 8vo. 2*s.* 6*d.*

THE DINING ROOM. By Mrs. LOFTIE. Illustrated. Fourth
Thousand. Crown 8vo. 2*s.* 6*d.*

THE BED ROOM AND BOUDOIR. By LADY BARKER.
Illustrated. Fourth Thousand. Crown 8vo. 2*s.* 6*d.*

DRESS. By Mrs. OLIPHANT. Illustrated. Crown 8vo. 2*s.* 6*d.*

PRIVATE THEATRICALS. By Lady POLLOCK. Illustrated.
[*Shortly.*

　　　[Other vols. in preparation.]

Atkinson. — AN ART TOUR TO THE NORTHERN
CAPITALS OF EUROPE. By J. BEAVINGTON ATKINSON.
8vo. 12*s.*
*"We can highly recommend it ; not only for the valuable informa-
tion it gives on the special subjects to which it is dedicated, but also
for the interesting episodes of travel which are interwoven with, and
lighten, the weightier matters of judicious and varied criticism on
art and artists in northern capitals."*—ART JOURNAL.

Atkinson (J. P.)—A WEEK AT THE LAKES, AND WHAT
CAME OF IT ; OR, THE ADVENTURES OF MR. DOBBS
AND HIS FRIEND MR. POTTS. A Series of Sketches by
J. P. ATKINSON. Oblong 4to. 7*s.* 6*d.*

Baker.—CAST UP BY THE SEA ; OR, THE ADVEN-
TURES OF NED GREY. By Sir SAMUEL BAKER, Pasha,
F.R.G.S. With Illustrations by HUARD. Sixth Edition. Crown
8vo. cloth gilt. 6*s.*
*"An admirable tale of adventure, of marvellous incidents, wild
exploits, and terrible dénouements."*—DAILY NEWS. *"A story of
adventure by sea and land in the good old style."*—PALL MALL
GAZETTE.

Barker(Lady).—A YEAR'S HOUSEKEEPING IN SOUTH
AFRICA. With Illustrations. Crown 8vo. 9*s.*
*"We doubt whether in any of her previous books she has written
more pleasantly than in this. . . . The great charm of these
letters is that she is always natural, and tells of what she sees and
hears in a strange country, just as if she were quietly chatting to
her friends by their own fireside."*—STANDARD.

Beesly.—STORIES FROM THE HISTORY OF ROME. By
Mrs. BEESLY. Fcap. 8vo. 2*s.* 6*d.*
*"A little book for which every cultivated and intelligent mother will
be grateful."*—EXAMINER.

Besant.—STUDIES IN EARLY FRENCH POETRY. By WALTER BESANT, M.A. Crown 8vo. 8s. 6d.

Betsy Lee ; A FO'C'S'LE YARN. Extra fcap. 8vo. 3s. 6d.
"*We can at least say that it is the work of a true poet.*"—ATHE-NÆUM.

Black (W.)—Works by W. BLACK, Author of "A Daughter of Heth."

THE STRANGE ADVENTURES OF A PHAETON. Eleventh Edition. Crown 8vo. 6s.
" *The book is a really charming description of a thousand English landscapes and of the emergencies and the fun and the delight of a picnic journey through them by a party determined to enjoy themselves, and as well matched as the pair of horses which drew the phaeton they sat in.*"—TIMES.

A PRINCESS OF THULE. Thirteenth Thousand. Crown 8vo. 6s.
The SATURDAY REVIEW says :—"*A novel which is both romantic and natural, which has much feeling, without any touch of mawkishness, which goes deep into character without any suggestion of painful analysis—this is a rare gem to find amongst the débris of current literature, and this, or nearly this, Mr. Black has given us in the 'Princess of Thule.'*" " *A beautiful and nearly perfect story.*"—SPECTATOR.

THE MAID OF KILLEENA, and other Stories. Cheaper Edition. Crown 8vo. 6s.
" *A collection of pretty stories told in the easiest and pleasantest manner imaginable.*"—TIMES. " *It was with something akin to joy that we drew our chair closer to the fire as the weary work of the novel critic gave place to the smile of satisfaction and pleasure, when, in the very first page of our book, we discovered that we had come again to those Western Isles in the quiet summer sea in the far North, and to those simple people amidst whose loving allegiance the Princess of Thule—Sheila—held her modest Court . . . We shall not be satisfied till ' The Maid of Killeena' rests on our shelves.*"—SPECTATOR.

MADCAP VIOLET. Eighth Thousand. Crown 8vo. 6s.
" *In the very first rank of Mr. Black's heroines ; proud as Sheila, and sweet as Coquette, stands Madcap Violet. The true, proud, tender nature of her, her beauty, her mischief, her self-sacrifice, endear her to the reader.*"—DAILY NEWS.

GREEN PASTURES AND PICCADILLY. Cheaper Edition. Sixth Thousand. Crown 8vo. 6s.

MACLEOD OF DARE. With Illustrations by Eminent Artists. 3 vols. Crown 8vo. 31s. 6d.

Blackie.—THE WISE MEN OF GREECE. In a Series of Dramatic Dialogues. By J. E. BLACKIE, Professor of Greek in the University of Edinburgh. Crown 8vo. 9s.

Blakiston.—MODERN SOCIETY IN ITS RELIGIOUS AND SOCIAL ASPECTS. By PEYTON BLAKISTON, M.D., F.R.S. Crown 8vo. 5s.

Borland Hall.—By the Author of "Olrig Grange." Cr. 8vo. 7s.

Bramston.—RALPH AND BRUNO. A Novel. By M. BRAMSTON. 2 vols. crown 8vo. 21s.

Brooke.—THE FOOL OF QUALITY; OR, THE HISTORY OF HENRY, EARL OF MORELAND. By HENRY BROOKE. Newly revised, with a Biographical Preface by the Rev. CHARLES KINGSLEY, M.A., Rector of Eversley. Crown 8vo. 6s.

Buist.—BIRDS, THEIR CAGES AND THEIR KEEP : Being a Practical Manual of Bird-Keeping and Bird-Rearing. By K. A. BUIST. With Coloured Frontispiece and other Illustrations. Crown 8vo. 5s.

Bunce.—FAIRY TALES, THEIR ORIGIN AND MEANING. With some Account of the Dwellers in Fairy Land. By J. THACKRAY BUNCE. Extra fcap. 8vo. 3s. 6d. [*Shortly.*

Burnand.—MY TIME, AND WHAT I'VE DONE WITH IT. By F. C. BURNAND. Crown 8vo. 6s.

Cameron.—LIGHT, SHADE, AND TOIL. Poems by W. C. CAMERON, with Introduction by the Rev. W. C. Smith, D.D. Extra fcap. 8vo. 6s.

Carroll.—Works by "LEWIS CARROLL :"—

ALICE'S ADVENTURES IN WONDERLAND. With Forty-two Illustrations by TENNIEL. 55th Thousand. Crown 8vo. cloth. 6s.
"*An excellent piece of nonsense.*"—TIMES. "*Elegant and delicious nonsense.*"—GUARDIAN. "*That most delightful of children's stories.*"—SATURDAY REVIEW.

A GERMAN TRANSLATION OF THE SAME. With TENNIEL's Illustrations. Crown 8vo. gilt. 6s.

A FRENCH TRANSLATION OF THE SAME. With TENNIEL's Illustrations. Crown 8vo. gilt. 6s.

AN ITALIAN TRANSLATION OF THE SAME. By T. P. ROSSETTE. With TENNIEL's Illustrations. Crown 8vo. 6s.

Carroll (Lewis).—*continued.*

THROUGH THE LOOKING-GLASS, AND WHAT ALICE FOUND THERE. With Fifty Illustrations by TENNIEL. Crown 8vo. gilt. 6s. 44th Thousand.
"*Will fairly rank with the tale of her previous experiences.*"—DAILY TELEGRAPH. "*Many of Mr. Tenniel's designs are masterpieces of wise absurdity.*"—ATHENÆUM.

THE HUNTING OF THE SNARK. An Agony in Eight Fits. With Nine Illustrations by H. Holiday. Crown 8vo. cloth extra, Gilt edges. 4s. 6d. 17th Thousand.
"*This glorious piece of nonsense. . . . . Everybody ought to read it—nearly everybody will—and all who deserve the treat will scream with laughter.*"—GRAPHIC.

Cautley.—A CENTURY OF EMBLEMS. By G. S. CAUTLEY, Vicar of Nettleden, author of "The After Glow," etc. With numerous Illustrations by LADY MARION ALFORD, REAR-ADMIRAL LORD W. COMPTON, the VEN. LORD A. COMPTON, R. BARNES, J. D. COOPER, and the author. Pott 4to. cloth elegant, gilt edges. 10s. 6d.

Christmas Carol (A). Printed in Colours from Original Designs by Mr. and Mrs. TREVOR CRISPIN, with Illuminated Borders from MSS. of the 14th and 15th Centuries. Imp. 4to. cloth elegant. Cheaper Edition, 21s.
"*A most exquisitely got-up volume.*"—TIMES.

Church (A. J.)—HORÆ TENNYSONIANÆ, Sive Eclogæ e Tennysono Latine redditæ. Cura A. J. CHURCH, A.M. Extra fcap. 8vo. 6s.

Clough (Arthur Hugh).—THE POEMS AND PROSE REMAINS OF ARTHUR HUGH CLOUGH. With a Selection from his Letters and a Memoir. Edited by his Wife. With Portrait. Two Vols. Crown 8vo. 21s.
"*Taken as a whole,*" *the* SPECTATOR *says,* "*these volumes cannot fail to be a lasting monument of one of the most original men of our age.*"

THE POEMS OF ARTHUR HUGH CLOUGH, sometime Fellow of Oriel College, Oxford. Fifth Edition. Fcap. 8vo. 6s.
"*From the higher mind of cultivated, all-questioning, but still conservative England, in this our puzzled generation, we do not know of any utterance in literature so characteristic as the poems of Arthur Hugh Clough.*"—FRASER'S MAGAZINE.

Clunes.—THE STORY OF PAULINE: an Autobiography. By G. C. CLUNES. Crown 8vo. 6s.

Coleridge.—HUGH CRICHTON'S ROMANCE. A Novel. By CHRISTABEL R. COLERIDGE. Second Edition. Crown 8vo. 6s. "*We have read it with more than average interest.*"—SATURDAY REVIEW. "*We can heartily commend this very charming book.*"— STANDARD.

Collects of the Church of England. With a beautifully Coloured Floral Design to each Collect, and Illuminated Cover. Crown 8vo. 12s. Also kept in various styles of morocco. "*This is beyond question,*" the ART JOURNAL says, "*the most beautiful book of the season.*" The GUARDIAN thinks it "*a successful attempt to associate in a natural and unforced manner the flowers of our fields and gardens with the course of the Christian year.*"

Colquhoun.—RHYMES AND CHIMES. By F. S. COLQUHOUN (née F. S. FULLER MAITLAND). Extra fcap. 8vo. 2s. 6d.

Cooper.—SEBASTIAN. A Novel. By KATHERINE COOPER. Crown 8vo. 6s.

Dante ; AN ESSAY. With a Translation of the "De Monarchia." By the Very Rev. R. W. CHURCH, D.C.L., Dean of St. Paul's. Crown 8vo. [*Immediately.*

Day.—GOVINDA SAMANTA; OR, THE HISTORY OF A BENGAL RAIYAT. By the Rev. LAL BEHARI DAY. Crown 8vo. 6s. "*The book presents a careful, minute, and well-drawn picture of Hindoo peasant life.*"—DAILY NEWS.

Days of Old ; STORIES FROM OLD ENGLISH HISTORY. By the Author of "Ruth and her Friends." New Edition. 18mo. cloth, extra. 2s. 6d. "*Full of truthful and charming historic pictures, is everywhere vital with moral and religious principles, and is written with a brightness of description, and with a dramatic force in the representation of character, that have made, and will always make, it one of the greatest favourites with reading boys.*"—NONCONFORMIST.

Doyle (Sir F. H.)—LECTURES ON POETRY, delivered before the University of Oxford in 1868. By Sir FRANCIS HASTINGS DOYLE, Professor of Poetry in the University of Oxford. Crown 8vo. 3s. 6d.

Elsie.—A LOWLAND SKETCH. By A. C. M. Crown 8vo. 6s.

Estelle Russell.—By the Author of "The Private Life of Galileo." New Edition. Crown 8vo. 6s.

Full of bright pictures of French life. The English family, whose fortunes form the main drift of the story, reside mostly in France, but there are also many English characters and scenes of great interest. It is certainly the work of a fresh, vigorous, and most interesting writer, with a dash of sarcastic humour which is refreshing and not too bitter. " We can send our readers to it with confidence." —SPECTATOR.

Evans.—Works by SEBASTIAN EVANS.

BROTHER FABIAN'S MANUSCRIPT, AND OTHER POEMS. Fcap. 8vo. cloth. 6s.

" In this volume we have full assurance that he has ' the vision and the faculty divine.' . . . Clever and full of kindly humour."— GLOBE.

IN THE STUDIO: A DECADE OF POEMS. Extra fcap. 8vo. 5s.

" The finest thing in the book is 'Dudman in Paradise,' a wonderfully vigorous and beautiful story. The poem is a most remarkable one, full of beauty, humour, and pointed satire."—ACADEMY.

Farrell.—THE LECTURES OF A CERTAIN PROFESSOR. By the Rev. JOSEPH FARRELL. Crown 8vo. 7s. 6d.

Fawcett.—TALES IN POLITICAL ECONOMY. By MIL-LICENT FAWCETT, Author of "Political Economy for Beginners.' Globe 8vo. 3s.

" The idea is a good one, and it is quite wonderful what a mass of economic teaching the author manages to compress into a small space. . . The true doctrines of international trade, currency, and the ratio between production and population, are set before us and illustrated in a masterly manner."—ATHENÆUM.

Fleming.—Works by GEORGE FLEMING.

A NILE NOVEL. Third and Cheaper Edition. Crown 8vo.

MIRAGE. A Novel. Cheaper Edition. Crown 8vo. 6s.

Fletcher.—THOUGHTS FROM A GIRL'S LIFE. By LUCY FLETCHER. Second Edition. Fcap. 8vo. 4s. 6d.

Freeman. — HISTORICAL AND ARCHITECTURAL SKETCHES; CHIEFLY ITALIAN. By E. A. FREEMAN, D.C.L., LL.D. With Illustrations by the Author. Crown 8vo. 10s. 6d.

" Those who know Italy well will retrace their steps with delight in Mr. Freeman's company, and find him a most interesting guide and instructor."—EXAMINER.

Garnett.—IDYLLS AND EPIGRAMS. Chiefly from the Greek Anthology. By RICHARD GARNETT. Fcap. 8vo. 2s. 6d.
"A charming little book. For English readers, Mr. Garnett's translations will open a new world of thought."—WESTMINSTER REVIEW.

Gilmore.—STORM WARRIORS; OR, LIFE-BOAT WORK ON THE GOODWIN SANDS. By the Rev. JOHN GILMORE, M.A., Rector of Holy Trinity, Ramsgate, Author of "The Ramsgate Life-Boat," in *Macmillan's Magazine.* Second Edition. Crown 8vo. 6s.
" The stories, which are said to be literally exact, are more thrilling than anything in fiction. Mr. Gilmore has done a good work as well as written a good book."—DAILY NEWS.

Guesses at Truth.—By TWO BROTHERS. 18mo. 4s. 6d. Golden Treasury Series.

Hamerton.—A PAINTER'S CAMP. Second Edition, revised. Extra fcap. 8vo. 6s.
"These pages, written with infinite spirit and humour, bring into close rooms, back upon tired heads, the breezy airs of Lancashire moors and Highland lochs, with a freshness which no recent novelist has succeeded in preserving."—NONCONFORMIST.

Harry.—A POEM. By the Author of "Mrs. Jerningham's Journal." Extra fcap. 8vo. 3s. 6d.

Heine.—SELECTIONS FROM THE POETICAL WORKS OF HEINRICH HEINE. Translated into English. Crown 8vo. 4s. 6d.

Higginson.—MALBONE: An Oldport Romance. By T. W. HIGGINSON. Fcap. 8vo. 2s. 6d.

Hilda among the Broken Gods.—By the Author of "Olrig Grange." Extra fcap. 8vo. 7s. 6d.

Hobday. — COTTAGE GARDENING; OR, FLOWERS, FRUITS AND VEGETABLES FOR SMALL GARDENS. By E. HOBDAY. Crown 8vo. 1s. 6d.
" A sensible and useful little book."—ATHENÆUM.

Home.—BLANCHE LISLE, and other Poems. By CECIL HOME. Fcap. 8vo. 4s. 6d.

Hood (Tom).—THE PLEASANT TALE OF PUSS AND ROBIN AND THEIR FRIENDS, KITTY AND BOB. Told in Pictures by L. FRÖLICH, and in Rhymes by TOM HOOD. Crown 8vo. gilt. 3s. 6d.
" The volume is prettily got up, and is sure to be a favourite in the nursery."—SCOTSMAN. *"Herr Frölich has outdone himself in his pictures of this dramatic chase."*—MORNING POST.

Hooper and Phillips.—A MANUAL OF MARKS ON POTTERY AND PORCELAIN. A Dictionary of Easy Reference. By W. H. HOOPER and W. C. PHILLIPS. With numerous Illustrations. Second Edition, revised. 16mo. 4s. 6d.

"*It is one of the most complete, and beyond all comparison, the handiest volume of the kind.*"—ATHENÆUM.

Hopkins.—ROSE TURQUAND: A Novel. By ELLICE HOPKINS. Cheaper Edition. Crown 8vo. 6s.

"*Rose Turquand is a noble heroine, and the story of her sufferings and of her sacrifice is most touching. A tale of rare excellence.*"—STANDARD.

Horace.—WORD FOR WORD FROM HORACE. The Odes literally versified. By W. T. THORNTON, C.B. Crown 8vo. 7s. 6d.

Hunt.—TALKS ABOUT ART. By WILLIAM HUNT. With a Letter by J. E. MILLAIS. Crown 8vo. 3s. 6d.

"*They are singularly racy and suggestive.*"——PALL MALL GAZETTE.

Irving.—Works by WASHINGTON IRVING.

OLD CHRISTMAS. From the Sketch Book. With upwards of 100 Illustrations by Randolph Caldecott, engraved by J. D. Cooper. Second Edition. Crown 8vo. cloth elegant. 6s.

"*This little volume is indeed a gem.*"—DAILY NEWS. "*One of the best and prettiest volumes we have seen this year. . . . . All the illustrations are equally charming and equally worthy of the immortal words to which they are wedded.*"—SATURDAY REVIEW.

BRACEBRIDGE HALL. With 120 illustrations by R. Caldecott. Crown 8vo. cloth gilt. 6s.

"'*No one who has seen 'Old Christmas,' issued last year with charming illustrations by Mr. Caldecott, is likely to forget the pleasure he derived from turning over its pages. Text and illustrations, both having a flavour of quaint, old-fashioned humour, fit into each other to perfection, and leave an impression absolutely unique. . . . This work is in no respect behind its predecessor.*"—GLOBE.

James.—Works by HENRY JAMES, jun.

FRENCH POETS AND NOVELISTS. Crown 8vo. 8s. 6d.

CONTENTS :—Alfred de Musset—Théophile Gautier—Baudelaire—Honoré de Balzac—George Sand—Turgénieff, etc.

"*There has of late years appeared nothing upon French literature so intelligent as this book—so acute, so full of good sense, so free from affectation and pretence.*"—ATHENÆUM.

THE EUROPEANS. A Novel. 2 vols. Crown 8vo. 21s.

Joubert.—PENSÉES OF JOUBERT. Selected and Translated with the Original French appended, by HENRY ATTWELL, Knight of the Order of the Oak Crown. Crown 8vo. 5*s.*

Keary (A.)—Works by ANNIE KEARY :—

CASTLE DALY : THE STORY OF AN IRISH HOME THIRTY YEARS AGO. New Edition. Crown 8vo. 6*s.*
"*Extremely touching, and at the same time thoroughly amusing.*"— MORNING POST.

JANET'S HOME. New Edition. Globe 8vo. 2*s.* 6*d.*

CLEMENCY FRANKLYN. New Edition. Globe 8vo. 2*s.* 6*d.*
"*Full of wisdom and goodness, simple, truthful, and artistic. . . It is capital as a story; better still in its pure tone and wholesome influence.*"—GLOBE.

OLDBURY. New and Cheaper Edition. Crown 8vo. 6*s.*
"*This is a very powerfully written story.*"—GLOBE. "*This is a really excellent novel.*"—ILLUSTRATED LONDON NEWS. "*The sketches of society in Oldbury are excellent. The pictures of child life are full of truth.*"—WESTMINSTER REVIEW.

A YORK AND A LANCASTER ROSE. Crown 8vo. 6*s.*
"*A very pleasant and thoroughly interesting book.*"—JOHN BULL.

Keary (E.) — THE MAGIC VALLEY; or, PATIENT ANTOINE. With Illustrations by E. V. B. Globe 8vo. gilt. 4*s.* 6*d.*
"*A very pretty, tender, quaint little tale.*"—TIMES.

Keary (A. and E.)—Works by A. and E. KEARY :—

THE LITTLE WANDERLIN, and other Fairy Tales. 18mo. 2*s.* 6*d.*
"*The tales are fanciful and well written, and they are sure to win favour amongst little readers.*"—ATHENÆUM.

THE HEROES OF ASGARD. Tales from Scandinavian Mythology. New and Revised Edition, Illustrated by HUARD. Extra fcap. 8vo. 4*s.* 6*d.*
"*Told in a light and amusing style, which, in its drollery and quaintness, reminds us of our old favourite Grimm.*"—TIMES.

Kingsley.—Works by the Rev. CHARLES KINGSLEY, M.A., Rector of Eversley, and Canon of Westminster :—

WESTWARD HO! or, The Voyages and Adventures of Sir Amyas Leigh. Forty-first Thousand. Crown 8vo. 6*s.*

TWO YEARS AGO. Ninth Edition. Crown 8vo. 6*s.*

HYPATIA ; or, New Foes with an Old Face. Ninth Edition. Crown 8vo. 6*s.*

Kingsley (C.)—*continued.*

HEREWARD THE WAKE—LAST OF THE ENGLISH.
Fifth Edition. Crown 8vo. 6s.

YEAST: A Problem. Tenth Edition. Crown 8vo. 6s.

ALTON LOCKE. New Edition. With a Prefatory Memoir by
THOMAS HUGHES, Q.C., and Portrait of the Author. Crown
8vo. 6s.

THE WATER BABIES. A Fairy Tale for a Land Baby. With
Illustrations by Sir NOEL PATON, R.S.A., and P. SKELTON.
New Edition. Crown 8vo. 6s.
"*In fun, in humour, and in innocent imagination, as a child's
book we do not know its equal.*"—LONDON REVIEW. "*Mr.
Kingsley must have the credit of revealing to us a new order of life.
. . . There is in the 'Water Babies' an abundance of wit, fun,
good humour, geniality, élan, go.*"—TIMES.

THE HEROES; or, Greek Fairy Tales for my Children. With
Illustrations. New Edition. Crown 8vo. 6s.
"*We do not think these heroic stories have ever been more attractively
told. . . There is a deep under-current of religious feeling traceable
throughout its pages which is sure to influence young readers powerfully.*"—LONDON REVIEW. "*One of the children's books that
will surely become a classic.*"—NONCONFORMIST.

PHAETHON; or, Loose Thoughts for Loose Thinkers. Third
Edition. Crown 8vo. 2s.
"*The dialogue of 'Phaethon' has striking beauties, and its suggestions may meet half-way many a latent doubt, and, like a light
breeze, lift from the soul clouds that are gathering heavily, and
threatening to settle down in misty gloom on the summer of many
a fair and promising young life.*"—SPECTATOR.

POEMS; including The Saint's Tragedy, Andromeda, Songs,
Ballads, etc. Complete Collected Edition. Extra fcap. 8vo. 6s.
The SPECTATOR *calls* "*Andromeda*" "*the finest piece of English
hexameter verse that has ever been written. It is a volume
which many readers will be glad to possess.*"

PROSE IDYLLS. NEW AND OLD. Fourth Edition. Crown
8vo. 6s.
CONTENTS:—*A Charm of Birds; Chalk-Stream Studies; The
Fens; My Winter-Garden; From Ocean to Sea; North Devon.*
"*Altogether a delightful book. . . . . It exhibits the author's best
traits, and cannot fail to infect the reader with a love of nature
and of out-door life and its enjoyments. It is well calculated to
bring a gleam of summer with its pleasant associations, into the
bleak winter-time; while a better companion for a summer ramble
could hardly be found.*"—BRITISH QUARTERLY REVIEW.

GLAUCUS; OR, THE WONDERS OF THE SEA-SHORE.
With Coloured Illustrations. Sixth Edition. Crown 8vo. 6s.

Kingsley (H.)—Works by HENRY KINGSLEY :—

TALES OF OLD TRAVEL. Re-narrated. With Eight full-page Illustrations by HUARD. Fifth Edition. Crown 8vo. cloth, extra gilt. 5s.

"*We know no better book for those who want knowledge or seek to refresh it. As for the 'sensational,' most novels are tame compared with these narratives.*"—ATHENÆUM. "*Exactly the book to interest and to do good to intelligent and high-spirited boys.*"—LITERARY CHURCHMAN.

THE LOST CHILD. With Eight Illustrations by FRÖLICH. Crown 4to. cloth gilt. 3s. 6d.

"*A pathetic story, and told so as to give children an interest in Australian ways and scenery.*"—GLOBE. "*Very charmingly and very touchingly told.*"—SATURDAY REVIEW.

Knatchbull-Hugessen.—Works by E. H. KNATCHBULL-HUGESSEN, M.P. :—

Mr. Knatchbull-Hugessen has won for himself a reputation as a teller of fairy-tales. "His powers," says the TIMES, "*are of a very high order ; light and brilliant narrative flows from his pen, and is fed by an invention as graceful as it is inexhaustible." "Children reading his stories," the* SCOTSMAN *says, "or hearing them read, will have their minds refreshed and invigorated as much as their bodies would be by abundance of fresh air and exercise.*"

STORIES FOR MY CHILDREN. With Illustrations. Sixth Edition. Crown 8vo. 5s.

"*The stories are charming, and full of life and fun.*"—STANDARD. "*The author has an imagination as fanciful as Grimm himself, while some of his stories are superior to anything that Hans Christian Andersen has written.*"—NONCONFORMIST.

CRACKERS FOR CHRISTMAS. More Stories. With Illustrations by JELLICOE and ELWES. Fifth Edition. Crown 8vo. 5s.

"*A fascinating little volume, which will make him friends in every household in which there are children.*"—DAILY NEWS.

MOONSHINE : Fairy Tales. With Illustrations by W. BRUNTON. Seventh Edition. Crown 8vo. cloth gilt. 5s.

"*A volume of fairy tales, written not only for ungrown children, but for bigger, and if you are nearly worn out, or sick, or sorry, you will find it good reading.*"—GRAPHIC. "*The most charming volume of fairy tales which we have ever read. . . . We cannot quit this very pleasant book without a word of praise to its illustrator. Mr. Brunton from first to last has done admirably.*"—TIMES.

TALES AT TEA-TIME. Fairy Stories. With Seven Illustrations by W. BRUNTON. Fifth Edition. Crown 8vo. Cloth gilt. 5s.

Knatchbull-Hugessen (E. H.)—*continued.*

"*Capitally illustrated by W. Brunton. . . . In frolic and fancy they are quite equal to his other books. The author knows how to write fairy stories as they should be written. The whole book is full of the most delightful drolleries.*"—TIMES.

QUEER FOLK. FAIRY STORIES. Illustrated by S. E. WALLER. Fourth Edition. Crown 8vo. Cloth gilt. 5*s.*
"*Decidedly the author's happiest effort. . . . One of the best story books of the year.*"—HOUR.

Knatchbull-Hugessen (Louisa).—THE HISTORY OF PRINCE PERRYPETS. A Fairy Tale. By LOUISA KNATCH-BULL-HUGESSEN. With Eight Illustrations by WEIGAND. New Edition. Crown 4to. cloth gilt. 3*s.* 6*d.*
"*A grand and exciting fairy tale.*"—MORNING POST. "*A delicious piece of fairy nonsense.*"—ILLUSTRATED LONDON NEWS.

Knox.—SONGS OF CONSOLATION. By ISA CRAIG KNOX. Extra fcap. 8vo. Cloth extra, gilt edges. 4*s.* 6*d.*
"*The verses are truly sweet; there is in them not only much genuine poetic quality, but an ardent, flowing devotedness, and a peculiar skill in propounding theological tenets in the most graceful way, which any divine might envy.*"—SCOTSMAN.

Leading Cases done into English. By an Apprentice of Lincoln's Inn. Third Edition. Crown 8vo. 2*s.* 6*d.*
"*The versifier of these 'Leading Cases' has been most successful. He has surrounded his legal distinctions with a halo of mock passion which is in itself in the highest degree entertaining, especially when the style of the different modern poets is so admirably hit off that the cloud of associations which hangs round one of Mr. Swinburne's, or Mr. Rossetti's, or Mr. Browning's, or Mr. Clough's, or Mr. Tennyson's poems, is summoned up to set off the mock tenderness or mock patriotism of the strain itself.*"—SPECTATOR.

Leland.—JOHNNYKIN AND THE GOBLINS. By C. G. LELAND, Author of "Hans Breitmann's Ballads." With numerous Illustrations by the Author. Crown 8vo. 6*s.*
"*Mr. Leland is rich in fantastic conception and full of rollicking fun, and youngsters will amazingly enjoy his book.*"—BRITISH QUARTERLY REVIEW.

Life and Times of Conrad the Squirrel. A Story for Children. By the Author of "Wandering Willie," "Effie's Friends," &c. With a Frontispiece by R. FARREN. Second Edition. Crown 8vo. 3*s.* 6*d.*
"*Having commenced on the first page, we were compelled to go on to the conclusion, and this we predict will be the case with every one who opens the book.*"—PALL MALL GAZETTE.

Little Estella, and other FAIRY TALES FOR THE YOUNG. 18mo. cloth extra. 2s. 6d.

"*This is a fine story, and we thank heaven for not being too wise to enjoy it.*"—DAILY NEWS.

Loftie.—FORTY-SIX SOCIAL TWITTERS. By MRS. LOFTIE. 16mo. 2s. 6d.

"*Many of these essays are bright and pleasant, and extremely sensible remarks are scattered about the book.*"—ATHENÆUM.

Lorne.—Works by the MARQUIS OF LORNE :—

GUIDO AND LITA : A TALE OF THE RIVIERA. A Poem. Third Edition. Small 4to. cloth elegant, with Illustrations. 7s. 6d.

"*Lord Lorne has the gifts of expression as well as the feelings of a poet.*"—TIMES. "*A volume of graceful and harmonious verse.*"—STANDARD. "*We may congratulate the Marquis on something more than a mere succès d'estime.*"—GRAPHIC. "*Lucidity of thought and gracefulness of expression abound in this attractive poem.*"—MORNING POST.

THE BOOK OF THE PSALMS, LITERALLY RENDERED IN VERSE. With Three Illustrations. Third Edition. Crown 8vo. 7s. 6d.

"*His version is such a great improvement upon Rous that it will be surprising should it not supplant the old version in the Scottish churches. . . . on the whole, it would not be rash, to call Lord Lorne's the best rhymed Psalter we have.*"—ATHENÆUM.

Lowell.—COMPLETE POETICAL WORKS of JAMES RUSSELL LOWELL. With Portrait, engraved by Jeens. 18mo. cloth extra. 4s. 6d.

"*All readers who are able to recognise and appreciate genuine verse will give a glad welcome to this beautiful little volume.*"—PALL MALL GAZETTE.

Lyttelton.—Works by LORD LYTTELTON :—

THE "COMUS" OF MILTON, rendered into Greek Verse. Extra fcap. 8vo. 5s.

THE "SAMSON AGONISTES" OF MILTON, rendered into Greek Verse. Extra fcap. 8vo. 6s. 6d.

Macdonell.—FOR THE KING'S DUES. By AGNES MACDONELL, Author of "Martin's Vineyard." Cheaper Edition. Crown 8vo. 6s.

Mackinlay.—POEMS. By JAMES M. MACKINLAY, M.A., Extra fcap. 8vo. 3s. 6d.

Maclaren.—THE FAIRY FAMILY. A series of Ballads and Metrical Tales illustrating the Fairy Mythology of Europe. By ARCHIBALD MACLAREN. With Frontispiece, Illustrated Title, and Vignette. Crown 8vo. gilt. 5*s.*

Macmillan's Magazine.—Published Monthly. Price 1*s.* Volumes I. to XXXVIII. are now ready. 7*s.* 6*d.* each.

Macquoid.—PATTY. By KATHARINE S. MACQUOID. Third and Cheaper Edition. Crown 8vo. 6*s.*
"*A book to be read.*"—STANDARD. "*A powerful and fascinating story.*"—DAILY TELEGRAPH.

Maguire.—YOUNG PRINCE MARIGOLD, AND OTHER FAIRY STORIES. By the late JOHN FRANCIS MAGUIRE, M.P. Illustrated by S. E. WALLER. Globe 8vo. gilt. 4*s.* 6*d.*
" *The author has evidently studied the ways and tastes of children and got at the secret of amusing them ; and has succeeded in what is not so easy a task as it may seem—in producing a really good children's book.*"—DAILY TELEGRAPH.

Mahaffy.—Works by J. P. MAHAFFY, M.A., Fellow of Trinity College, Dublin.
SOCIAL LIFE IN GREECE FROM HOMER TO MENAN-DER. Third Edition, enlarged, with New Chapter on Greek Art. Crown 8vo. 9*s.*
"*Should be in the hands of all who desire thoroughly to understand and to enjoy Greek literature, and to get an intelligent idea of the old Greek life.*"—GUARDIAN.
RAMBLES AND STUDIES IN GREECE. Illustrated. Second Edition, revised and enlarged, with Map. Crown 8vo. 10*s.* 6*d.*
" *A singularly instructive and agreeable volume.*"—ATHENÆUM.
" *This charmingly picturesque and lively volume.*"—EXAMINER.

Massey.—SONGS OF THE NOONTIDE REST. By LUCY MASSEY, Author of "Thoughts from a Girl's Life." Fcap. 8vo. cloth extra. 4*s.* 6*d.*

Masson (Mrs.)—THREE CENTURIES OF ENGLISH POETRY : being selections from Chaucer to Herrick, with Introductions and Notes by Mrs. MASSON and a general introduction by PROFESSOR MASSON. Extra fcap. 8vo. 3*s.* 6*d.*
" *Most excellently done. The selections are made with good taste and discrimination. The notes, too, are to the point. We can most strongly recommend the book.*"—WESTMINSTER REVIEW.

Masson (Professor).—Works by DAVID MASSON, M.A., Professor of Rhetoric and English Literature in the University of Edinburgh.

Masson (Professor)—*continued.*
WORDSWORTH, SHELLEY, KEATS, AND OTHER
ESSAYS. Crown 8vo. 5s.
CHATTERTON : A Story of the Year 1770. Crown 8vo. 5s.
THE THREE DEVILS : LUTHER'S, MILTON'S, and
GOETHE'S ; and other Essays. Crown 8vo. 5s.

Mazini.—IN THE GOLDEN SHELL ; A Story of Palermo. By
LINDA MAZINI. With Illustrations. Globe 8vo. cloth gilt. 4s. 6d.
" *As beautiful and bright and fresh as the scenes to which it wafts
us over the blue Mediterranean, and as pure and innocent, but
piquant and sprightly as the little girl who plays the part of its
heroine, is this admirable little book.*"—ILLUSTRATED LONDON
NEWS.

Merivale.—KEATS' HYPERION, rendered into Latin Verse.
By C. MERIVALE, B.D. Second Edition. Extra fcap. 8vo.
3s. 6d.

Milner.—THE LILY OF LUMLEY. By EDITH MILNER.
Crown 8vo. 7s. 6d.

Milton's Poetical Works.—Edited with Text collated from
the best Authorities, with Introduction and Notes by DAVID
MASSON. Three vols. 8vo. 42s. With Three Portraits engraved by
C. H. JEENS. (Uniform with the Cambridge Shakespeare.)
" *An edition of Milton which is certain to be the standard edition
for many years to come, and which is as complete and satisfactory
as can be conceived.*"—EXAMINER.
Golden Treasury Edition. By the same Editor. With Two
Portraits. 2 vols. 18mo. 9s.

Mistral (F.)—MIRELLE, a Pastoral Epic of Provence. Translated by H. CRICHTON. Extra fcap. 8vo. 6s.

Mitford (A. B.)—TALES OF OLD JAPAN. By A. B.
MITFORD, Second Secretary to the British Legation in Japan.
With Illustrations drawn and cut on Wood by Japanese Artists
New and Cheaper Edition. Crown 8vo. 6s.
" *They will always be interesting as memorials of a most exceptional
society ; while, regarded simply as tales, they are sparkling, sensa-
tional, and dramatic, and the originality of their ideas and the
quaintness of their language give them a most captivating piquancy.
The illustrations are extremely interesting, and for the curious in
such matters have a special and particular value.*"—PALL MALL
GAZETTE.

Molesworth. — Works by Mrs. MOLESWORTH (ENNIS
GRAHAM) :—
GRANDMOTHER DEAR. Illustrated by WALTER CRANE.
Extra fcap. 8vo. cloth gilt. 4s. 6d.   .· [*Just ready.*

Molesworth (Mrs.)—*continued.*

TELL ME A STORY. Illustrated by WALTER CRANE. Globe
8vo. gilt. 4s. 6d. Second Edition.
"*So delightful that we are inclined to join in the petition, and we
hope she may soon tell us more stories.*"—ATHENÆUM.

"CARROTS": JUST A LITTLE BOY. Illustrated by WALTER
CRANE. Eighth Thousand. Globe 8vo. gilt. 4s. 6d.
"*One of the cleverest and most pleasing stories it has been our good
fortune to meet with for some time. 'Carrots' and his sister are
delightful little beings, whom to read about is at once to be become
very fond of.*—EXAMINER.

THE CUCKOO CLOCK. Illustrated by WALTER CRANE. Eighth
Thousand. Globe 8vo. gilt. 4s. 6d.
"*A beautiful little story. . . . It will be read with delight by
every child into whose hands it is placed. . . . Ennis Graham
deserves all the praise that has been, is, and will be, bestowed on
'The Cuckoo Clock. Children's stories are plentiful, but one like
this is not to be met with every day.*" —PALL MALL GAZETTE.

Morgan.—BARON BRUNO; OR, THE UNBELIEVING
PHILOSOPHER, AND OTHER FAIRY STORIES. By
LOUISA MORGAN. Illustrated by R. Caldecott. Crown 8vo. gilt. 5s.
"*The prettiest collection of stories we have seen for a long time.
One and all are graceful and dreamy little prose-poems with some-
thing of the bewitching pathos of Hans Christian Andersen's
'Little Mermaid,' and 'Eleven Swans.'*"—EXAMINER.

Moulton.—SWALLOW FLIGHTS. Poems by LOUISA CHAND-
LER MOULTON. Extra fcap. 8vo. 4s. 6d.
The ATHENÆUM says :—"*Mrs. Moulton has a real claim to attention. It is not too much to say of these poems that they exhibit
delicate and rare beauty, marked originality, and perfection of
style. What is still better, they impress us with a sense of vivid
and subtle imagination, and that spontaneous feeling which is the
essence of lyrical poetry.*"

Moultrie.—POEMS by JOHN MOULTRIE. Complete Edition.
2 vols. Crown 8vo. 7s. each.
Vol. I. MY BROTHER'S GRAVE, DREAM OF LIFE, &c.
With Memoir by the Rev. Prebendary COLERIDGE.
Vol. II. LAYS OF THE ENGLISH CHURCH, and other Poems.
With notices of the Rectors of Rugby, by M. H. BLOXHAM.
F.R.A.S.

Mrs. Jerningham's Journal. A Poem purporting to be the
Journal of a newly-married Lady. Third Edition. Fcap. 8vo.
3s. 6d.

"It is nearly a perfect gem. We have had nothing so good for a long time, and those who neglect to read it are neglecting one of the jewels of contemporary history."—EDINBURGH DAILY REVIEW. *"One quality in the piece, sufficient of itself to claim a moment's attention, is that it is unique—original, indeed, is not too strong a word—in the manner of its conception and execution.'*—PALL MALL GAZETTE.

Mudie.—STRAY LEAVES. By C. E. MUDIE. New Edition. Extra fcap. 8vo. 3s. 6d. Contents :—"His and Mine"—"Night and Day"—"One of Many," &c.

This little volume consists of a number of poems, mostly of a genuinely devotional character. "They are for the most part so exquisitely sweet and delicate as to be quite a marvel of composition. They are worthy of being laid up in the recesses of the heart, and recalled to memory from time to time."—ILLUSTRATED LONDON NEWS.

Murray.—ROUND ABOUT FRANCE. By E. C. GRENVILLE MURRAY. Crown 8vo. 7s. 6d.

"A most amusing series of articles."—ATHENÆUM.

Myers (Ernest).—Works by ERNEST MYERS :—

THE PURITANS. Extra fcap. 8vo. cloth. 2s. 6d.

POEMS. Extra fcap. 8vo. 4s. 6d.

" The diction is excellent, the rhythm falls pleasantly on the ear, there is a classical flavour in the verse which is eminently grateful, the thought and imagery are poetical in character."—PALL MALL GAZETTE.

Myers (F. W. H.)—POEMS. By F. W. H. MYERS. Containing "St. Paul," "St. John," and others. Extra fcap. 8vo. 4s. 6d.

"It is rare to find a writer who combines to such an extent the faculty of communicating feelings with the faculty of euphonious expression."—SPECTATOR.

Nichol.—HANNIBAL, A HISTORICAL DRAMA. By JOHN NICHOL, B.A. Oxon., Regius Professor of English Language and Literature in the University of Glasgow. Extra fcap. 8vo. 7s. 6d.

Nine Years Old.—By the Author of "St. Olave's," "When I was a Little Girl," &c. Illustrated by FRÖLICH. Fourth Edition. Extra fcap. 8vo. cloth gilt. 4s. 6d.

It is believed that this story, by the favourably known author of "St. Olave's," will be found both highly interesting and instructive to the young. The volume contains eight graphic illustrations by Mr. L. Frölich. The EXAMINER *says: "Whether the readers are nine years old, or twice, or seven times as old, they must enjoy this pretty volume."*

Noel.—BEATRICE AND OTHER POEMS. By the HON. RODEN NOEL. Fcap. 8vo. 6s.

Noel (Lady Augusta).—OWEN GWYNNE'S GREAT WORK. Cheaper Edition. Crown 8vo. 6s.

Norton.—Works by the Hon. Mrs. NORTON :—

THE LADY OF LA GARAYE. With Vignette and Frontispiece. Eighth Edition. Fcap. 8vo. 4s. 6d.
"*Full of thought well expressed, and may be classed among her best efforts.*"—TIMES.

OLD SIR DOUGLAS. New Edition. Crown 8vo. 6s.
"*This varied and lively novel—this clever novel so full of character, and of fine incidental remark.*"—SCOTSMAN. "*One of the pleasantest and healthiest stories of modern fiction.*"—GLOBE.

Oliphant.—Works by Mrs. OLIPHANT :—

AGNES HOPETOUN'S SCHOOLS AND HOLIDAYS. New Edition with Illustrations. Royal 16mo. gilt leaves. 4s. 6d.
"*There are few books of late years more fitted to touch the heart, purify the feeling, and quicken and sustain right principles.*"—NONCONFORMIST. "*A more gracefully written story it is impossible to desire.*"—DAILY NEWS.

A SON OF THE SOIL. New Edition. Crown 8vo. 6s.
"*It is a very different work from the ordinary run of novels. The whole life of a man is portrayed in it, worked out with subtlety and insight.*"—ATHENÆUM

THE CURATE IN CHARGE. Crown 8vo. 6s. Sixth Edition
"*We can pronounce it one of the happiest of her recent efforts.*"—TIMES.

THE MAKERS OF FLORENCE: Dante, Giotto, Savonarola, and their City. With Illustrations from Drawings by Professor Delamotte, and a Steel Portrait of Savonarola, engraved by C. H. JEENS. Second Edition with Preface. Medium 8vo. Cloth extra. 21s.
The EDINBURGH REVIEW *says* "*We cannot leave this subject without expressing our admiration for the beautiful volume which Mrs. Oliphant has devoted to the ' Makers of Florence'—one of the most elegant and interesting books which has been inspired in our time by the arts and annals of that celebrated Republic.*"

YOUNG MUSGRAVE. Cheaper Edition. Crown 8vo. 6s.

Our Year. A Child's Book, in Prose and Verse. By the Author of "John Halifax, Gentleman." Illustrated by CLARENCE DOBELL. Royal 16mo. 3s. 6d.
"*It is just the book we could wish to see in the hands of every child.*"—ENGLISH CHURCHMAN.

B 2

Palgrave.—Works by FRANCIS TURNER PALGRAVE, M.A., late Fellow of Exeter College, Oxford :—

THE FIVE DAYS' ENTERTAINMENTS AT WENTWORTH GRANGE. A Book for Children. With Illustrations by ARTHUR HUGHES, and Engraved Title-page by JEENS. Small 4to. cloth extra. 6s.

"*If you want a really good book for both sexes and all ages, buy this, as handsome a volume of tales as you'll find in all the market.*"—ATHENÆUM. "*Exquisite both in form and substance.*" —GUARDIAN.

LYRICAL POEMS. Extra fcap. 8vo. 6s.

"*A volume of pure quiet verse, sparkling with tender melodies, and alive with thoughts of genuine poetry. . . . Turn where we will throughout the volume, we find traces of beauty, tenderness, and truth; true poet's work, touched and refined by the master-hand of a real artist, who shows his genius even in trifles.*"—STANDARD.

ORIGINAL HYMNS. Third Edition, enlarged, 18mo. 1s. 6d.

"*So choice, so perfect, and so refined, so tender in feeling, and so scholarly in expression, that we look with special interest to every-thing that he gives us.*"—LITERARY CHURCHMAN.

GOLDEN TREASURY OF THE BEST SONGS AND LYRICS. Edited by F. T. PALGRAVE. 18mo. 4s. 6d.

SHAKESPEARE'S SONNETS AND SONGS. Edited by F. T. PALGRAVE. Gem Edition. With Vignette Title by JEENS. 3s. 6d.

"*For minute elegance no volume could possibly excel the 'Gem Edition.'*"—SCOTSMAN.

THE CHILDREN'S TREASURY OF LYRICAL POETRY. Selected and arranged with Notes by F. T. PALGRAVE. 18mo. 2s. 6d., and in Two Parts, 1s. each.

HERRICK : SELECTIONS FROM THE LYRICAL POEMS. With Notes. 18mo. 4s. 6d.

Pater.—Works by WALTER PATER, Fellow of Brasenose College, Oxford :—

THE RENAISSANCE. Studies in Art and Poetry. Second Edition, Revised, with Vignette, engraved by C. H. Jeens. Crown 8vo. 10s. 6d.

"*Mr. Pater's Studies in the history of the Renaissance, constitute the most remarkable example of this younger movement towards a fresh and inner criticism, and they are in themselves a singular and interesting addition to literature. The subjects are of the very kind in which we need instruction and guidance, and there is a moral in the very choice of them. From the point of view of form and literary composition they are striking in the highest degree. They introduce to English readers a new and distinguished master in the great and difficult art of writing prose. Their style is marked by a flavour at once full and exquisite, by a quality that mixes richness with delicacy and a firm coherency with infinite subtlety."*—FORTNIGHTLY REVIEW.

DIONYSUS ; and other Studies. Crown 8vo.   [*Shortly.*

Patmore.—THE CHILDREN'S GARLAND, from the Best Poets. Selected and arranged by COVENTRY PATMORE. New Edition. With Illustrations by J. LAWSON. Crown 8vo. gilt. 6s. Golden Treasury Edition. 18mo. 4s. 6d.
" The charming illustrations added to many of the poems will add greatly to their value in the eyes of children."—DAILY NEWS.

Peel.—ECHOES FROM HOREB, AND OTHER POEMS. By EDMUND PEEL, Author of "An Ancient City," etc. Crown 8vo. 3s. 6d.

Pember.—THE TRAGEDY OF LESBOS. A Dramatic Poem. By E. H. PEMBER. Fcap. 8vo. 4s. 6d.
Founded upon the story of Sappho. "He tells his story with dramatic force, and in language that often rises almost to grandeur."— ATHENÆUM.

Phillips.—BENEDICTA. A Novel. By Mrs. ALFRED PHILLIPS. 3 Vols. Crown 8vo. 31s. 6d.

Philpot. — A POCKET OF PEBBLES, WITH A FEW SHELLS ; Being Fragments of Reflection, now and then with Cadence, made up mostly by the Sea-shore. By the Rev. W. B. PHILPOT. Second Edition, picked, sorted, and polished anew ; with Two Illustrations by GEORGE SMITH. Fcap. 8vo. 5s.

Poole.—PICTURES OF COTTAGE LIFE IN THE WEST OF ENGLAND. By MARGARET E. POOLE. New and Cheaper Edition. With Frontispiece by R. Farren. Crown 8vo. 3s. 6d.

Population of an Old Pear Tree. From the French of E. VAN BRUYSSEL. Edited by the Author of " The Heir of Redclyffe." With Illustrations by BECKER. Cheaper Edition. Crown 8vo. gilt. 4s. 6d.
" A whimsical and charming little book."—ATHENÆUM.

Prince Florestan of Monaco, The Fall of. By HIMSELF. New Edition, with Illustration and Map. 8vo. cloth. Extra gilt edges, 5s. A French Translation, 5s. Also an Edition for the People. Crown 8vo. 1s.

Quin.—GARDEN RECEIPTS. Edited by CHARLES QUIN. Crown 8vo. 2s. 6d.
" The most useful book for the garden that has been published for some time."—FLORIST AND POMOLOGIST.

Realmah.—By the Author of "Friends in Council." Crown 8vo. 6s.

Rhoades.—POEMS. By JAMES RHOADES. Fcap. 8vo. 4s. 6d.

Richardson.—THE ILIAD OF THE EAST. A Selection of Legends drawn from Valmiki's Sanskrit Poem, "The Ramayana." By FREDERIKA RICHARDSON. Crown 8vo. 7s. 6d.
"*It is impossible to read it without recognizing the value and interest of the Eastern epic. It is as fascinating as a fairy tale, this romantic poem of India."*—GLOBE. "*A charming volume, which at once enmeshes the reader in its snares."*—ATHENÆUM.

Rimmer.—ANCIENT STREETS AND HOMESTEADS OF ENGLAND. By ALFRED RIMMER. With Introduction by the Very Rev. J. S. HOWSON, D.D., Dean of Chester. Royal 8vo. with 150 Illustrations by the Author. Cloth elegant, 21s.
"*All the illustrations are clear and good, and they are eminently truthful. . . . A book which gladdens the eye while it instructs and improves the mind."*—STANDARD. "*One of the most interesting and beautiful books we have seen this season. . . . It is full of knowledge, the result of exact and faithful study, most readable and interesting; the illustrations are simply exquisite."* —NONCONFORMIST.

Robinson.—GEORGE LINTON; OR, THE FIRST YEARS OF AN ENGLISH COLONY. By JOHN ROBINSON, F.R.G.S. Crown 8vo. 7s. 6d.
"*If one may speak confidently on such a matter from one's own experience, it must be a rare thing for a critic to put down a novel, having read every word of it, and find himself at the end asking for more. Yet this is what happened to us with George Linton."* —SPECTATOR.

Rossetti.—Works by CHRISTINA ROSSETTI :—
POEMS. Complete Edition, containing "Goblin Market," "The Prince's Progress," &c. With Four Illustrations. Extra fcap. 8vo. 6s.

SPEAKING LIKENESSES. Illustrated by ARTHUR HUGHES. Crown 8vo. gilt edges. 4s. 6d.
"*Certain to be a delight to many a juvenile fireside circle."*— MORNING POST.

Ruth and her Friends. A Story for Girls. With a Frontispiece. Seventh Edition. Extra fcap. 8vo. 4s. 6d.
"*We wish all the school girls and home-taught girls in the land had the opportunity of reading it."*—NONCONFORMIST.

Scouring of The White Horse; or, the Long VACATION RAMBLE OF A LONDON CLERK. Illustrated by DOYLE. Imp. 16mo. Cheaper Issue. 3s. 6d.

Shairp (Principal).—KILMAHOE, a Highland Pastoral, with other Poems. By JOHN CAMPBELL SHAIRP, Principal of the United College, St. Andrews. Fcap. 8vo. 5*s.*

"Kilmahoe is a Highland Pastoral, redolent of the warm soft air of the western lochs and moors, sketched out with remarkable grace and picturesqueness."—SATURDAY REVIEW.

Shakespeare.—The Works of WILLIAM SHAKESPEARE. Cambridge Edition. Edited by W. GEORGE CLARK, M.A. and W. ALDIS WRIGHT, M.A. Nine vols. 8vo. cloth.

The GUARDIAN *calls it an "excellent, and, to the student, almost indispensable edition;" and the* EXAMINER *calls it "an unrivalled edition."*

Shakespeare's Plays.—An attempt to determine the Chronological Order. By the Rev. H. PAINE STOKES, B.A. Extra fcap. 8vo. 4*s.* 6*d.*

Shakespeare Scenes and Characters.—A Series o Illustrations designed by ADAMO, HOFMANN, MAKART, PECHT, SCHWOERER, and SPEISS, engraved on Steel by BANKEL, BAUER, GOLDBERG, RAAB, and SCHMIDT; with Explanatory Text, selected and arranged by Professor DOWDEN. Royal 8vo. Cloth elegant. 2*l.* 12*s.* 6*d.*

Also a LARGE PAPER EDITION, India Proofs. Folio, half-morocco elegant. 4*l.* 14*s.* 6*d.*

Shakespeare's Tempest. Edited with Glossarial and Explanatory Notes, by the Rev. J. M. JEPHSON. New Edition. 18mo. 1*s.*

Slip (A) in the Fens.—Illustrated by the Author. Crown 8vo. 6*s.*

"An artistic little volume, for every page is a picture."—TIMES. *"It will be read with pleasure, and with a pleasure that is altogether innocent."*—SATURDAY REVIEW.

Smedley.—TWO DRAMATIC POEMS. By MENELLA BUTE SMEDLEY, Author of "Lady Grace," &c. Extra fcap. 8vo. 6*s.*

"May be read with enjoyment and profit."—SATURDAY REVIEW.

Smith.—POEMS. By CATHERINE BARNARD SMITH. Fcap. 8vo. 5*s.*

Smith (Rev. Walter).—HYMNS OF CHRIST AND THE CHRISTIAN LIFE. By the Rev. WALTER C. SMITH, M.A. Fcap. 8vo. 6*s.*

Southesk.—THE MEDA MAIDEN : AND OTHER POEMS. By the Earl of Southesk, K.T. Extra fcap. 8vo. 7*s.*

" *It is pleasant in these days, when there is so much artificial and sensuous verse published, to come across a book so thoroughly fresh and healthy as Lord Southesk's.* . . . *There is an infinite charm about them in their spontaneity and their healthful philosophy, in the fervent love for nature which is their distinguishing character- istic, and the manly and wholesome tone which pervades every page.*"—SCOTSMAN.

Stanley.—TRUE TO LIFE.—A SIMPLE STORY. By MARY STANLEY. Cheaper Edition. Crown 8vo. 6s.
" *For many a long day we have not met with a more simple, healthy, and unpretending story.*"—STANDARD.

Stephen (C. E.)—THE SERVICE OF THE POOR; being an Inquiry into the Reasons for and against the Establishment of Religious Sisterhoods for Charitable Purposes. By CAROLINE EMILIA STEPHEN. Crown 8vo. 6s. 6d.
" *It touches incidentally and with much wisdom and tenderness on so many of the relations of women, particularly of single women, with society, that it may be read with advantage by many who have never thought of entering a Sisterhood.*"—SPECTATOR.

Stephens (J. B.)—CONVICT ONCE. A Poem. By J. BRUNTON STEPHENS. Extra fcap. 8vo. 3s. 6d.
" *It is as far more interesting than ninety-nine novels out of a hundred, as it is superior to them in power, worth, and beauty. We should most strongly advise everybody to read ' Convict Once.'* "
—WESTMINSTER REVIEW.

Streets and Lanes of a City: Being the Reminiscences of AMY DUTTON. With a Preface by the BISHOP OF SALIS- BURY. Second and Cheaper Edition. Globe 8vo. 2s. 6d.
" *One of the most really striking books that has ever come before us.*"
—LITERARY CHURCHMAN.

Thompson.—A HANDBOOK TO THE PUBLIC PICTURE GALLERIES OF EUROPE. With a brief sketch of the History of the various schools of Painting from the thirteenth century to the eighteenth, inclusive. By KATE THOMPSON. Second Edition, Revised and Enlarged. Extra fcap. 8vo. 6s.
" *A very remarkable memoir of the several great schools of painting, and a singularly lucid exhibition of the principal treasures of all the chief and some of the smaller picture galleries of Europe. This unpretending book which does so much for the history of art is also a traveller's guide-book; a guide-book, moreover, so con- venient in arrangement and comprehensive in design that it will not fail to become the companion of the majority of English tourists.* . . . *The large crowd of ordinary connoisseurs who only care to know a little about pictures, and the choicer body of intelligent students of all artistic objects that fall in their way, will*

*extol the compact little volume as the model of what an art
explorer's* vade mecum *should be. It will also be found in the
highest degree serviceable to the more learned connoisseurs and
erudite authorities on the matter of art.*"—MORNING POST.

Thring.—SCHOOL SONGS. A Collection of Songs for Schools.
With the Music arranged for four Voices. Edited by the Rev. E.
THRING and H. RICCIUS. Folio. 7*s.* 6*d.*

Tom Brown's School Days.—By AN OLD BOY.

Golden Treasury Edition, 4*s.* 6*d.* People's Edition, 2*s.*
With Seven Illustrations by A. HUGHES and SYDNEY HALL.
Crown 8vo. 6*s.*
" *The most famous boy's book in the language.*"—DAILY NEWS.

Tom Brown at Oxford.—New Edition. With Illustrations

Crown 8vo. 6*s.*
" *In no other work that we can call to mind are the finer qualities of
the English gentleman more happily portrayed.*"—DAILY NEWS.
"*A book of great power and truth.*"—NATIONAL REVIEW.

Tourgenief.—VIRGIN SOIL. By I. TOURGENIEF. Translated by ASHTON W. DILKE. Crown 8vo. 10*s.* 6*d.*
" *If we want to know Russian life and society in all its phases . . .
we cannot do better than take up the works of the greatest of
Russian novelists, and one of the greatest in all European literature, Ivan Tourgenief.*"—DAILY NEWS.

Trench.—Works by R. CHENEVIX TRENCH, D.D., Archbishop
of Dublin. (For other Works by this Author, see THEOLOGICAL,
HISTORICAL, and PHILOSOPHICAL CATALOGUES.)

POEMS. Collected and arranged anew. Fcap. 8vo. 7*s.* 6*d.*

HOUSEHOLD BOOK OF ENGLISH POETRY. Selected and
arranged, with Notes, by Archbishop TRENCH. Second Edition.
Extra fcap. 8vo. 5*s.* 6*d.*
" *The Archbishop has conferred in this delightful volume an important
gift on the whole English-speaking population of the world.*"—
PALL MALL GAZETTE.

SACRED LATIN POETRY, Chiefly Lyrical. Selected and
arranged for Use. By Archbishop TRENCH. Third Edition,
Corrected and Improved. Fcap. 8vo. 7*s.*

Turner.—Works by the Rev. CHARLES TENNYSON TURNER :—
SONNETS. Dedicated to his Brother, the Poet Laureate. Fcap.
8vo. 4*s.* 6*d.*
SMALL TABLEAUX. Fcap. 8vo. 4*s.* 6*d.*

Tyrwhitt.—OUR SKETCHING CLUB. Letters and Studies on Landscape Art. By Rev. R. St. JOHN TYRWHITT, M.A. With an Authorized Reproduction of the Lessons and Woodcuts in Professor Ruskin's "Elements of Drawing." Second Edition. Crown 8vo. 7s. 6d.

Under the Limes.—By the Author of "Christina North." Second Edition. Crown 8vo. 6s.
"*One of the prettiest and best told stories which it has been our good fortune to read for a long time.*"—PALL MALL GAZETTE.

Villari.—IN CHANGE UNCHANGED. By LINDA VILLARI. Author of "In the Golden Shell," &c. Two vols. Crown 8vo. 21s.

Wandering Willie. By the Author of "Effie's Friends," and "John Hatherton." Third Edition. Crown 8vo. 6s.
"*This is an idyll of rare truth and beauty. . . . The story is simple and touching, the style of extraordinary delicacy, precision, and picturesqueness. . . . A charming gift-book for young ladies not yet promoted to novels, and will amply repay those of their elders who may give an hour to its perusal.*"—DAILY NEWS.

Webster.—Works by AUGUSTA WEBSTER :—
"*If Mrs. Webster only remains true to herself, she will assuredly take a higher rank as a poet than any woman has yet done.*"— WESTMINSTER REVIEW.

DRAMATIC STUDIES. Extra fcap. 8vo. 5s.
"*A volume as strongly marked by perfect taste as by poetic power.*"— NONCONFORMIST.

A WOMAN SOLD, AND OTHER POEMS. Crown 8vo. 7s. 6d.
"*Mrs. Webster has shown us that she is able to draw admirably from the life; that she can observe with subtlety, and render her observations with delicacy; that she can impersonate complex conceptions and venture into recesses of the ideal world into which few living writers can follow her.*" —GUARDIAN.

PORTRAITS. Second Edition. Extra fcap. 8vo. 3s. 6d.
"*Mrs. Webster's poems exhibit simplicity and tenderness . . . her taste is perfect . . . This simplicity is combined with a subtlety of thought, feeling, and observation which demand that attention which only real lovers of poetry are apt to bestow.*"—WESTMINSTER REVIEW.

PROMETHEUS BOUND OF ÆSCHYLUS. Literally translated into English Verse. Extra fcap. 8vo. 3s. 6d.

Webster (Augusta)—*continued.*

"*Closeness and simplicity combined with literary skill.*" — ATHE-NÆUM. "*Mrs. Webster's 'Dramatic Studies' and 'Translation of Prometheus' have won for her an honourable place among our female poets. She writes with remarkable vigour and dramatic realization, and bids fair to be the most successful claimant of Mrs. Browning's mantle.*"—BRITISH QUARTERLY REVIEW.

MEDEA OF EURIPIDES. Literally translated into English Verse. Extra fcap. 8vo. 3s. 6d.
"*Mrs. Webster's translation surpasses our utmost expectations. It is a photograph of the original without any of that harshness which so often accompanies a photograph.*"—WESTMINSTER REVIEW.

THE AUSPICIOUS DAY. A Dramatic Poem. Extra fcap. 8vo. 5s.
"*The 'Auspicious Day' shows a marked advance, not only in art, but, in what is of far more importance, in breadth of thought and intellectual grasp.*"—WESTMINSTER REVIEW. "*This drama is a manifestation of high dramatic power on the part of the gifted writer, and entitled to our warmest admiration, as a worthy piece of work.*"—STANDARD.

YU-PE-YA'S LUTE. A Chinese Tale in English Verse. Extra fcap. 8vo. 3s. 6d.
"*A very charming tale, charmingly told in dainty verse, with occasional lyrics of tender beauty.*"—STANDARD. "*We close the book with the renewed conviction that in Mrs. Webster we have a profound and original poet. The book is marked not by mere sweetness of melody—rare as that gift is—but by the infinitely rarer gifts of dramatic power, of passion, and sympathetic insight.*" —WESTMINSTER REVIEW.

A HOUSEWIFE'S OPINIONS. Crown 8vo. 7s. 6d.

When I was a Little Girl. STORIES FOR CHILDREN. By the Author of "St. Olave's." Fifth Edition. Extra fcap. 8vo. 4s. 6d. With Eight Illustrations by L. FRÖLICH.
"*At the head, and a long way ahead, of all books for girls, we place 'When I was a Little Girl.'*"—TIMES. "*It is one of the choicest morsels of child-biography which we have met with.*"—NONCONFORMIST.

White.—RHYMES BY WALTER WHITE. 8vo. 7s. 6d.

Whittier.—JOHN GREENLEAF WHITTIER'S POETICAL WORKS. Complete Edition, with Portrait engraved by C. H. JEENS. 18mo. 4s. 6d.
"*Mr. Whittier has all the smooth melody and the pathos of the author of 'Hiawatha,' with a greater nicety of description and a quainter fancy.*"—GRAPHIC.

Willoughby.—FAIRY GUARDIANS. A Book for the Young.
By F. WILLOUGHBY. Illustrated. Crown 8vo. gilt. 5s.
"*A dainty and delicious tale of the good old-fashioned type.*"—
SATURDAY REVIEW.

Wolf.—THE LIFE AND HABITS OF WILD ANIMALS.
Twenty Illustrations by JOSEPH WOLF, engraved by J. W. and E.
WHYMPER. With descriptive Letter-press, by D. G. ELLIOT,
F.L.S. Super royal 4to, cloth extra, gilt edges. 21s.
*This is the last series of drawings which will be made by Mr. Wolf,
either upon wood or stone.* The PALL MALL GAZETTE *says:
"The fierce, untamable side of brute nature has never received a
more robust and vigorous interpretation, and the various incidents
in which particular character is shown are set forth with rare dramatic power. For excellence that will endure, we incline to place
this very near the top of the list of Christmas books." And the
*ART JOURNAL *observes, "Rarely, if ever, have we seen animal
life more forcibly and beautifully depicted than in this really
splendid volume.*"

Also, an Edition in royal folio, Proofs before Letters, each Proof
signed by the Engravers.

Woolner.—MY BEAUTIFUL LADY. By THOMAS WOOLNER.
With a Vignette by A. HUGHES. Third Edition. Fcap. 8vo. 5s.
"*No man can read this poem without being struck by the fitness and
finish of the workmanship, so to speak, as well as by the chastened
and unpretending loftiness of thought which pervades the whole.*"
—GLOBE.

Words from the Poets. Selected by the Editor of "Rays
of Sunlight." With a Vignette and Frontispiece. 18mo. limp., 1s.
"*The selection aims at popularity, and deserves it.*"—GUARDIAN.

Yonge (C. M.)—Works by CHARLOTTE M. YONGE.

THE HEIR OF REDCLYFFE. Twenty-third Edition. With
Illustrations. Crown 8vo. 6s.

HEARTSEASE. Fifteenth Edition. With Illustrations. Crown
8vo. 6s.

THE DAISY CHAIN. Sixteenth Edition. With Illustrations.
Crown 8vo. 6s.

THE TRIAL: MORE LINKS OF THE DAISY CHAIN.
Fourteenth Edition. With Illustrations. Crown 8vo. 6s.

DYNEVOR TERRACE. Seventh Edition. Crown 8vo. 6s.

HOPES AND FEARS. Sixth Edition. Crown 8vo. 6s.

Yonge (C. M.)—*continued.*

THE YOUNG STEPMOTHER. Sixth Edition. Crown 8vo. 6s.

CLEVER WOMAN OF THE FAMILY. Fifth Edition. Crown 8vo. 6s.

THE DOVE IN THE EAGLE'S NEST. Seventh Edition. Crown 8vo. 6s.
" We think the authoress of ' The Heir of Redclyffe' has surpassed her previous efforts in this illuminated chronicle of the olden time."—BRITISH QUARTERLY.

THE CAGED LION. Illustrated. Fourth Edition. Crown 8vo. 6s.
" Prettily and tenderly written, and will with young people especially be a great favourite."—DAILY NEWS. *" Everybody should read this."*—LITERARY CHURCHMAN.

THE CHAPLET OF PEARLS; OR, THE WHITE AND BLACK RIBAUMONT. Crown 8vo. 6s. Sixth Edition.
" Miss Yonge has brought a lofty aim as well as high art to the construction of a story which may claim a place among the best efforts in historical romance."—MORNING POST. *" The plot, in truth, is of the very first order of merit."*—SPECTATOR. *" We have seldom read a more charming story."*—GUARDIAN.

THE PRINCE AND THE PAGE. A Tale of the Last Crusade. Illustrated. Third Edition. 18mo. 2s. 6d.
" A tale which, we are sure, will give pleasure to many others besides the young people for whom it is specially intended. . . . This extremely prettily-told story does not require the guarantee afforded by the name of the author of ' The Heir of Redclyffe' on the title-page to ensure its becoming a universal favourite."—DUBLIN EVENING MAIL.

THE LANCES OF LYNWOOD. New Edition, with Coloured Illustrations. 18mo. 4s. 6d.
" The illustrations are very spirited and rich in colour, and the story can hardly fail to charm the youthful reader."—MANCHESTER EXAMINER.

THE LITTLE DUKE : RICHARD THE FEARLESS. Sixth Edition. Illustrated. 18mo. 2s. 6d.

A STOREHOUSE OF STORIES. First and Second Series. Globe 8vo. 3s. 6d. each.
CONTENTS OF FIRST SERIES :—History of Philip Quarll—Goody Twoshoes—The Governess—Jemima Placid—The Perambulations of a Mouse—The Village School—The Little Queen—History of Little Jack.

Yonge (C. M.)—*continued.*

"Miss Yonge has done great service to the infantry of this generation by putting these eleven stories of sage simplicity within their reach." —BRITISH QUARTERLY REVIEW.

CONTENTS OF SECOND SERIES :—Family Stories—Elements of Morality—A Puzzle for a Curious Girl—Blossoms of Morality.

A BOOK OF GOLDEN DEEDS OF ALL TIMES AND ALL COUNTRIES. Gathered and Narrated Anew. GOLDEN TREASURY SERIES). 4s. 6d. Cheap Edition. 1s.
"We have seen no prettier gift-book for a long time, and none which, both for its cheapness and the spirit in which it has been compiled, is more deserving of praise."—ATHENÆUM.

LITTLE LUCY'S WONDERFUL GLOBE. Pictured by FRÖLICH, and narrated by CHARLOTTE M. YONGE. Second Edition. Crown 4to. cloth gilt. 6s.
"'Lucy's Wonderful Globe' is capital, and will give its youthful readers more idea of foreign countries and customs than any number of books of geography or travel."—GRAPHIC.

CAMEOS FROM ENGLISH HISTORY. From ROLLO to EDWARD II. Extra fcap. 8vo. 5s. Third Edition, enlarged. 5s.

SECOND SERIES. THE WARS IN FRANCE. Third Edition. Extra fcap. 8vo. 5s.
"Instead of dry details," says the NONCONFORMIST, *"we have living pictures, faithful, vivid, and striking."*

THIRD SERIES. THE WARS OF THE ROSES. Extra fcap. 8vo. 5s.

P's AND Q's ; OR, THE QUESTION OF PUTTING UPON. With Illustrations by C. O. MURRAY. Third Edition. Globe 8vo. cloth gilt. 4s. 6d.
"One of her most successful little pieces . . . . just what a narrative should be, each incident simply and naturally related, no preaching or moralizing, and yet the moral coming out most powerfully, and the whole story not too long, or with the least appearance of being spun out."—LITERARY CHURCHMAN.

THE PILLARS OF THE HOUSE; OR, UNDER WODE, UNDER RODE. Fourth Edition. Two vols. crown 8vo. 12s.
"A domestic story of English professional life, which for sweetness of tone and absorbing interest from first to last has never been rivalled."—STANDARD. *"Miss Yonge has certainly added to her already high reputation by this charming book, which keeps the reader's attention fixed to the end. Indeed we are only sorry there is not another volume to come, and part with the Underwood family with sincere regret."*—COURT CIRCULAR.

Yonge (C. M.)—*continued.*

LADY HESTER; OR, URSULA'S NARRATIVE. Third Edition. Crown 8vo. 6s.

" We shall not anticipate the interest by epitomizing the plot, but we shall only say that readers will find in it all the gracefulness, right feeling, and delicate perception which they have been long accustomed to look for in Miss Yonge's writings."—GUARDIAN.

MY YOUNG ALCIDES ; OR, A FADED PHOTOGRAPH. Sixth Edition. Crown 8vo. 6s.

" Marked by all the perfect and untiring freshness that always charm us in Miss Yonge's novels."—GRAPHIC. *" The story is admirably told, and extremely interesting."*—STANDARD.

THE THREE BRIDES. Eighth Edition. 2 vols. Crown 8vo. 12s.

MACMILLAN'S GOLDEN TREASURY SERIES.

UNIFORMLY printed in 18mo., with Vignette Titles by Sir NOEL PATON, T. WOOLNER, W. HOLMAN HUNT, J. E. MILLAIS, ARTHUR HUGHES, &c. Engraved on Steel by JEENS. Bound in extra cloth, 4s. 6d. each volume. Also kept in morocco and calf bindings.

" Messrs. Macmillan have, in their Golden Treasury Series, especially provided editions of standard works, volumes of selected poetry, and original compositions, which entitle this series to be called classical. Nothing can be better than the literary execution, nothing more elegant than the material workmanship."—BRITISH QUARTERLY REVIEW.

The Golden Treasury of the Best Songs and LYRICAL POEMS IN THE ENGLISH LANGUAGE. Selected and arranged, with Notes, by FRANCIS TURNER PALGRAVE.

" This delightful little volume, the Golden Treasury, which contains many of the best original lyrical pieces and songs in our language, grouped with care and skill, so as to illustrate each other like the pictures in a well-arranged gallery."—QUARTERLY REVIEW.

The Children's Garland from the best Poets. Selected and arranged by COVENTRY PATMORE.

" It includes specimens of all the great masters in the art of poetry, selected with the matured judgment of a man concentrated on obtaining insight into the feelings and tastes of childhood, and desirous to awaken its finest impulses, to cultivate its keenest sensibilities."—MORNING POST.

The Book of Praise. From the Best English Hymn Writers. Selected and arranged by LORD SELBORNE. *A New and Enlarged Edition.*

" All previous compilations of this kind must undeniably for the present give place to the Book of Praise. . . . The selection has been made throughout with sound judgment and critical taste. The pains involved in this compilation must have been immense, embracing, as it does, every writer of note in this special province of English literature, and ranging over the most widely divergent tracks of religious thought."—SATURDAY REVIEW.

The Fairy Book; the Best Popular Fairy Stories. Selected and rendered anew by the Author of "John Halifax, Gentleman."
"*A delightful selection, in a delightful external form ; full of the physical splendour and vast opulence of proper fairy tales.*"— SPECTATOR.

The Ballad Book. A Selection of the Choicest British Ballads. Edited by WILLIAM ALLINGHAM.
"*His taste as a judge of old poetry will be found, by all acquainted with the various readings of old English ballads, true enough to justify his undertaking so critical a task.*"—SATURDAY REVIEW.

The Jest Book. The Choicest Anecdotes and Sayings. Selected and arranged by MARK LEMON.
"*The fullest and best jest book that has yet appeared.*"—SATURDAY REVIEW.

Bacon's Essays and Colours of Good and Evil. With Notes and Glossarial Index. By W. ALDIS WRIGHT, M.A.
"*The beautiful little edition of Bacon's Essays, now before us, does credit to the taste and scholarship of Mr. Aldis Wright. . . . It puts the reader in possession of all the essential literary facts and chronology necessary for reading the Essays in connection with Bacon's life and times.*"—SPECTATOR.

The Pilgrim's Progress from this World to that which is to come. By JOHN BUNYAN.
"*A beautiful and scholarly reprint.*"—SPECTATOR.

The Sunday Book of Poetry for the Young. Selected and arranged by C. F. ALEXANDER.
"*A well-selected volume of Sacred Poetry.*"—SPECTATOR.

A Book of Golden Deeds of All Times and All Countries Gathered and narrated anew. By the Author of "THE HEIR OF REDCLYFFE."
"*. . . To the young, for whom it is especially intended, as a most interesting collection of thrilling tales well told ; and to their elders, as a useful handbook of reference, and a pleasant one to take up when their wish is to while away a weary half-hour. We have seen no prettier gift-book for a long time.*"—ATHENÆUM.

The Poetical Works of Robert Burns. Edited, with Biographical Memoir, Notes, and Glossary, by ALEXANDER SMITH. Two Vols.
"*Beyond all question this is the most beautiful edition of Burns yet out.*"—EDINBURGH DAILY REVIEW.

C

The Adventures of Robinson Crusoe. Edited from the Original Edition by J. W. CLARK, M.A. Fellow of Trinity College, Cambridge.
"*Mutilated and modified editions of this English classic are so much the rule, that a cheap and pretty copy of it, rigidly exact to the original, will be a prize to many book-buyers.*"—EXAMINER.

The Republic of Plato. TRANSLATED into ENGLISH, with Notes by J. Ll. DAVIES, M.A. and D. J. VAUGHAN, M.A.
"*A dainty and cheap little edition.*"—EXAMINER.

The Song Book. Words and Tunes from the best Poets and Musicians. Selected and arranged by JOHN HULLAH, Professor of Vocal Music in King's College, London.

"*A choice collection of the sterling songs of England, Scotland, and Ireland, with the music of each prefixed to the Words. How much true wholesome pleasure such a book can diffuse, and will diffuse, we trust through many thousand families.*"—EXAMINER.

La Lyre Française, Selected and arranged, with Notes, by GUSTAVE MASSON, French Master in Harrow School.
A selection of the best French songs and lyrical pieces.

Tom Brown's School Days. By AN OLD BOY.
"*A perfect gem of a book. The best and most healthy book about boys for boys that ever was written.*"—ILLUSTRATED TIMES.

A Book of Worthies. Gathered from the Old Histories and written anew by the Author of "THE HEIR OF REDCLYFFE." With Vignette.
"*An admirable addition to an admirable series.*"—WESTMINSTER REVIEW.

A Book of Golden Thoughts. By HENRY ATTWELL, Knight of the Order of the Oak Crown.
"*Mr. Attwell has produced a book of rare value . . . . Happily it is small enough to be carried about in the pocket, and of such a companion it would be difficult to weary.*"—PALL MALL GAZETTE.

Guesses at Truth. By TWO BROTHERS. New Edition.

The Cavalier and his Lady. Selections from the Works of the First Duke and Duchess of Newcastle. With an Introductory Essay by EDWARD JENKINS, Author of "Ginx's Baby," &c.
"*A charming little volume.*"—STANDARD.

Theologia Germanica.—Which setteth forth many fair Lineaments of Divine Truth, and saith very lofty and lovely things touching a Perfect Life. Edited by DR. PFEIFFER, from the only complete manuscript yet known. Translated from the German, by SUSANNA WINKWORTH. With a Preface by the REV. CHARLES KINGSLEY, and a Letter to the Translator by the Chevalier Bunsen, D.D.

Milton's Poetical Works.—Edited, with Notes, &c., by PROFESSOR MASSON. Two vols. 18mo. 9s.

Scottish Song. A Selection of the Choicest Lyrics of Scotland. Compiled and arranged, with brief Notes, by MARY CARLYLE AITKIN.

" *Miss Aitkin's exquisite collection of Scottish Song is so alluring, and suggests so many topics, that we find it difficult to lay it down. The book is one that should find a place in every library, we haa almost said in every pocket, and the summer tourist who wishes to carry with him into the country a volume of genuine poetry, will find it difficult to select one containing within so small a compass so much of rarest value.*"—SPECTATOR.

Deutsche Lyrik.—The Golden Treasury of the best German Lyrical Poems, selected and arranged with Notes and Literary Introduction. By Dr. BUCHHEIM.

" *This collection of German poetry is compiled with care and conscientiousness. . . . . The result of his labours is satisfactory. Almost all the lyrics dear to English readers of German will be found in this little volume.*"—PALL MALL GAZETTE.

Robert Herrick.—SELECTIONS FROM THE LYRICAL POEMS OF. Arranged with Notes by F. T. PALGRAVE.

" *A delightful little book. Herrick, the English Catullus, is simply one of the most exquisite of poets, and his fame and memory are fortunate in having found one so capable of doing honour to them as the present editor ; who contributes a charming dedication and a preface full of delicate and sensitive criticism to a volume than which one would hardly desire a choicer companion for a jour ney or for hours of ease in the country.*"—DAILY NEWS.

Poems of Places.—Edited by H. W. LONGFELLOW. England and Wales. Two Vols.

" *After a careful perusal we must pronounce his work an excellent collection. . . . In this compilation we find not only a guide-book for future travels, but a fund of reminiscences of the past. To many of us it will seem like a biography of our best and happiest emotions. . . . For those who know not all these places the book will be an excellent travelling companion or guide, or may even stand some in good stead in place of travel.*"—TIMES.

Matthew Arnold's Selected Poems. Also a Large Paper Edition. Crown 8vo. 12s. 6d.

The Story of the Christians and Moors in Spain. —By CHARLOTTE M. YONGE. With a Vignette by HOLMAN HUNT.

Lamb's Tales from Shakespeare.—Edited with Preface by the Rev. ALFRED AINGER, Reader at the Temple.

MACMILLAN'S GLOBE LIBRARY.

Beautifully printed on toned paper and bound in cloth extra, gilt edges, price 4s. 6d. each; in cloth plain, 3s. 6d. Also kept in a variety of calf and morocco bindings at moderate prices.

BOOKS, Wordsworth says, are
> "the spirit breathed
> By dead men to their kind;"

and the aim of the publishers of the Globe Library has been to make it possible for the universal kin of English-speaking men to hold communion with the loftiest "spirits of the mighty dead;" to put within the reach of all classes *complete* and *accurate* editions, carefully and clearly printed upon the best paper, in a convenient form, at a moderate price, of the works of the MASTER-MINDS OF ENGLISH LITERATURE, and occasionally of foreign literature in an attractive English dress.

The Editors, by their scholarship and special study of their authors, are competent to afford every assistance to readers of all kinds : this assistance is rendered by original biographies, glossaries of unusual or obsolete words, and critical and explanatory notes.

The publishers hope, therefore, that these Globe Editions may prove worthy of acceptance by all classes wherever the English Language is spoken, and by their universal circulation justify their distinctive epithet ; while at the same time they spread and nourish a common sympathy with nature's most "finely touched" spirits, and thus help a little to "make the whole world kin."

The SATURDAY REVIEW *says:* " *The Globe Editions are admirable for their scholarly editing, their typographical excellence, their compendious form, and their cheapness.*" The BRITISH QUARTERLY REVIEW *says:* "*In compendiousness, elegance, and scholarliness, the Globe Editions of Messrs. Macmillan surpass any popular series of our classics hitherto given to the public. As near an approach to miniature perfection as has ever been made.*"

Shakespeare's Complete Works. Edited by W. G. CLARK, M.A., and W. ALDIS WRIGHT, M. A., of Trinity College,

Cambridge, Editors of the "Cambridge Shakespeare." With Glossary. Pp. 1,075.

The ATHENÆUM *says this edition is "a marvel of beauty, cheapness, and compactness. . . . For the busy man, above all for the working student, this is the best of all existing Shakespeares." And the* PALL MALL GAZETTE *observes: "To have produced the complete works of the world's greatest poet in such a form, and at a price within the reach of every one, is of itself almost sufficient to give the publishers a claim to be considered public benefactors."*

Spenser's Complete Works. Edited from the Original
Editions and Manuscripts, by R. MORRIS, with a Memoir by J. W. HALES, M.A. With Glossary. pp. lv., 736.

*"Worthy—and higher praise it needs not—of the beautiful ' Globe Series.' The work is edited with all the care so noble a poet deserves."—*DAILY NEWS.

Sir Walter Scott's Poetical Works. Edited with a
Biographical and Critical Memoir by FRANCIS TURNER PALGRAVE, and copious Notes. pp. xliii., 559.

*" We can almost sympathise with a middle-aged grumbler, who, after reading Mr. Palgrave's memoir and introduction, should exclaim —'Why was there not such an edition of Scott when I was a schoolboy?' "—*GUARDIAN.

Complete Works of Robert Burns.—THE POEMS,
SONGS, AND LETTERS, edited from the best Printed and Manuscript Authorities, with Glossarial Index, Notes, and a Biographical Memoir by ALEXANDER SMITH. pp. lxii., 636.

*"Admirable in all respects."—*SPECTATOR. *" The cheapest, the most perfect, and the most interesting edition which has ever been published."—*BELL'S MESSENGER.

Robinson Crusoe. Edited after the Original Editions, with a
Biographical Introduction by HENRY KINGSLEY. pp. xxxi., 607.

*" A most excellent and in every way desirable edition."—*COURT CIRCULAR. *"Macmillan's ' Globe' Robinson Crusoe is a book to have and to keep."—*MORNING STAR.

Goldsmith's Miscellaneous Works. Edited, with
Biographical Introduction, by Professor MASSON. pp. lx., 695.

*" Such an admirable compendium of the facts of Goldsmith's life, and so careful and minute a delineation of the mixed traits of his peculiar character as to be a very model of a literary biography in little."—*SCOTSMAN.

Pope's Poetical Works. Edited, with Notes and Intro-
ductory Memoir, by ADOLPHUS WILLIAM WARD, M.A., Fellow of St. Peter's College, Cambridge, and Professor of History in Owens College, Manchester. pp. lii., 508.

The LITERARY CHURCHMAN *remarks: " The editor's own notes and introductory memoir are excellent, the memoir alone would be cheap and well worth buying at the price of the whole volume."*

Dryden's Poetical Works. Edited, with a Memoir, Revised Text, and Notes, by W. D. CHRISTIE, M.A., of Trinity College, Cambridge. pp. lxxxvii., 662.

"*An admirable edition, the result of great research and of a careful revision of the text. The memoir prefixed contains, within less than ninety pages, as much sound criticism and as comprehensive a biography as the student of Dryden need desire.*"—PALL MALL GAZETTE.

Cowper's Poetical Works. Edited, with Notes and Biographical Introduction, by WILLIAM BENHAM, Vicar of Addington and Professor of Modern History in Queen's College, London. pp. lxxiii., 536.

"*Mr. Benham's edition of Cowper is one of permanent value. The biographical introduction is excellent, full of information, singularly neat and readable and modest—indeed too modest in its comments. The notes are concise and accurate, and the editor has been able to discover and introduce some hitherto unprinted matter. Altogether the book is a very excellent one.*"—SATURDAY REVIEW.

Morte d'Arthur.—SIR THOMAS MALORY'S BOOK OF KING ARTHUR AND OF HIS NOBLE KNIGHTS OF THE ROUND TABLE. The original Edition of CAXTON, revised for Modern Use. With an Introduction by Sir EDWARD STRACHEY, Bart. pp. xxxvii., 509.

"*It is with perfect confidence that we recommend this edition of the old romance to every class of readers.*"—PALL MALL GAZETTE.

The Works of Virgil. Rendered into English Prose, with Introductions, Notes, Running Analysis, and an Index. By JAMES LONSDALE, M.A., late Fellow and Tutor of Balliol College, Oxford, and Classical Professor in King's College, London ; and SAMUEL LEE, M.A., Latin Lecturer at University College, London. pp. 288.

"*A more complete edition of Virgil in English it is scarcely possible to conceive than the scholarly work before us.*"—GLOBE.

The Works of Horace. Rendered into English Prose, with Introductions, Running Analysis, Notes, and Index. By JOHN LONSDALE, M.A., and SAMUEL LEE, M.A.

The STANDARD *says,* "*To classical and non-classical readers it will be invaluable as a faithful interpretation of the mind and meaning of the poet, enriched as it is with notes and dissertations of the highest value in the way of criticism, illustration, and explanation.*"

Milton's Poetical Works.—Edited with Introductions by Professor MASSON.

"*A worthy addition to a valuable series.*"—ATHENÆUM.

"*In every way an admirable book.*"—PALL MALL GAZETTE.

MACMILLAN'S POPULAR NOVELS.

In Crown 8vo. cloth, price 6s. each Volume.

BY WILLIAM BLACK.

A PRINCESS OF THULE.

MADCAP VIOLET.

THE MAID OF KILLEENA; and other Tales.

THE STRANGE ADVENTURES OF A PHAETON.
Illustrated.

GREEN PASTURES AND PICCADILLY.

BY CHARLES KINGSLEY.

TWO YEARS AGO.

"WESTWARD HO!"

ALTON LOCKE. With Portrait.

HYPATIA.

YEAST.

HEREWARD THE WAKE.

BY THE AUTHOR OF "JOHN HALIFAX, GENTLEMAN.

THE HEAD OF THE FAMILY. Illustrated.

THE OGILVIES. Illustrated.

AGATHA'S HUSBAND. Illustrated.

OLIVE. Illustrated.

BY CHARLOTTE M. YONGE.

THE HEIR OF REDCLYFFE. With Illustrations.

HEARTSEASE. With Illustrations.

THE DAISY CHAIN. With Illustrations.

THE TRIAL: More Links in the Daisy Chain. With Illustrations.

HOPES AND FEARS.

DYNEVOR TERRACE.

MY YOUNG ALCIDES.

THE PILLARS OF THE HOUSE. 2 Vols.

CLEVER WOMAN OF THE FAMILY.

THE YOUNG STEPMOTHER.

THE DOVE IN THE EAGLE'S NEST.

THE CAGED LION. Illustrated.

BY CHARLOTTE M. YONGE—*continued.*
THE CHAPLET OF PEARLS.
LADY HESTER ; or, Ursula's Narrative.
THE THREE BRIDES. 2 Vols.

BY MRS. OLIPHANT.
YOUNG MUSGRAVE.
THE CURATE IN CHARGE.
A SON OF THE SOIL.

BY ANNIE KEARY.
CASTLE DALY.
OLDBURY.
A YORK AND A LANCASTER ROSE.

BY GEORGE FLEMING.
A NILE NOVEL.
MIRAGE.

TOM BROWN'S SCHOOL DAYS.
TOM BROWN AT OXFORD.
PAULINE. By G. C. CLUNES.
THE FOOL OF QUALITY. By H. BROOKE.
UNDER THE LIMES.
CHRISTINA NORTH.
ELSIE. By A. C. M.
REALMAH. By the Author of "Friends in Council."
PATTY. By Mrs. MACQUOID.
HUGH CRICHTON'S ROMANCE. By C. R. COLERIDGE.
OWEN GWYNNE'S GREAT WORK. By LADY AUGUSTA NOEL.
A SLIP IN THE FENS. Illustrated.
MY TIME, AND WHAT I'VE DONE WITH IT. By F C. BURNAND.
ROSE TURQUAND. By ELLICE HOPKINS.
OLD SIR DOUGLAS. By the Hon. Mrs. NORTON.
SEBASTIAN. By KATHERINE COOPER.

MACMILLAN AND CO., LONDON.